TORIAN

EDEN SUMMERS

PROLOGUE

TORIAN

I've done some heavy shit in my time.

I've taken the lives of many and ordered the death of more.

I was barely out of my teens when I had to take down one of my own men—a guy I'd trusted—because he'd dared to touch my sister. He'd raised a hand to Layla, and in return, I'd raised a gun to his temple and didn't bat an eye when I pulled the trigger.

My father instilled that sense of protection in me. Which, I guess, makes my task today more than a little ironic.

The man who taught me everything, who shaped my prejudices and guided me through my entire life, needs to be shut down for the betrayal he's inflicted on his children.

Today, I will punish my father out of respect for all of us. And that, by far, is the heaviest shit I've ever had to deal with. Not just the thought of confronting his actions, but addressing the betrayal —his against me, and mine against him.

At one time, he was all I knew. Everything I looked up to. All I aspired to be. There was no greater man than the mighty Luther Torian.

Now, he's everything I despise and all I crave to defeat.

My only concern is the consequences.

If I had my way, I'd tap the brakes and allow myself more time to work out this plan. But stalling isn't an option after I made a promise to an irrational sister who was hell-bent on taking the task into her own hands.

I won't allow anyone else to sentence him. I don't care how big the grievance. He's mine to deal with.

My mentor. My flesh. My blood.

If anyone is going to instigate a war of loyalties among the men in my organization, it will be me. And I've never been more aware of the dangers of a possible split than I am now, standing beneath a portable gazebo, before a polished coffin, waiting for my uncle's funeral to begin, in front of a crowd filled with potential enemies.

Richard Torian was an unscrupulous bastard.

A rapist.

A pedophile.

But both he and my father have always provided an unyielding level of protection toward our family that very few people dared to breech.

Without them, my stronghold will take a major hit.

Me, my sisters, my niece—all of us will be vulnerable unless I make the right choices.

"Unkie Cole, where's Aunt Keira?" Stella drags her feet toward me, peering up with pained eyes.

"I'm sure she isn't too far away." I lean forward, palm her delicate chin, and encourage her focus to remain on mine. "How are you holding up, pumpkin?"

She nods, silently lying to me as she blinks through grief-stricken tears.

The heartache she harbors for a man who never existed cuts me to the core. She isn't aware of Richard's perversions, the ones that brought pleasure to him and agony to others. Hopefully, she never will be.

"She's doing okay." Layla grabs her daughter's shoulders and encourages the child to retreat from me. It's a subtle shun. A barely recognizable retaliation in front of a crowd filled with dark suits and darker souls. "Aren't you, sweetheart?"

I stifle a snarl while Stella nuzzles her face into her mother's stomach.

My sister isn't letting go of her grudge against me any time soon. She's made it clear she doesn't appreciate me hiding family secrets from her. Secrets that weren't mine to share. And, like every woman on the face of the earth, she's clutching the grievance as if it's a fucking lifeline.

"Lay off him, my love." Her husband, Benji, places his hands on her waist. "The situation was complicated."

"*Your* situation will be complicated if you don't make intelligent choices about where your loyalties lie." She scowls straight ahead, fixing her attention on something in the distance.

Benji's hands drop from her body, his nostrils flaring in a show of annoyance. He's not romantic or sweet. He's not weak or defenseless either, and definitely not the type to withstand female ultimatums. Especially not in front of me.

He's harsh. Aggressive. And threatening at the best of times.

When he opens his mouth to retaliate, I shoot him a look—one that orders him to be smart and keep quiet.

I know exactly where his loyalties lie. I always have. It's the reason I gave him my blessing to marry my sister.

Besides, this isn't the place to air relationship issues. God knows I've got enough shit to deal with without their egos fighting for supremacy.

"Unkie Cole?"

I sigh, this time ignoring the pull of angelic eyes as I glance across the crowd. "Yeah, little one?"

"Aunt Keira is late."

"I know. Just try to be patient for me. I promise she will be here."

Keira is definitely late, but she'll show.

That boyfriend of hers will be at her side, too, when I'd much prefer he took up residence in the free plot beside my uncle.

I haven't hidden my animosity toward Decker. In fact, I've made it clear I'd like to take the fucker swimming. While he wears cement blocks for shoes.

He's a traitor. Not to mention a smart-ass who makes me want to extract every one of his teeth. *Slowly.*

The only thing keeping him alive is his dedication to my sister.

He saved Keira's life. And, okay, he saved my ass, too.

But my generosity is wearing thin with every breath he takes.

"Want me to make some calls?" Luca asks over my shoulder. "She was riding with Hunt and Sarah."

"Give them a few more minutes." I bite back the annoyance from my voice. Luca is starting to grate on my nerves.

Fuck.

With the mess in my head, everyone is rubbing me the wrong way. I understand he's still trying to find his feet in the position of my right-hand man; he just needs to do it quicker. Before I lose my shit.

Maybe it was a mistake giving him Hunter's previous role. I demoted my long-time enforcer to prove a point about loyalty. I demand allegiance. Honesty. Reliability. Hunt had wavered on all three counts. The non-compliance wasn't something I could ignore.

Nobody fucks with me.

Not even a little bit.

But Luca will be a suitable placeholder until my point is made. He's an ex-SEAL who entered the fold due to his relationship with Benji—his brother.

I'm always willing to take on new members who vouch for others with their lives. It makes for easy leverage.

But Luca's loyalty has always been clear. He's already had the psychological manipulation implanted in him from the government, making him the perfect soldier.

He's just asking too many fucking questions when all I want is silence.

The funeral can't start without Keira. And as much as I'd prefer to put this morning in my rearview, I don't have the luxury of wishing away the minutes.

She isn't the only person missing from the festivities.

My father is yet to arrive.

Maybe he's not going to show.

I could've sworn he wouldn't miss his brother's funeral, despite the threat of the authorities breathing down his neck.

Each second that ticks by acts like a tightening vise around my chest. I haven't heard a word from him since I called to relay the details of the graveside service. Not one fucking word.

There have been no whispers of travel arrangements. Or sightings among the many people I pay for information.

As far as I'm aware, he's still in the Greek islands, pretending to kick back and soak up the scenery, when what he's really doing is tainting our family name.

Desecrating my mother's memory.

He's branded me and my sisters, associating all of us with the sex slave trade.

To anyone else, it might not seem a far stretch from the schemes I've spent years cultivating. And maybe drug distribution, money laundering, racketeering and extortion—to name a few— aren't all that distant from the brutality of women, but to me, they're fucking worlds apart.

Extortion is about exuding power and claiming money. The distribution of drugs, again, is about power and money. Everything I do holds the same values.

I never target those who are fragile and innocent.

I'm not weak.

Yet my father holds entirely different views, or so it seems. The man who I thought was beyond strength and power is nothing but a pitiful, spineless fool.

He preys on those who can't protect themselves while succumbing to perversions ninety percent of the population can keep in check.

There's no power in that. Only deficiency.

The thought of being associated with those activities makes my skin crawl.

Luca inches closer. "They're here."

I glance toward the narrow road leading through the cemetery and find Hunter's black Suburban pulling into the only remaining parking space reserved for family.

Decker rides shotgun. The women must be behind the back tinted windows.

Two doors open and Hunter and Sarah make their way toward the crowd, while my sister remains in the car, taunting my impatience.

"Want me to get them to hurry up?"

I pretend not to hear yet another one of Luca's questions and breathe deep to find some calm.

Despite my diminishing tolerance, I know Keira doesn't deserve to be rushed. She loathes Richard more than I do. She has every reason to.

My struggle is centered on something entirely different.

Something more brutal.

I fear what I will become once I condemn my father.

I grew up worlds apart from my sisters. I didn't have my mother's guidance. The kindness. The nurturing. The fucking morals that have begun to drive me bat-shit crazy. I remained tightly guided under my father's influence.

He molded me into a resilient warrior.

His spitting image.

The perfect protégé.

I learned about the drug trade while kids my age were getting beat up in middle school. There was no gentle upbringing. I shuffled through crime-scene photos like other teens flicked through *Playboy*. I was born to live in my father's footsteps. Taught to lead. To control. To conquer.

The only softness I knew was my predecessor's greatest lesson, the one that continues to ring in my ears to this very day, haunting me—*money is power, but family is everything.*

Family. Is. Everything.

Giving him what he deserves means I'm spitting in the face of the only warmth I know.

My reputation for ruthlessness will be cemented—the horrors etched in stone.

But maybe the lesson was strategic on my father's behalf.

I wouldn't be surprised if he taught me the highest value of family because he knew the day would come when I would question if he deserved his next breath.

And I am questioning it.

I'm questioning every thought. Every feeling. Every twinge of consciousness.

I guess the moral crisis is a blessing in disguise. It means I haven't reached his level of savagery.

Not yet.

"Here they come," Luca mutters.

"I can fucking see that." I don't need a blow-by-blow update. *Jesus.* I'm not blind.

Layla glares at me. "Watch your mouth in front of Stella."

I roll my eyes and hold in a sigh. Her parenting isn't a battle I'm willing to fight. We need to be strong. To be unified. I'll release my thread-bare frustration soon enough, and God help the poor motherfucker who has to deal with the nuclear detonation.

"I apologize." I grind the words through gritted teeth as Keira slides from the car.

Surprise, surprise, Decker meets her at the side of the vehicle with an outstretched hand.

That guy never ceases to piss me off.

I hate how she submits to him too easily. And maybe I envy it a little, too.

She's happy with this asshole. Despite the reasons for her being here today, beyond the weary eyes and wearier expression, she's at peace. And that solace can't be easy to find when you know your father is responsible for the death of your boyfriend's sister.

Yep. My father led Penny from the country using fake promises of a bright future in modelling.

Last I heard, her DNA was found in a mass grave.

What a great foundation for a flourishing relationship.

I drag my attention from the smitten couple who choose to stand away from our family gathered beneath the gazebo, and focus past the crowd, staring into the distance. I ignore the pound of a building headache. I block out the increased chatter from friends and strangers alike. I try to clear my head of the noise even though my mind pummels me with a million unanswered questions regarding my father's whereabouts.

Fucking hell.

He's not coming.

Which means Keira is going to crumple. Momentarily. Then bounce back even harder with a vengeance.

She will nag and nag at me to finish this. And if I don't act quick enough, she will revert to making threats to take the matter into her own hands.

I don't know what's worse—the thought of the guilt that could consume me once I deal with my own father or the fear Keira will attempt an attack before I have the chance.

I can't allow her the opportunity.

I've already failed her many times before. I won't let her be in harm's way again.

"You can start." I jerk my head toward the funeral officiant murmuring with mourners. "The last of our family has arrived."

Layla shoots me a look of concern. "You're not going to wait?"

My pulse is triggered by her panic, the frantic beats ratcheting up another notch. "There's no need. If he's not here already, he's not going to show."

The admission should bring relief. I wanted more time, right? This was what I'd been praying for. So why do I feel defeated?

The officiant steps forward, a leather-bound book clutched in his hands. He greets the crowd of people I barely recognize and speaks scripted lies, his showmanship engaging everyone in attendance as he weaves something closer to a fairy-tale than reality.

I watch Keira as the funeral drags on. I don't know how to make this right. To ease her burden. But maybe this is for the best.

I need to keep her safe. *All of us safe.*

Delaying the drama with my father will afford me the opportunity to build more loyalties. To cultivate a better plan.

As if hearing my thoughts, she freezes in place and grabs the crook of Decker's arm. She stares blankly ahead, her lips parted, her eyes wide.

She could be lost in past nightmares or predicting the horrors of the future for all I know, but I follow her gaze across the open expanse of the cemetery only to find the devil stalking toward me.

"Shit." The curse brushes past my clenched teeth.

Layla shoots me another glare, then quickly mimics my line of sight.

"Oh, God," she whispers.

My father strides toward us, passing angel statues and monuments to lives lost, his shoulders stiff beneath his expensive suit. It's been many months since I've seen him. Not enough to lessen the sense of authority he brings. Or the gut-wrenching animosity I feel.

I've never battled with such vastly conflicting emotions as I do right now.

The anger. The resentment.

The fucking brutal pain.

He used to be a storm of power and hostility, the attributes intimately entwined to make him a force to be reckoned with. At least that was what I'd thought, until he started delving in things only a weak man would entertain.

Now I see it as nothing more than a show.

A facade to hide his deficiencies.

Two men flank him, providing protection, their faces unfamiliar.

All three of them approach, inspiring a wave of whispers to break out among the mourners. The respect my father wordlessly demands is enough to make the officiant stop his fabricated remake of Richard's life and stand at attention.

Game on.

It's time for me and my sisters to fake our loyalty.

"Dad." Layla's the first to greet him, the two of them sharing an awkward embrace that is interrupted by Stella squeezing between them.

"Grandpa? I didn't think you were going to make it."

"I couldn't stay at home when I knew you needed me." He runs a hand through her hair, the action taunting my restraint. "Nothing could stop me from coming to take care of my little button."

My niece beams up at him, her grief seeming momentarily forgotten.

"Father." I hold the disgust from my tone and reach out a hand. "I'm glad you could make it."

"Thank you for taking care of everything. Even though you didn't bother to wait for me." He clasps me in a grip with unyielding strength. "We've got a lot to discuss once this is over."

His tone almost holds a threat as he steps back to settle between me and Layla, his men moving in behind him. He encourages Stella to stand at his feet with the wave of a hand, and holds the little girl's shoulders as the crowd stares.

Vengeance rushes through my veins. Anguish pounds in my chest.

"Where's Keira?" His question is low. Almost indecipherable.

"To your left." I jerk my chin in her direction and find her huddled into Decker, her suffering seeming to outweigh everyone in attendance despite her lack of grief.

What everyone doesn't realize is her tears are for the man beside me. The one she wants to see six feet under.

"She's temperamental at the moment." I don't know what else to tell him. Obviously, the truth isn't an option. "She hasn't been doing well."

He nods. "I should've come back sooner. Girls always need their father at a time like this."

I could laugh. I probably should. That way, the building resentment might have an outlet. Instead, I grit my teeth and try to ignore the men behind me, despite their proximity raising the hair on the back of my neck.

I don't trust them. I don't even trust my own flesh and blood after a lifetime trusting nothing but.

"Are you okay if we continue?" the officiant asks.

"Yes." I incline my head and the man proceeds with his elaborate fiction about Richard while I focus on pushing myself toward a resolution my sister will appreciate.

Hunter is already on standby. All I need to do is say the word and this train wreck will start rolling forward.

I'll get my father alone, confront him about the mess he's made, then look him in the fucking eye when I tell him his fate.

It's the only way. With respect and honor.

I refuse to make a sneak attack. I can't stab him in the back even though he's stabbed me in mine.

The officiant's words trail off, and I fight to understand the sudden quiet. Then the coffin lowers, the foot of space it descends enough to make Stella wail. Her grandfather comforts her by rubbing his hands down her arms. The same hands that have molested many and scarred more.

He shouldn't be touching her—shouldn't be anywhere near her innocence. The horrified look Layla gives me tells she's come to the same judgment.

"I'd now like to call upon anyone who would like to place petals or sand in the grave as a personal goodbye." The officiant meets my gaze, offering my family the first opportunity to take from his small wicker basket.

Luther sidesteps Stella to move forward, away from his guards. He grabs a handful of petals as he passes, every person in attendance watching his movements. He scatters the offering, the gentle show of mourning leaving a bitter taste in my mouth, before he kisses his clenched fist and thumps it down on the coffin.

The bang reverberates through the crowd, stealing gasps and making the people before me jump in unison. None more so than Keira.

But it's not her shock stealing my attention. It's the man behind her who jostles his way to the front of the crowd, bumping Decker's shoulder in the process.

He's either drunk or suicidal. Maybe both.

"Luther Torian?" He calls the name loudly, without remorse.

My father bristles, every inch of him tightening in what I learned at an early age to be vehemence. He scowls, not hiding his hostility.

The man doesn't quit his approach. He strides forward, holding his hand out for my father to take.

That's when it hits me.

The reality.

The trap.

Right before the man says, "I'm Special Agent Anthony Easton, and you're under arrest for human trafficking." The fucker clasps my father's palm with his right hand and retrieves a pair of cuffs with his left. "And solicitation involving minors under the age of sixteen."

A mutiny of whispered retaliation rises from the crowd, the noise building into chatter. The only quiet souls are my siblings and the people who know the severity of this situation. Not just the criminal charges, but the complication of a prison sentence.

"You have the right to remain silent."

"No." I storm forward. "*Stop.*"

This asshole isn't going to steal vengeance away from me. My father's punishment is my decision to make. If Luther is taken into custody, there's no doubt he'll escape, then disappear.

"What the fuck do you think you're doing?" I hold my anger in check, my voice coming out in a lethal calm.

The agent doesn't pause. "Anything you say can and will be used against you in a court of law."

My father's men move forward, only to stop dead at the sudden shift in the crowd. A mass of strangers nudge their way through the familiar faces, holding their FBI badges high.

Jesus. *Fuck.*

I chance a glance at Keira, finding her in panic mode, her body facing Decker, her hands wrapped in his white button-down as if begging for help.

Hunter and Sarah look at me for guidance. Luca and Benji, too.

They're all waiting for instructions. All my men are.

But what do I tell them? What the fuck do I do?

This can't end in a blood bath. Not with women and children in attendance. We can't fight our way out of this.

The agent continues reciting the Miranda rights as he hikes my father's hands behind his back. Not one word leaves the mighty Luther Torian's lips. There's no spite. Not even a glimpse of the rage I'm feeling.

Everything is locked down. Shut off.

I meet his stare and jerk my chin the slightest inch, letting him know I'm strong. Fucking defensive. He needs to think I'm on his side. That's the only play I have. The only strategy available.

"Everyone, move," a woman shouts. "Make way."

The female agent steals my attention as she spreads her arms wide and keeps my extended family at bay.

I stalk to her, my fists clenched at my sides. "What the hell do you think you're doing?" I keep my tone level. "This is a fucking funeral."

She raises a brow. "Please accept my sincerest apologies for the inconvenient timing." She flicks her attention toward my father and proceeds to ignore my existence.

Who the fuck does she think she is?

We're not a family to be messed with. Not even by the Feds.

"We've done this dance a dozen times before," I seethe. "You make an arrest. Then the charges are dropped. But this is going too fucking far. You can't come here and tear apart a place of mourning. Do you have any idea who you're messing with?"

Her lips kick into a sultry smile, exposing a viper beneath the feminine facade. "I know exactly what I'm doing, Mr. Torian. I'm putting a sick son of a bitch behind bars for a very long time. If I were you, I'd get my legal team in order. It's not just your father who's going to need it."

My pulse doesn't spike; it fucking detonates. The simmering madness I've been carrying turns into full-scale psychosis.

I see red. I hear static. I crave revenge.

"You've got some nerve, throwing your weight around, sweetheart." I scrutinize her eyes, looking deep into the hazel-green depths to try and grasp the slightest glimmer of fear. But this woman isn't scared of me. She's not even threatened. Not yet, anyway. "The FBI has nothing on me and my family. Never have. Never will."

"I wouldn't be so sure." Her grin remains in place. "In fact, I think we're going to be seeing a lot of each other in the near future." She glances away, seeming unconcerned with the threat standing right in front of her as she watches my father being hauled around headstones.

"Until next time, Mr. Torian." Briefly, those taunting eyes meet mine and she winks. "Enjoy your day."

She strides away, head high, shoulders straight, and a careless sway to her hips.

I clench my fists tighter, my nostrils flaring.

Maybe I'm closer to my father's perversions than I thought, because I want nothing more than to take her down. To watch her suffer. To make her pay.

But this woman is far from weak. There's no hint of vulnerability.

"What did she say to you?" Keira reaches my side, Decker close at her back, Sarah and Hunt following behind.

"A lot of things." I grind my teeth, still fighting for the illusive calm that's nowhere in sight. "She has the impression we're going to be seeing a lot of each other in the future."

"She said that?" Sarah snarls over Decker's shoulder. "She comes to your uncle's funeral, arrests your father, then lays more threats?"

Yes. That's exactly what she did.

With a fucking wink.

"What are you going to do?" Decker juts his chin at me. "Apart from the legal team moving into action, what's your plan?"

I return my focus to the female agent sauntering toward the mass of parked cars along the narrow cemetery road.

She poked a bear.

Fucking taunted a predator.

"I'm going to give that woman exactly what she wants."

1

TORIAN

ONE WEEK LATER

I DRUM MY FINGERS ALONG THE STEERING WHEEL OF THE rental, deliberately keeping my hands busy.

One lapse in concentration and I'll succumb. I'll pull over and slide out of this car to approach my favorite special agent on her ritual five-mile jog instead of stalking her from afar.

The temptation of being face-to-face has taunted me for days. But this morning isn't the right moment to have our reunion.

Not yet.

I need to bide my time and ignore the enticing sweat-slicked exercise gear hugging her body like a second skin.

I thought I'd be immune to her haughty sterility by now. Desensitized. Turns out, she's had the opposite effect.

I'm itching to play with her. To mess with her head, just like she's messed with mine.

Every morning, she runs circles around the city streets, each step like fuel to a fucking wet dream. Her cheeks are slicked with wisps of dark, shoulder-length hair, her skin flushed.

She pushes herself to the limit, always slaying the same path, never stopping, not even pausing for breath. She doesn't smile at people as they pass. There's no friendly hello or gentle finger wave.

Ms. Fox is the queen of hostility, keeping herself at a distance from any unnecessary human contact.

Turns out, she doesn't have a lot of friends. Not that her solo status is a surprise, with her prickly personality. The woman doesn't just have resting bitch face; it's more an expression of overly enthusiastic aggression.

There's minimal family, too.

Her mother is dead, and her ex-FBI father left the scene a while ago, with the suspicion of his crimes probably more familiar to me than they are to his own daughter.

She's all alone, which makes these secret moments of ours all the more intimate.

It's just the two of us.

Me and her.

Even though she's not aware.

The best time to watch her is early morning. At sunrise. When her clothes are flattering and her motivation is high.

She's far more alluring now than during office hours when she hides her figure behind masculine business suits.

Ninety percent of the time she insists upon dressing like a man. It's clear she's overcompensating for the lack of appendage between her thighs. The FBI is a men's club. Always has been. Probably always will be.

A woman with her lack of physical flaws would struggle to gain respect since she's a walking, talking turn-on. I think that's why she never gentles her expression. She's always harsh: either aggressive with her arrogance or spiteful with her intimidation.

There's no softness to her. It's all stiff shoulders and tight features.

But not for too much longer. I'll weaken her. Soon.

She's going to regret fucking with me.

I'll make sure of it. Take pleasure in it.

I just need to ignore the building anticipation urging me to get this show underway, and enjoy the foreplay.

It's not like I'm stupid enough to think she's oblivious to the eyes she has on her.

She's a smart woman. She's aware her actions have consequences.

Right now is the perfect example. She slows to a walk as she approaches her favorite coffee shop, her gaze trekking the street as she pushes open the glass door.

She's always searching.

She never finds what she's looking for.

I use a different car each day. Sometimes I'm on foot. Today, though, I pull to the curb at the end of her block and focus inside the cafe, watching as she takes her headphones out to place them in her pocket.

She knows someone is close. How couldn't she?

The list of criminals she's fucked over is a mile long, and I'm at the top of her list. This pretty little thing would be well aware of my history of retaliation. My reputation speaks for itself.

But is she aware I haven't outsourced the surveillance to my men?

Not entirely, anyway.

It isn't Hunter who witnesses the dimming of her apartment light every night. Luca and Decker don't trail her through her morning routine.

I do.

The last week of predatory stalking has become a favored pastime. A sport. I've grown to appreciate the shared parts of our lives.

It's even got to the point where my pulse spikes whenever I lay eyes on her. The dose of anticipation increases every damn day.

It's a fucking drug.

I live for it.

Crave it.

I'm impatient, waiting for the moment when I get to wipe her smug smile from my memory. The one she etched into my mind at my uncle's funeral. I'll replace the expression with something beautiful. Something full of fear and panic.

The shock of parted lips.

The horror of wide, shimmering eyes.

She needs to learn the dynamic here in Portland. I want to

show her who holds the power. I plan to teach her that lesson over and over until her soul is crushed with the weight of her mistakes.

The Feds can't threaten me.

They have no control here. Not over my family.

They may provide a temporary inconvenience. But that's all it is. An annoyance. A mere disruption to a flawless system.

"You're mine, Ms. Fox."

I continue with the *tap, tap, tap* of my fingers, the beat growing faster to match my pulse. My fun for the day is going to end soon. I can feel the seconds ticking down.

When my cell rings from the passenger seat, I glare through the annoyance, never taking my gaze from Anissa as she hands payment to the cashier.

I already know who's responsible for the intrusion. Hunter. It always is at this time of morning.

I snatch the device and connect the call. "What is it?"

"Are you ready for me to take over?"

I withhold my instinctive response.

I could spend all day staring at this woman, daydreaming about the moment I get to speak to her again. The threats I'll promise. The taunts I'll make. But exposing my obsession is a weak move. I need to remain focused.

My father is still in custody. And Keira is a constant thorn in my side, her lack of faith in me growing every day.

"Yeah," I mutter. "Soon. Where are you?"

"In a rental on the other side of the street. A woman in red is just about to walk by me."

I drag my focus from the café to the sidewalk, finding the lady in red, then Hunt behind the wheel of a beat-up blue minivan.

"Nice wheels."

"Thanks," he grates. "I'm switching it up to stay off the radar."

"Where's your babysitter?" I return my attention to the shopfront and ignore the way my chest tightens when my gaze locks onto my target.

Hunt knows I'm referring to his fiancée. What I hope he doesn't realize is my attempt to waste time as I steal a few more precious moments with my prey.

"Sarah decided to bow out of the surveillance gig for a few days. There's not enough action to keep her happy."

"Interesting." I watch as my mark smiles at the barista, grabs her coffee, and hustles from the cafe. There's no bagel this morning. Or maybe she buys a croissant. I never know what she carries in her paper bag. "You better make sure you've got Sarah on a tight leash. If she starts whispering in Keira's ear I'll—"

"She's not doing a damn thing to Keira. I've got her under control."

"About time."

"Speaking of time. Have you heard any news on your father's court appearance? Do we have a date?"

Anissa approaches the street and looks both ways. Like always, I stiffen, wondering, waiting to see if she'll find me sitting here.

I'm like a fucking junkie in need of a fix.

But she doesn't discover my hiding place. She doesn't even come close as she starts to cut through the light traffic to get to her apartment on the other side of the street.

"I'll have more information today. Don't worry; you'll be the first to hear."

"The first?" Hunt pauses, and I can already sense the direction of his thoughts. "What happened to your new lapdog?"

"My new one?" His annoyance at Luca's promotion has been a constant point of contention. He doesn't appreciate being second best, which was the entire point of the exercise. "Are you implying you were the previous lapdog?"

"I've never been your bitch," he growls. "Never will be. Unlike Luca, I've got a fucking backbone. But you know as well as I do that I'm the best person to have at your side."

"He does his job. I have no complaints. And I'm pretty sure you were one of his cheerleaders when he got you and Sarah out of that warehouse alive." I cut the ignition and slump back in my seat. "You, on the other hand, fucking betrayed me."

"Jesus Christ," he mutters. "Not this shit again."

"It will continue to be this shit until I quit questioning your loyalty."

Anissa reaches the door of her apartment building and stops

before the security panel to enter her three-digit code. I can't help reciting the numbers in my head as her finger works across the buttons. *One-four-eight*. Her deceased mother's birthday.

It was too fucking easy for Decker to get the information. A heat-sensor camera focused on the keypad was all it took. The additional pinhole device he planted between the brickwork was overkill. But I've taken advantage of the screen time it provides.

I watch her more often than I care to admit, trying to read what's going on behind those hard eyes.

Like every morning this week, she disappears inside with another cautionary glance over her shoulder. And like every morning this week, I ignore my disappointment at her not finding me.

In another forty-five minutes, she'll be back, showered, dressed, and wearing one of those fucking suits I've grown to hate. But I won't be here. I need to return to the family restaurant and concentrate on the things that matter.

Things like my father's fucking court case, and the shipment of blow that came in ten bricks short.

"Just let me do my fucking job," Hunt growls.

"Unfortunately, I can't. Trust is important. I hope this is a lesson you won't forget."

Like Keira, he recently showed his allegiance to someone other than me. Information was withheld. Friendship came before the family.

That shit is never acceptable. And he should know; he was the one who previously punished those who betrayed me.

"Don't even fucking start," he snarls. "We've gone over this. I've told you. I've explained. So either man the fuck up and let it go. Or tell me to cut and run, and I'll walk out of here and never look back. I'm sick of being treated like an ex you want to bang when it's convenient, but can't stand the sight of every other second of the day."

"Nice analogy," I drawl. "Fits perfectly."

He mutters a string of curses under his breath. And yeah, I get it. He's pissed at me. He's pissed at himself.

That's the price he has to pay for making mistakes.

If I let it slide without penalty, any motherfucker will think he can run rings around me. Hunt's just lucky very few people know about his blunder.

"Look, we're as good as we're going to get for now." I glance up at Anissa's window on the fifth floor, hoping to catch another glimpse. "Luca will remain at my side. But I have plans for you. Ones I can't entrust with anyone else."

"What plans?"

"We'll speak later."

I won't discuss the necessity for a recruitment drive, even on a burner. Not when I've been paranoid enough to switch phones every other day.

We have to boost our numbers. Expand our presence. Increase our power. All outstanding favors need to be claimed. Anyone with even a glimpse of loyalty has to be enlisted into my outer circles to keep my family safe.

And Hunt is the guy I want on the job. He sees through the bullshit, sometimes better than I do. And when my focus is shot to shit, it's a smart move to let him do what he does best.

"Fine. I'll meet you back at the restaurant this afternoon." There's another pause. "You can leave now. I've got her covered."

I don't appreciate the nudge. Or the reminder he's going to be taking over my part in this game.

I hate anyone else's involvement. If I had my way, I'd be the only player. I want full responsibility.

Unfortunately, my empire won't run itself.

"I'll leave when I'm ready," I mutter.

Which doesn't feel like it's going to be anytime soon.

I disconnect the call and throw the cell to the passenger seat.

My hands return to the steering wheel, my fingers tapping out an agitated rhythm, but it's the devil on my shoulder causing the burn in my chest.

I've denied the impulse to mess with her for longer than I thought possible. I've fought and fought the nagging urge even though anticipation has had me by the balls.

I don't think fighting will be enough today.

I need something more. The slightest hint of her apprehension. The sweetest taste of her fear.

I'm going to have to succumb.

Just a little.

As much as I don't want to buckle, it's time to start toying with my prey.

2

ANISSA

YOU RUN LIKE A GAZELLE. I SHOULD KNOW—I'M SOMEONE WHO loves to hunt.

I sprint out the last of my five-mile run. It isn't difficult. Spurring my legs to move faster despite the fatigue is easy when I'm being followed.

I've known for almost two weeks. Since before the flowers started to arrive with their taunting notes.

Being aware of my tail before they deliberately announced their existence wasn't because my watchers are novices. In fact, it's the opposite.

I've never seen them. It's the raised hair on the back of my neck making their presence known. Pure instinct.

I'd anticipated the retaliation after my outburst at the funeral. I hadn't been able to bite my tongue. For once, I lacked my usual restraint because victory had been too invigorating not to bask in its glory.

One failed investigation after another had led to Luther's arrest. Finally, we'd taken him into custody, and I'd struggled to curb my need to gloat.

It then proved impossible when his son, the formidable Cole Torian, had tried to talk his way out of the situation using intimidation and threats. That dark, soulless gaze had been fixed on me. Conniving. Vindictive. He'd wanted to squash me like a bug, and in that moment, I decided I'd prefer him to see me as more of a lion than a cockroach.

I'd stared the devil in the eye, and without any subtlety, I kinda told him to go fuck himself, adding a provoking wink for good measure.

Euphoria had shot through me, the thrill entirely worth the death sentence his expression had promised. At least, that was what I'd thought at the time.

Now, I'm not so sure.

Your body is a masterpiece, but your screams will be my symphony.

The deliveries keep coming. Every day for the last five days. Roses, lilies, carnations, irises. Yesterday, tulips.

After the first bouquet, I didn't accept another offering. I refused the blooms and only took the cards. Those tiny envelopes, with their delightful messages from my secret admirer, are all the evidence I need.

I just have to find a way to tie them to a source.

Problem is, I'm not entirely sure who the sender is. The florist won't help without a warrant, and the list of potential candidates is mighty long. Even narrowing my search to the latest investigation leaves me with more options than I'd like—Luther, Cole, and Decker. I've also made threats toward Hunter and Sarah, so those two can't be ignored.

Any one of them would want revenge. It's merely a case of who's willing to claim it.

The advantage is in their court, especially when I haven't mentioned the constant tail to my supervisor.

I can't.

I kept the heated exchange with Cole from my report, too.

My presence in this department has been a point of contention since my father left his badge behind to join the dark side. Without a word, he disappeared, removing every penny from his bank account to start a new life among the crime rings he'd spent the majority of his adult life trying to disband.

Now he's dead to me. As far as I'm concerned, I lost both

parents the night my mother died, but the taint of his actions still linger.

Nobody here trusts me. Well, I don't trust that they trust me. Not really. They don't have my back, and I don't fucking care. I've always worked on my own anyway.

It's their judgment that kills me. They think I'm a traitor, too. They expect that I'm a hair-trigger away from packing my bags and switching to a life of crime.

It didn't fucking help when my only informant inside the Torian organization chose to take the same path as my father. Apparently, I'm a magnet for turncoats.

Or, if I listen to the taunting whispers inside the bureau, I'm a recruiter for the other side.

A fucking leper.

So keeping my slip-up from the funeral to myself is important. And I refuse to let anyone think I'm weak and in need of surveillance. I can handle these threats on my own.

Do you dream of me? Because I dream about what I'm going to do to you.

My anger leaves no room for fear.

Instead, I work harder, sprinting faster, pushing myself further until I reach the café doors in a panting, sweating mess.

I suck gulps of air into my lungs as I wipe the dampness from my face and succumb to the uncomfortable shiver at the back of my neck.

I glance over my shoulder and scan the sidewalk.

They're here. Somewhere. They, he or her.

It doesn't matter that I can't see the culprit. There's only a street filled with parked cars and what appears to be innocent pedestrians pacing along the cement, but they're here. I can feel it.

The mornings and evenings are the worst. I don't know why. I don't think I want to know. It's bad enough that my entire body gets blanketed in goose bumps whenever I leave my apartment to exercise, and then again when I return home from work.

Their presence shadows the start and end of every day.

But it can't last forever. Whoever it is will grow tired before I become scared.

Not long now, little fox. Not long at all.

I push open the café door and walk inside, determined to put their existence to the back of my mind.

Today is about celebration. Luther Torian is making a court appearance, and I get to witness the magnificence. Nothing can drag me down from the heightened anticipation of seeing him in cuffs. His suffering will make my hardships worthwhile.

The barista meets my gaze as I approach, her subtle nod a confirmation of my order. She's run off her feet. Like always. The line of customers are banked up like a traffic jam.

There's a reason I come here to join the weary queue, and it has nothing to do with the convenience of the café being directly across the street from my apartment and everything to do with the strong coffee and creamy aftertaste.

"The usual?" the cashier asks over the hiss of steam from the machine making the heavenly liquid.

"Yeah. Thanks." I shove a hand into the gauze pocket in the side of my leggings, my fingers grazing the crinkled bills as a skitter of awareness shoots up my spine.

A figure moves to stand close. The large frame right by my side.

"Allow me," a man offers.

I freeze, watching as a hand reaches out, offering payment, the material of a tailored suit jacket entering my peripheral vision.

I know the voice. I've heard it ring in my ears. Whisper into my dreams. Murmur through my nightmares.

It's the friendly tone that's unfamiliar. The deep, smooth words drift over my skin, making the hairs on the back of my neck dance.

"No. Thanks." I scoot my money along the counter. "I've got this."

I don't look at him. I won't risk letting him hear my thoughts.

"I insist." He inches his fingers farther, creating a race toward the cashier that I'm loath to participate in.

"Again, *thanks*," I grate, "but the Bureau frowns upon agents accepting gifts from criminals." I speak loud enough for my accusation to be heard by the line of people waiting for their morning solace.

It's another taunt. A mistake. One I'm too pathetic to resist.

I glare at the cashier, silently demanding she take my money while I wait for Cole Torian to retaliate.

Instead, he chuckles, the thickly rich sound sinking into me along with the woodsy scent of his expensive cologne. "I've got a clean record, Niss. So there's no need to fear."

He lets the sentence linger. The last word hovers in the air between us like a threat before he gently nudges in front of me and places his cash directly in the hand of the slack-jawed woman I seriously want to slap.

I should turn around and walk out. I should... But my addiction to caffeine and the allure of withstanding his intimidation becomes a living, breathing thing inside me as I stalk to the serving station to await my order.

I continue my refusal to make eye contact. I won't give him the satisfaction of my attention, not when I'm unsure if my emotions are masked.

"Why are you walking away?" He follows behind me, stopping on the fringes of my personal space. "You said we were going to be seeing a lot of each other. Then you didn't call. You didn't text. I'm beginning to think you led me on."

My pulse spikes and I pivot to face him. "Don't—"

I snap my mouth shut at the grin he beams at me. The provoking, manipulative curve of lips.

"Don't what?" His deep blue eyes glisten, his enjoyment crystal clear.

My heart rate becomes a crescendo, the growing beats transforming into a throbbing pound in my ears.

He's playing with me. Toying. And it's all my fault.

I started this game. I whacked the hornet nest and thought I could get away with it. But I'm not going to be terrorized. Not now. Not ever.

I'm immune to his charm. I don't see the beauty in him, not like all the women around me seem to.

Those dark eyes are threatening, not mesmerizing. The thick

eyelashes. The chocolate hair. The richly tanned skin with enough stubble to increase his masculinity. It all means nothing.

Nothing.

He's packaged strategically. To lure his prey.

And I won't be enticed toward that web.

"Mr. Torian." I raise my voice above polite conversation in an attempt to gain an audience. "I don't think it's appropriate for you to be speaking to me seeing as though your actions are constantly under FBI scrutiny."

His shoulder lifts in a faint shrug. "You've got nothing to worry—"

"And don't you have more important things to do this morning?" I speak over the top of him, one brow cocked. "I thought you'd be making your way to court. Your father's case is going to make headlines. It's definitely an event I won't miss."

Those dark ocean eyes remain on mine. The smile holds in place. But something waivers. There's the slightest change in him to make the charming expression turn forced.

Good.

I've struck a chord.

If he doesn't leave, I'll strike many more.

"I understand the hostility." He reaches out an arm and checks his watch. "And yes, I assume my father is being transported to the courthouse as we speak. That's why I'm here. I'd like to offer a truce."

"A truce?" The question escapes my lips without my permission.

"Yes." He loses the grin and quits the playboy act to stare at me with a solemn facade. "I want to clear my name and any misconceptions you might have. I don't want to be associated with my father's crimes."

"Misconceptions?"

The cashier slides my coffee and an apricot Danish encased in a paper bag across the collection counter and murmurs my name.

"I don't have any misconceptions." I step forward to claim my bag and travel cup, then indulge in a sip. "Only cold, hard facts. I know exactly what type of man you are. There's no need to waste your breath."

He follows me, stepping close and lowering his voice. "You may not agree with the way I do business, but I'm not anything like my father."

"The way you do business?" I keep repeating him. I can't help it. His insanity is worth hearing more than once. "That's a delusional way of describing what you do."

"I'm nothing but a ruthless businessman."

"Ruthless, with stalking tendencies, right?"

The accusation isn't a stab in the dark. He came here looking for me, which means he already knew my routine.

"I wouldn't call this stalking." He flashes me a flawless grin. "I asked a colleague or two about your habits, and they led me here. I don't think there's anything wrong with that, do you?"

I wave a hand in the direction of his face. "Intimidation, threats, lies, and now flirtation? You really do have a remarkable set of skills. But none of them will work on me. I suggest you quit while you're ahead."

I start for the doors, his footsteps following close behind.

"You've got the wrong idea. I just want to talk."

Despite the calm tone, there's a wealth of authority in his voice. He's used to being obeyed. He's perfected the art of coercion.

"I'll tell you whatever you want to know." He maneuvers around me, cutting me off before I reach the door. "What do you have to lose?"

"My integrity." I stop, not wanting to barrel into him. I'm sure his heat is enough to scar. "My self-respect."

"You don't know me." Again, he's calm. Collected. He's entirely locked down, but there's the slightest hint of panic in his eyes.

He needs this.

Why?

"I don't want to know you," I drawl.

He raises his chin as if offended. "I understand that. But you want to know the facts, right? You want to learn the truth."

I scrutinize him, trying to understand his hidden motives. He's not making sense. Cole Torian doesn't beg. He never shows weakness.

Something must be amiss in his magical world of criminal activity to have him scrambling for my attention.

The possibilities eat away at my curiosity. That hyper-sensitive skin at the back of my neck regains its tingle.

"I've already told you I've got places to be this morning." I focus outside, trying to fight the wicked web he's weaved. "I can give you five minutes. Nothing more."

"That works for me."

He takes the lead, moving away from the door. But I can't follow. My feet are cemented in place, the instinct to flee scratching at my skin.

I should call this in. Or request assistance. Even a silent witness.

Then again, it's just a conversation. No other agent would show anything but excitement at this opportunity. Unless they had a tarnished reputation.

"Anissa?" His voice brushes my ear, the material of his suit grazing my arm. "We can take the empty table next to the window."

"Yeah. Okay." I nod, my mind made up, and push past him to lead the way toward the front corner of the cafe, the glass window providing an unrestricted view of the sidewalk.

I take the far seat and place my paper bag on the table, my back to the wall while his remains exposed to the room.

"I assume you won't protest the need to record this conversation." I pull my cell from the Velcro strap stretched across my bicep and place it between us.

"Not at all."

I expected a refusal. This man is definitely full of surprises today.

"Good." I place my coffee down and swipe through the cell screen until I find the voice recorder. "You can get started whenever you're ready."

He eyes me, those navy depths examining me closely. "You're going to fight this friendship every step of the way, aren't you?"

I don't bite. I refuse.

He's trying to get me to admit to a non-existent relationship, one that will worsen my position within the Bureau, and I won't let it happen.

He won't gain the upper hand here.

I sigh. "What's this about, Cole? What's the game?"

"There's no game." He leans back in his chair, the picture of relaxation. "I just want to make both our lives easier. You keep trying to pin me for crimes I haven't committed. You even planted an informant to gain evidence that doesn't exist. What will it take to make this stop?"

I press my lips tight, feigning contemplation while I push aside the unwanted reminder of my defective narc. "I don't know, maybe when you quit breaking the law we can all get along."

"Then why do I get the distinct impression you won't be satisfied until you see me behind bars?"

"Maybe that's what you deserve."

He cocks his head. "Because you think I'm guilty of the same atrocities as my father."

I sigh. "I think we're getting sidetracked here. My opinion doesn't count. The evidence is all that matters."

"And there is no evidence. You'll never tie me to my father's crimes."

"Is that because you're smarter at covering your tracks?"

His eyes narrow. His irritation quick to ignite. "No, it's because I was never involved." His tone is vehement, the words dripping with conviction.

I could almost believe him. *Almost.* If I were high and insanely stupid.

Unfortunately for him, I'm neither.

"Even if you didn't participate, there's no way you wouldn't have been aware of what Richard and Luther were doing. And the fact you stood by while women were manipulated, escorted from the country, then sold as sex slaves, makes you an accomplice."

"There." He points a finger at the table. "That right there is an unfounded misconception."

"For now," I drawl. "It's only a matter of time before misconceptions become facts."

His jaw tics, his building anger entirely delicious. "I'm a businessman, Niss. A successful entrepreneur. I don't have the time or inclination to keep up-to-date with my father's activities."

"I don't think entrepreneurship extends to the drug trade. Do you?"

His nostrils flare. "That's yet another unfounded accusation."

"That part of your reputation is far from unfounded." I take a sip of coffee, trying to disguise my annoyance. "Do you think we're not aware of how you run your business? You set up your lower ranks to take the fall. That's all part of the deal. You pay them beyond their wildest dreams, but the drawcard is the possibility of prison time if the shit hits the fan. Isn't that what happened to Trenton White and Samuel Puglisi? One of your deals went bad, and they took the hit. But hey, I guess you should be commended for looking after their wives and children while they rot in a cell."

Cole sighs, and reaches out his arm, taking another look at his watch.

I should be doing the same. The court case will start in roughly ninety minutes. Just enough time for me to shower, dress, and get my ass across town.

"Regretting your decision already?" I muse. "Did my insight hit a little too close to the mark? Or have you had enough of this delightful conversation already?"

"I see this as less of a conversation and more of a trial." He crosses his arms, making the collared shirt beneath his jacket cling tight to his chest. "When you're ready to stop the accusations and have a civilized discussion, please let me know."

"Don't reach for the sympathy card, Cole. Not with all the horrors your family have inflicted."

I take a gulp of java, throwing it back like a shot.

Fuck him.

Seriously, fuck this manipulative prick for thinking he can gain any understanding from me.

He won't change my opinion. I'll never see him as anything other than a waste of possibilities.

It's obvious he's attractive. His intelligence isn't in question either. A stupid man could never have risen in power, expanding his family's grasp further and tighter, without a glimpse of brilliance.

But he could've been so much more. An academic. A doctor. A politician. Even an entrepreneur who made millions from something legitimate instead of criminal.

"I'm not after sympathy, Nissa."

That's another thing I despise. The deliberately taunting way he takes liberties with my name. Nobody calls me Niss. Or Nissa. I've only ever been Anissa. Or Fox.

"Good." I hold his gaze and smile. "Because you'll never get it."

My cell vibrates on the table, the incoming call from my supervisor. "I need to take this."

Cole sits forward. "By all means, answer the call, but I'm not going to wait around." He pushes his chair back, poised to stand. "Either you talk to me, or him."

Him. Taggert.

I'm not surprised he recognized the name on my screen.

"You're not making it a hard decision when you haven't told me anything of value." I raise a brow, waiting as my cell continues to trill. "I'm still not sure why you're wasting my time."

"It wouldn't be a waste, Nissie, if you asked questions instead of running your mouth."

Nissie.

Fucking. Nissie.

This asshole has crawled under my skin like a plague of parasites. Problem is, I've already succumbed. I'm here, ready and waiting. And if I leave without a thread of valuable insight, I'll look an even bigger fool.

"Fine." I reject the call. "You claim you didn't know what your father was doing. How is that possible?"

He stills, not only in his movements, but in his expression.

He's considering lying to me.

Not a smart move when my patience is threadbare.

"I confess." He raises his hands in surrender. "I *was* aware."

My heart stills in shock and I glance down at my cell. *Fuck.*

The recording stopped when the call came through.

Fuck. Fuck. *Fuck.*

"You didn't get that on the record?" he taunts. "What a shame."

I breathe through the anger, not letting him get to me. "How long before?"

"Since Richard went to hospital." He glances at his watch again, seeming bored with the topic. "My father offered me the lucrative position my uncle held within their organization. Apparently, there's a lot of money in sex trafficking."

I don't appreciate the candor. The complete and utter lack of empathy.

"Have some respect," I seethe. "A lot of those women were raped and murdered for sport. I don't know how you can look yourself in the mirror with their torture on your conscience."

"I knew about it, but I wasn't involved. Never have been and never will be."

"How noble of you." My sarcasm is profound. I could win an Academy Award for the performance. I could also have a stroke from the potency of my rage. "Do you really expect praise just because you didn't take a golden handshake from the scum of the earth? Those women continued to suffer until me and my colleagues could pull together enough evidence to arrest your father."

His eyes narrow, the intense depths turning spiteful. "Are you that naive to think his arrest helped their situation?" He scoffs. "You've got no idea what you've done by putting him behind bars."

"Then tell me."

There are still a million leads to follow in Luther's case. A myriad of tangled threads to unravel before we determine how many women he abducted. And we're not getting anywhere with his father's refusal to answer questions.

"Tell me what we've done," I repeat.

The trill of my cell breaks the moment, stealing away the glimmer of insight I'm dying to hear. I lower my gaze to read *Taggert* across the screen again. *Shit.* He's going to be pissed I've ignored him, but I'm finally getting somewhere. The smoke and mirrors are subsiding to reveal the truth I need.

"Please continue." I reject the call and return my gaze to Cole's. "What's changed now that Luther is behind bars?"

Yet again he's looking at his watch, his patience seeming to grow thin. "Forget it. You're needed elsewhere and I've got places to be."

"No, it's fine. I'll return the call once we're finished."

Another cell tone interrupts us, but this time it isn't mine.

"Excuse me." Cole reaches into his jacket and pulls out his phone. "Unfortunately, I'm going to have to take this."

He pushes to his feet, placing distance between me and the information I need when he connects the call. "Yeah?"

He listens for long moments, his brow furrowed. "Okay. I understand. I'll see you soon."

He lowers the device, presses the screen to end the call, and places the cell back inside his jacket. "I'm sorry. I need to leave."

"What?" I push to my feet. "You're the one who wanted this. Not me."

"Again, I apologize. It can't be helped." He gives me a sad smile, one that drips with satire. "Maybe we can reschedule."

Reschedule?

This asshole has been stalking me, invading every inch of my privacy. And now he has the balls to fuck with me?

"Or maybe not," he drawls. "Either way, don't be a stranger." He winks, and the gesture is so familiar I want to stab myself for doing it to him at the funeral.

He lured me here, provoking me, and I fell for it.

He starts for the door, dismissing me as if I don't exist.

"What the hell was this, Cole?" I stalk after him. "Did you come here just to waste a few minutes of my day? Because I can assure you, it takes more than that to piss me off."

"This hasn't been a waste." He keeps walking, only to stop suddenly before me. "Actually, before I leave, there's one thing I've been meaning to ask you."

I glare, my fury rising because I don't understand his motive.

He's inspired a wealth of questions inside me only to deny me at the last second, and now he wants me to play nice?

He turns to face me, his brows tight as if he's deep in thought. "Why do you insist on wearing those masculine pantsuits to work when the little black dress in the back of your closet would look ten times better?"

My stomach drops. It completely bottoms out.

Everything inside me hollows as I quickly realize this meeting wasn't about misconceptions; it was purely about payback. His presence is entirely based on a threat.

He stares, waiting for a reply I can't give. I *won't* give.

I'm not going to release a breath of panic, or utter a word of fear. Not even when I picture him in my apartment. In my fucking closet.

"Forget it." His eyes dance with mirth. His mouth kicks at one side. "I can see I've touched a nerve. But it's definitely something you should think about. You've got great legs; you should show them off."

I fight to keep my mouth shut, my shoulders strong, and my restraint locked tight.

I won't falter.

I won't show fear.

"Enjoy your day, little fox."

3

ANISSA

I HUSTLE FROM THE CAFÉ, MY HANDS SHAKING AS I CROSS THE street and escape into the tainted sanctuary of my apartment building.

The tremble isn't from fear.

Oh, no. I refuse to let him get to me that way.

What I feel is fury. Spite. And a huge desire for retaliation.

I ride the elevator to the fifth floor and quickly rush to open my apartment. I'm already running late, which I'm sure was Cole's plan, but I refuse to miss Luther's day in court, even when the desire to figure out how Cole got into my home is gnawing at me.

I run down the hall to my kitchen, slam my cell on the counter, then strip, leaving my sweat-soaked clothes strewn all over the floor. Then it's a mad dash to the bathroom, where I stop on the threshold at the sound of my cell.

"Damn it." I rush back to the kitchen and read the screen. *Taggert.* "Shit."

One missed call is acceptable. Two means I'm in trouble, but three is a clear sign I'm about to get my ass whipped.

I swipe to connect and raise the phone to my ear. "I'm running late," I start before he can get an accusatory word in. "There was a slight change in plan."

"What kind of change?" he growls.

I contemplate keeping the truth to myself. If I could slide this under the rug along with everything else, my life would be less complicated. Unfortunately, I've hidden too much to keep track of. "I ran into Cole Torian. He sought me out and wanted to talk."

Silence greets my admission. Cold, judgmental silence.

"I took the opportunity to try and get some information out of him."

"And did you?" His tone is lethal, laced with anger and not even a hint of curiosity.

"I'm not sure. I'll need to do some research. For all I know, he was wasting my time in a vain attempt to intimidate me."

"And let me guess; you were there on your own."

"Yes, but—"

"Get to the office," he snarls.

"Sir, let me explain."

"Get to the office. *Now*."

I squeeze my eyes shut and clench my free hand into a fist. "But I planned on going to Luther's—"

The line disconnects and I'm left to despise his increased animosity toward me.

I've been a target for Taggert's anger for too damn long, and this shit is growing old. Fast. He has no right to judge me for my father's actions. I've done nothing wrong.

Nothing but let a smart-mouthed informant slip through my fingers.

I slam my cell down on the counter and stalk to the bathroom. This time, I don't even contemplate a much needed shower. I bathe Irish-style, dousing my sweat in a truckload of deodorant, before I dress in one of Cole's favorite pantsuits and head for the door.

I don't even do my hair or spare a few minutes for makeup.

If Taggert wants to see a dragon, I'll give him one.

I reach the Bureau less than twenty minutes later and walk into my department on the third floor to find a frenzy of scrambling colleagues. Agents rush to answer phone calls. Assistants hustle to get coffee. And I start to second guess my decision to use the quiet car ride to mellow myself out instead of listening to the radio.

Something has happened.

Something that has put me in the firing line.

I cut through the war zone, increasing my pace through the middle of the partitioned desk spaces until I reach Taggert's office at the end of the building.

He's already glaring at me as I approach, his face flushed.

"Good morning," I mutter in greeting. It's a far stretch from sarcasm, but he wouldn't have missed my contempt.

"Close the door behind you."

I ignore the instinct to panic and do as he requests, closing us into the confined space and coming to stand between the two leather chairs situated before his desk. "What's going on?"

"You tell me." He leans forward, placing his elbows on the desk to steeple his fingers. "I want to know where the fuck your head's at."

"I'm sorry, but I missed the news flash. I don't know what's going on."

"Then tell me what you do know. What happened between you and Cole Torian?" he asks, as if my actions are a dirty little secret. Like I've committed a cardinal sin.

"He approached me after my run. He wanted to talk. He paid for my coffee, despite my firm refusal. End of story. I thought it would be a great opportunity to get information."

"And did you?" he drawls. "Did you actually get any information, Fox?"

"I already told you. I need to do some digging first."

He huffs out a derisive laugh. "Let me save you the time. Whatever he told you was bullshit."

"You don't know that." He couldn't. He doesn't have a clue about the basis of our conversation. "He said he—"

"He used you." The derision remains in his voice, growing thicker with each passing syllable. "He played you."

I stiffen, not appreciating the accusation even though I already know it's true.

"He was trying to keep you busy."

"He was?" My pulse grows frantic. My heart squeezes. "For what reason?"

"His father's transport van was ambushed on the way to the court house."

I don't react. I won't flinch despite the words that act like a physical blow.

"You were Cole's fucking alibi."

I raise my chin, taking the punishment as it pummels me from the inside out. "How?" My voice cracks, exposing my proximity to breaking point. "How could that happen?"

"We're still working on it. All I know is that the driver is dead and another guard has been rushed to hospital."

Nausea thickens at the back of my throat, the bitter taste growing stronger. I lower my gaze, no longer able to look him in the eye. "And Luther? What about him?"

"Gone."

I press my lips shut, fighting the need to scream. My head grows heavy, my arms and legs, too. I'm weighed down by failure. But the shame is heavier, threatening to suffocate me.

I'd known Cole had deliberately sought me out. I'd never assumed it was a coincidence. I'd just had no clue how badly he wanted to screw me over.

He'd wanted my degradation. My complete and utter humiliation.

And now he has it.

"I'll find him," I vow. "I'll get Luther back."

I have to. There's no other choice. My reputation was on its last legs before today; now it's completely shattered. I need to be the one who makes this right.

"No." Taggert's rejection hits hard. "You're going to do the opposite. I need you to take some time off."

"You're suspending me?" My gaze snaps to his. "No. Please." I take a step forward. "Don't do this."

"It's not a suspension. It's time off. You haven't taken a break in over a year."

"Forced leave is as good as a suspension. All it does is save you the paperwork."

He gives me a brittle smile. "And I thank you for it."

I keep shaking my head. Keep refusing.

No. No. No.

This is bullshit.

"It's only until Monday. You need the week to get your head on straight because it's clear you can't think to save your life at the moment."

"I don't need—"

"It's not up for discussion." He lowers his hands to the desk and pushes to his feet. "Monday. No sooner. Do you hear me?"

I grind my molars harder and harder until my jaw aches in protest.

Fuck him. Fuck Cole. Fuck the whole Torian family along with the Bureau.

I've lived and breathed their justice all my life. I knew I would be an FBI agent from the first time my dad showed me his badge with an insane amount of pride. This is my home. My existence. And it's imploding around me.

I swing around and stalk to the door, yanking it wide. The slam of the flimsy wood is my only response, the resounding bang drawing the attention of the entire department. My fellow agents stop and stare, not bothering to hide their judgment, although I'm pretty sure they don't even know what I've done. Not yet. At least, not this time.

Their intolerance is engrained.

I continue my trek toward the elevator, holding my head high despite the disgrace. How the hell am I going to face them on Monday? The distance will only make the situation worse. I'd prefer to deal with their animosity now. To answer all the questions before they have time to fester.

"You okay?" Luther Torian's arresting agent jogs to catch up with me, squeezing close to my side along the narrow walkway.

Anthony Easton is the closest thing I have to a... I don't know what to call him. He's not a friend. But he's not an asshole either.

"No." I keep pounding out the distance across the building, not willing to lose my shit in front of an audience.

"What's going on?" He follows me past the open cubicles. His heavy footfalls match mine. "Is Taggert riding your ass again?"

"Nope, not riding it. He's setting it loose."

"What?" He grabs my arm, forcing me to stop as he steps in front of me. "What does that mean?"

The concern in his expression is a trigger to the growing storm inside me. I feel my restraint slipping. One more nudge and I'll go over the edge.

"It's nothing. Don't worry. I'm just going to take the week off. That's all."

"But you don't take time off." His brow furrows. "Tell me what happened. Is he blaming you for this morning because he thinks we would've had foresight if your informant hadn't bailed?"

"Oh, God." I scrub a hand down my face. "I hadn't even thought of that."

This is too much. I can't fucking take it.

I shove past him, the remaining distance to the elevator covered in a blur.

"What the fuck is going on, Fox?" Anthony continues to follow. "Just tell me what he thinks you did."

"It's not what he thinks," I mutter. "I'm actually guilty this time."

"Of what?"

I don't want to say it. But the truth will come out while I'm gone, and I'd prefer if it wasn't explained with Taggert bias. "Cole approached me this morning. He said he wanted to talk, when what he really wanted to do was use me as an alibi for his father's escape. He's taunting me. Deliberately messing with my life."

"Oh, shit."

"Yeah, oh shit." I slam my hand against the elevator call button. "I'm not even on desk duty. Taggert wants me out of here until Monday."

He cringes. "Maybe that's for the best. You know how nasty some of these pricks can get."

"And you think me not being here will change that? It's only going to delay the inevitable and leave me out of the search for Luther." A search that I need to be a part of, goddammit.

"Forget the search. We'll catch him before the day's out. You need to concentrate on holding that temper of yours in check."

I glare at him. I keep glaring until the elevator doors open and I step inside. "I'll see you on Monday."

He moves between the doors and spreads his legs to hold them at bay. "Don't let this get to you."

I roll my eyes. That ship has well and truly set sail.

"And keep your head up," he continues. "If you can, enjoy the break while you have it. I can't remember the last time you took a vacation."

That's because I don't take them. The last thing I need are long stretches of inactivity where I'm at the mercy of my thoughts.

"Bye, Easton." I rest against the back of the enclosed space, waiting for him to move.

"Yeah, okay." He retreats. "I'll keep you updated."

It's on the tip of my tongue to tell him not to bother but the truth is, I'm dying inside knowing I won't have access to every detail of this case. "I'd appreciate it."

He juts his chin in response as the doors close between us, and all I'm left with is the walk of shame from the building.

Every step across the parking lot is filled with thoughts of retaliation. I know it's not normal for a federal agent to seek revenge. And it certainly isn't healthy. The problem is, it's what I crave, and the one thing I need to distance myself from.

These types of thoughts are for criminals. Ones like Cole Torian who take the law into their own hands.

That's never been me.

Despite my father's blood running through my veins, I'd never stoop to his level. The FBI motto is carved into my soul—fidelity, bravery, and integrity.

My fidelity is unbreakable. My bravery is in abundance. And my integrity is entirely intact.

But those attributes don't stop me from fantasizing about going entirely postal on Cole's ass. I could fucking kill that smug son of a bitch.

I stalk across the parking lot to climb into my car, grip the steering wheel, and scream. I release my rage in a mass of earsplitting decibels. I shriek until my throat sears in protest. Then my anger escalates because I have no way to let it out.

The Torian family has been a thorn in my side for too long. Too damn long to take a back seat now. Luther is out there. He could be anywhere. With anyone. About to do anything to sate his perverted nature.

And I can't do a goddamn thing about it.

I start the ignition and slam my foot down on the accelerator, letting the rev of the engine match the roar of my heart. I'm going to take that asshole down.

I'll drag each and every one of those motherfuckers under— Cole. Hunter. The Torian sisters and the Hart brothers. I don't care if Layla's daughter gets placed in foster care. Her life will be all the better for it.

I'll destroy their family, like they destroyed so many. And I'll keep a fucking smile on my face as I do it.

I shove the car into reverse, escape the parking space, and squeal my tires out into the Portland traffic.

Is Taggert going to be pissed at my lack of control? Hell, yeah.

Do I give a flying fuck? Not a single one.

I head out of the city toward the open road, weaving in and out of traffic like a speed racer. I drive and drive and fucking drive, praying that a traffic cop will pull me over and give me an outlet for my rage. But, just like with everything else today, I don't get what I want.

Nobody approaches me. The cars I pass barely pay me attention.

I drive for more than fifty miles, and all my heart rate does is climb. There's no calm to be found. No relief. I'm still fuming when I turn the car around and retrace the miles back into Portland.

I can't stop seeing Cole's face. That provoking wink plays on a continuous loop in my mind.

I don't know what to do. There's nothing I *can* do. So I give in to temptation and head for Hillsboro Airport. I slow as I pass the wire fence to make sure cops are lying in wait for a mastermind criminal who is likely to charter a private plane out of here.

Local authorities are already on the scene. Sniffer dogs, too.

The show of force settles my nerves a little. But not enough to discourage me from taking the forty-minute drive to Troutdale Airport to do the same surveillance.

Once I find more police and unmarked cars on the scene, I crumple. I pull to the curb and slump over the steering wheel, totally and utterly disgusted in myself.

I can't do this.

I need to... *shit*. I don't know what I need, and I don't think I'm going to find the answer anytime soon.

I lean back in my seat and keep clinging to the wheel, hoping and praying something will relieve the tightened ache inside my chest. Then I pull back onto the road and try to maintain a relaxed commute.

I take a left, then a right, then a left, driving aimlessly while my pulse finally begins to quit the marathon pace. I weave through Portland. Back and forth. Side to side. I pass playgrounds and schools. Churches and sporting fields.

I don't pay attention to where I'm going. Not for a long time. Not until I find myself on a familiar street, with an even more familiar building coming up on my left.

The harmonious heart rate I worked toward starts to pound a deeper beat. A faster tempo. Slowly, I inch past the extravagant Torian family restaurant, my gaze firmly affixed to the people inside.

Couples eat. Families dine. Waitresses stroll around with trays of drinks and plates of food.

They're all naive. Ignorant to the criminal pockets they're filling.

It's disgusting.

It shouldn't be legal.

These people should know who they're giving their money to. The crimes they're supporting. The evil they're encouraging.

My stomach churns with the need to do something. My insides turn and tumble, demanding more of me than I'm supposed to give.

More and more and more until I'm forced to pull over and take action.

4

ANISSA

I cut the ignition despite the guilty nudge from my self-preservation that tells me not to. I open my door and climb out even though my throat tightens in protest. And I stalk down the sidewalk, undeterred by my reflection in the neighboring buildings that clearly point out I look like Medusa after a five-week bender.

Before I know it, my palms are splayed on the glass door of the Torian restaurant and I'm pushing my way inside.

Heads turn in my direction, the curious stares of strangers kicking my insanity back a notch.

I'm making a mistake.

I shouldn't be here. But neither should these people.

"Table for one?" A suit-clad young man approaches me, his smile more of a troubled grimace.

This guy knows crazy when he sees it, and I'm sure he's getting an eyeful looking at me.

"No... Thanks." I glance around the lavish restaurant, hating the sparkling cutlery and immaculate tablecloths. It's too pure. "I'll take a seat at the bar."

I start toward the place in question.

One drink and I'll leave. I'll douse my roller-coaster blood pressure with a taste of liquor and be on my way.

"Excuse me, miss." He rushes after me. "I'm sorry, but we only provide table service. There's no seating at the bar."

I stop dead in my tracks and try to ignore the irritating tic plucking the skin at the top of my left cheek. This poor schmuck is going to be the innocent bystander who receives the heavy weight of my wrath if he doesn't back off.

"Miss?" he repeats. "Let me seat you at a table."

"I don't want a table."

I won't be another nameless, faceless customer.

I turn to face him, pulling my badge from the inside pocket of my suit jacket. "FBI." I force a fake smile. "I'm going to take a seat at the bar."

He straightens, his back turning ramrod. "Okay... Sure." He nods, over and over. "Go ahead."

"Thank you." I keep my lips gently curved. I'm sure it exudes goodwill and peace to all as I eye those in the vicinity who think I'm the latest live-stream entertainment. "I appreciate the hospitality."

I continue to the back corner, to the beautifully crafted wooden bar with its shelves lined with expensive bottles of liquor. But the host was right; there's not a damn stool in sight. Not even one.

I slide my badge along the counter and make eye contact with the slick-haired bartender cutting up limes, letting him know I'm taking all the liberties my badge will afford me. "A mimosa, please."

He pauses his task to wipe his hand on his black slacks. "You realize we—"

"Don't do bar service? Yeah. I get it." I tap my badge. "Today, you're making an exception."

He quirks a brow, annoyed or maybe slightly impressed, as he grabs a bottle of champagne from the fridge beneath the bar and begins making my drink.

"We don't see a lot of your type around here." He adds orange juice to my glass and then slides it over.

"My type? You mean federal agents?"

"No." He grins. "I mean disheveled women who start drinking —" He checks his watch. "—before noon."

Before noon? Okay, so time hasn't slid by as fast as I thought, but they're already doing lunch service which means it can't be far off. "I'm getting in before the rush."

I grab my drink and turn to rest my back against the counter while I take the first sip. The bubbles explode on my tongue, the sugary sweetness a welcomed reprieve against my sore throat.

I contemplate addressing the room in a come-to-Jesus speech about the dangers of drugs and how supporting local crime only increases their reach. I think of how I'll shock them into losing their appetites as my delicate sips turn into large gulps.

I'm throwing back the last drops of alcoholic goodness when the bartender takes residence in my peripheral vision and asks, "Another?"

"Yeah." Fuck it. Why should I leave? "Keep 'em coming."

I'm not doing anything wrong by being here. The restaurant won't be on Cole's radar when he has his father's escape to occupy him. He's probably out living it up with his psychotic family. Drinking their own alcoholic beverages in celebration instead of commiseration.

Good for him.

Cole won this round fair and square. He poked and prodded until he gained my attention. Then he made a complete and utter fool out of me for giving him even a slight second of my day.

He'd insisted on talking to me. He wasn't going to take no for an answer.

First, he attempted to charm his way in, then he teased my curiosity with his uncharacteristic behavior. He didn't give up, his determination entirely subtle in the moment, but fucking obvious in hindsight.

Goddammit.

How many times had he glanced at his watch? On alert. Waiting.

He was counting down the minutes until his father was out of custody so he could cut and run.

He could've used any public place for his alibi. Anywhere with surveillance and a constant stream of witnesses would've worked.

Instead, he'd deliberately sought me out, kept me distracted, and ensured I didn't answer my phone.

Fucking asshole.

I gulp at my second mimosa, downing the contents like a shot as a waitress walks in my direction, her gaze deliberately skirting mine. She continues by me with a guilty look on her face and stops at the opening of the bar to wave the bartender toward her.

She pulls him close and whispers in his ear, her eyes darting in my direction every few seconds.

Subtle. Real fucking subtle.

The bartender doesn't react, his face not giving a hint to their conversation apart from telling me it's all about little ol' me. He nods. Whispers. Nods again. Then the woman walks away, her face downcast.

Interesting.

I slow my consumption, taking smaller sips, and watch the guy go back to his chore of chopping limes. Something has changed. Something that could be entirely based on my paranoia. Or maybe not.

He's stiff in the shoulders. His cuts are slower. His face is deliberately blank.

I glance around the restaurant, my gaze latching onto the host at the door. His eyes widen when I catch him staring at me, then he quickly looks away. I frown, and focus on the nearest employee. A waitress. She places a plate of food down in front of a customer, but her attention is on me. At least until we lock eyes then, just like the guy at the door, she quickly averts her gaze.

Even more interesting.

I take another sip as I continue my scrutiny and lock eye after eye, only to have every staff member show fear at the connection.

"Can I have another, please?" I place the flute on the bar, my fingers resting on the stem.

"Are you sure?" The bartender's brows are pulled tight in a wince. "Why don't you take a breather and I'll go out back and find you a stool?"

I cock my head, studying him. "I don't need a breather. And I'm okay without a stool."

He scrubs his hands on his pants again and clears his throat.

"Look, ma'am, I'm sorry, but I've been told I can't serve you another drink."

I continue to analyze the slight change to his expression. The discomfort. The uncertainty. But it's my own curiosity taking precedence. "I'm not drunk. Why am I being refused service?"

"I... Um..." He glances toward the swinging doors leading to the kitchen. "I'm not sure. I'm just told the order came from management."

I don't react.

Instead, I think.

I put two and two together and pretend the addition hasn't resulted in a lotto win.

"Is Cole here?" I keep my tone light. Calm. I don't show an ounce of the exhilaration currently flooding my veins at the thought of the smug piece of shit hiding out in the building somewhere.

"I..." He scrubs his hands against his pants for a third time. "Let me get you that stool." He starts for the end of the bar. "I won't be long."

He walks away, taking long strides across the open expanse of the restaurant to disappear behind the swinging doors.

I lock down my emotions, determined not to jump to crazy conclusions while my limbs tingle, and the slightest buzz begins to take over my head.

Normally, Cole would be back there somewhere. Not in the kitchen. He would be in the surrounding rooms he uses as offices to run his operation. But not today. It's stupid to think he'd be anywhere in the vicinity while his father is being hunted.

No, that smug piece of shit would be somewhere strategic.

He's smart. Really smart.

That's why I've always been drawn to this case. The Torian family aren't simple. They know what they're doing and have a brilliant method to their madness.

But what if he is?

What if Cole is here? Watching me? Laughing at me?

He would think I was weak and pathetic for succumbing to my anger. And he'd be right.

I *am* weak.

I *am* pathetic.

I'm also a little psychotic, just like him, but my psychosis remains on the right side of the law. I'm crazy with the need to take him down. I'd do anything. *Give* anything.

I grip the bar and dig my fingertips into the wood as I stare at my reflection behind the wall of mirrors partially covered by glass. I look like hell. My eyes are wild, my cheeks rosy. And my hair. *Jesus.* The chin-length strands are a tangled mess that would probably seem trendy if I had a speck of makeup on to help me appear slightly respectable.

I'm the living, breathing definition of what Cole has made me —distraught.

Tormented.

I really should go.

"I'm told you need a stool."

The briefest snippet of a horror re-run brushes my ears. That voice. The provoking lilt. The arrogant tone.

I remain still despite the threat at my back and the mass of wasps swarming in my stomach.

"Where is he?" I whisper.

"Where is who?" Cole drawls.

I close my eyes, succumbing to the comfort of darkness for a few seconds before I turn to face the picture of arrogance standing right before me in his perfect suit.

"I would've thought you were far too proud to play dumb, Mr. Torian." My voice climbs, letting those in the vicinity hear our conversation. "Is he here? Do you have him hiding out back?"

He inches closer, leaning into me so we're almost chest to chest. His cologne regains its hold in the air around me, the woodsy scent settling into my lungs. "As much as you seem to be enjoying yourself at my bar, why don't you follow me and take a look for yourself? We can talk in private. Just the two of us."

The words are intimate. Almost like a lover's promise.

"Just you and me?" I mimic his sultry tone, refusing to retreat even though he's deliberately smothering my personal space.

"Without witnesses or anyone to hold you accountable for what you might try to do to me?"

He chuckles, the warmth of his breath brushing my cheek, triggering an ambush of goose bumps to skitter across the back of my neck. "A woman like you wouldn't be able to fathom the type of things I want to do."

He's toying with me again. Playing the master manipulator. Attempting to inspire fear.

"I'm not scared of you."

"No." He inclines his head in agreement, his mouth kicking at one side. "I'm well aware you shiver for different reasons."

I glare, my lips parting, about to spew my bottled hatred.

"You didn't come here to make a scene, Niss." He enunciates the nickname with deliberate affection, dangling it like a noose. "You came here to my restaurant, despite the risks involved, because we have unfinished business you want to resolve. So let's resolve it."

He turns and strides away, heading toward the swinging kitchen doors.

I'm sure the attention of every person in a one-mile radius is on him, taking in the perfect fit of his tailored suit, the styled hair, the thick, broad shoulders.

He doesn't wait to see if I follow. He knows I will. This asshole is well aware he's got the upper hand, and it needs to stop. But how? He'll only gain more power if I walk away.

I'm left with no choice. I have to give chase.

I stalk after him, catching up at the kitchen door he holds open for me. The bartender stands inside, his eyes curious.

"Thanks for the drinks," I mutter. "You can put them on Cole's tab."

Torian chuckles, the thickly rich sound another taunt to slap away my attempt to anger him. He leads me through the spotless kitchen, the staff staring at me with intrigue.

Their attention is reassuring. He can't pay everyone for their silence. Someone in here has to cling to a moral or two. So if I wind up in a ditch in the early hours of the morning, Cole won't get away with it.

"This way." He holds open another door with a dimly lit hall on the other side.

This time I take the lead, not letting the darkened shadows spook me.

"Keep going until you reach the last door on the right."

I glance over my shoulder. "And what if I want to check these other rooms?"

"Have at it. But I think you're smart enough to know there's nothing illegal on this premises."

Another taunt. More softly spoken ridicule.

God, I detest this man.

I continue to the end of the hall and pause, waiting.

"After you." He indicates the door with the wave of a hand, his gaze narrowed as if daring me to continue.

I don't play into his intimidation. I refuse to whimper in fear.

In fact, I scoff, practically laughing in the face of it, and step closer to the door.

I grab that handle, twist, and shove inside, a woman on a mission, only to stop dead at the wall of muscle that greets me.

The three men put an immediate halt on their murmured conversation, their menacing faces turning to take me in, their relaxed expressions morphing to incredulity as recognition hits.

"Don't stop now, little fox," Cole whispers in my ear. "Make yourself at home."

5

TORIAN

My men glare at the female intrusion, their hatred palpable, their shock evident. I can only assume they don't understand why I'd willingly lead an FBI agent into our sanctuary without a warrant.

I'm not too clear on the tactic myself.

It's part of the fun, I guess. Leading the prey behind enemy lines.

"What the fuck is she doing here?" Decker snarls.

Her chin hikes. That's all she does. It's her only sign of defense.

And it's nowhere near enough to sate my thirst.

"Back off. She's with me." I walk around her, placing distance between us in the hope it will increase her apprehension. "We'll finish our conversation later. I've got confidential things to discuss with my favorite special agent."

"Are you kidding?" Luca asks. "You can't be left alone with her."

"He's right." Hunt questions my sanity with the tight pinch of his brows. "You need a witness. Who knows what shit she'll try to pin on you."

"Don't worry. This is a friendly visit." I tilt my chin toward the door, wordlessly telling him to get moving. "Isn't it, Niss?"

She ignores me, her attention remaining on the men a few feet away.

One in particular.

Decker.

"Leave us," I reiterate, adding steel to my tone.

Two of my trio know better than to push my patience, and reluctantly head toward the door. The third always has the opposite reaction, so it's no fucking surprise when Decker remains in place.

"She can't be trusted," he seethes.

"Thanks for the concern. But I'll take it from here."

"This is bullshit." He clenches his fists at his sides, Hunter and Luca waiting for him at the door. "She'll throw you under a bus the first chance she gets." A wealth of hatred ebbs from him, his hostility barely leashed.

She doesn't react. Not in concern, anyway. If anything, she relaxes into the animosity, her shoulders losing their tight edge. "And here I was thinking you've been pining over me like I've been pining for you."

His upper lip curls as he takes an aggressive step forward, and this time, I don't warn him to back down.

I watch their interaction play out, transfixed, my gaze glued to every flicker in her expression.

She intrigues me, and I'm not entirely sure why. Maybe it's the absence of self-preservation. Or how she lacks the fragility I'm used to from women. Either way, her oddly captivating personality has my attention.

I observe the gentle increase in her breathing. The twitch of her fingers against the hem of her suit jacket. Nothing goes by unnoticed, not even the slight curve to her lips.

But still, there's no fucking fear, and the famine is killing me.

She thrives on this—the fight, the aggression. Anger seems to be her favored emotion. Her happy place.

"Leave," I repeat. "I can take care of myself."

Decker's upper lip continues to curl. "Watch her." He backtracks, pointing a menacing finger in her direction. "This bitch has claws."

"And I remember you enjoying them not too long ago," she purrs.

They've slept together?

Of course they have.

Decker has the uncanny ability to taint everything I crave. And yes, the games I want to play with her are near the top of that list.

"Out," I snap. "Now."

He swings around, storms for the door, and nudges past Hunter. They leave in a group, the latch clicking shut behind them.

For a few moments, the room is quiet. The air is filled with something thick and thrilling.

"Take a seat." I continue toward my desk, my pace slow, before I turn to sit my ass against the polished wood.

"I'd prefer to stand." She takes in her surroundings, her gaze trekking over the bookshelves and expensive artwork.

She's more controlled than I thought. Or more stupid.

The jury's still out on that one.

But her fearlessness is magnificent. I could watch her battle intimidation every day of the week and never grow tired.

"That's an admirable group of men you've got there," she murmurs. "Not only threatening an FBI agent, but a woman. Is that something they're trained to do during the induction process?"

I snicker. I gather it's the response she wanted because there's no way she could make me angry. Not again.

"No, those skills are engrained. I doubt they're teachable. But I should probably look into it for future recruitment, right?" I cross my legs at the ankles, exuding relaxation. "Especially when the level of bullying from your people is continuously increasing."

"Your people." She scoffs, her brows rising as she continues her examination of my private space. "I don't think you can consider it bullying when you spend every waking minute breaking the law. Most people would refer to it as justice."

"Good to know."

She sucks in a deep breath, as if bored, and lets it out on a sigh. She's playing the game, too. Trying to appear disinterested while in the lion's den.

"Why are you here, Anissa?"

"Why?" Her tone drips with sarcasm. "I don't know. I guess I thought it was a lovely day for a visit." She turns to face me, her fake tranquility vanishing with the narrowing of her gaze. "Why don't you save us both a lot of time and just tell me where Luther is?"

I grin, my expression having the opposite effect on hers.

Those eyes turn hostile. Her jaw tics.

"You're such a tight ball of hostility, aren't you?" I journey my gaze over her body, taking the liberty to let my attention linger on the parts I like most.

I wonder if she'd mind me hiring her a personal shopper. These suits of hers really are pathetic. Sexy, yet pathetic. What hot-blooded woman doesn't want to show a bit of leg? Especially with the set of pins she has hiding under that stiff material.

"Tell me, little fox, do you drink to drown your sorrows?"

She doesn't reply.

Silence reigns for long, drawn-out seconds.

I raise my gaze over the hips hugged in navy, along the white blouse showing the faintest outline of a lace bra beneath, past the tight line of her lips, to her cold, calculating squint.

"Did I hit a point of contention?" I smirk. "Have I already driven you to the bottle?"

Her mouth curves. "You couldn't drive me to do anything. You don't scare me, despite how hard you try."

"Understood." I nod. "So I assume you won't mind me reporting this incident as harassment."

"By all means." Her chin hitches, the action a beaming tell. "Go ahead. I'm not going to stop you."

"You don't even want to try? I'm sure we could come to a mutually beneficial agreement to make up for you badgering my staff."

Her eyes dance, and the renewed kick to her lips gives me the slightest glimpse of a dimple in her right cheek. "It's already clear your obsession with power is an overcompensation for something you lack. And I've been dissatisfied too many times to struggle my way through a pity fuck. So by all means, report me. But I assure you, I can do whatever the hell I like. I haven't broken any rules."

She keeps throwing cheap insults at me, and I seriously think she expects me to react.

It's disappointing.

Truly.

She needs to be aware of my control.

"Interesting." I uncross my legs and grab the desk at my sides. "I thought there were strict rules within the Bureau. I didn't know you could do whatever you liked. It sounds like the perfect job. Maybe I should become an agent."

She releases a breathy laugh and heads toward the only window in the room, flicking the curtain aside to peer across the staff parking lot. "I'm sure you already have enough people inside those walls doing the dirty work for you."

I nod, slow and subtle. "Maybe you're right."

Again, her chin hitches. There's no other sign of her fury, just the damn chin that demands my tight hold.

"I suppose I should thank you for the flowers," she murmurs. "That's the polite thing to do, isn't it?"

"Flowers?" I push from my desk and stroll around to sit in the office chair behind it. "I have absolutely no idea what you're talking about."

She sighs, not buying my bullshit, and steps away from the window. "This was a mistake."

"Of course it was. You never should've tried to take me on, especially not at my uncle's funeral."

"I didn't try to take you on," she snaps. "Your father came out of hiding for the first time in months. I couldn't have cared less if he was celebrating the birth of a grandchild, or lying on his death bed. He's a vile waste of oxygen who needs to be behind bars. And anyone who disagrees should be there with him."

I raise my arms in front of me, holding out my wrists. "Then lock me up, honey, because I strongly disagree."

She bares her teeth, and the vicious snarl she releases does things to me that defy logic.

This is what I wanted. The brilliant rage. The blinding beauty.

It wipes away the memory of the provoking smirk she inflicted upon me and replaces the expression with something I'll cling to for a damn long time.

All I need now is her fear.

"One day I will, asshole." She stalks for the door. "I bet my life on it."

"Oh, no, this isn't over." Far from it. I shove from my chair and take two quick strides to step in front of her, blocking her path before she reaches her escape. "We're not done."

Her eyes flare as she stops. "Move."

"No. You came here because you want something from me. What is it?"

"I already told you," she growls. "I wanted to know where you're hiding him, but obviously you're not going to do the world a favor and fill me in."

"Bullshit." I lean closer, getting right in her face. "You came here for something else. You were trying to turn the tables. To get back at me for humiliating you earlier. You came storming in here with your over-cocked attitude and attempted to intimidate my customers."

"Like hell I did. I came here because a man died today. And another is fighting for his life." She throws her arms wide. "Hell, for all I know, he may already be dead. And for once, I wanted to see the affect the brutality had on you. *For once,* I wanted to know if you were anything but a heartless piece of shit."

"You expect my remorse when I'm not responsible?"

A jilted breath brushes past her lips, half laugh, half hatred. "You approached me at the exact moment it happened. You kept me busy the entire time." She holds my gaze, her cheeks turning a dark shade of pink. "You're guilty, Cole Torian. And suspension or not, I'm going to take you down."

Suspension?

I pull back to scrutinize her. I take in all the features I haven't had enough time to appreciate. Her short, sleek hair, the black strands cut at different lengths to give a loose, messy vibe. But it's those eyes, the same ones that slayed me this morning, that keep me engaged now. They're a captivating color—a mix between hazel and green.

"Stop looking at me like that, and get out of my fucking way." She sidesteps, waiting for me to move.

"I can't. I thought I knew everything there was to know, but now I'm baffled."

She huffs. "Move."

I lean back against the door, my head cocked, my brows furrowed. "This morning I was certain nothing could be more of a turn-on than your unjustified arrogance. But here you are, entirely defeated, humiliated, and flushed with rage, and I've gotta say, I think I made the wrong assumption. Nothing is more attractive than you at your lowest."

Her face transforms into a mask of shock. Then utter rage.

My pulse kicks in anticipation. In pure, undiluted pleasure.

She's going to break. To fucking explode. And I can't wait for the detonation.

Each second that passes makes my heart beat faster, my limbs pulse harder.

Do it, little fox. Let me have your worst.

"You—" She snaps her mouth shut and sucks a deep breath through her nose, gaining restraint.

"Me, what, Nissie?"

Her jaw works overtime, those beautiful lips pressed tight. But still, she clambers for control, scrambling for dear life. "*Move.*"

"We're not done."

"No?" Her eyes narrow. "What's left to say? Do you want to throw some more threats around? Maybe remind me how much you like hunting?"

I frown. "I do enjoy hunting. How did you know?"

The rage continues to bubble, the heat in her cheeks growing despite her attempts to chill. "Move, or I'll use whatever force necessary."

"And add to the harassment case already hovering over your head?"

Her hands shake. And her face—God, her face makes her seem

like a bull about to slay a pen of matadors. This woman is lit and about to blow.

She lunges for the nearest bookshelf and grabs a novel, throwing the projectile at my head. The heavy weight misses by half a foot, its only achievement a weighty thunk against the wood.

"Jesus," I scoff. "I hope you're more accurate with your gun."

"Do you want to find out?"

I laugh.

I think I do. I have a strange urge to be in her line of fire, as I push her closer toward the edge. She'll have the lethal weapon, but I'll be the one in control, calling the shots.

"I can't wait to snap those cuffs around your wrists." Those green eyes turn manic, her smile crazed. "I'm going to take pleasure in nailing you to the wall."

"By all means." I crook a finger at her. "Have at it. I've often thought about nailing you myself."

She grabs book after book, throwing one after another until I score a spine in the gut and another on the thigh. She's deliberately aiming low. Trying not to leave the damning evidence of a bruise. Or maybe just aiming for my cock.

But why not reach for her gun? Suspension or not, why isn't she phoning this in?

My threat of reporting her must be far more terrorizing than I'd thought.

How perfect.

This feisty little thing might be on the verge of losing her badge.

"Okay. Okay. Let's call a truce." I hold up my hands in surrender. I won this round; I don't need to beat a dead horse. "You can't blame me for levelling the score. You picked this fight. Not me."

She turns rigid, her eyes flaring again, only this time it's in horror. Pain. "This is you levelling the score?"

"Yes. We both enjoy winning. There's nothing wrong with that." I itch to swipe the hair from her cheeks. To frighten her with a gentle touch. "We're even. For now."

"Even?" Her voice is raw. "You killed an officer and another may already have died. But now we're even for my few taunting words?"

She doesn't give herself credit. She did more than taunt me with a few words.

I haven't come close to losing my calm in public since I was a teenager, yet this woman inspired madness and incredible instability in me. I could've raged at that funeral—not because of the injustice or the unfortunate timing, but because of Anissa. Because of her perfect provocation.

She's unaware of her power, which, for me, is a good thing.

"I've told you, I had no involvement in my father's escape." I lower my arms to my sides. "But if you'd like me to send a floral arrangement to the deceased's family, I'll happily oblige."

"How do you sleep at night?" She reaches for another projectile, this time retrieving a small clay statue.

To anyone else, it would be considered a novelty item. An inexpensive trinket.

To me, it's more.

The woman and child figurine was given to me by my mother. It's the only weakness I allow inside these walls.

"I'm not sure what you expect from me, Niss." I move away from the door, no longer willing to antagonize her when she holds a fragile treasure in her shaking hands. "I actually came to you this morning with information. The FBI has made mistakes regarding my father's arrest. Mistakes that those women will pay for."

"Is that another threat?" She slams the figurine down on the shelf and storms toward the exit. "Because I'm goddamn sick of your threats, Cole."

"It's no threat." I hold her gaze, staring deep into the tumultuous sea of her eyes, hoping to tempt her into staying. "It's a peace offering. I'm happy to tell you everything I know. Maybe over dinner? Tonight?"

She snatches at the door handle. "Sell the story to some other sucker. I'm not that gullible."

"Wait. What makes you think you've got me perfectly pegged?"

"Let's call it months of meticulous investigation." She draws out the words like a queen talking to a servant. It's fucking brilliant.

"There are two sides to every story."

"Right." She swings open the door. "And you're the poor defenseless drug lord who deserves a break?"

"Maybe. You won't know unless you give me the chance to plead my case." I shrug. "Who knows if some random fact might hold the key to capturing my father all over again?"

She glowers. "I'm not taking the bait."

"That's a shame." I flash a smirk even though I'm disappointed our encounter is coming to an end. I didn't expect this meeting to be as long, or as spicy. It's above and beyond my expectations, and I'll miss the theatrics once she's gone. "But the offer still stands. Feel free to contact me whenever you're ready to work on leaving this animosity behind us. I assume the Bureau has my cell number on file."

She chokes out a breathy laugh and gives a roll of those beautiful emerald eyes before she makes for the hall. "Goodbye, Cole."

6

ANISSA

I tried to stay away.

That night, I fought anger and determination as I paced my bedroom. I battled against the passion to provide justice and the need to obey Taggert. I also struggled under the heavy weight of shame.

But I remained inside those four apartment walls. I didn't leave. I stayed out of the investigation despite the instinct to act.

The only connection I had to their world were the news broadcasts reminding me of my failures.

Nobody had a lead on Luther.

He'd disappeared. *Poof.* Gone. Right into thin air.

My fellow FBI agents were on the case, along with local law enforcement, airport security, and sniffer dogs, just to name a few. Everyone was entrusted to help find him.

Everyone except me.

The next morning, I wasn't going to wallow. I wouldn't let him beat me into depression. Moving forward was my only option.

I woke at the usual time, jogged the same five miles, not diverting a single foot off my regular path. And every step I took felt wrong. My thoughts weren't even right. Everything that filled my head had been about Cole. The ridicule. The manipulation.

I pushed myself to run through all the pummeling memories, spurring my legs faster.

I wouldn't stop my exercise routine on his account.

I refused.

Yet the streets I crossed and the people I passed seemed different.

I no longer had the tingle at the back of my neck. My senses weren't hyper-alert. The feeling of being hunted had vanished.

By the time I reached the café, I knew why my intuition was off-kilter.

I was alone.

Nobody followed me. There was no need to watch me anymore. No unexpected visitors waited to buy me a coffee. The flowers with their threatening notes had stopped, too. And why wouldn't they?

Cole had won.

He'd set a goal and claimed victory.

The reprieve should've been a blessing and a leap in the right direction for my safety. So why did it compound my failure?

Instead of rejoicing with goddamn relief because a psychotic fuck had grown tired of me, I became consumed with isolation. Slammed with abandonment issues.

The overwhelming sense of solitude didn't make sense.

The grief from my mother's death returned. The anger over my father's betrayal cut deeper. And the reminder I had no job to escape to made me entirely unhinged.

That day, I'd been a fucking mess.

But again, the next morning, I refused to wallow.

I ran my five miles, hoping against hope for the skin to crawl at the back of my neck. I prayed for the skitter of awareness. For the brush of my sixth sense.

Nothing came.

I had no connection to the case and no outlet for my spiraling mind.

Easton didn't call to give me updates like he'd promised. There were no e-mails or texts or carrier pigeons. Everyone and everything had turned against me, leaving me secluded.

I couldn't hack it.

I kept that routine for three days—three full days when I battled to contain my hysteria. But I couldn't do it for a fourth.

Friday morning started with a pre-dawn escape to Cole's exclusive neighborhood. It was only meant to be a drive-by—a brief insight to reassure my frustration that the good guys were keeping him under control with constant surveillance.

Instead, I found nothing.

No cars. No cops. No fellow agents struggling through an early-morning stakeout.

Nobody watched the son of the escaped sex trafficker, and I couldn't understand why.

I parked on the nearest side street, close enough to the corner to have a slightly restricted view of the ostentatious mansion purchased with dirty drug money.

He wasn't inside. He couldn't be. Cole Torian was somewhere else, enjoying his victory while the good guys watched from their secret hiding spots.

I told myself over and over, until the garage door rose and his glistening black Porsche drove out.

And that's how I came to be sitting here, out the front of a local nightclub fifteen hours later, watching Cole escort a sophisticated, young brunette inside.

I'm not proud I disobeyed Taggert's orders to shadow a suspect. But do I regret it?

Hell, no.

I didn't see one agent today. Not at Cole's restaurant. Not when he returned home at dinner. Nobody is riding his ass and it doesn't make sense.

For the fifteenth time, I palm my cell and click through to Easton's contact details. I've attempted to dial his number every hour, almost on the hour. Pride has been the only leash holding me back.

I don't want to beg for information. Being ostracized is bad enough without having to grovel for insight, but I can't remain isolated a moment longer.

I press "connect" and the dull ringtone filters into my ear. Each subtle vibration of the cell feels like a siren announcing my weakness. It nestles deep, tearing apart my self-esteem.

The final click of the connection makes me hold my breath.

"You shouldn't be calling me," he mutters in greeting.

I close my eyes, taking the kick to my teeth without a flinch. "And I wouldn't be if you'd kept your promise to feed me information."

He sighs, the sound long and loud. "I couldn't. Taggert made it clear you're not to be contacted. He's pissed. *Really* pissed. Nobody is willing to mess with him right now."

I run a hand over my face, attempting to scrub away the remorse. The last thing I should be doing is dragging Easton down with me. I'm well aware of the risk I'm placing on his job, yet here I am, unable to disconnect the call.

"I did try." Guilt laces his tone. "Despite the warning, I came to see you today, but you weren't home."

"Really?" The news is the slightest balm on my battered ego. "I've been out."

"Where?"

"Just out."

There's a long-drawn breath of silence. "I don't want to know, do I?"

I sigh and slink farther down in the driver's seat. "It's better if you don't."

"Dammit, Fox. What the hell are you doing?"

"Nothing." I grind my teeth through the need to defend myself. I ball my fists, and still, the frustration escalates. "Nobody is watching him. *Why* is nobody watching him?"

"Jesus fucking Christ, you're going to get your ass kicked. If Taggert finds out—"

"He's not going to find out. And I'm not doing anything wrong. In fact, I'm the only one doing my job. Why the hell doesn't anyone have eyes on him?"

"Because he didn't have anything to do with the escape. Not only was he with you at the time, but we've listened to all the phone recordings while Luther was incarcerated. They never discussed any plans. Neither one of them even alluded to what was happening. And Cole never stepped foot in that jail."

"That doesn't mean a damn thing, and you know it."

"All Cole's men have airtight alibis. Their stories check out."

So either someone is feeding them the right story to tell, or the FBI are dropping the ball. Hell, it sounds like they're not even taking the fucking field.

"Still doesn't mean a damn thing." I turn my attention to the nightclub, the slow-moving line out front growing by the minute. Maybe I need to go in there and make my presence known. I can't let Cole think his family is winning. He should be scared. Intimidated.

"Look, I shouldn't be telling you this," Easton admits, "but we've been warned. Someone went over Taggert's head and told the department to back off unless we have a lead. And we don't."

Mother.

Fucker.

"You should've told me that in the first place," I grate. "It makes more fucking sense."

"You're a loose cannon when it comes to these people. And I get it. I'm frustrated, too. But you only have to wait until Monday. It's three days. So let me shield you from this shit until then."

Three days.

Three fucking days where I'll go insane without more insight.

"No, please." I wince through the plea. "You need to tell me something. Anything. I don't care what it is. I just need an update to tide me over."

"Fox..."

"Come on. How long have we worked together? Doesn't that count for something?"

"You know I've got your back. That's why I've kept my mouth shut. You're going to get in some deep shit if you keep poking your nose around this investigation. The stakes are building too high, and anything that distracts Taggert from the case is going to send him postal."

My pulse kicks up a notch. "So something else has happened. Something that isn't public knowledge."

"Fox," he warns.

I sit up and frantically try to force my brain to find leverage. "*Please. Please. Please.*" God, the begging makes me feel dirty.

Fucking filthy. "I can help. You know I can. Nobody knows this family better than I do."

"Jesus," he hisses. "You must be desperate."

"You have no idea." I hold my breath through the growing silence, and my leg jolts, out of control. I'm shaking, my need for a fix uncontrollable.

"More women have gone missing," he mutters.

I slump as the information sinks in.

"Young, attractive women from stable families," he continues. "These aren't runaways or girls likely to get caught up in trouble. We're leaning toward abduction. And all of them have happened since Luther escaped."

My throat goes dry, and the memories of past crime scenes come back to haunt me.

I've been inside homes used for the exchange of sex slaves. I've witnessed mass graves filled with the remnants of tangled female bodies.

These women could be next, and what's worse is the suffering they might endure before they finally receive the peace that comes with death.

"It could be a coincidence," he murmurs. "You know how these things go. It wouldn't be a shock if this turned out to be entirely unrelated."

"But you don't think so?"

"No. I think Luther is sending a message."

One that announces to the world he's above the law and shouldn't be fucked with.

A duplicate message to the one Cole has already given me.

"How many?" My heart beats rapidly in my throat as seconds pass. "How many women, Easton?"

"Two. Every day. For the last three days. Wednesday, Thursday, Friday. All of them from Portland. Whoever responsible isn't even spreading them out across the state."

My heart drops at the additional stab to my ego. I've been wasting away the hours while these women get abducted, and still, Taggert doesn't want me involved.

"What about today?" My thoughts snap to the woman who

70

accompanied Cole inside the club. The beautiful brunette. "Have there been any additional reports?"

"Just one. We're waiting on a second. I don't think the pattern will change anytime soon."

Seven women.

With more likely to fall victim.

I can't sit on my hands any longer. Nobody should.

"I need to help." I'll take Cole up on his offer. I can sit down with him and use my own manipulative magic to get inside information. I won't need much. The slightest slip could lead to their downfall. One tiny straw to instigate an avalanche. "I *can* help."

"Don't even think about it. It's not worth it. If Taggert finds out, you're gone. Not only from the department, but maybe from the Bureau entirely. He's gunning to take you down. Don't give him the opportunity."

"It's been days. Am I meant to sit on my ass and wait while more women are taken?"

"No, you're meant to detach from the situation and rely on us to do the work. You're not the only agent in Portland. We've got this."

I scoff. I'll believe in their abilities when they're focused on something other than their hatred for me.

"Promise me, Fox. Tell me you're not going to do anything crazy."

I keep my mouth shut. My teeth are snapped tight. I don't want to make a vow I can't keep.

"Fox, fucking swear it or I'll come find you. I'm not joking."

"It's not that easy."

The Torians have been a part of my life since I was on the cusp of my teenage years. I still remember the night when Cole's mother died from a gunshot wound. I remember, because my father cried that night. He'd walked through the front door, his eyes red and glistening, then slumped into my mother's arms.

I wasn't told why.

As a child, I wasn't told much of anything, especially about my father's position within the FBI. I had to figure it out from the newspapers. The following day, I'd seen his photo on the front page, his solemn face encapsulated for the world to see as he helped investigate a young woman gunned down before her time.

I've hated them since then. They're a vile family whose actions are gruesome enough to make an unshakable man like my father tear up.

But I can't let my cravings for justice blind me to the warnings from Taggert. I have to be cautious. Smart.

Easton's right, no matter how much I want to deny it.

"Don't be a fucking moron," he snarls.

"Fine. I swear it." I slam my palm against the steering wheel and glare toward the front of the club. "I'll speak to you later."

I don't wait for him to respond. I disconnect the call and throw my cell to the passenger seat.

I know he's only trying to look out for me, but there are so many other things I'm aware of too. For example, I'm blindingly aware Cole is involved in every deceitful action attributed to his family. I'm also mindful of his influence and reach. And it's crystal fucking clear he has no plans to change his criminal ways.

I don't care if there's no evidence of his involvement in Luther's escape.

He participated.

I can feel the potency of his treachery in my blood. Can taste it with every breath.

There has to be an evidence trail.

He can't keep everyone quiet forever. More witnesses have to come forward. DNA had to be left at the scene. It's only a matter of searching harder, for longer.

I turn on the radio to distract myself from the maddening loop of frustration and focus on the front of the club for hours.

I don't leave. Not when my eyes grow tired or my butt goes numb. I have nowhere else to go apart from an empty apartment filled with reminders of my failure.

I'm still sitting there at three in the morning when a familiar man walks out the front doors and farewells the bouncer with a hand clasp and a pat on the back.

After all this time, Cole remains crisp. Entirely impeccable.

I don't know how the asshole does it. He never appears anything other than immaculate. The hair. The style.

He's a flawless illusion. Perfect on the outside with a charred soul hidden beneath.

The only thing missing is a woman at his side.

He's alone.

The gorgeous brunette isn't with him, and I doubt she would've rejected his advances. He isn't the type of man anyone denies. And I find it hard to believe he chose to end the night on his own.

So where is she?

My palms sweat as my mind runs wild with possibilities.

Is the club a cover? Is she trapped somewhere inside, her screams muted by loud music? Was his companion the next victim?

He walks for his car in the reserved space a few feet from the entrance of the club and slides into the driver's seat. We both start our ignition in unison.

I promised not to do anything crazy, but following him home doesn't break that vow.

I hang back, waiting until he's almost out of view before I tag along for the ride.

As expected, he drives more cautious than normal. He navigates toward his suburb, sticking to the speed limit like a good little boy, which only makes me more suspicious.

Why would he pretend he's driving Miss Daisy unless he didn't want to draw attention to himself and the abduction he just instigated?

Three a.m. delirium has me convinced he did something to that woman. And even if he didn't, I refuse to let him curl up in bed thinking he's getting away with his crimes.

Something has to be done.

But what?

I creep my car closer as we approach his street, giving up the pretense of an early morning drive to make it clear he's being followed.

He doesn't react. There's no increase in speed or diversion to put me off his trail.

I can still picture him behind that wheel, all smug and self-assured, acting entirely untouchable.

It drives me fucking crazy.

It drives me so fucking crazy I break my promise and plant my foot on the accelerator.

I zoom along his desolate street, overtaking him to pull to a stop in front of his driveway. I block his entrance and storm out of my car, frustration and resentment seeping from my pores.

His window lowers as I turn toward him, the sight before me more daunting in its appeal than I remember. He's gorgeous. Perfect teeth. Smooth skin. Healthy tan. So much masculine stubble along that incredible jaw line.

God, I want to break this motherfucker. I want to break him more than words can express.

"What a pleasant surprise," he purrs. "To what do I owe the pleasure?"

He's all sophisticated charm and oozing chivalry. The heavy flirtation doesn't skip my attention either, but two can play that game.

"Having a good night?" I close my door and start toward him.

"It's definitely shaping up to be memorable." His mouth kicks in a wicked grin. "I've been waiting for you to face me again."

I gasp in fake concern. "I hope you haven't been holding your breath."

"Only since I spied you out the front of my house this morning."

Shit.

I ignore the heavy pulse in my chest and saunter toward the Porsche. "Well, here we are. Reunited at last."

"And ready for round two?" he muses. "Or is this round three?"

I answer the provocation with a breath of a laugh. "Did you have a good night? I assume the date didn't go well."

"Date?"

I reach his door and grip the window ledge to peer down at him. "You took a woman to the club. Two of you went in. Only one came out." I watch for a flicker in his expression, hoping for a clue that never comes. "I was wondering if she was your next victim."

"Victim? You speak as if women aren't begging to get in my bed." He snickers. "And that woman in particular wasn't one of them. Her name's Beth, and she's a bartender. I gave her a ride for her birthday, because she wants to have a few drinks after the doors close. I'm sure she's still in the VIP lounge if you feel inclined to stalk her, too."

What I feel inclined to do is shove that cocky attitude down his throat.

His self-assurance makes it hard not to believe his story. There's not a single hint of guilt or apprehension.

"You know, you never cease to surprise me, little fox."

"Yeah?" I add sugar to my tone. "Why is that? Did you think I'd give up after our last encounter? Are you really delusional enough to believe you intimidate me?"

"Not at all." The smirk reaches his eyes, the deep blue glistening as a dimple becomes visible in his left cheek. "What surprises me is that your jealousy is ten times sexier than your anger."

Jealousy?

Not even if hell froze over, buddy.

He's baiting me. Tap, tap, tapping at my grated nerves.

I won't bite.

"Do you know what I find really sexy?" I ask. "The thought of slapping a set of cuffs on you and watching you rot in prison."

"Don't tease, gorgeous. You've got no idea how hard it makes me."

I struggle to hold my smile when all I want to do is snarl. The mental pictures of his erection aren't easily ignored with my frazzled brain.

He makes fire burn in the pit of my stomach, the flames growing, licking higher with every second his arrogant expression remains fixed in my direction.

He's a sociopath.

An emotionless, narcissistic predator.

"You're incredible." So undeniably, unbelievably remarkable. Like a rotting corpse desecrating the purity of heaven.

"I like to think so," he drawls. "But tell me why you agree."

I crouch, leaning down until I'm at eye level. "With the amount of suspicion piling up behind you from the new flood of missing women, I would've thought you'd be cautious." It's a bluff. A rather large one, considering I'm the only agent paying him attention. "But not you. You keep swinging around that ego of yours like it's a foot-long dick."

His features tighten, the smirk more of a gnashing of teeth, the stare edging toward a scowl.

I've struck a nerve.

Good.

"What missing women?" He asks the question on a breathy sigh, as if he's suddenly grown tired of my company when he'd delighted in it moments earlier. "What crime are you trying to pin on me now?"

Surprise, surprise. Feigned ignorance. I can't say it's a favored facet of this man, but it's better than when he's antagonistic.

"I'm sure it's nothing." I wave away the comment, taking his smug, superior attitude and running with it. "What's a few cases of abduction among friends?"

His jaw tightens. His nostrils flare.

"Did you come here for a reason, Ms. Fox? I mean, other than adding to the harassment case you continue to build. Are you searching for a nightcap? I think a good fucking is exactly what you need to distract you from making more false accusations."

"Tempting." I nod. "Seriously, tempting. But not tonight. I actually came here because I need to apologize for my behavior. The last time we spoke, you offered an olive branch and I threw it back in your face. I was hoping the offer might still be open."

The tightness fades from his features, and he settles back into his comfortable role of arrogant asshole. "Dinner?"

"Yes, dinner." I nibble my lower lip, pure and innocent. "You said you wanted to clear up any misconceptions I have and to also enlighten me on your father's disappearance."

He inclines his head. "I remember. I promised to tell you everything I know about his escape."

"So, is the offer still open?"

He shrugs. "That depends on what I get in return."

I gasp in fake outrage. I even clutch at my chest for dramatic effect. "Do you mean to tell me the pleasure of my company isn't enough of an incentive?"

"Possibly." He ponders the question, or maybe he ponders the situation in general, those eyes taking me in, seeing everything. His gaze rakes my body, narrow with speculation. Down my chest, over my hips, and farther, to my thighs. "What happens if I want something more substantial?"

"Like?" I'm not signing my own death certificate. I might be slightly crazed with dedication. I'm not fucking stupid.

"Leave it to me. But don't worry, I'll make my terms known before you're asked to sign in blood." He flashes a bright-white smile. "Would tonight suit?"

"Tonight is perfect." I stand and retreat a step to counter the overwhelming rush of triumph. He doesn't know what he's getting himself into.

In fact, from his pretentious expression, it looks as though he considers himself the victor.

No way in hell.

All I need is a clue. Just one.

It doesn't matter if he strings together a conversation full of lies. I'll figure out the pattern. I'll find what he's hiding. All I have to do is keep him engaged and control my temper.

"Then it's a date," he drawls. "I'll send a car to pick you up at seven."

Again, I refuse to bite at the taunt. He can play his games.

I'm sure they'll be his downfall.

"I'll be ready." I continue walking backward toward my car, keeping him in my sights while he chuckles and raises his tinted window.

It's not until I'm behind the driver's seat, inching down the road, my vision stalking the rearview, that I realize I'm tingling with adrenaline. That's when the apprehension kicks in. Not because meeting with him will be dangerous, but because it suddenly feels like this is a game to me, too.

7

ANISSA

Unease accompanies me the entire way home, the dull throb pulsing through my veins.

This isn't me—the taunting. The facade.

Okay, maybe that's a lie.

Just a tiny one.

When working with informants, I need to be able to bend them to my will. It takes a certain level of manipulation to convince them to talk when they don't want to. And yes, it becomes a game of mastery.

But I never indulge criminals.

Especially not antagonistic pricks like Cole.

I'm giving him exactly what he wants—my attention.

I can't win without engaging in battle. The situation is a double-edged sword that requires a foolproof strategy.

I can't get him out of my head. Not once I reach my apartment, and definitely not while I'm in the shower, attempting to scrub my skin of his effects.

When I turn off the lights and climb into bed, he's all I see. Every time I close my eyes, he's staring back at me with that devilish smile. The satanic smirk. All I hear is the deep purr of his voice. It whispers in my ear, making the hair on my arms stand on end.

I'm still awake when the sun rises. I don't pass out until after the busy rush of peak-hour traffic fills my head to distract me from the nagging thoughts of a predator.

It's quieter when I wake, the bedside clock glowing red to announce it's two in the afternoon. But that's good. It means I have less time to worry about the risky choices I've made and all those I'll be forced to make in the near future.

Every time I think about Taggert, I distract myself with exercise. I punish myself with sit-ups or squats. I even lower myself to the pain of burpees. I let the burn take away the thought process, because I can't change my mind.

I'm doing the right thing.

I know I am. Despite breaking a promise to Easton.

I don't lose sight of my goal, not through the slow afternoon hours when I try to strategize. And not when my pulse beats faster as the time of reckoning approaches.

I dress simple. Black slacks, white blouse, and two-inch heels, with a faint hint of makeup to mask the sleep deprivation.

For the briefest second, I'm tempted to put on a business suit, until I force myself to realize the appeal is based on nothing but a cheap thrill.

I'm as eager to antagonize him as he is with me. It has to stop. At least on my behalf.

This is serious. I can't keep walking into every trap he lays before me. The lives of so many women are at stake. Not just the nine who have been reported missing over the last five days. It's also all those who remain in the clutches of Luther's sex-trafficking syndicate.

When seven o'clock draws near, I catch the elevator downstairs, my cell in my pocket, my purse and keys in hand.

I don't wear a wire. I don't even contemplate going behind Cole's back to record our encounter.

I'm sure he's smart enough to have contingencies in place to scramble any signal. And if he doesn't, then he has no intention of spilling secrets. My aim is to trick him into revealing the truth. Taunt and torment.

I push through the glass lobby door and step outside, finding the streetlight beaming down to highlight a nightmare.

Double-parked right in front of the building is a sleek, black limousine drawing the attention of people passing by like a stripper handing out hundred-dollar bills.

This isn't the car Cole sent. It can't be.

Neither one of us want to be seen together. The prince of the underworld and a special agent with the FBI. Whispers of an alliance wouldn't be good for either of us.

I glance down the street, then back in the opposite direction, searching for another option as the driver climbs from the limo.

"Ms. Fox?"

I ignore the call as my irritation climbs to new heights.

Should I flee inside to escape being seen? Should I give up because I didn't anticipate yet another game?

"Ms. Fox?"

Shit.

Why the hell am I surprised?

I suck in a deep breath and stand tall, meeting the driver's gaze. "Yes?"

He smiles, the expression filled with gentle kindness. Obviously, he's not a seasoned asshole like his employer.

"It's nice to meet you." He swings an arm in the direction of the back door. "Are you ready to leave?"

No.

Hell fucking no. But do I have a choice?

Wherever my tormentor is, I bet he's laughing his ass off.

"I'm ready." I'm not going to let the prick win this early.

I make my way toward the limo, pause when the driver opens the door, and then slide straight inside. I'm closed into the shadows within seconds, immediately finding the significant space occupied by another soul.

Cole sits on the leather seat running the length of the vehicle, his expression filled with smug satisfaction as he swirls a finger of scotch in the glass resting atop his palm.

"Good evening." I measure my breathing, not willing to show I'm off balance. It's too early for him to be getting to me. "Thanks for the ride. I didn't think you'd go to this much trouble in an effort to impress me."

"Then you must doubt your allure." He takes a drink, the action highlighting the rough tease of stubble along his jaw. "You look nice."

I ignore the compliment as the vehicle begins to move, the slow glide either marking the start of another mistake or the beginning of my victory.

"Would you like to join me in a drink?" He indicates the stocked bar with a tilt of his scotch. "I took the liberty of pouring you a glass of Beluga. I vaguely recall vodka being your poison of choice."

It's not a vague recollection. Or a guess.

It's a fucking statement of knowledge.

I'm sure he's learned everything there is to know about me. I just don't want to contemplate how.

"That's right." I drag my gaze toward the lone glass sitting in front of expensive bottles of liquor, the ice swimming amongst a sea of clear liquid. "But I'm not in the mood to drink right now. Maybe later."

There's another tweak to those lips. "You can pour your own, if that's what you're worried about."

I mimic his expression. Smug. Self-assured. Fucking confident. "I'm not worried."

I'm almost certain he has no plans to kill me. This is nothing more than a show of power. He's succumbing to the weakness of messing with me, which can only work in my favor.

He's a slave to these games.

It's only a matter of time before he makes a mistake.

"Good." He licks his lower lip. "My aim for tonight is to build trust between us."

"That sounds nice."

He continues to eye me over the rim of his glass, drinking in slow sips.

His attention is consuming. It's almost tangible. The potency of his gaze wraps around me, slightly restricting.

He isn't distracted by the passing traffic or the blare of a nearby horn. He keeps watching me. Reading me. He coils his presence around me so tightly, without a single word, that I grow discomforted by the silence.

"Where are we going?" I turn my attention to the window and focus on the passing buildings. He will surprise me with the location. He'll either take me to a place in full view of the public eye. Or somewhere entirely remote. Because he thinks both locations will daunt me.

And he's right.

I don't want anyone seeing us together. If my actions get back to Taggert, I can kiss goodbye all new information on any case revolving around the Torians. I'll be locked out, if I don't lose my job entirely.

The only problem is, being away from civilization provides yet another risk.

"Cole?" I keep my attention on the other side of the tinted windows as we cross the Willamette River and merge onto the I-85. "Where are we going?"

"It isn't far. And we won't be alone. There will be witnesses to ensure your safety."

His attempt at reassurance doesn't hit its mark. I'm not going to let him lull me into a false sense of security.

"I remember at one point you said I could choose the time and location."

"Yes. I did." The flirtation leaves his voice. "But the situation has changed. Things are more complicated now."

"They are?" I turn to him, his eyes immediately meeting mine as I frown in feigned confusion. "How so?"

He keeps staring at me, keeps attempting to read what I try to hide. The taunting expression has vanished and what greets me now is nothingness. No seduction. No arrogance. He's reined it all in.

"We've had our fun, Anissa. Now it's time to get down to business."

My brows raise at the change in gears. "You mean you're ready to tell me about your father's escape?"

His detox from humor doesn't shift. Nothing but hard severity stares back at me. "I'm going to be up-front and explain, with all honesty, that I have no valuable information to give you in relation to that matter. I wasn't included in his plans."

Bullshit.

Bull. Shit.

I don't fucking believe him. I never will. Not on this.

I keep my frustration under wraps, unwilling to divert from my plan. Cool, calm, charismatic. That's the way it's gotta be. I'm determined to match his demeanor every step of the way. He can set the tone, but it won't stop me from laying the trap.

"Then why am I here?" I ask.

He takes another drink and returns to swirling the liquid inside the glass. "Because we both want the same thing."

My mind works overtime while I attempt to work out his meaning.

Is he thinking what I think he's thinking? Does he believe his flirtation is enough to seduce an FBI agent?

Oh, hell no.

"If you're talking about—" I shudder at the mere thought.

If he has the misconception that my panties are melting because of his bad-boy reputation, he's going to get a rude awakening. I'd prefer to commando roll from this moving vehicle and aim for the tires of the next oncoming truck than have sex with him.

"No, I'm not talking about fucking." A half-hearted grin breaks his seriousness. "But if it's at the forefront of your mind, maybe we should get it out of the way."

I scoff.

Well, it's more of a sputter.

He is *not* going to get the better of me. I'm not going to break character. "What do we both want, Cole?"

Cool, calm, charismatic.

Those three words will be imprinted on my brain before the end of the night.

His grin kicks up again, the flicker slight before it fades to nothingness. He breaks the potent fix of our stare and focuses out the window, detaching from the conversation.

Usually, he's fully engaged. Yet, tonight he seems distracted.

He's such an accomplished actor I'm not sure what to believe.

He keeps building the tension to the point where it crackles in the space between us before a sudden detox. There's always so much push and pull. A tedious game of tug-of-war I keep succumbing to.

He lets out a huff of exhaustion. "Neither one of us wants to see another abduction."

It takes all my control not to drop the civil act and loudly voice a call of bullshit right in his deceptive face. With this man, I swear I could call it over and over, but it wouldn't stop the lies falling from his lips. Everything he says is fiction. I wouldn't be surprised if he wasn't aware of reality anymore.

"Are you referring to the women you knew nothing about a few hours ago?" I contemplate taking the drink he offered. Safety be damned. I'm going to need it to get through a meal if I'm already struggling in the limo ride.

"Yes. I've since been informed."

For a moment, I hear static. There's no traffic. Not even the subtle crunch of asphalt. Only annoyance as he uses those women as a ploy.

"You want to help?" My question holds a hint of incredulity, the friendly charade temporarily faltering. I can't help mentally inching toward his trap. I know it's there. He's baiting me, and it's tempting to take a hearty bite.

"You judge me too harshly," he mutters. "I'm not the man you think I am."

Doubtful.

Very doubtful.

"I didn't know anything about the abductions until you mentioned it." He fixes me with narrowed eyes. "Apparently, I've been more distracted than I thought."

"Now all of a sudden you're informed?"

"That's right." He nods. "My sources have given me substantial information that I'm happy to pass on. But now that I think about it, I'm not sure it will do you any good seeing as though you're on leave." He delivers the provocation with a straight face, even though I'm sure he's delighting in my situation.

"How many days until you can return to the office, Ms. Fox?"

"I'm sure you already know, Mr. Torian."

His breathy chuckle brushes my senses, tattooing my ears. But it's the allure of intel that sends my pulse higher.

I focus on settling my eagerness and strive to hear the deception. The manipulation. I try so fucking hard to work out his next trick, when all I want is a clue to help those women.

"You're right." He finishes the liquid in his glass. "It seems I've spent more time being informed about you than anything else."

"Should I be flattered?"

He shrugs. "I'm confused to be honest. Who would've thought an aggressive FBI agent would be so entertaining?"

"Maybe it's your inability to break me that holds the allure. You've probably never met a woman you couldn't walk over."

"Anything can be broken. But I didn't agree to tonight to continue our fun-filled arguments. I'm here for my own reasons."

"Which are?"

Those deep eyes slowly turn back to the window, and for a moment, I wonder if he's striving for sympathy.

"I don't appreciate being labelled a sex trafficker. I don't appreciate that word being used in conjunction with my family at all. I need the judgment to stop."

The statement is more bait.

More taunting, tempting, teasing bait.

I can't bite.

I couldn't care less about his reputation. It's the convincing reasoning that holds my interest. If he would've claimed to care about the welfare of those women, I would've known he was lying.

Now, I'm not so sure.

"I'm capable of many things, Cole, but I don't think changing your reputation is one of them."

"You wouldn't have to. If I share this insight with you, an arrest will be made. I only need you to withhold any ties it has to my family."

I can't do that.

I won't.

But I'm willing to lie to get what I want.

"Okay..." Hope grows wings inside my chest, the gentle flutters increasing the need for oxygen. "Go ahead. I'm listening."

"Not in here. We need to discuss this somewhere neutral and out of listening distance from anyone likely to eavesdrop."

Seclusion. That's what he's aiming for. "Are you saying your own driver can't be trusted?"

"It's not him I'm worried about. I don't believe you're careless enough to meet me without backup, and you should know I'm the same. We need somewhere we can both feel comfortable to speak openly."

His assumption about my carelessness is incorrect. I've gone above and beyond stupidity by meeting Cole without informing anyone. I wasn't going to shoot an e-mail to Taggert. And I didn't want Easton to know I broke my promise.

I'm here entirely on my own, using his presumptions to keep me safe, along with a tracker app on my cell that sends half-hourly location coordinates to my work e-mail. But that security net isn't going to be helpful until after someone realizes I'm missing. I'll already be in a ditch somewhere, my body decomposing by the time anyone thinks to ask for permission to check my inbox.

"You want to get me alone," I muse. "You have to understand how careless it would be if I agreed." I scrutinize him, using everything I've learned over the years in an attempt to find the truth. I need to determine reality from fiction, deceit from fact. "And I'm also confused at why you would come to me for help. It's no secret I'm not your biggest fan."

"For starters, you came to me."

Okay, so he's got me there.

"But the main reason is because of the animosity you wave around like a red flag in front of a bull. You're my toughest critic. I prefer to tackle the hardest tasks instead of wasting time building up to it."

I may be his toughest critic, but I'm also the type of gal who doesn't budge an inch when a man has proven to be untrustworthy. Yet, here I am, falling under his spell.

I want to believe him. The need burns inside my stomach, growing hungrier by the second.

And why wouldn't I?

Obtaining answers about the abducted women goes above and beyond my objective for this meeting. Yes, I'd been aiming to get information to find his father, or take down Cole, but helping those women is far more important.

"So where's this secluded, neutral place you have in mind?" I rub a hand along the back of my neck, easing the prickle of goose bumps. "How far away is it?"

His lips part, but then the limousine pulls to a stop.

He doesn't answer my question. Instead, his mouth thins into a tight line as he juts his chin toward the window, instructing me to take a look.

My chest tightens before I even bother to comply. It's the change in the air between us that unsettles me. Intuition has my nerves hyper-sensitive as I glance outside and become overwhelmed with a heavy sense of dread.

Stretched out before me is a private airport with a jet waiting on the other side of the fence, our names practically written all over it.

8

TORIAN

She keeps staring out the window, the increasing rise and fall of her chest the only indication of her unease.

Manipulating her is a beautiful thing. Molding and shaping this woman's perception is growing beyond an addiction. It's an obsession.

Only this time, there's some truth beneath the deception.

She surprised me with the news of the missing women. I hadn't been aware of the problem. Nobody had fucking told me. Which meant I initially thought it was a provocation.

Unfortunately, I learned otherwise when my informants corroborated the news.

The tally of abductions continues to climb, along with the suspicion my father is responsible. Which only makes me fucking furious because the stigma always attaches itself to me.

"This information will help us both." I speak softly, not wanting to spook her any more than necessary. "If I'm not mistaken, you need something to get back in the good books with your boss."

Her eyes narrow into spiteful slits as she loses her hold on this playful act we've got going.

"I'm not trying to bait you." Not right now, anyway. "I'm only laying out the facts before you attempt to shut me down. For once, we have to work together." I murmur the admission because saying it with conviction is a struggle.

I've never turned to the authorities for help.

Never wanted to. Or needed to.

Even now, it sickens me.

But the truth is, I do need her. The necessity has gone beyond entertainment.

"No." She shakes her head, the refusal barely audible. "I'm not getting on that thing with you."

My optimism takes a hit, the injury striking hard.

I hadn't expected her to skip across the tarmac and rush up the stairs to enter the aircraft. I'd anticipated rejection. I'd predicted it. But my confidence in convincing her had been stronger when she wasn't sitting across from me, her shoulders straight with conviction.

"It's a safe environment." I don't move an inch. I'm not going to scare her into running. "If we're airborne, neither of us have to worry about being followed. I won't have to question whether or not your FBI buddies are tailing us, and you don't need to be concerned about being ambushed by my men. This is the smartest, safest move."

I pause, waiting for a response that doesn't come. She just keeps staring out the window, while her expression turns stoic.

"If I'm going to give you incriminating information, I'm going to do it in a controlled environment, with all my bases covered."

"How incriminating?" she murmurs.

"Incriminating enough to go to the expense and effort of hiring a private jet."

She nibbles her lower lip, raking those teeth deep enough I'm sure I'll see blood.

I'm fully aware her companionable attitude tonight is all for show. She's a tight bundle of aggression under the friendly act. Nothing has changed between us, at least not from her side of the battlefield.

"It's not my jet." I'll keep gently prodding until I get the response I need. "I don't know the pilot, and he doesn't have any loyalty to me."

"It's neutral ground," she drawls. "Just without the ground part."

"You'll be safe, Anissa. I promise."

"It's not about safety."

Like hell it isn't.

She's on the cusp of fear, yet not quite close enough to sate my hunger. She refuses to show weakness, and I can relate to the aversion. I rarely allow anyone access to my underbelly.

Her strength is admirable though. Or it would be if I wasn't so fucking eager to witness her crumple.

"Then why are you stalling?" I ask.

She winces and sinks those teeth farther into her lip.

"Nissa?" I keep waiting for an answer, my patience waning. "If you're not scared of me, what's stopping this from happening?"

Her gaze snaps to mine. "You like thinking I'm scared of you, don't you? It's a thrill. Taunting me is your favorite game."

"*Was* my favorite game," I correct. "We're moving on, remember?"

"Yeah," she mutters. "I remember."

"I'll be clear and admit this is an exercise where we're using each other. Pure and simple. I have information to help those women, and you have the ability to steer evidence away from me and my sisters. That's all this is. Don't make it out to be anything sinister."

Her tongue swipes over the flesh she's been torturing and it drives me to madness. "Where would we go?"

"Wherever you like, as long as it's not here—Seattle, LA, San Fran. I can arrange a driver to meet us at the airport when—"

"No. We don't land." She sits up straight. "We take off, discuss whatever needs to be discussed, then we return."

I incline my head, the heat of adrenaline spurring to life inside my veins. "We can do that."

She narrows her gaze and seems to attempt to siphon my trickery with the sheer force of her evil eye. She's looking for an excuse to deny me. *Any* excuse.

But I can see now that her stubborn determination will get her on the tarmac. She'll climb aboard the aircraft thanks to her sheer dedication to the task of taking down my father. And yes, me as well.

"If you fuck with—"

"What is your obsession with us fucking?" I give a lazy smirk. "It's crazy how often sex is on your mind."

"Don't. Even." She snarls the words with vehemence. It's incredibly provocative even though I'm sure she's completely unaware.

The constant ferocity of her denials makes my dick twitch.

"I won't." I vow an end to the flirtation with a definitive cross of a finger over my chest. "We've both had our fun and made our hostility clear. Now it's time to set that aside and move on."

She sighs and focuses back out the window. "I can't believe I'm even contemplating this."

Contemplate, little vixen. Then hurry up and make a fucking decision.

"I assure you, I want these women found as much as you do." I slide along the bench seat and open the door. "I can step outside to give you privacy if you'd like to call someone and let them know where you're going to be."

There's another huff of laughter. "Don't bother."

I guess she suspects the limo is bugged. And she's right. I'm curious to know who she would contact. I'd love to find out who her go-to person is—the one soul she relies upon now her mother is dead and her father is in hiding.

That nugget of information hadn't been something Decker could source with his expensive surveillance equipment. Not when she's such a solitary person.

She doesn't go out with friends, makes little to no personal calls, and doesn't live it up on her days off.

"Are you sure? This will be your last opportunity to contact someone. I want to make sure all devices are locked in the cockpit while we're onboard."

She meets my gaze with a forced smile. "It's fine. I'll make sure I speak to company staff, along with the pilot before we leave. I won't agree to take off unless I feel comfortable."

I incline my head and climb outside, holding the door wide for her to follow. "That sounds like a good idea."

She keeps those shoulders tight and her back stiff as we enter the small charter building to go through the security process. She hands over her gun, our belongings are scanned, and we're escorted through a metal detector. There's no protest when a pat down is requested. There's also nothing inappropriate found on her person, easing my concerns of her wearing a wire.

I wait patiently as she grills staff on their association with me.

How do you know Mr. Torian?

How often does he fly with you?

The security officer answers her with subtle annoyance—no, he doesn't know me. And he can't recall ever seeing me before.

Or so he says.

We're almost on our way, about to reach the glass sliding doors leading to the tarmac, when she stops and turns back toward the room.

"Is everything okay?" I lean close, whispering the question near her ear. "You're not having second thoughts, are you?"

"I passed second thoughts a long time ago. This goes well beyond that."

"Is there anything I can do to reassure you?" It's surprising how easy the offer to comfort her flows from my lips. This act is so enjoyable, I guess it has become engrained.

"No." She eyes everyone in sight, as if instructing them to remember what she looks like.

It's disappointing.

She should know by now that I could cover up our time together if I wanted. There's rarely anything money can't buy, and with the help of the police in my pocket, I'm almost untouchable.

It also makes life easier when the staff here know and trust me. This company is mine, after all. My name might not be on the documentation, but I sure as hell own it.

I have legitimate businesses everywhere. Gas stations. Freight carriers. Pharmacies. All of which remain under the radar from law enforcement.

There's minimal association between me and the people at the helm of these companies to maintain my anonymity. They give me their assurance they will work honestly, while they trust me to commit to my vow that they will never see the bright light of day again if they even think to fuck me over.

Profit for conformity.

That's all it is. I help them work toward a comfortable future, and they allow me to gain necessary information and untraceable supplies.

The authorities have no clue of the hold I have on this city. Not the slightest glimpse.

My influence is woven through every brick, along every street and sidewalk.

I *am* this city, despite my current need to get away.

"Why don't you make that call? It might settle your nerves." I place my hand at the low of her back and watch her stiffen further.

"I'm not nervous." She swings around and steps out of reach in her approach to the door. "And I don't need to make a call. I'm already covered."

I strongly disagree.

I found Benji's car edging its way into the private airport parking lot as we walked into the building, but I didn't see any other vehicle. Either the Feds are better at hiding than my own men, or she isn't covered as well as she thinks.

"Let's do this." She leads the way toward the jet, not stopping until she reaches the staircase.

"After you." I wave a hand, indicating for her to proceed. "Go speak to the pilot. Inspect the cabin. Do whatever's necessary to make yourself feel comfortable before we take flight."

"I will." She narrows her eyes. "Just remember, climbing onboard doesn't mean I've agreed to go with you."

"I'm well aware."

She takes the first step, her hips holding a gentle sway as she ascends before me.

I don't follow for a few minutes, giving her space to talk privately with the flight team before I make my way to the liquor cabinet in the main cabin.

I don't use the opened bottles. I reach for the Macallan in the back and pour myself a generous glass of fifty-five-year-old scotch.

I'm seated in one of the cream leather chairs when she walks toward me, then directly past to disappear into the bathroom. She bangs and clatters around in there, making me smirk as she no doubt searches for another reason not to trust me.

She won't find anything in there, and I'm pretty sure she already knows it.

The dramatic display is her not-so-subtle way of showing me I'll have to work hard if I expect her to believe a word I say. From the looks of the co-pilot retrieving the staircase and locking us in, it seems she's already given the all-clear for take-off.

I continue drinking, paying her no attention when she returns like a whirlwind, skittering her way around the cabin to lift seat cushions and look behind the television.

"What are you searching for exactly?" I ask.

"Nothing." She doesn't stop her inspection.

"Then why don't you join me for a drink?" I raise my glass in toast. "There's a fully stocked bar. Help yourself."

She pivots toward me, her arms crossed over her chest, plumping her breasts beneath the sheer blouse. I don't pretend not to notice. In fact, I make it known those tits of hers are fucking mesmerizing for so long she rolls her eyes and slaps her arms back down to her sides.

"For once, I think you're right. I doubt I'm capable of getting through a conversation with you without the help of a slight buzz." She makes for the liquor, retrieves a glass, and pours herself at least a double from an opened vodka bottle sitting in the display. "Cheers." She tilts the glass as if toasting the cabinet itself, then throws back a gulp.

Yet again, this woman surprises me.

"Top up your glass before you take a seat. It won't be long before we're in the air."

The cabin jolts on cue, the aircraft slowly moving forward.

"Great." She throws back another gulp, pours more liquor, then approaches to take the seat opposite me, the toes of our shoes barely inches apart.

"Your phone?" I ask. "I'd like to put it in the cockpit."

"I already gave it to the pilot." She holds my stare, taunting me to call her bluff.

I don't bother. Telling her I needed the cell stowed was more of a strategy to forewarn her I would be in control in this environment. And she agreed regardless.

The device itself was never an issue.

"I also told him our flight plans." She places her glass in the cup holder and clasps her belt. "He didn't seem to think doing circle work around the Portland area would be an issue."

"Efficient." I give her a slow grin. "I like it."

She ignores my subtle flirtation, choosing to stare out the window.

She isn't unaffected though. I'm wearing her down—slowly digging my claws beneath her smooth skin.

"Good evening, folks," the pilot announces over the speakers. "Please take your seat and buckle up. It shouldn't be long until we're cleared for take-off."

I follow orders and hide my annoyance at the interruption. I'm finally gaining momentum. I can't risk her having the time to change her mind.

"Do you enjoy flying?" I watch the tarmac roll, the daylight completely faded to night.

"Usually, yes. But I have a feeling the private jet experience will be slightly different."

This one definitely will be.

I have no idea when we'll land, and the thought of returning to Portland isn't something worthy of inspiring excitement. This place doesn't feel like home anymore. Instead, it resembles a war zone.

Keira keeps riding my ass. Layla continues to fight with her husband. Stella doesn't understand why she can't speak to her grandfather.

Our family is in turmoil, and I'd like nothing more than to be a thousand miles away.

The tether tying us together has vanished. We're separate entities instead of one unit, and I'm the poor sucker who needs to pull everyone back into place.

Me, and the woman seated directly in front of me.

Her left hand grips the armrest as the aircraft accelerates, the entire cabin shaking. She doesn't look scared. But she's not comfortable either.

"Is the vodka to your approval?"

She keeps her focus on the world outside, her chest rising and falling with slow breaths. "Yes. It's beyond my pay grade, if that's what you're asking."

"No. That's not what I was asking. I only wanted to make sure you were enjoying yourself."

"I'm having a wonderful time." Her sarcastic tone implies otherwise. "We should do this more often."

I can't help a grin.

I fucking can't.

Her suffering is cathartic. Pure and utter bliss.

"Why don't we? We could make this a weekly ritual. You can share the inside scoop on the Bureau and I'd vow to listen to you more intently than any other man has ever listened in your entire life. Just you and me—"

"Give it a rest." There's laughter in her voice as she rolls her eyes. "You're entirely shameless, aren't you?"

No. Not at all.

The shame I harbor is marrow deep, eating me from the inside out. "I think you mean I'm entirely charming."

"Actually, entirely self-centered is a better fit." She purses her lips, claiming victory, and this time I'll let her have it. The little wins are all she's going to get. "I suggest we get to the point before this slides out of hand. Talk to me about your father."

The jet's acceleration increases, faster and faster. The speed, the approaching victory, along with the unfiltered defiance staring back at me has my cock pulsing.

It's ridiculous.

She's an enemy. One who likes to remind me of the vast differences in our morality. And still, the appreciation I feel in this moment thrums through my veins.

"It's barely eight. What's the rush?"

She cringes, and the air that leaves her lungs is forced out, as if she's in pain. "Come on, Cole. I know you like games, but I can't sit here and pretend to play along when the lives of women hang in the balance."

"I can't share information without trust, Nissa. We need to get to know each other first."

Her fingers clench tighter around the armrest. "I thought you already knew everything about me. What could I possibly share to earn your trust?"

"It's not information as such. It's whether or not you'll give me the truth when I need it."

She takes another sip of vodka, growing unsettled.

She's struggling not to show weakness, and I'd admire her strength if I wasn't so hungry to witness her buckle.

"Okay. Fine. Let's get this over and done with."

I incline my head. "Good. You can start off by telling me how many men you've slept with."

Her face snaps tight with incredulity. "I'm not playing those sorts of games with you."

"It's not a game. Like I said, it's about trust. And don't discount the fact that you can learn a lot about a woman by the number of men she's allowed into her bed."

"Like what?" she growls.

I chuckle, in my fucking element with the appearance of her feisty attitude. "Like if she's a risk-taker or high-strung."

"You're telling me a woman who doesn't have a long list of lovers is high-strung?" She scoffs. "That's probably the most narrow-minded thing I've ever heard. A low tally could simply mean the few men she's slept with didn't know her ass from her clit, so she didn't bother wasting any more time."

I wonder if that's her. If she's a woman with a low tally because the men she's slept with didn't have a clue how to inspire her pleasure.

"True," I admit. "But a healthy number speaks of trust toward the opposite sex."

She laughs this time, and the humor almost reaches her eyes. "Again, I disagree. It could simply mean a woman is confident she can protect herself. Among other reasons." She rolls her eyes again. "You can't claim to need that information to get to know me, Cole.

Some women pay no thought to the men they sleep with, while others examine everything. You can't pigeon-hole me from these questions. It's ridiculous."

She's right. I only wanted to hear her talk about sex. To lighten the mood. To mess with her head a little more.

"Okay, then, I'll ask another. What is—"

"Oh, no, buddy. You had your turn. It's my go now."

Perfect. I'm dying to hear what she wants to know. Out of all the questions she could ask, what draws her attention the most?

"Tell me about the first crime you ever committed."

I expected the hostility. I actually anticipated more, but I straighten, feigning offence as the jet evens out. "I assume this is off the record."

"Of course." There's a quirk to her lips. "This is about trust, remember?"

An ache forms beneath my sternum. I'm not sure if it's caused by her arrogance, the curve of her lips, or the way her gaze makes her appear fully invested. Her features are no longer mismatched. I've learned she can fake a smile like nobody's business, but those eyes never lie.

"Okay." I nod and take a gulp of scotch. "I stole from my local church."

"Wow. When you commit a crime you really start at the top, don't you?"

"It sure seemed like it at the time. I think I was eight. Maybe nine. And the piece of chalk I pocketed felt as if I'd lifted a million dollars."

Her face falls into a glower. "That's hardly a crime, Cole."

"But it's the truth. Which is more than I can say for you with your non-answer."

She snickers and quickly hides the response behind a sip of vodka.

She makes it hard not to stare. It's not often that she laughs or smiles. Not without derision or spite.

This right here is something I've never seen before. Maybe something even more enjoyable than the misery I've been searching for. To have an FBI agent comfortable in my presence is quite an achievement.

"You can now unfasten your seatbelts and move around the cabin," the pilot announces. "It should be a steady flight for quite some time."

The interruption acts as a trigger to reality. Her face falls, the glimpse of happiness replaced with detachment.

"Do you want a top up before we continue?" I unclasp my belt and tilt my glass in her direction.

"I shouldn't." She scrutinizes me, the flicker of indecision working over her features as she glances from me to her vodka then back again.

"You shouldn't or you don't want to?"

"Does it make a difference?"

"Yes, of course it does." I stand and peer down at her. "If you don't want to, that's fine. But if you're not drinking because you feel there's a certain way we need to interact, or you're scared, or on edge—"

"I'm not scared. Or on edge." Her chin hikes, her ego coming into play entirely on cue. "And no matter how many times you question me about it, my feelings aren't going to change. I'm not scared of you."

"Then I can only assume attraction is stopping you from sharing another drink with me." I start toward the liquor cabinet and grab my scotch from the back. "Are you worried you'll succumb to my charm?"

"I'm more worried about leprosy."

She always has a comeback. Her necessity to have the last word is obvious. But those words draw a reaction out of me every time, either enjoyment or competition. I'm always impatient to hear how she'll respond next.

I grab my drink and the bottle of vodka before I return to my seat.

"Are you sure you don't want another?" I hold out the temptation, knowing full well she craves the alcoholic buzz. "Not even a little bit?"

She huffs out a breath and raises her glass. "Fine. Give me a top up, just don't pour too much."

I nod, placing my drink down in the cup holder to give her my full attention. Our eyes hold as I open the bottle, and she doesn't stop me when I pour a generous dose.

"That should keep you occupied for a while."

"I'm sure it will." She gives a gentle smile in thanks. Again, I know it's fake. She despises me under those heavy layers of goodwill.

"Have I earned your trust yet?" she murmurs. "Can we finally address why we're both here?"

This is the tricky part.

The pivotal point.

I break eye contact and retrace my steps, placing the vodka back in the cabinet.

"The trust isn't only for my benefit, Nissa. I need you to feel the same way about me, too. Otherwise what's the point in sharing information you won't believe?"

"Why wouldn't I believe it?" She narrows her gaze. "I think we've come as far as we're going to get today with our faith in each other. We've been civil for, what?" She glances at her watch. "More than an hour now. I think that says a lot."

"I guess it does."

She sits forward in her seat, moving closer. "So, tell me, why don't you think I'll believe you?"

"Because the information isn't going to be what you want to hear."

She bristles and slumps back in her chair. "You're going to try and convince me your father isn't involved."

"Yes."

"Then you're right." Her voice grows bitter. "I don't believe you. Just like I don't believe you had nothing to do with his escape."

I chuckle, but the enjoyment is forced. I'm growing tired of this. "I guess this means we've returned to square one."

"This isn't a joke." She throws back a gulp of vodka, the slightest tremble taking over her hand. "And I'm sick of your goddamn games. You need to tell me something. Anything."

"I just did." I keep my tone measured. Level. "What can I do when you're determined not to believe me?"

"You can start by telling me anything with a glimpse of truth to it. Tell me something I can believe," she begs. "Something true."

Her pleas are music to my ears, sweet and powerless.

"How 'bout I come clean and tell you my comment about the little black dress in your closet was nothing more than a calculated guess?"

She stiffens, her lips pressing into a tight line of disbelief.

"What woman doesn't own one of those dresses?" I smirk. "And I made an assumption about your preference for vodka. I haven't invaded your privacy as much as I wanted you to believe."

She keeps eying me, no doubt pondering my honesty, her tongue snaking out to quickly moisten her lower lip.

"But I did send you those flowers," I admit, "and I enjoyed coming up with the notes. I even watched you myself. Every morning on your run, and every night when you returned home. The rest of the time, my men kept an eye on you."

She swallows, her delicate throat working overtime. "I appreciate the honesty."

I want to laugh. I've divulged my secrets, along with incriminating information, and all I'm getting is appreciation? "You're a hard woman to please, Ms. Fox."

"And you're a hard man to trust, Mr. Torian."

Being hard is definitely becoming an issue. The more time I spend with this viperous enemy, the more she holds my attention.

"But I will trust you," she lies, her voice breathy with the rush of anticipation. "Now, please, tell me what you know."

9

―――――

ANISSA

Cole holds my gaze, his eyes intense. "The person responsible is trying to impress my father."

All my instincts tell me to shoot him down in flames. To deny every single word he says. But I can't.

Game or not, manipulation or sincere confession, I have to remain open to the possibility he's telling the truth.

I force myself to be patient—cool, calm, and collected—and sip my drink as the aircraft pivots to the left.

This situation is going to be difficult to explain to Taggert. Not only did I disobey his orders, but I kinda spat all over them when I boarded this exquisite jet and began doing circle work above the Portland skyline.

All I can do is hope the information provides enough evidence to take down a highly sought-after criminal. Maybe then my disobedience might be excusable, or at least ignorable.

"How do you know?" I take another sip, letting the burn of vodka energize me.

"Information isn't hard to obtain when you know where to look." He shrugs. "Unlike the authorities, people actually want to talk to me."

"You mean they're threatened to spill their guts, otherwise you'll do it for them. Literally."

He raises a brow, gently scolding. "For a smart woman, you have a very narrow-minded view of right and wrong."

"How can it be considered narrow when the majority of the population holds the same view? You're the one making up your own rules."

His eyes consider me with patience while he swirls his glass. "When I ask for information, I give a reward in exchange. Not just occasionally. Always. People want to help me. Yet, in your case, you threaten and intimidate for what you need, and still continue to call yourself the right side of the law."

He's delusional.

A gorgeously charming slip of reality.

"You may reward your informants, but those people know there will be hell to pay if they don't talk."

"Not true." He gives a subtle shake of his head. "I'm not the monster you think I am."

"No, I'm sure you're far worse."

"I'm a businessman, Anissa. And I do my job well. I can only assume you're one of those people who believes money is the devil."

Not money, just you. "That's not the case. But I do think there are more important things in life."

"Like?"

"That's a long list." I'm getting distracted. I'm not usually prone to straying from a conversation, especially not when evidence is involved. "Can we stay on topic, please?"

"Humor me. Tell me one or two things more important than money."

I pause. For some reason, I know I shouldn't blurt out an answer. This isn't merely chatter to him. He's trying to learn more about me. To understand who I am.

I take another sip and ponder my response through a brain that begins to feel sluggish. "Family, for starters."

He nods. "I can agree with that."

A funny, twisting feeling takes over my stomach.

His relaxed sincerity is getting to me. When compared to his antagonistic flirtation and his unpalatable games, he now seems entirely endearing.

Even though I loath to admit it, he's not a terrible conversationalist.

"I'd have to say family are at the top of all my lists," he adds. "Nothing is more important."

"I already knew as much." The Torians are famous for many things, but criminal activity and family honor are their calling cards.

I think that's the main reason my father became heavily invested in the death of Cole's mother. I'd never seen him affected emotionally like he had been that day. I'd assumed he was living in fear of the street war predicted by the newspapers, even though the scaremongering had proven unnecessary.

The bloodshed had been strategic.

Specific.

Contained.

Every victim could be tied to Denise's death. Nobody else had been hurt on either side of the battlefield.

Not the Torian men. Their enemies. Or the police.

Well, not that the hospitals had reported.

The Torian protection umbrella stretches past blood, covering all those loyal to the family.

I guess it's kinda like God promising the bliss of Heaven to anyone who vows their life to him. And when it comes to Cole, the god complex entirely fits. I've never met anyone with a more holier-than-thou attitude, even when it's clear he has no morals.

"What's so funny?" He cocks his head to the side, scrutinizing me. "What brought on that amazing smile?"

Shit.

I raise my glass, hiding my mouth behind another sip of alcohol.

I'm losing track of why I'm here. We're talking about dirty money, threatening civilians, and abductions, yet my mind keeps wandering. What's worse is that I haven't had to keep a constant leash on my animosity.

I've been civil without having to act.

There's no venom from either of us. No anger or annoyance.

For a short space of time, even though I've been well aware of who I'm speaking to, I fell under the spell of his charisma.

What the hell is wrong with me?

"It's nothing." I shake my head and a sudden case of vertigo sends me reeling. For a moment, I have to fight to blink back clarity. "Holy shit."

I'm drunk. Already.

This isn't right.

I stare at my glass, trying to recount how much liquor I've consumed.

"Are you okay?" Cole's tone is dire as he leans forward and brushes a hand over my knee. "You do realize the oxygen up here messes with the alcohol. That vodka will hit you a lot quicker than normal."

"Yeah."

I watch his fingers, entranced. They're large. Strong.

Big, solid hands capable of many, many bad things. Yet there's comfort in his touch.

This man, with his threats and lies and dripping innuendo, is capable of softness.

Fuck. I need to sober up.

"I guess I forgot." I squeeze my eyes shut and the vertigo disappears with the darkness.

What I'm left with is an overwhelming sense of stupidity.

I tried to drown my annoyance and trepidation with vodka, and *yippee,* it worked, but now I'm dizzy drunk without even being buzzed.

"Do you want me to get you a bottle of water?"

The kindness in his voice doesn't sit right. It's too nice. Too uncharacteristic.

This isn't the Cole Torian I know. Well, it's not the man I've researched. He's meant to be callous and spiteful. Just like the man I verbally sparred with in his restaurant.

"Water would be great. Thanks."

I hear the squeak of his chair, the soft pad of footsteps, and the gentle suction of a fridge door opening and closing.

Goddammit, I need to pull my shit together. This isn't professional. I've found a cash cow of information, and I'm kicking it in the teeth.

Not that it's deliberate. I can usually hold my liquor. One or two drinks a night is my daily sedative to help me get to sleep. And here I am, floundering like a teenager on their first bender.

I massage my forehead, trying again to figure out my intake.

I threw back a generous amount initially, needing an immediate hit to lessen all the emotions. Then Cole topped me up with the same amount, which is still half full.

That makes... What? Two standard drinks in quick succession? Maybe three?

"Here." Coldness presses against my upper arm, the chill from the bottle seeping through my blouse.

"Thanks." I meet his gaze as I grab the offering. "I'm sure I'll be okay in a minute. I guess it's the oxygen thing. Or a lack of food. I haven't eaten much today."

"Then it isn't a good idea to keep circling the skies." His brow remains pinched. "Why don't we land and get a bite to eat? We've only got snacks onboard."

"No. I'm fine. Honestly." I crack the lid and drink the water, wiping my hand over my mouth when I finish. "Where were we?"

I need to concentrate on why I'm here.

This isn't an exercise in growing numb to Cole's monstrous influence. He's still a heinous criminal.

He leans back in his seat, eyeing me with fatherly worry. It's annoying.

It's fake, Anissa.

Fake. Fake. Fake.

"Do you have a name for this person who's trying to impress your father?" I take another gulp and another, impatiently waiting for the water to wash away the liquor's effects. "Do you have any proof?"

"I have everything you need. I even have an address of where he's keeping his victims."

"What?" The question bursts free, sounding more like an accusation. "You know where they are, yet we're up here talking instead of taking action? Why didn't you phone it in to the authorities?"

"I need to know you will hold up your end of the deal first."

"My end?" My vision blurs, his face growing cloudy.

I'm drunk. Seriously smashed.

It's fucking embarrassing.

I chug more water, hoping it will clear the confusion, but my sight doesn't improve.

"I need you to clear the stigma around my name. I'm not involved in this, and neither is my father. That needs to be noted and the information shared. I don't want this sex-trafficking bullshit associated with me a moment longer."

I frown. "But your father is guilty."

I unclasp my belt in a vain attempt to help ease the overwhelming discomfort. I feel wrong. My limbs are heavy. My head's a foggy mess. I can barely hold on to the topic of conversation. It keeps slipping away, like sand through my fingers.

"We need to land. I have to call this in." I place the bottle down beside me and push from my seat, intent on walking to the cockpit, when the jet takes a nosedive.

I lunge for the headrest, clinging tight with the sudden descent.

I struggle to battle the swirl and fight from passing out. But when I glance at Cole, he looks at me as if I'm insane. He's not gripping the armrests or staring in panic. From what I can see through the blur, he's relaxed. Calm. In control.

The jet isn't spinning.

It's me.

All me.

I fight against the darkness and make myself concentrate. I pull together the only thoughts I can cling to—the alcohol, the sudden insanity.

This shouldn't be happening.

I squint through muddled vision and stare at Cole.

"What did you do?" I whisper the accusation as I struggle to make out his features.

Lazy assurance blinks back at me, his gentle expression transforming into a smug grin that robs me of any comfort.

"*You,*" I seethe. "You drugged me."

Oh, God.

I cling tighter to the seat as he stands, his nearness increasing the rapid sway of my head.

I fight to understand. I struggle and snatch for clarity yet I can't grasp hold. Everything is a riddle. A convoluted game.

I poured the first drink. I watched him like a hawk with the second.

He didn't slip anything into my glass. I know he didn't.

I fucking *know*.

"It's okay." He grasps my wrist.

I slap at him, trying to bat away the contact, and fail miserably. Every move I make takes the effort of a marathon. My co-ordination is off. I struggle to lift my arms, move my legs, keep any type of focus.

"You son of a bitch." I turn toward the cockpit and stumble forward. "Help me... Help."

"It's too late for that."

No. No. *No*.

I shake my head and it increases the turmoil. I sway with the movement. Stumble some more.

Holy shit, I'm in trouble.

I should be scared. I should be fucking petrified. Instead, I'm consumed with blinding rage.

I continue to fight against his hold, unable to see, barely able to think. "Don't touch me."

My voice grows hollow, barely recognizable. I'm not sure I even have the energy to yell.

I bump into things. I hit my knee, my thigh, while Cole's grip remains gentle on my arm.

There's no vision at all now, only the rampant thump of my heart in my ears and so much anger.

"Sit back down, Nissa." His words haunt me, echoing over my pulse. "Don't make this any harder than it needs to be."

I fling out a hand, and it connects with something solid.

Muscle.

Tightness wraps around my wrists and I'm dragged, pulled against something warm.

I attempt to fight. In my mind, I'm battling the enemy with all my might, but in reality, I'm not sure I even move.

I can't.

My head droops against his chest. I can smell him. Can scent the dizzying masculinity of his cologne. "Fuck you."

"Shh." His breath caresses my cheek. "Give in, little fox." His arms wrap around me, holding me close. "Stop fighting."

"No," I mumble, my lips numb. "You're going to..."

The words don't come. I hear them, think them, but they don't leave my mind. They're stuck in the growing darkness, clambering to break free.

I want him to know how much he will regret this.

He's going to pay... But the heaviness... The encroaching shadows.

I collapse, falling into his hold, succumbing to obscurity.

"It's okay," he murmurs in my ear. "I've got you."

10

ANISSA

I wake in comfort. The softness of a delicate pillow cradles my cheek, the gentle press of silk sheets brushing my neck.

I jerk upright, opening my eyes to an immaculate room brightened by the sunshine pouring in behind thick, elegant curtains.

I don't know this place. I've never seen any of the furniture before. Not the polished, dark wood dresser. Or the carved antique chair in the corner.

But more unnerving than the unfamiliar setting is the uncomfortable dawning I've lost at least eight hours of my life if the brightness of the sun is any indication.

I remember Cole picking me up in a limo, taking me to the airport, and then being on a private jet. We were civil. He offered to help find the missing women.

No. He had information to assist in saving them.

Important information.

Then... I struggle to remember what comes next.

I'd been drinking. I'd poured myself a glass of vodka. Then Cole gave me one more.

There's no way I would've consumed enough to make me pass out. I've *never* passed out.

That asshole must have slipped me a roofie.

I throw back the covers, and the rush of movement makes my wrists protest. They ache. Throb. I glance down to see red streaks marking my skin, the damage peeking out from beneath the cuffs of my blouse.

My stomach lurches at the thought of what was done to me. The possibilities batter my mind. I rush from the bed, my feet hitting plush carpet.

My shoes... I've got no shoes.

Thank fuck my clothes are still intact. But someone took my goddamn shoes.

Cole.

Why?

Why the hell would he drug me and bring me back to his house? Why the hell would he do any of this?

I pace as I frantically contemplate. I need to settle myself before I storm from the room to face him.

He didn't hurt me. Not apart from the marks on my wrists.

Maybe he didn't drug me either.

Maybe... *Fuck.*

The possibilities are endless, and my wild imagination isn't helping.

I inhale deep, measuring my breath. I'm not going to hyperventilate over this. Not yet. There's no reason to panic until I know what happened.

Doesn't mean I shouldn't protect myself.

I crouch, reaching for the ankle holster hiding my pepper spray. I'm not surprised to find it isn't there. There's only more tenderness to match my wrists.

"Cole, what the hell have you done?" The question whispers from my parched lips.

I must have been bound, hog-tied, while left fully dressed and without any indication of sexual violation.

He then made sure I was comfortable. My binds were removed. I was placed in an expensive bed. In an extravagant room.

The evidence is contradictory. Hog-tied and comforted. Drugged yet nurtured.

The pounding beneath my skull doesn't make the puzzle any easier to figure out.

Maybe he realized he made a mistake. He could've been worried about my safety.

Did he want to keep an eye on me?

I can't help trying to convince myself of the placations. But that's exactly what they are. I'm grasping for the best-case scenario.

Worst-case?

I shudder, my chest hollowing.

Am I victim number ten?

I glance around, taking more notice of my surroundings. This isn't a prison cell. It's an elegantly furnished bedroom, oozing sophistication.

It isn't a place that promotes confinement.

There's a window, for heaven's sake. And yes, Cole's house is big, but it isn't a palace with walls too high to scale down.

If I wanted, I'm sure I could open the window and escape to the lawn below. Then all I'd have to do is walk to the nearest house to ask for assistance.

Easy.

I'm certain there's a simple explanation for all of this. I'll be laughing over my wild imagination as soon as the dust settles.

I bridge the distance to the window and pull aside the curtain. The material grates along a metal track, causing a growl of noise to spike my apprehension. But it's the view that ignites panic.

I see water. An open expanse of deep blue that doesn't resemble anything close to the Willamette River.

This is the ocean. Lots and lots of ocean as far as the eye can see.

"Holy shit." I gasp.

The view doesn't resemble anything close to the beaches along the Oregon coast. There's no sand. Only rock. And the shore is close to the house. This doesn't look like any place I've visited before.

Everything inside me hollows—my stomach, my chest, my lungs. Confusion and hysteria battle for supremacy through a rapidly pounding heart.

I grasp the pane and pull, opening the window a crack.

Fresh air engulfs me, the warm breeze hotter than the cooler

Portland weather. But the temperature shouldn't be my focus. I have to remind myself the window opened.

It fucking opened.

I'm not a prisoner. My thoughts return to this being a simple misunderstanding... With burns on my wrists.

I start toward the door, my steps slow as I pull myself together.

I'm not going to show fear. Nothing has changed. I'll remain cool, calm, and charismatic... *Yeah, because that worked so fucking well for me last night.*

I grasp the door handle, the brass twisted in an elegant style, and slowly lower the lever. I don't make a noise as I pull the obstruction open a crack and listen for clues.

At first, there's nothing—only the rustle of breeze in the distance. The gentle *whoosh* of air is comforting, portraying freedom.

I inch the door wider and peek outside, finding a dimly lit hall, the runner along the carpet plush and, yet again, elegant. To the right, large, ornate paintings are spaced along the walls. Some sort of Roman warrior statue stands atop a pedestal, staring back at me from the very far end.

To the left, there's more hall, much, much more, with a break in the middle leading into a light-filled area.

A clatter sounds in the distance. The noise associated with a kitchen. Then there's a clink of cutlery.

Food.

My stomach rumbles in optimism.

I pull the door wide and tiptoe from the room, creeping my way toward the opening in the hall. My wrists and ankles throb with each twinge of movement. My heart thunders, each step bringing a harder beat.

The further I trek, the brighter the light seeps in, the louder the breeze gets, the more definitive those food-prep noises become.

There's no hint of danger, only the prickle at the back of my neck making my nerves sensitive to everything around me.

I pause before the opening of the hall, pressed tight against the wall while I remain in the shadows. For long heartbeats, I stay frozen, breathing deep, preparing myself for the worst before I glance around the corner and find Cole in an immaculate kitchen.

He's standing before a cooktop in the middle of an island counter, a stainless canopy rangehood above his head as he grips a frying pan with one hand and a spatula in another.

The sight is almost comical. Entirely bizarre.

He's different—almost unrecognizable in a short-sleeved collared shirt, his dark hair damp and casually mussed.

It's the first time I've seen him without a suit. He seems almost naked in comparison, his arms holding more muscle than I would've imagined. If I'd ever imagined them. Which I haven't.

"You hungry?" He doesn't take his attention from the pan, and my pulse rate increases with the thought of someone else being here with us.

A threat.

An accomplice to my abduction.

"I've been waiting for you to wake up," he continues. "I hope you like eggs."

I don't move.

"Anissa?" He glances in my direction, and I plaster myself back against the wall.

Shit.

I'm unprepared.

I don't know what to do. What to say. I have no idea how to react, but I refuse to appear weak.

"You must be starving." His voice is entirely casual.

Fuck.

I can't stand here forever. The lack of movement is more telling of my vulnerability than words could ever be.

I suck in a deep breath and bounce my butt off the wall, striding out into the open space. "What time is it?"

Sheer curtains billow in front of an open glass door leading outside. I see the faint outline of deck chairs, a beach umbrella, maybe even the corner of a pool. But nothing beyond. No hint or clue as to my location.

He flips something in the pan, the accompanying sizzle crackling in my ears. "That depends." His tone is ominous.

No, I'm wrong. It's not his tone. It's his words. They almost resemble a threat.

"What time is it?" I repeat with a bite of impatience.

"Like I said, that depends." He flicks his gaze toward me, giving me a glimpse of lazy contact before he returns his attention to the food. "Are you referring to Pacific time or Eastern European?"

Eastern European?

I chuckle even though my stomach free falls, his taunt hitting its mark. "Why would I want to know Eastern European, Cole? Where are we?"

"The Greek islands." He offers the insight without faltering. Just blurts that shit as if it doesn't have the ability to inspire a heart attack.

I swallow over the desert claiming my throat. "Quit playing games. I didn't have a passport. I wasn't even conscious. You're not going to get me to believe we're in another country."

He raises his brows and holds my gaze. Waiting.

There's nothing smug about his expression. It's not taunting or impatient.

I guess it's curious.

Why is it curious?

I glance toward the billowing curtains again and try harder to make out the background beyond the pool loungers.

He wants me to go outside. He expects me to panic and rush toward clarity, only to laugh in my face when I realize we're somewhere close to home. Maybe Astoria or Cannon Beach. A few hours' drive from familiarity.

The need for answers kills me, the tendrils of possibility coiling around my chest to squeeze tight. I can't help giving him what he wants.

I start for the glass doors, slow and gradual, hoping to keep my self-respect intact.

"You don't want to have breakfast first?"

There's another sizzle from the pan but I ignore it, along with the question as I reach the curtains and pull them aside. The double glass doors are open, allowing me to step outside onto the warm cement tile.

An outdoor oasis spreads before me. A crystal-clear pool. Manicured waist-high hedges. A spa.

This place resembles some sort of mini resort. It's a multi-million-dollar property with another view of the ocean from this side of the building.

I walk around the pool, heading toward a path between the hedges that leads somewhere outside this hellish paradise.

The air is different here. Crisper. Cleaner. The salt of the ocean lingers with every breath. It doesn't feel like I'm Stateside. Or that could be Cole working his way into my head to trigger my paranoia.

He keeps manipulating me, messing with my thoughts.

I increase my pace, finding a stone path leading through long, wild grass. The expanse of land opens up before me, an unfettered view of ocean across 180 degrees.

I break into a jog, following the trail toward a pier. My feet hit the wooden planks hard in my rush to the very end. My body is a mix of numb limbs and throbbing arrhythmia as I turn in a full circle to find more water. It's everywhere. In every direction, apart from the restricted view behind the stunning beach house.

What the hell have you done, Cole?

I shove my hands through my hair, trying to rack my brain for a possible name to my location. We could be on the tip of the coast somewhere. A secluded hideaway exclusive to the rich and famous.

I stalk from the pier, bypassing the path to jump along the rocky shore. I pass shrubs and more wild grass in my search for humanity. I lunge over crevasses carved out by the tide. I push my legs harder, accelerating into a jog. All that does is help me see more water.

There's nothing else out here.

No land. No escape. No options.

I pivot and sprint in the opposite direction, cutting through vegetation, my feet punished by prickles and stones until I reach the perfectly manicured grass of the yard. I dash around the pool to take another path on the far side, leading in the opposite direction, only to be devastated by the sight.

More water.

We're surrounded.

The ground beneath my feet is nothing but a tiny island.

More are scattered in the distance, with a large expanse of land stretching along the horizon. Any chance of escape too far away.

Escape isn't within my grasp.

Even if I had assurance the water wasn't littered with hungry sharks, I could never swim that far. There's no hope of paddling to safety.

No hope for anything.

My breathing comes short and sharp. Each exhale is a shudder.

I'm stuck here. On an island. With a murderous criminal.

I drag my feet to the shore and crumple, slumping onto the rock to stare blankly across a building nightmare.

This feels like an alternate reality. I stepped onto that jet and my life changed. It fractured.

All because I couldn't keep my nose out of it.

I had to go after Cole. I had to succumb to that nagging twinge deep down inside me. For what? What had I hoped to achieve? Why didn't I stay away?

I undo the buttons on the wrist cuffs of my blouse and inspect my skin in the bright light of day. They're burns. Potential rope marks. I twist my arms back and forth, cursing Cole for every inch of damaged flesh.

This isn't right. I don't understand his angle. How can he benefit from holding me hostage?

I lower the cuffs back in place and begin undoing the buttons down the front of my blouse, determine to inspect every inch of my skin for possible violations. My stomach is clear, without a blemish, but I have to do a double-take when I tilt my head to look at the side of my waist.

My skin bears a bruise, the area circular, under an inch in diameter. I crane my neck for a better look, and hold my breath at the sight of a puncture mark.

Oh, God.

Bile goes into mass production in my stomach. Nausea takes over.

Did he bother to use a clean needle?

My breathing becomes ragged. My arms tremble.

There's no way he's going to get away with this.

Once he takes me home, he'll be charged with a string of offences. I'll take pleasure in outlining all the crimes he's made against me.

A prison sentence is inevitable. I'll make sure of it... Unless he doesn't plan on taking me home at all.

I give way to the buckle of my legs and descend to the rocky shore, sitting my ass down to pull my knees to my chest.

Could he seriously be contemplating keeping me here? Killing me?

My death wouldn't achieve anything, except maybe mild satisfaction on his behalf. And even if he successfully disposed of my body, there's no way he wouldn't be linked to my disappearance.

I battle confusion, my head growing heavy the more my speculation builds.

I can't make sense of his actions. No matter what way I look at this, his motives seem careless and unplanned. If he wanted to kill me, he could've achieved his goal easier in Portland. He has an enforcer on staff to handle those situations. They've perfected the art of getting away with murder.

So why bring me here? What is his objective?

I don't know how long I sit there, wallowing in impending doom with the sun directly overhead to sizzle my skin when I hear an abnormal buzzing, burring sound.

I snap my gaze to the left, a speedboat catching my eye in the distance.

It's approaching.

I'm on my feet in seconds, my heart racing as I flail my arms in an attempt to draw attention. The hope of savior brings time to a grinding halt. The progression takes forever, the boat barely seeming to move despite its generous size.

It's definitely not small, and the closer it gets the more luxurious it appears. A rail borders the elongated front with enough room for a tanning area, while the back and upper deck, have more free space than my apartment.

Much more than a speedboat, it's a knight in sea-sprayed armor.

I continue to wave my arms, swinging them wildly while I jump, jump, jump.

The boat progresses closer and closer, spurring my hope higher and higher, until it pivots within half a mile of the shore, heading somewhere behind my private island hell.

"*Where are you going?*" I scream.

I collapse back onto the rock, listening to the burr of the boat as it fades, then abruptly stops.

One minute the sound is there, then it's gone. I tilt my head, wondering if my mind is playing tricks on me.

No. It's not.

The boat must have diverted to the pier.

I scramble onto my feet and sprint, heading back along the path I came. Through the yard, alongside the pool, and down the other trail. I silently pray as I pant out the distance, hoping and wishing for a quick salvation.

And there it is, my savior, docked at the very far end of the pier.

I glance over my shoulder as I run, cautious of my captor trying to stop me, but he's nowhere in sight.

Hopefully the sizzling of the frying pan is too loud for that motherfucker to hear me speed out of here. And if I'm really lucky, he'll choke on whatever breakfast he's slaved over.

This time, when my feet hit the wooden planks, my heart soars.

Two men are aboard the fancy boat. They're both in the back, one bent over, tending to something at his feet. The other smiles at me as I approach, the laugh lines of a man well into his fifties filling me with relief.

"*Kali mere, omorfo thyma.*" He waves at me in greeting.

I stupidly wave back, momentarily stunned because I don't know a lick of Greek. Not one single word.

"I need help." I pause, waiting for a glimpse of understanding.

His smile grows wider, the bright white of his teeth in heavy contrast to the dark tan of his skin.

"I have to get to the mainland. Do you have a phone?"

I have to tell someone my location. Nobody knows where I am. Nobody even knows I was docile enough to meet up with Cole.

"Cell phone," I repeat as I stop beside the boat. "Tel-uh-fohn?"

The man continues to smile. No, he's almost laughing.

I frown, not appreciating his humor over my lack of communication when my captor could come after me at any minute. "Ih-mur-juhn-see."

"He's not going to help you."

I turn my attention to the man bent over two large duffels.

His voice is pure American English. Not a hint of an accent.

He straightens, lifting one of the bags onto his shoulder. Our eyes meet and familiarity brings an icy chill to my bones.

Luca Hart.

One of Cole's men.

His lips are set in a tight line, his brow pulled tight. "I suggest you go back inside." He lugs the duffel onto the pier, then does the same with the second. "You're not going anywhere today."

"I need help," the old man mocks in a high-pitched, almost unrecognizable accent. "Ih-mur-juhn-see. Ih-mur-juhn-see." He releases a belly laugh, the noise ricocheting through my head and turning my cheeks to flame.

I retreat a step, then another.

I've been furious before. Recently, I've been caught in one red-hot rage after another. But what I feel right now goes beyond that.

It's fire and ferocity. Venom and vengeance.

This man is taking joy from my life-threatening situation.

He wants my fear, and I sure as fuck won't give it to him.

"Thanks for the ride." Luca climbs from the boat and drags one of the duffels from the pier over his shoulder. He jolts with the weight, and I force myself not to think of what could be hidden inside.

"Anhjoy." The old predator grins.

Enjoy? Fucking asshole.

"Yeah... Thanks." Luca nudges past me and stalks toward the house, not sparing me a second glance.

They're cocky as hell, with no concern over my possible escape.

They think I'm stuck here, but I refuse to believe it.

The statistics on survival for abducted victims is low once they're taken to a new location. It's imperative I find a way off this island. Cole has all the power here.

I need to demand assistance.

This old wrinkled fuck isn't going to get away with leering, laughing, and loading me with his caustic vibes.

"I need help," I repeat, this time with a venomous tone as I approach the boat. "You need to give me your phone."

I move to climb aboard, swinging one leg over the side of the vessel to place my foot on a padded bench seat beneath. "And take me to the mainland."

I chance another glance over my shoulder, making sure Luca isn't rushing back to stop me, before raising my other leg.

The unmistakable click of a cocking gun makes me freeze.

My heart stutters and I struggle not to become a victim of hysteria when I tilt my face to find a barrel aimed right between my eyes.

"Off," he grunts. "Off my boat."

I raise my hands slowly. "Please lower your weapon."

"Off." He jerks the gun toward the pier. "Off. Off."

"Okay. I'm getting off." I measure my movements, backtracking gradual and steady. I can feel the aim between my eyes. The pressure heavy.

I watch him, watch the gun, watch anything and everything in the hopes the scrutiny will save me.

One foot reaches the pier, closely followed by the other.

Even without the threat of me being on the vessel, the man keeps me in his sights and sidesteps until he's under the shade of the cabin, directly in front of the steering wheel.

There's no smile anymore. No taunting laugh or infuriating leer.

But there's annoyance.

He's angry I spoiled his fun.

"I'm an American citizen," I repeat. "I work for—"

My words are cut off by the roar of the boat's engine. Then he's taking off, speeding away in a mass of swirling whitewash and taking any hope of escape with him.

I stand there for so long, watching him drive out of view. Then longer, until I'm unable to hear another sign of life. Or freedom.

The anger doesn't dissipate. It builds, growing alongside my frustration.

My life can't be in danger. It can't be, despite the gun that threatened to blow my brains out moments ago. Cole isn't a stupid man. Thinking he can kill me and get away with it is ludicrous.

Yet, he's brought me here against my will, exposing himself to a whole new level of crime.

The staff at the airport saw us together.

The pilots. The limo driver.

Someone will talk.

Someone *has* to talk.

My pulse grows frantic, beating out of control.

Cole and his family have gotten away with a multitude of offences. He's a walking, talking bucket list of unpunished criminal activity.

God, if his father can escape incarceration for sex trafficking and solicitation, what's to stop Cole from covering up the disappearance of a disgraced FBI agent?

"Fuck." I swallow over the horrid taste at the back of my throat and clasp my hands behind my head.

I need to think.

Think. Think. Think.

This is just another taunting game.

He'll try to pretend I agreed to this impromptu vacation. Maybe he even has a video of me, drugged and disorderly, slurring through an agreement to accompany him here.

He would've covered his ass somehow, which means this is only temporary.

Once he's had his fill of entertainment, I'll be worthless. Meaningless.

My hands fall to my sides, and my focus shifts to the lone duffel still sitting on the wooden planks before me. I sink to my haunches, determined to find something useful—a weapon, a phone, I'd settle for matches to set this island ablaze—as I pull the zipper.

Material comes into view as I yank the opening wide. Material I begin to recognize as I scrounge around inside.

These are my clothes. My blouses. My jeans. My fucking underwear. Along with a large clip-lock bag containing my hair and toothbrushes, hair-ties, and moisturizer. Almost anything and everything that lived on the top of my bathroom vanity.

They've been in my apartment, scavenging through my belongings.

Cole thought of everything. This wasn't a spur-of-the-moment plan. He must have had each step and contingency in place. Maybe even from the moment he met me in the coffee shop.

He anticipated my retaliation. He knew I'd come after him when he made me his alibi. He created the perfect opportunity to offer me information in exchange for another meeting. He predicted I'd take him up on his offer. He fucking read me like a book.

I became distracted by my need for justice and never noticed the moves he made toward a far bigger game.

"Fucking hell." I wipe a hand over my face and drag my feet back down the pier.

I don't bother with the duffel. I leave it where it lays. Luca might expect me to haul my own luggage inside, but they'll both get a surprise when they realize I have no intention of going back inside at all.

If they want entertainment, they won't get it from me.

There will be no begging for freedom or bending to their will.

If Cole Torian wants to continue to make a fool out of me, he will need to come find me first.

11

TORIAN

Luca eyes me from the sofa, his stare holding a hint of judgment. "How long are you going to keep her outside? There's no fresh water out there, and she's been in the sun all day."

"Keep her?" I continue to cut the fruit housekeeping stocked in the fridge. "The only thing keeping her outside is her stubborn pride."

"You sure she's not scared?"

I scoff. "That woman wouldn't feel fear if it bit her on the ass."

"And you're not worried she'll do something stupid?"

"Not at all. What's she going to do? Build a raft and paddle her way off the island?"

He holds up his hands in surrender. "It's just getting dark, that's all."

I'm well aware.

I've waited all day to speak to her. I've deliberately given her space. I wanted her to have time to think. I also needed my own breathing room.

This morning didn't go to plan.

Luca was meant to be here before she woke up. I wanted the island contained. Free from the possibility of escape.

The confrontation with the boat driver shouldn't have happened.

It was neither predicted nor appreciated.

I'd walked outside to check on her after Luca updated me on

the situation, only to find a gun pointed at her head. Her life whittled down to the hair trigger of a simple ferry man.

It took all my restraint to watch the interaction play out, my hands clenched at my sides, my jaw wired shut.

Common sense demands nobody would dare kill a woman of mine, captive or not, but common fucking sense seems to be in short supply these days.

"In half an hour, it's going to be pitch black out there," Luca adds. "And if you do finally decide to search her out, it's going to be the prime opportunity for a woman like that to do a surprise shank attack."

A woman like that—determined, vindictive, strong.

"I'm well aware." I finish slicing the watermelon and place it on a plate beside nectarines, grapes, and cherries, then grab a bottle of water from the fridge. She's spent too long without food and water. And with or without Luca's prodding, I had every intention of going out to face her as soon as I'd finished preparing her something to eat.

I palm the filled plate and place the bottle under my arm, then start for the open doors.

"You're going?" he asks.

I don't answer. Luca's unhealthy obsession with preparation needs to be worn down. He doesn't always have to know what I'm doing.

He sits up straight. "If you're not back in an hour, I'll come rescue you."

"Don't bother. If she outsmarts me, she deserves to get away with it."

He doesn't respond, neither confirming or denying the instruction.

It's so he can claim ignorance later if he does have to rush to my aid.

His loyalty has recently stretched far beyond anything given from my other men, even though everyone in my employ is impeccably devoted. I think he's been waiting for something to focus on since his discharge from the SEALs, and thankfully, me and my family became his distraction. He's becoming an asset. A dedicated soldier.

I walk outside, around the pool area, right up to the manicured hedge used as a makeshift boundary to the yard, and scope out the desolate island.

There's no sign of life.

She's not on the pier or along the shore as far as the eye can see. She could be on the other side of the house, but I doubt it.

I'll bet her hiding place is among the only group of trees straight ahead. I wouldn't be surprised if she'd monkey-d her way up one of them, determined to stay out of reach.

I slip through a break in the hedge and walk through tall grass, the long strands whipping at my jeans in the breeze. The wide trunks and billowing branches provide a secluded canopy out here —the perfect shelter. Or an ideal base camp for war.

I'm a few feet from the boundary of trees when I hear a nearby rustle of undergrowth. *Bingo*. She's here. And hopefully not about to swing from a vine to ruin the fruit platter I spent way too long creating.

"I come in peace." I hold the plate up with one hand and the bottle of water high in the other.

More rustling sounds, then the snap of a twig.

"I've got food." I take another step and another. "You need to eat."

There's no response. I guess I don't expect one. Not if it isn't violent.

I reach the first tree and peer around to see what's hidden inside the circular canopy. I don't react at the sight of her standing with her back to one of the trunks, her body in a fighting stance, a sharpened stick clutched in her fist.

I don't allow myself the luxury of an opinion. I'm not going to fixate on the tangled mess of her short, dark hair. Or the gentle glow of her skin that says she's spent too much time in the sun.

I'm not going to acknowledge how impressed I am at the pile of makeshift weapons at her feet, the sharpened branches resting into a subtle pyramid. And I'm definitely not going to be annoyed by her constant need to fight.

I'm nothing.

I can't mess with her anymore. Things have changed.

"Drop the weapon, little fox. The chances of you succeeding are slim to none. But the likelihood I'll retaliate is one-hundred percent."

"Slim to none?" She quirks a brow. "I can deal with those odds."

I clamp my lips shut, determined not to grin, and throw the bottle of water at her feet. "Drink."

She scoffs. "And be drugged again? No, thank you."

"There's no drugs. It's time to move forward."

She doesn't budge, remaining in her battle position, slowly twisting her stabbing stick between the fingers of her right hand.

"Okay. I see you're reluctant to trust." I hold up my free hand, solemnly vowing my surrender. "That's understandable. But why don't you sit for a while and give me the chance to explain?"

"If you think I'll believe your words will ever hold any truth, you're delusional. Have you heard the story of the boy who cried wolf?"

"Yes, I'm familiar."

"Then you'll also be familiar with what happens to that little fucker." Her words are vicious, snapped between fierce lips. "And do you know what else, Cole?"

I keep my mouth under control, fucking determined not to smirk. There's something invigorating about her. Something in her violent energy that makes me burn. "What, Nissa?"

"He deserved it. And you will, too."

"When I get eaten by a wolf?"

"You are the wolf," she grates. "But you'll get what you deserve. I have no doubt."

I raise my brows, impressed at yet another new level to her anger. She's a feisty little thing. "Are you finished with the fairy-tales?"

"Fuck you."

I can't help it. A grin breaks free. "I'll take that as confirmation."

I glance around, searching for a place to sit—a rock, a ledge, something—because I have a strange feeling we're going to be stuck in a verbal sparring match for quite some time. "Don't go postal on me, but I'm going to come a little closer to put this plate down near your feet. I'd prefer if you didn't try to stab me in the jugular."

"I'd prefer if you crawled into a hole and died." She shrugs. "I don't think either of us are going to get what we want."

I chuckle. It can't be helped. "You're always filled with spirit, aren't you, Niss?"

"And you're always filled with sh—"

"Okay. Enough." I raise my voice, demanding control. "You need to eat." I take a step forward.

"Don't bother." She holds her weapon higher. "I'm not going to consume anything you've prepared. I've already learned from that mistake."

"Then you'll die from a lack of sustenance. Is your stubborn pride really that strong?"

"Stubborn pride?" She huffs out a derisive laugh. "It's called self-fucking-preservation. You got me suspended, broke into my house, and went through my belongings—my fucking underwear. You then plied me with a date-rape concoction. Kidnapped me. Injected me with drugs and—"

"There were no drugs or date-rape concoctions." I inch a step forward. "Only sedatives."

"I have track marks," she snarls.

"You have an injection site from a liquid sedative. I needed to make sure you remained asleep while we transported you."

"Bullshit."

"No, not bullshit. Do you seriously feel like you've had a narcotic hit?"

"How would I know? I'm not a user like you." She keeps the stick clenched in her hand and her stance strong.

"You'd know. Most drug highs usually demand an adverse payment. All those good feelings are reimbursed in the aftermath when you feel like hell."

"I certainly don't feel peachy, Cole."

I won't laugh again. I can't. I'm almost certain she will take the lousy odds and attempt a stabbing spree. "They were only sedatives. Nothing more sinister."

"That doesn't make what you've done any better. I'd been drinking. Everyone knows sedatives and liquor don't mix. What if I was allergic? Or had a reaction? Despite you being oblivious to the severity of what you've done, I could've died."

"That would've been unfortunate." I attempt another step, not taking my gaze off her, having the perfect view of her expression-filled face as a new layer of rage seems to set in. "I wouldn't have let anything happen to you, Nissa."

I crouch and place the plate a few feet from the pile of sticks. She eyes the offering and swallows hard.

It's clear she's starving. I'm sure she's suffering from thirst, too.

"What if I eat first?" I shouldn't care about her struggle. Not when it's now self-inflicted. All she needs to do is take a piece of fucking fruit. "You tell me what I should eat, and I'll eat it."

"How 'bout a bag of dicks?"

I grin. The constant snap, snap, snap of her remarks is a beautiful thing. "How 'bout a grape instead?" I reach for the plate and pop the fruit into my mouth. "And a cherry?" I steal another piece, chewing the juicy morsel before spitting the seed near her bare feet. "Anything else?"

She continues to inspect the plate, her tongue nervously snaking out to swipe her lower lip. "The watermelon."

Good. Those two words are a lifeline to civility.

I obey, grabbing a chunk from the top of the pile.

"No. Not that one." She points her stick to the opposite side of the plate. "Take one from the bottom."

I incline my head, happy to oblige, and finish the watermelon piece in two bites. "Believe me now?"

She doesn't answer as I withdraw, but she does creep forward to grab the plate, placing the stick under her arm for safekeeping. The cautious retreat back toward the tree is done in silence, her gaze never leaving mine.

"You don't need to keep glaring at me, sweetheart. You've made it crystal clear you're pissed off."

She sits on the ground, her bare feet covered in dirt. "Pissed off doesn't come close, *pumpkin.*"

She grabs a slice of nectarine and cautiously inspects it, her focus returning to my face as she raises the food to her mouth.

I continue to place space between us while the fruit inches closer to those lips, the slow motion fucking with my mind, increasing my pulse. I never would've thought healthy eating could be this intriguing, but here I am, transfixed as she takes her first bite.

The slightest glimpse of bliss crosses her features in the roll of her eyes, the closing of her lids. I wait for a moan, for a needy groan of satisfaction. I can already hear it. Right there, on the tip of her tongue.

"Don't forget the water," I remind her.

Those luminous green eyes snap open. "Leave me alone."

"I wish I could." I glance to the ground, finding a relatively short expanse of grass, then sit my ass down. "Unfortunately, we're just getting started."

She doesn't respond with interest. Not even intrigue. I doubt she has any intent to listen to what I have to say, but she'll soon learn she has no choice. I can't let her go unless she believes my story. And she won't believe my story unless she's willing to listen.

"Nissa..." Where do I start? *How* do I start?

What she said last night was true. I've never interacted with a woman I couldn't walk over. Hunter's fiancée, Sarah, is the closest I've come to finding a female with balls, but she can still be tamed.

Everyone can be leashed.

Yet, this woman is different. So fucking different I struggle to predict what she'll do next. Or understand how I should manage her. She doesn't have clear indicators. At least not to me.

That's why I'm not going to bother beating around the metaphorical bush.

"The only insight I had into my father's escape came from his legal team," I start. "And I use the word 'insight' loosely."

"You're wasting your breath. I've gone beyond the point of being able to listen to you."

"I was told to keep myself busy in a public place before the court case."

130

She lets out a derisive huff. "And that didn't tip you off?"

"I made assumptions. But I didn't know."

"You knew enough to be held accountable for not informing the authorities." She pops a cherry into her mouth, her expression filled with superiority. "You may not have pulled the trigger that killed the guard, but you're guilty just the same."

I grind my teeth at her judgment.

I think this is the only time she gets to me. *Really* gets to me. When she looks down at my life, I see red. Until her, nobody has come close to making me feel inferior, and I want nothing more than to prove her wrong in whatever way possible.

She thinks she's better than me. That her way of thinking exceeds mine. That her form of justice is superior.

Like fuck.

She has no right to climb aboard her high horse.

"I said I didn't know the details. I never said I didn't want him free."

"And finally, the truth comes out," she drawls. "It's what I've known all along."

"You don't know shit." I force my mouth shut, clamping my teeth tight to stop another outburst.

For long moments, she taunts me with the raise of a haughty brow, popping one grape after another while I stew under her bigotry.

"I know you attack the lovely state of Oregon with your drugs."

And here we go with the illicit-substance debate. It's one of my favorites.

"The drug trade isn't an attack on anyone. It's an addiction not unlike caffeine or nicotine. The only difference is you consider it illegal."

"It *is* illegal. And heroine is nothing like coffee or cigarettes. Hard drugs kill people. They ruin families and create more violence and crime. You're literally poisoning the masses."

"And what about the poison you indulged in last night? You had no problem throwing back that Beluga. Alcohol also kills people, destroys families, and inspires violence. But because it's legal, you've got no problem with it. There's no logic to your rules."

Her nostrils flare. "There's a big difference."

"No, there's not." I've honestly never understood the distinction. "They both take away control from the user, act as a toxin against the body, and cause addiction."

She shakes her head, her jaw working overtime. "If you ever had to make the devastating discovery of a dead coke-head's frozen body on the streets, or had to watch a baby struggle through an addiction her mother gave her in the womb, your opinion wouldn't be the same."

She glares at me for a second, then lets out a bitter laugh. "What am I thinking? You're Cole Torian; you wouldn't give a shit about a homeless person, let alone a newborn. You've got no heart."

Maybe she's right.

Maybe I don't.

To me, the thought of the underprivileged valuing drugs above food, shelter, or health is fucking infuriating. They have no control. No sense. It's pathetic. And the mothers who shoot up while carrying a child should be sterilized.

But their actions have nothing to do with me. Never have.

"I provide a product. I don't force people to buy it. I can't be held responsible when a woman decides her next fix is more important than her fetus. And I certainly don't give a fuck when the homeless choose one more hit over a warm bed and a free meal from a shelter. It's their choice."

"There aren't enough shelters—"

"Don't fucking argue about things you know nothing about. I fund a local shelter, Ms. Fox. I get their reports and feedback. I know exactly how many people turn up in need of a bed and a warm meal, yet they arrive high as a fucking kite when they know it's against the rules. Then it's society's fault for not looking after them. They blame everyone but themselves. I don't create these fucking problems, Nissa. The users do."

"You taunt the weak. If your product wasn't available, they wouldn't succumb."

"You think the problem will disappear if I do?" I ask. Her comment is disappointing. Entirely naive and almost pitiful to

132

hear. "All that will achieve is a war between rivals wanting to claim the position my family has held for generations. That's when your precious crime rate would skyrocket. Drive-bys would be an hourly occurrence. The streets would be bathed in blood until someone claimed power. But the problem would never disappear. Drugs are a necessary evil, whether you like it or not."

I let the information sink in.

She may detest the way I do business, but my crimes keep the peace. That's why I have willing police in my pockets. That's why the authorities help me, despite my illegal actions.

"*I'm* a necessary evil, little fox. And if you take the time to think about it, without society's blinders, you'll realize I'm right."

She shakes her head and slumps back against the tree. "Not going to happen."

"Then you're not only narrow-minded, you're a fool."

"And you're not only delusional, you're narcissistic." She crosses her arms over her chest, plumping her breasts beneath the blouse. "I bet the next thing you'll do is try to convince me you've done nothing wrong by abducting me. You haven't broken any laws. You haven't violated my freedom or safety. You're entirely innocent and free from blame."

I divert my gaze to the setting sun between the trees, unwilling to let her any further under my skin. We'll soon be in darkness. Nothing but the black of night and a wealth of hatred. As if our current situation wasn't already a volatile concoction.

"Again," I murmur, "it was a necessary evil."

Silence descends.

She doesn't reply. There's no curiosity. No apparent impulse to learn more.

"I understand you're not willing to give me a chance because you're clouded by misconceptions and preconceived notions. You're caught up in the regulations of a naïve society."

"I'm not willing to give you a chance? Really?" Her words are barely above a whisper. "Do you hear yourself?"

I return my gaze to her face, the shadows of approaching night creeping over her features.

"I agreed to have coffee with you. I boarded a jet even though the dangers were blindingly clear." She eyes the water bottle at her feet, suspicion and need pulling at her features. "I went with you, despite everything you'd previously done to me. I've given you chance after chance—"

"You're not kidding anyone," I growl. "You didn't want to meet with me to give me a chance. You were only hoping for the opportunity to take me down."

She grins, the curve of her lips sinister. "And now I have it. Because of this, you're going to be locked up, right alongside your father, for a damn long time."

This loop of hatred is unending. Tiring. I guess I have a limit when it comes to bitchy bad-assery, and she's reached it. I'm also growing annoyed at her stubborn nature. She's preoccupied with thirst, her gaze continuously straying to the bottle mere inches from her feet. Yet she won't fucking take it.

"Just drink the water, for Christ's sake." I scrub a hand down my face in an attempt to wipe away the frustration.

"And wake up tomorrow in another foreign country with my arms shredded from rope burns?"

"Shredded?" My attention snaps to the wrists covered by her white blouse. "Show me."

"Go to hell." She scowls, disbelieving my concern even though the emotion nips at my heels.

She hadn't been bound for my pleasure. The binds were necessary. Vital. There hadn't been a choice.

"I didn't mean for you to get hurt." A nagging pulse starts under my sternum, the throb digging deep.

Physical torture isn't a part of this. Yes, there's been mental manipulation and psychological fuckery. But that doesn't mean hurting her was in the plan.

"Only sedated and abducted," she drawls.

I ignore the barb, determined to pull this conversation back on track. "If you can't trust the unbroken seal on the bottle, then we can finish this inside where you have access to running tap water. Or do you think I would've drugged our entire water supply just to play games?"

"I wouldn't put it past you." She reaches for the bottle and cracks the lid. "I guess I don't have anything left to lose. You've already violated me in every way imaginable."

Hardly.

I could've done far worse, especially if I had my father's proclivities. "In the end, I'm sure you'll appreciate what I'm trying to achieve, despite the way I had to go about it."

"No, I won't." She drinks, taking large gulps before swiping a hand over her mouth. Then she returns her attention to the fruit, taking small bites of watermelon.

She's not going to let up with the attitude.

After all the scheming and plotting, I'm beginning to think my plan won't work.

I've made a mistake. She won't listen.

"Better?" I ask.

She sighs. "Just say whatever you have to say, Cole. I'm growing tired of this."

Me, too.

Jesus Christ. Me fucking too.

"There's no point." I push to my feet. "You're not ready to hear me."

Maybe she never will be. Which puts us both in a difficult position.

"Look, I'm sorry things have turned out this way." I brush the dirt and leaves from my ass. "But for you to get home safely, we need to be able to work together. You have to forget the circumstances surrounding your arrival and concentrate on *why* this is necessary."

I pause, giving her the opportunity to continue the conversation. To reach out for a fucking olive branch. Instead, she remains quiet, glaring into the approaching night.

"Fine. I guess you've made your choice." I start for the edge of the tree canopy, each step a conscious reminder of how flawed my patience has become. "I'm going back to the house where there's plenty to eat and drink. If I were you, I wouldn't stay out here long. If the bugs don't get you, the wildlife will."

12

ANISSA

I don't say a word as he strides away.

I remain seated, stuck in sullen silence as the sunlight fades and darkness rapidly descends. The shadows grow taller, wider, as the gentle lap of the ocean becomes louder.

I'm entirely lost.

Physically and mentally.

I'm angry at myself. At Cole. And Luca. Not to mention that old fucking asshole on the boat.

But the aggression toward my captor is tainted with curiosity.

There was something different about him tonight. A change in demeanor I'm not familiar with.

He needs me for something. What? I'm not sure.

I clung too tight to my pride to ask. Or even listen.

I refused to surrender. I still don't want to budge an inch. Now, I'm stuck in ignorance.

It doesn't take long for the smell of a home-cooked meal to fill the air, brushing away the scent of salt and replacing it with enough herbs and spices to make my mouth salivate.

The fruit wasn't enough. It barely touched the sides of my hunger, and my throat remains dry with no more water to soothe the ache.

I'm growing cold. I'm dirty as hell. My feet throb. And I'm tired—the type of weary tiredness that starts in the bones and works its way out.

Yet, I can't will myself to get up and walk into that house with my tail between my legs. I don't want to go crawling back to him, even after his deluded attempt to make peace.

I'm always at war with him, regardless of the topic or the location. It's fight, fight, fight, and I'm not sure I know how to act any different.

Work together?

I scoff every time I contemplate the comedic partnership.

I can't work with him. I wouldn't even know how. Not when he's manipulated and fooled me enough times to eviscerate my self-respect.

The problem is, he brought me here for a reason. He wouldn't risk his freedom for a game. He couldn't. He acts invincible, but believing he can get away with the abduction of an FBI agent is insane.

He must need me for something.

And I'm certain I won't leave this island until he gets what he wants.

I close my eyes and rerun our conversation in my mind.

He was emotional. More prone to anger than his usual state of being calm and in control. He'd also seemed genuinely surprised and disturbed at the mention of my injuries.

I didn't mean for you to get hurt.

I can't believe his kindness at the moment. There's only speculation.

He tied me up. Drugged me. Took me from the US, without my consent or a passport.

But since waking in a foreign country, I guess I could agree he hasn't hurt me.

He didn't lock me in the bedroom. There weren't any restraints keeping me captive. He left me alone all day, not chasing me down or demanding anything from me. He gave me space, and later, food and water. He also arranged for my clothes to be brought here.

I can only conclude he wants my comfort.

I just wish I knew why.

The grass rustles in the breeze while I continue to speculate, the cool chill sinking into my arms. The temperature only drops with the passing hours.

At one point, I think I hear my name called in the distance. The temptation of a warm bed almost has me responding. But I remain in place, dozing against the trunk of the tree until the rustle of grass grows, the sound loud enough to bring me back to consciousness.

This time it's a contained noise. Not caused by the breeze. It's specific. To my right. Approaching.

"Cole?"

I sit up straight, the star-filled night subtly illuminating the darkness.

"Luca?"

My heartbeat increases, not quite loud enough to silence the *rustle, rustle, rustle*.

"I know you're there." I raise my voice and slowly inch to my feet, grabbing one of my sharpened sticks from the pile. "I can hear you."

There's no response. Not in words or in continued sound.

Everything falls quiet. There's only the lap of the ocean and my pounding pulse thundering in my ears.

"Is this another game? Am I meant to be scared?"

If so, he might be succeeding.

My imagination runs wild wondering what he's trying to achieve this time. Am I expected to run? Is this one of those games where rich fuckers pay to hunt people down?

A twig breaks to my left. A crunch of grass follows.

I twist toward the noise and scan the horizon for a silhouette.

Someone is out here.

I'm not alone.

"Cole?" I hold my stance, frozen, barely breathing. I stay there for long minutes, becoming one with the night. "I've got a weapon."

I cling tight to the stick, my palm growing slick with sweat. There's another rustle. A crunch. A snap.

Air congeals in my lungs, making it hard to breathe.

"I'm—"

Something slides over my foot. Heavy and smooth.

I scream, not even thinking before I break into a run and escape the circle of trees. Pain slices through my bare feet. I step on pebbles, rocks, prickles, and still I keep running. I stumble over unlevelled ground, tumbling to the grass, the stick stabbing the dirt with the heavy weight of my shoulder falling on top of it.

I cry out, the impact sending an explosion of pain to slice through my collarbone and down my arm.

"Jesus. *Fuck.*" I drop the stick and roll onto my back. I clutch at my shoulder, my fingers gliding over dry material, not blood, despite feeling like I've been shot.

There's another rustle, a snap, and I'm on my feet again, ignoring the injury to continue sprinting toward the house. My vision through the darkness vanishes as I focus on those bright lights, but I don't care.

I keep running toward the only refuge available.

Air pants from my lungs as I push myself faster, bumping into the hedge, before my sore shoulder collides with something solid and unyielding. I twirl with the impact. I probably perform a perfect pirouette before starting another rapid descent toward the ground, only to be stopped by strong hands gripping my arms to pull me upright.

"Cole?"

In this moment, I don't feel any anger. Or fear. Or resentment.

I've been running toward safety—toward *him*—and I can't deny the overwhelming rush of relief.

"No, not Cole."

Luca.

His deep voice brings an icy chill.

I yank my arms from his grasp, wincing at the throb in my shoulder, and stumble backward, my feet connecting with soothing tile.

"Calm down," he warns. "You're safe."

I continue retreating, not believing him. "Where's Cole?"

He steps toward me, his profile gaining more definition as my eyes adjust. He's wearing a thread-bare tank and boxers, exposing inch after inch of muscle, which seems like a threat to my safety. "Inside. Asleep."

It doesn't feel right that the man who abducted me now suddenly seems like my only solace. In fact, it feels downright pathetic, but there's no one else. *Nothing* else.

All I have to cling to is the brief glimpse of Cole's kindness and his solemn promise that he has no intention of hurting me.

"Are you okay?" Luca's voice softens. "I heard you scream."

My cheeks heat.

I'd thought I was under attack, when it's more likely I've scared the hell out of whatever creatures call this island home.

"Anissa?" His shadowed hand reaches out.

"Stop." Whatever he's trying to achieve—my trust, my comfort —he's not going to succeed.

"Okay." His arm falls to his side. "Are you ready to come into the house? There's leftover dinner in the fridge."

Through the heavy rush of adrenaline and the rapid heartbeat, my stomach still has the ability to grumble at the thought of food.

God, I'm starving.

"Come on." He turns, leading the way toward the house.

I don't want to follow. I shouldn't.

My head tells me to go back into the darkness and learn to live with the wildlife, while my aching limbs, tired bones, and hollow stomach encourage my feet to inch forward.

I can't stay strong without food. I need fresh water, otherwise my health will deteriorate quickly.

He walks through the open glass doors, the sheer curtain gently billowing around him as I tag a few feet behind.

I'm blinded by the lighting. Every lamp has been switched on. Every overhead glistening halogen beams down with a warm glow. Did they leave them on for me?

"What do you want to eat?" Luca starts toward the kitchen. "There's leftover tacos. Or fruit. Chocolate. Cake. You name it."

"No." My mouth would salivate over week-old bread at the moment. But sustenance needs to wait. "I want to see Cole first."

If he's asleep, he needs to wake to the sight of me. I have to see his instinctual emotion, the sleep-roughened truth, before he can hide it behind lies.

Luca nods and diverts his path, continuing toward the start of the hall I'd walked down earlier. I hustle to keep up, my feet beginning to protest, my shoulder incessant with its dull throb.

He flicks on another light, and this time I'm prepared. My sight rapidly adjusts and I can see the large length of space stretched out before me, the overbearing art lining the walls.

I'm led right to the very end, to a lone closed door.

"He's in here?" I stop a few feet away, still needing space.

"Yeah. Just knock to wake him."

I ignore the instruction and snatch at the handle, pushing the door wide.

Light invades the darkened room, highlighting a monstrous four-poster bed and an equally monstrous man snapping upright from beneath the covers. Shirtless.

I'm stunned.

Speechless.

A mass of chest, stomach, and arm muscles are on display. Thick muscles I never would've expected hidden beneath those expensive suits he always wears.

I knew his mind was lethal, but the strength laid out before me proves his body is, too. All this time I thought he liked to flaunt his strength when the reality now seems far different. He's hidden his capabilities. At least his physical ones.

I don't wait for him to invite me in.

I stalk forward, reaching the bottom corner of the bed before he's had time to blink away sleep. He's an entirely different man with his hair mussed and eyes squinted. I could be fooled into thinking he has vulnerabilities when I see him like this.

"Why am I here?" I grip the elegantly carved wooden pole holding up the canopy. "I need to know the point of all this?"

He quickly wins the battle to wake up, the docile expression transforming to a frown as his attention treks over my face. My blouse. My arms.

There's no anger or spite in his features. His animosity isn't evident. All that stares back at me is concern.

"What's going on?" he demands. "What happened?"

"Nothing—"

"I heard her scream," Luca interrupts from the door. "She came running toward the house in a panic. I tried to get her to eat, but she wanted to see you first."

I clench my teeth against the pathetic truth, and tell myself their opinion doesn't matter. They can believe what they like about me. I'll happily prove them wrong.

In fact, it's better if they start to think I'm weak.

"Thanks," Cole directs toward Luca, but his eyes never stray from mine. "Go to bed. I can handle this from here."

There's no reply. Not in words. The light pad of retreating footsteps are the only response, the sound quickly fading to leave us alone in silence.

"Go to the kitchen." He swings his legs to the side of the bed and grabs the covers, poised to fling them away. "I'll meet you there in a minute."

I don't move. I'm not willing to let him out of my sight. If he's going to grab a weapon, I want to know where he retrieves it from. I'm done with being clueless. "I'll wait."

"Suit yourself." He throws back the quilt and shoves to his feet, exposing an entirely naked ass.

"Holy shit." I avert my gaze as heat not only floods my cheeks, but my entire body. "You could've warned me."

"I did. Forgive me for being subtle."

There isn't a damn thing subtle about that sculpted body.

Not a damn thing.

Every inch of him is toned. Calves. Thighs. Hips.

He pulls on a pair of jeans, the thrust and tug of legs and arms visible in my periphery. "Let's get you some food." He strides for the door and treks his hands through his hair, regaining some of his air of perfection.

"I want answers first." I tag along after him. "Food can wait."

"You can have both at the same time."

He flicks off the hall light as we enter the main room, and stalks straight for the fridge. He pulls out container after container, placing them on the island counter, before returning to grab a jug of water and a bottle of juice. "Help yourself."

I lift the offerings, glancing inside the plastic tubs to inspect the contents while he grabs a plate and a glass from a nearby cupboard to sit them in front of me.

"Juice or water?" He places a hand on both jugs, waiting.

It still doesn't feel right to accept anything from him. Even a simple glass of OJ seems like a bribe, but I can't be stubborn a moment longer.

"Water."

He lifts the jug and begins to pour as if he's entirely at home. "You were outside a long time. I thought you would've succumbed earlier when you needed to make use of the facilities."

I glare. "I made do." I had to resort to squatting against a tree and using leaves instead of toilet paper.

He doesn't laugh, but I see the mirth in his eyes.

Asshole.

I reach for the closest container and prepare to open the taco mince, only to wince at the protest from my shoulder. It throbs with the movement, letting me know a wicked bruise will be waiting for me if I ever get the chance to look at myself in a mirror again.

"You're hurt." Cole dumps the jug on the counter and stalks around the island toward me. "What happened?"

"Nothing." I backtrack, staying out of reach until he stops.

"Anissa." I'm not sure if my name is a plea or a warning as he wipes a rough hand through his hair. He's the picture of exhausted frustration. "Tell me what happened. If you're hurt, I can arrange for a doctor to see you."

A doctor?

Hope distracts me from the pain.

I analyze his tone, his features, his...everything. Is the kindness a ploy? A tactic?

"I tripped and landed awkwardly. I strained or pulled a muscle in my shoulder."

"Show me," he demands.

"Like hell."

143

He might be eager to flaunt his nudity, but that shit isn't mutual.

"I'm not asking for a lap dance. I only want to take a look at your shoulder." Annoyance seeps into those ocean eyes, and I kiss goodbye to the thought of a doctor's visit.

"It's nothing." Nothing that will have me stripping in front of him, anyway. "Can you please just let me eat?"

His jaw tics, and he takes a few steps back to snatch the container from the counter. "I'll do it for you." He pops the lid and places the taco mince in the microwave, the spiced scent filling the air in seconds and sending my stomach into an unending loop of somersaults.

"I won't be able to eat all that," I admit.

"Eat what you can. I'm not concerned about waste."

He's not concerned about anything. Not wasted food, or the expense of a private jet, or abduction. Life is void of problems for him. And he's definitely not in a hurry to talk, seeing as though he remains quiet while he retrieves tortillas from a cupboard, then opens more containers filled with diced tomatoes and thinly sliced lettuce.

I climb onto a stool hidden beneath the counter, my need for answers temporarily diverted by the heavenly aroma of food.

When he slides the heated mince toward me, I try my best not to show how starving I am by making the slowest taco in living history.

I have no doubt he can see right through me, especially when my hand shakes as I spoon the tomato onto the tortilla. It's a foregone conclusion when I take my first bite and bliss explodes on my tongue, dragging a moan from the deepest depths of my gratitude.

It feels like I haven't eaten in weeks. Every mouthful is euphoric. And all the while, Cole watches me, his attention rarely leaving my face.

"I'm ready to listen." I take a sip of water to clear my throat. "I was frustrated earlier, but now I'm willing to hear what you have to say."

"Once you finish eating." His focus turns to my mouth. My lips.

It's daunting. Far more disconcerting than when he raises his voice or plays his conniving games.

I'm under his control, a slave to his whims, and with all that power he's going to sit there at whatever hellish hour this is, and watch me down a taco or two?

"Please, Cole." I'm not too proud to beg when his attention makes goose bumps erupt over my skin. He's unsettling me. Unnerving.

"Have one more," he demands.

I sigh and finish the first taco in two more bites, then quickly make a second. "You enjoy watching people eat?" I ask and take another mouthful.

He moves to lean back against the main kitchen counter with a shrug. "I enjoy watching *you* eat. It's comforting after being concerned about you all day."

I don't scoff, despite wanting to. I don't roll my eyes either.

I keep eating. Bite after bite until my plate is bare. "I'm done," I murmur. "Please start talking. I won't argue with you this time."

"You had every reason to argue with me, Nissa. I won't expect anything less now, and I shouldn't have expected anything less earlier."

"But you did?" I scrutinize him. "You expected me to react differently?"

"I thought you'd wake up ready to fight," he admits. "I anticipated things to be heated for a few hours. Maybe you'd throw a lamp or a few plates. But I didn't expect you to run. And I sure as shit didn't think you'd have a gun pointed at your head before dinner."

I stiffen, and my shoulder pinches in protest. "You saw that?"

His eyes narrow, as if sensing my pain. "I caught the final moments between you and the boat driver before he took off. Trust me, having him threaten you wasn't in my plan."

He's remorseful. At least, that's what he wants me to believe.

"So what *was* your plan?" I hold his gaze, relying on his expression to lead the way, not his words. I watch his breathing, how often he swallows. I take note of everything, because he's already fooled me so many times before.

All I see is discomfort.

Awkward frustration.

He sucks in a deep breath, expanding his chest then letting the air out on a sigh. "It's a long story. Are you sure you don't want to get some sleep first?"

"All I want is to go home. I'm willing to live without sleep and discuss whatever needs to be discussed until that can happen."

His chin tilts, raising the slightest inch. Without him knowing, he's made it crystal clear this conversation isn't going to be my ticket home.

"Just tell me." I slide from the stool and grab my dirty plate to round the counter. "Start from the very beginning if you have to."

"Like I told you before, I didn't know the details of my father's escape. I've had very little contact with him. But I'd been warned to keep myself busy. To remain in the public eye. Seeking you out to be my alibi was out of spite, not only for the way you spoke to me at my uncle's funeral, but because you fucked up so many of my plans by making the arrest."

He pauses, seeming to doubt whether I can handle what he's about to say next.

He shouldn't.

After everything he's put me through, words could barely faze me at this point.

"Keep going." I place the dripping plate on the sink and return to my stool, ignoring the close-up view of all the threatening muscles. "I'm listening."

"What you and your FBI buddies don't realize is that there's no place for my father's actions within my organization. I don't condone his behavior. In fact, me and my siblings are furious. We hadn't been aware of what he was doing—"

"You knew before the funeral." It's not a question, and not a statement either. "I refuse to believe you were oblivious."

"You're right." He inclines his head. "I'd been informed a few weeks prior. But there hadn't been enough time to decide what to do."

"You knew for weeks and didn't do anything?" It should've taken hours to act. Mere minutes. "Seconds is all I would've spared to pick up the phone and make a call to the authorities."

His jaw tics. "Let me make this clear, Anissa. I have no intention of letting my father get away with his crimes, especially when they tarnish my family name, but all the authorities have done is fuck this up. The FBI has made one mistake after another. Their growing level of incompetence is the reason I'm fucking thankful he's now free."

My chest expands in anger, my blood running hot. I fight against the need to defend myself and my colleagues. Not only that, I'm beyond skeptical at his claim to want justice against his father.

His family has never shown a glimpse of morality. And even if I could skirt reality for a moment and become a believer, it's equally ridiculous for Cole to think he has the right to take the law into his own hands.

"And you think you can do a better job than we have?" The faintest hint of incredulity taints my voice. "I'm sorry, Cole, I'm trying really hard to be patient, but what you're suggesting is delusional."

"You want to talk about delusions?" He slides from the stool and stands, gripping the counter in both hands. "How 'bout we start with the Feds who locked up a sex trafficker with no thought to the women he had imprisoned?"

"We imprisoned him *because* of those women. He can't hurt anyone when he's behind bars."

"Bullshit. You put them in more danger when you arrested him."

I snap upright. "How? They're free. They've been returned to their families."

He laughs. It's a bitter, resentful sound that unsettles me.

"The information you passed on to Greek authorities led to the freedom of six victims, right? *Six.*" He clucks his tongue. "Do you really think a man like my father had such a small grasp?"

No, I didn't.

We didn't.

The FBI knows there are more victims out there. It's only a matter of time before we find them. And even with their location unknown, it was better to arrest Luther while we searched for more evidence than to build a case while he continued to terrorize.

"Tell me what you know," I plead. "How did we put women in more danger?"

"You're smart." He meets my gaze, his eyes begging me to figure it out on my own. "What do you think criminals do when they discover the authorities are onto them?"

He leans back against the fridge, crossing his arms over his chest. "You say he couldn't hurt anyone while he was behind bars, but did you consider what the men working for him would do when they figured out you were closing in on the scheme? Or did you kid yourself into thinking he worked alone?"

My throat dries.

I see spite in his eyes. The torment of harsh truths.

It sinks into me, tainting all chance of hope.

"Come on, Nissa. Take a guess at what a lowlife criminal would do with the evidence."

"I don't know." I don't want to give oxygen to the possibilities. Not when my mind has fixated on the worst possible outcome.

"But you could anticipate a reaction, right? You would've thought about what his men would've done."

I don't answer.

With any arrest, there are possible repercussions. Sometimes it's inevitable. We have to weigh the odds and hope for the best.

"What do you think happens to sex slaves when the men imprisoning them think the Feds are closing in?" He pushes from the counter and stalks forward to rest his elbows on the island counter, getting closer to eye level. "What does any criminal do with evidence when they think they're about to get caught?"

I shake my head, not letting him push my buttons. "Stop it."

I refuse to play along to yet another game.

"That's right, little fox." His lips curve into a feral smile. "Finally, the truth is starting to wiggle its way through your naive concept of justice." He mutters the words, his anger simmering below the surface. "If my father's men had a location which they thought caused suspicion, it would've been burned to the ground. They would've killed those they couldn't hide. Somewhere out there is a mass grave full of tortured women, and it's the FBI's fault."

"No." I keep shaking my head. "If a mass of imprisoned women were murdered, we would've heard about it."

"Are you trying to tell me the Greek police have been eagerly gushing to help you? If I took a guess, I'd say they've fought against your investigation every step of the way, letting you know it's their jurisdiction, not yours. Thus the basis of them only finding six victims—the bare minimum to get you assholes off their back."

I'm loath to admit the truth. Not because being wrong is an issue, but because him being right means women have died.

He gives a sad smile, as if understanding my suffering. "The police were never going to rat on one of their biggest sources of income. Your interference only helped to line their pockets with more money."

My stomach twists in knots, the tacos preparing to make a comeback. "Do you have proof?" My voice is weak. Fractured. "Is there evidence women were murdered?"

"I don't need evidence to know they would've been disposed of. Just like I didn't need evidence to know my father would escape. It's logical. It's human nature in my world."

I'm beginning to believe his continued references to this alternate society are necessary. Maybe he does live in a reality completely different to mine. One where people can talk about murder and rape without any emotional attachment.

"That's not human nature," I whisper. "It's psychotic."

"Yes, it is."

"Are all the people in your world psychopaths?" It's a legitimate question, not an attempt at humor.

Regardless, he laughs. "I think that depends on your definition. It's clear you've judged me to fit the—"

"I didn't say that." I may have thought it more times than I can remember, but I've never truly wanted to believe this man was devoid of emotion.

And I can't now, not when my life is in his hands.

"You didn't need to." He sobers, turning his focus away to stare toward the living room. "You're very good at showing your criticism with a single look."

"Your name has been mentioned with suspicion around the deaths of many men. You're not innocent in all of this. Drug dealers. Businessmen. Police officers. Even government officials."

"Men," he snarls. "*Guilty* men. Those who have stolen from me. Or tried to stab me in the back. Not innocent fucking women, Nissa." He spits the nickname as if it's poison. "What about my commitment to my sisters? What about my devotion to protecting them? And my niece..." He winces. "A fucking niece who I would give my life for. How can I be psychotic when my family are my life?"

"Your father shares the same family. Those sisters are his daughters. Your niece is his only grandchild. I'm sure he'd lay down his life to protect them, too; it doesn't make him any less of a monster."

His lip curls and I'm caught on the edge of anticipation, waiting for him to defend himself.

I want him to.

Each time he exposes me to a remorseful side, I relax a little. I don't fear for my safety as much.

I need more of that reassurance.

God, how I need it.

"You don't have a response?" I ask. "Aren't you going to tell me I'm wrong?"

"You're so fucking wrong," he snarls. "But I'm sick of defending my reputation. It's pointless and entirely unnecessary when I didn't bring you here to gain your respect."

"Then why am I here? Why did you risk life behind bars?"

His nostrils flare. "Because you're going to be my proof of following through on a promise."

The skin at my nape prickles. I'm not sure what he means, but I'm certain it's not something I want to be a part of. "Am I meant to guess or are you going to clarify?"

"I made a vow to deal with my father—to punish him for what

he's done. And you're going to assure those I've promised that I handled the situation accordingly."

There's so much anger in his tone. A ton of vehemence. A wealth of hate.

I swallow over the retreat of moisture in my throat.

Determination stares back at me with eyes so deep and blue.

I don't want to ask. I don't think I want to know.

"Nissa, I brought you here so you could see me shutting down my father's operation." He looks away and sucks in a deep breath, letting it out on a frustrated exhale. "I brought you here to witness his murder."

13

TORIAN

She doesn't react.

There's no disbelief, or humor, and yet again, not a glimpse of fear.

The only change comes with the slight decrease in color to her face. Her sun-ravaged skin grows pale, her ruby lips a million times darker in contrast as she swallows.

"You don't need to respond. All I want is for you to remain open to the conversation."

"Open," she repeats on a faint murmur.

She's overwhelmed with shock, or disbelief, her green eyes glazing in confusion.

I push from the counter, needing distance. "I brought you here, despite our differences, because this will give us what we both want. I will have a reliable witness. And in return, you get the justice you crave."

She shakes her head, her brows pinched. "Your justice. Not mine. This goes against everything I believe in. And even if I thought you were telling the truth, which I don't, I wouldn't be able to support your plan. This is fucking ridiculous."

"I don't need your support. Or your interaction. I only need your presence."

She lowers her gaze, her head still repeating the back and forth motion. "This is a game. It's not real."

"It's not a game—"

"You've said that before." Her head snaps up, her eyes fierce with spite. "You've told me no more games. No more lies. No more bullshit. But it never fucking stops."

"I fucked up," I admit. "I succumbed to the need to retaliate one too many times. Taunting you became my only stability after my father's arrest. So tell me what I need to do to earn your trust."

"Trust? Are you kidding?" She straightens, showing conviction. "It makes no sense."

"It makes perfect sense. I need to prove my father is dead. And you—"

"Bullshit, Cole. I'm not here to be a witness. I don't believe it for a second. You could get Luca to do that. Hell, you could get the asshole from the boat. Or a local. Anyone can be your damn witness. Or you could take a fucking photo, for Christ's sake. Or a souvenir." She lets out a maniacal bark of a laugh. "Why not chop off your dad's ear as proof?"

"I won't allow evidence to leave the crime scene." I mutter the words, slow and lethargic, trying to counter the fast pace of her rambling. "Not even a photo. The information will be shared without the horrors of body pieces or traumatic photos as proof."

"How kind of you." She shakes her head, over and over, her eyes narrowed on me. "I still don't believe this isn't some kind of trick."

I sigh, my fury and frustration mingling. "Nissa, the information can't come from one of my men. Their word means nothing when everyone already knows they would say or do anything for me. The same goes for those who could be paid off or intimidated. But an FBI agent with integrity, unwavering morals, and no fear of me? Now that's the perfect candidate to tell the truth, don't you think?"

"An FBI agent who would have no choice but to arrest you if you went ahead with this."

Her response is disappointing. I feel the hit to my chest like a physical blow.

I'd hoped she would see this as a victory. Not another opportunity to be antagonistic. "You can't. We're in Greece. You have no authority here."

"I'm well aware, but I could make a citizen's arrest until police arrive."

"The same police who've worked with my father for years?" I raise a brow. "That will either get you killed or sent to work in the same sex slums that have lined their pockets for years. Either way, you'll disappear and never set foot in the States again. They're the enemy here. Not me."

"You're both the enemy." She scoffs. "This is crazy."

"Maybe. But it's necessary. I didn't want to go down this path, but there's no other option."

"This isn't an option at all, Cole. And to be honest, if it's true, it sounds like a show of utter weakness. Who are you doing this for? What associate has enough power over you to convince you to kill your own father?"

I flinch. I can't help it. The comment on my weakness hits a target she didn't know existed. "You don't need to concern yourself with my reasons."

She holds my stare, the groove of her brow digging deeper. She's starting to believe me. Understanding dawns in her features, the anger turning to concern.

"You're serious," she murmurs. "You actually want me to witness your father's murder."

I leave her in silence, letting her come to terms with the truth.

"This is crazy." She shakes her head. "It still makes no sense when there's the much better alternative to get him back behind bars. If you work with the authorities—"

"Don't even start." I clench a fist at my side. "Have you listened to a word I've said?"

"I've listened to every insane word that's come out of your mouth. I've listened even though I'm here as your prisoner. But that isn't going to stop me from telling you this is wrong. And what you expect from me is completely delusional. I won't help you. I won't confirm anything. I can't."

I smirk, the expression so fucking tight, because looking at her in animosity is far better than exposing my fear of failure. "It isn't wrong. You're the one who's misguided. The authorities are

154

worthless. There won't be any justice at all, unless I'm the one who claims it."

She stares, almost glares, her self-assurance growing with my conviction.

We remain in the battle for visual supremacy for long moments, those big eyes focused on mine, her ruby lips pursed.

She'll crack.

She has to, because I won't.

"Okay. Fine." She throws up her hands. "Let's talk this through. Hypothetically."

I incline my head. "Hypothetically."

Her eyes roll as she huffs. "Your plan is to kill your father while I watch. Then I can spread the good word about your deeds like you're the Wizard of fucking Oz. But what happens to those women? You said the FBI endangered those left behind by arresting Luther. What will happen to them once he's dead?"

"His death will inspire chaos. The men left behind will fight for power. They'll slaughter one another in their attempt to climb to the top. Local residents will be affected. Then the media will get involved, and police will be forced to act, in return freeing those women."

"You're working on assumptions and speculation?" she accuses.

"If things don't fall apart naturally, I'll call in reinforcements to shut it down. I'm not going to let this continue. Not under my name."

She stares at me. Stares right through me. "This is insanity."

"No. It's the only fucking option. And nobody but a trusted few need to know. Once you relay the truth of what I've done to those necessary, you can pretend you were never here."

Her eyes snap back to reality. "You think I'm capable of hiding this? For you?"

"Not for me, Nissa. For those women. For justice against my father. The consequences for being a snitch aren't worth trying to take me down for a good deed."

Her eyes flair with the threat. Air leaves her lungs on a heave and she looks away, her anger seeming to bubble.

"You'll never get him back behind bars." I lower my voice, trying to provide a calming buffer to the tumultuous battle in her eyes. "He's already fled the US. And even if you have some incredible stroke of luck and convince someone here to arrest him, he's never going to talk. He won't tell you where the rest of the women are. But he'll open up to me. He'll spill his secrets."

Her gaze snaps to mine. Speculative. Hopeful. "You'll get that information?"

"I can."

The muscles in her jaw tense. "Don't try to trick me with a strategic word choice. Tell me. Right now. If I do this for you, will you get that information for me?"

My pulse kicks with her determination. Despite her being a pain in my ass, her dedication is inspiring. "Yes."

Her chin hitches.

She's hooked, even though she doesn't want to be.

"Then you'll slaughter him?" Her tone holds a new level of criticism, the dose thick and brutal. "Your own father. In cold blood."

Fuck her. Seriously, fuck her misguided naivety.

Nobody can judge me for my plans more than I've already judged myself.

At one point, Luther Torian was all I had.

He kept my mind active after my mother's death. He taught me to be strong for the sisters who buckled under the weight of their emotions. He showed me how to clasp revenge in both fists with patience and efficiency.

He was my mentor.

Now, he's my adversary.

"This isn't a bad deed, Anissa. I'm not planning a terrorist attack or instigating nuclear war. All I'm doing is taking down a criminal. A rapist. A murderer. The same man who escaped your custody and claimed more victims while under your watch."

It isn't a hard concept to grasp. To me, it's common fucking sense. The more I have to convince her, the stronger I am in my own convictions.

"I have to think." She frowns, the battle for understanding reclaiming her features. "I need time."

"We don't have any. My father would already have heard about my arrival." I start toward her. "He'll wait a day, maybe two, to make sure I wasn't followed, then he's going to come out here. You need to be onboard with the plan before he shows up."

"You should've thought about that before you deceived me a thousand times." She walks around the island counter, placing more distance between us. "I need time. Otherwise, I'll give you a flat refusal now and deal with the consequences."

"You don't want that." It's a slight threat. The barest nudge toward a better resolution. "You can't tell me you'd prefer my father to walk away unscathed instead of receiving the lethal punishment he deserves. You know what he's done. There's no—"

"Don't guilt me into making this decision. You're threatening my career. You're trying to destroy my morals. I can't simply sit back and watch you break the law."

"But you're happy to sit back and let those women continue to suffer? That's some fucked up logic, Nissa."

"Go to hell." She hits me with a scathing glare. "You know they're more important to me than anything else." She swings around and stalks for the hall. "But I said I need time, and that's what I'm going to get."

Christ, she's stubborn.

So fucking stubborn.

"He's going to turn up unannounced. You need to be prepared."

"No." Her stride doesn't falter as she speaks over her shoulder. "What I need is clarity, because at the moment, my head is filled with static. Either leave me alone until I can think straight or take no as my answer."

My limbs grow tense. Every nerve and muscle pulls tight. "I can give you a few hours."

"You'll give me as long as I need." She turns to face down the hall, and disappears from site.

I listen to her fading footsteps, then hear a door open and close, shutting me out entirely.

Nobody has ever dared to disrespect me the way this woman

157

does. Male. Female. Fed or criminal. She's fucking delusional with her self-assurance, and I can't help respecting her for it.

I fucking hate it, but I still respect it.

No more negotiation will happen tonight. No matter how necessary it is to my success.

"Fuck." I pace the kitchen, running my hands through my hair. "*Fuck.*"

I swipe at the counter, sending containers flying, the destruction smashing to the floor. Glass scatters. Food splatters. A huge fucking mess is laid bare at my feet, and it's more psychological than physical.

I can't let her get to me.

Anger is a weakness. A deficiency. I'm above the emotion, yet Anissa siphons it from me without effort.

She fucks with my head. Messes with my decisions. She shouldn't even be here. Dragging her along was an act of irrationality—of fucking instability. If I thought she wouldn't have me in cuffs at the next available opportunity, maybe I'd admit defeat and send her home... Maybe.

Then again, her defiance is like a drug.

I can't stop craving another hit despite the dangers.

I grip the counter, my hands clenched against the marble until my breathing slows and my pulse settles. There's power in action, not reaction.

I need to get back to basics.

Think. Strategize. Plan.

"I gather your chat didn't go well."

I cringe at the sound of Luca's voice and keep my hands clasped against the counter. I don't have the patience to speak to anyone right now. There's no calm to be found.

His footsteps approach. "Get some sleep. She'll be less scared in the morning."

"She doesn't get scared," I seethe. Or weak. Or vulnerable. Or any other emotion you'd fucking expect from a woman abducted from her own country.

"Then she'll be less of a bitch." He passes behind me, moving toward the destruction on the floor. "Go get some sleep. I'll clean up the mess."

He lowers to his haunches and reaches for a shard of glass, then another, stacking them in his palm.

"Get going." He doesn't bother to look at me as he speaks. "You need the rest more than I do."

My blood boils with his placating attitude. The coddling. Who the fuck does he think he is?

No, it's me. I'm running off the rails.

I dig my fingertips harder against the marble and clench my teeth.

She's eating away at my temper to the point where my patience is non-existent.

I wouldn't have thought I'd need more space when I'm secluded in the middle of nowhere, but even a remote island feels suffocating with the cloying churn of my mind.

I shove from the counter and stalk for the hall. I don't slow until I reach her door, then I listen for a moment, hearing the grate of a zipper and the pad of soft footfalls.

She's not throwing furniture or screaming in anger. Her control is better than mine, which only makes my blood burn hotter as I stalk away.

I don't stop myself from slamming my bedroom door before I punish myself with a long, cold shower.

Sleep isn't an option. There's no use when I'm wound up. Instead, I grab my Mac and slide into bed, logging into the surveillance app to pull the feed from her room into view.

There're two angles, one from the front-left corner, another from the back right. I can see every square inch of space, and she's not in any of it.

The instinct to panic is overwhelming and entirely unjustified.

She can't escape.

All the windows are alarmed. There's no boat. I worked hard to lock away any sharp objects. All the knives and razors, along with the cleaning products, are stored in a safe place.

If she's going to attempt to kill me, she'll need to do it with a lamp, or a fucking bedside table.

I continue to remind myself of the precautions, but my apprehension doesn't ease. My pulse rate only increases, pounding through my temples.

I'm seconds from sliding out of bed to go in search of her when the adjoining bathroom door opens on the screen before me, and she walks into view, tousling her wet hair with a towel, while another is wrapped around her body.

All my panic stops.

Everything does.

My thoughts. My pulse. My breath.

Her skin shines with moisture. Her cheeks are flushed. She looks different. Unguarded. Fucking tempting.

She crouches before the duffel on the floor, dropping the towel from her hair beside her before she shifts through clothes to pull out underwear, then a gray shirt and shorts. Pajamas. But she does it all with her left hand, while the right arm remains tucked against her chest.

That sore shoulder of hers is more than a pulled muscle.

She's hurt, and I don't appreciate not knowing the extent of her injuries.

I squint, trying to get a better view of the skin around her right collarbone. The pixilation doesn't give a pristine image; it's slightly blurred up close, and yet I can still see the darker tinge to the flesh on her shoulder.

"Pulled muscle, my ass."

She stands, throwing the clothes to the bed, then reclaiming the underwear.

I know what comes next, and I don't bother to look away. I don't spare a thought for her privacy as she drops the second towel, exposing a flawless body. Smooth legs. Flat stomach. Pert, delectable tits with dark, beaded nipples.

She leans over and toes her feet into the white, silken panties, shimmying them all the way up those toned thighs to cover the trim patch of hair at her mound.

Next she grabs the gray shirt, pulling the material over her head. Then the short shorts that she yanks on to settle over her hips.

Either she hasn't discovered the pinhole cameras hidden within her room, or this unrestricted show is deliberate. A taunt. Does she expect me to be the pervert who watches her undress? Does she assume I'm a deviant like my father?

Fuck her.

My surveillance is entirely cautionary.

I need to be aware of her location at all times. I have to keep a close eye on her.

It's fucking necessary.

It's... "*Fuck.*"

I slam the Mac closed and shove it to the far side of the mattress as I slink farther down the bed.

My father is the pervert. The deviant. Not me.

So why the hell am I walking in his footsteps with fucking brilliant precision?

I understand him in this moment. I get his perversions because even now, with the threat of becoming him a heavy weight over my conscience, I still have to fight not to take another look.

I'm being driven by weakness. Haunted by temptation. I've become what I despise and it's all her fault.

Anissa has me coiled tight. She drives my thoughts out of control. She makes me question everything.

I'm beginning to wonder if she's been a part of my game, or if I've been participating in hers. Is she winning this round? Has she claimed control?

Decker warned me about this. He told me she was a snake. A viper. A fucking bitch.

She's sneaky. Manipulative. Smart.

But not smarter than me. Or stronger.

I haven't lost this battle.

Not yet.

I don't hear from her for the rest of the night. There's only the faint fall of Luca's footsteps down the hall, then nothing until I wake mid-morning from a broken sleep and find her door still closed.

I force myself not to pause and listen. Instead, I make a beeline for coffee and find the kitchen spotless.

Luca cleaned the glass from the floor and the splatter from the cupboards. It's as if I never lost my temper, despite the memory of the weakness nagging at me.

I sit outside for hours, reclined on a pool lounger while I get to work replying to e-mails from my legitimate businesses. It's close to lunch when my cell rings and Hunter's name stares back at me from across the screen.

"What is it?" I ask in greeting.

"Rumor has it you went on a date with our least-favorite FBI agent the other night."

"And?" The animosity that faded overnight begins to rear its ugly head. I don't fucking get it. One mention of Anissa and I'm ready to break skulls.

"I want to know if I should be shutting down the claims or letting them fly. I don't give a shit where you shove your dick; all I need to know is if you want the crazy news public."

"I'm not shoving my dick anywhere." My nostrils flare with renewed aggression. I shouldn't need to justify myself. "If anyone dares to comment, let them know I'm working her over. I'm bringing her to our team."

"That's a tough feat if we're talking about the same woman Decker has been bitching about."

"Are there any other opinions you'd like to share before I hang up?"

"Well, seeing as though you asked," he growls, "I'd appreciate being told where the fuck you are. You don't usually disappear without letting me know the details."

He doesn't need the information, and I shouldn't bother telling him. But my mouth opens, and the taunting admission grates between my teeth. "Greece."

Silence follows my answer, the tense void building with the passing seconds.

"Torian—"

"Don't start," I warn. "I don't want to hear it."

"Too bad," he snarls. "Why the fuck aren't I there with you? You need me."

I let out a scoff. "I've learned that your presence isn't as fundamental as I once thought."

"Fuck you." Anger drips from his tone. "Are you seriously going to do this without me? Is that chump Luca there instead?"

"Focus on recruitment," I demand. "You've got more important work to do in Portland."

"Fuck—"

I disconnect the call, the provocation not filling me with the enjoyment I'd anticipated. There's only building frustration.

Hunter knows exactly why I'm here. My inner circle has been waiting for me to make this move for a while now. He'll also be aware it's a better plan to attack my father in Greece. I'll make dad disappear in private. Only my faithful few have to know.

I place the cell back in my jeans pocket and navigate my Mac to the surveillance feed from Anissa's room.

She's awake, seated on the floor, her back against the wall, her head in her hands. She isn't crying. Her shoulders don't shake. But her turmoil is clear. She still hasn't come to terms with her situation. Who knows if she ever will.

I let the sight of her sink into me, becoming more mesmerized with each passing minute.

I note everything. The messy light wave to her short hair. The loose-fitting red top that covers her shoulder injury from view.

She's wearing tight, black pants, cut off below the knee. Those active-wear type things that make me think she plans on exercising.

Running.

From me.

The thought creates a dull throb behind my sternum. I don't know whether it's inspired by pleasure or disappointment. Fighting with her is such a contradiction. I enjoy every minute, and hate it all the same. I want her anger, yet there's frustration and fucking guilt there, too.

We're not so different.

We both cling to strong values. We're governed by strict rules. We would fight to the death for what we hold dear.

We just happen to believe in completely opposing views.

"Boss." Luca walks from the open doorway looking like shit in nothing but navy shorts. "I gather you spoke to Hunt."

"About ten minutes ago. Why?"

"He called." He wipes a hand down his sleep-roughened face, then scratches his fingers across stubble almost growing into a beard. "He isn't too happy about me being here."

"He needs to get used to taking on a different role." I focus back on the computer and find Anissa's head resting against the wall, her emotionless face on display as she stares blankly across the room.

Luca slumps onto the lounger beside me. "That's pretty much what I said."

I frown, not taking my gaze off my captive as I try to read what's going on in that mind of hers. "You told him that?"

"I told him to fuck off." He shrugs. "It's pretty much the same thing. Have you spoken to your FBI agent this morning?"

My FBI agent.

The question is a trigger.

Everything is a fucking trigger.

"No," I grate. "She hasn't been out of her room."

"Does she know why she's here?" He stretches out along the lounger, his hands behind his head.

I slowly close the Mac screen, biding my time to ease into a conversation I don't want to participate in. "She knows enough. The finer details aren't her concern."

"Are you sure? She seems the type to want transparency. Especially when she sees you as nothing more than a criminal."

"I *am* a criminal."

"Yeah, you are, but she might attempt to trust you if she's given more details than a vague reference to her being a witness."

He listened to my conversation with her last night?

I'm not surprised. I expect him to have his finger on the pulse while we're here. It's his job. I just don't appreciate knowing he's been a fly on the wall when I'm alone with her. "You could hear us from your room?"

"Bits and pieces. I lipread some."

"You've been on the surveillance feed." It's not a question, only a necessary purge of information that smashes to the forefront of my mind.

"I set my phone to receive movement notifications. Every time she rolled in her sleep, I made sure to check she wasn't making her way into the hall to cause trouble."

"And what about before that? When she was awake?" I stare at him, my heartbeat throbbing down my neck, pounding in my ears. "And this morning? Were you watching then, too?"

Did he watch her get dressed? Has he seen her naked?

Jesus fuck.

I want to hurt him.

With or without his answer, I itch to punch my knuckles through his face.

"By the time I finished in the kitchen last night, she was in bed with the light off." He holds my gaze, his expression locked tight, as if sensing my desire to commit murder. "The same goes for this morning. She was asleep the whole time I checked on her. And once I got the notification you were moving around the house, I crashed, figuring you could keep watch on your own."

His answer eases the rage seeping through my marrow. Slightly.

Is this jealousy?

Am I fucking jealous over the enemy?

"What's going on with you?" His brows pull tight as he slides his arms down to his sides. "Is she getting in your head?"

Getting? No. She's already burrowed all the way in, grinding against every nerve.

But I'm sick of his questions. I'm fucking tired of people thinking I need to justify my actions.

"Stay off the feed." I keep my voice neutral. Level. Calm as fucking Larry. "Leave me in charge of it."

"That's no problem at all." He doesn't stop with the scrutiny. "But are you okay? This is some pretty heavy shit you have to deal—"

"Fuck off with the pep talk. I don't need it."

Movement nudges my peripheral vision, and I tilt my gaze to

see Anissa standing in the open doorway leading outside, her stare pinning me in place.

Dark hair frames her cheeks, and the sunburned skin she earned yesterday has turned to a healthy tan, making those green eyes all the more luminous.

I don't speak.

I don't move.

I don't do anything capable of making her feel like I'm flaunting my control over her, despite wanting to do exactly that.

She steps onto the tile, still favoring one arm, which she holds closer to her side than the other as she walks forward.

"How did you drug me?" She stops at the end of the lounger to look down her nose at me.

Her question is multifaceted. I can see it in her eyes.

She wants to know if I'm capable of the truth. If I can be honest and refrain from messing with her head.

"I watched you," she murmurs. "You didn't put anything in my glass. I made sure of it. So was it something I touched or inhaled? You said you didn't know I drank vodka."

"I didn't know." I place the Mac on the ground and swivel my legs off the lounger, needing to tilt my head to meet her gaze. "Like I already told you, I guessed. That's why I had all the bottles on the plane spiked. Except mine. I took a chance that you wouldn't want to share my scotch."

"And if I did?"

"I would've found another way." I let a slow grin curve my lips. "Maybe I would've convinced you to come here without needing medicinal assistance."

"And you would've crashed and burned. There's no way I would've come here willingly." She crosses her arms over her chest, attempting to shut me out.

I claim her need to ward me away as a small victory. A glimpse to her unease.

"I was joking." I push to my feet. "The drugs were my only preparation."

"Premeditation," she clarifies.

166

"Tomato, tamato. I prefer to steer clear of terms used in a court—"

"What about the women?" She raises her voice, cutting me off. "The abduction victims back in Portland. Did you lie about them, too? Were you responsible for their disappearance?"

I sigh, yet again disappointed at her stubborn need to continuously burn me at the stake. The hours apart have only given her more ammunition.

"No, Nissa. I wasn't responsible. An ex-con from Seattle had those women. Like I said, he was trying to impress my father in an attempt to be brought into the fold."

"*Had* the women?" She latches onto the word, her eyes narrowing. "Where are they now?"

"Nothing gets by you, does it?"

"Answer the question," she demands.

I snicker, only because it will piss her off even more.

Does it help with our situation? No.

Will it delay the necessary resolution? Yes.

But can I help it?

I'm not even going to pretend I have any control over my mouth when she's around. I don't know how to quit taunting her.

"You want us to work together." She throws the words at me like an accusation. "You say I can't go home unless I help you. Well, you need to help me first. Help me fucking understand."

I glare, her fiery temperament invigorating me more than I'd like to admit.

"They're safe," I mutter. "I'd already made arrangements to secure their release before we left Portland."

She stands a little taller, her breasts plumped above the shelf of her arms. "Prove it."

Impatience becomes a living, breathing force inside my veins. I want to deny her. To shove my authority down her throat. But that won't work in my favor.

"I'm going to leave you two alone." Luca pushes to his feet. "I'll be inside."

"No." She raises her voice. "Stay."

His gaze flicks to me, requesting a response.

"It's okay." I shrug, faking a level of calm I'm far from feeling. "If she wants you here, you stay."

I pull my cell from the back pocket of my jeans and scroll through my contacts to find Hunter's number. I connect the call and place the sound on loud speaker. "I'm not sure if he's going to be in the mood to talk."

The call doesn't last one full ring before Hunter is growling down the line. "Did your bitch boy rat on me?"

"He may have mentioned you reaching out," I drawl.

"Well, if you're going to ride me for telling him what he needs to hear, I guess it's my turn to hang up."

"Quit the theatrics. I need you to tell me what went down last night with Sayker."

There's a pause. A silent heartbeat.

"Just the CliffsNotes." I lock eyes with Anissa and raise my brows to ask if the short version is enough.

She swallows. Nods.

"Was there something wrong with my first recount?" Hunt asks.

"No. I was distracted and can't remember everything. Just repeat what happened."

"We found the women in a house in Centennial. They were hidden in the basement. Bound, gagged, and scared as fuck. Their captor was dealt with. The women were freed. End of story. Unless you want me to give you the blow-by-blow of my lovely lady and her newfound skills with a paring knife."

"Save your lady stories for another time. You've told me all I need to know." I disconnect the call and return the device to my pocket. "Is the information to your approval?"

She glances between me and Luca, back and forth, over and over before shaking her head. "It's only words. There's no proof."

"It's on the news." Luca pulls a cell from his shorts pocket, then types and scrolls over the screen. "Here, I'll show you."

I bristle when he hands her the device. As far as I'm concerned, that phone could lead to her escape. He shouldn't be willingly handing it over. Or I'm just pissed he thought of it first. That he's the one convincing her when I failed.

She focuses on the screen, swiping down every few seconds. "It says the perpetrator hasn't been found."

"He has. By us." I cross my arms over my chest. "We dealt with him our way."

"Your way?" She looks up at me through thick lashes. "You mean he's dead."

I don't answer. If she wants to continuously judge me as ruthless, so be it. It's not an unworthy title. It just happens to be incorrect this time.

"No. He's not dead." Luca holds out a hand to reclaim the device. "But he won't think about hurting women again."

She returns to the visual tennis match, glancing between us, her gaze searching for more answers.

"He's not dead," I repeat. "Be satisfied with the information. It's better for everyone involved if you don't know more."

She deflates, her shoulders and chest falling in defeat before she walks back into the house without a backward glance.

Luca watches her leave, his focus remaining on the door after she disappears behind the sheer curtains. For a man who doesn't give a shit about anything but work, he sure likes to pay her attention.

"You need to give her more information," he murmurs. "She doesn't believe one word you tell her." He turns to me, his face stern. "Whatever this tactic is, it's not working, and we're running out of time. If Luther turns up and she's not—"

"Back the fuck off," I warn. "I didn't bring you here as a strategist. Or a fucking therapist. Now move." He blocks my way from between the two loungers.

"Okay, but—"

"Don't fucking *but* me." I take a menacing step forward and get in his face. "Lay off or find yourself on the next flight out of here."

He straightens, not listening to the threat. "You're spiraling out of control. I don't know what the fuck is going on with you and her, but this isn't you."

A rush of blood floods my head, the surge of rage intense and entirely overwhelming.

I shove him, making him back up a step. The guy is bigger than me. Broader. An inch taller. More muscles.

I don't give a fuck.

I push again, and this time he begins to move a second before my hands connect with his chest, preempting the strike.

"I don't know why you're looking for a fight," he continues to back up, moving out of the way. "But you're not going to find it with me."

I snicker. "You're scared?"

"Torian, I'm a fucking SEAL. You don't stand a chance."

"You *were* a fucking SEAL. You were dishonorably discharged, asshole."

His mouth snaps shut. His jaw clenches.

The show of barely restrained anger acts like adrenaline in my veins. It eases the unrelenting pressure. It gets her out of my brain for the briefest seconds, providing a slight reprieve.

"I respect you," he seethes. "And I've vowed to work by your side, not under your fists."

I continue stalking forward, praying for him to take the first swing. I'm not a fighter. Never have been. Not physically. But for once, I need the distraction. I want the pain and brutality. "You're a fucking pussy."

"No." He stops dead, his eyes narrowed. "I've got self-fucking-control, and usually you do, too. Hit the weights room instead."

I shove him again. Hard.

I need an outlet. I have to find a way to get Anissa out of my system.

"Hit the fucking weights room, Torian." He puffs out his chest, waiting for another shove. "Do you want to be like this when your father shows? Is that what you're looking for? An excuse to fuck this up?"

Everything stops. My thoughts. My pulse.

The chase for numbing adrenaline becomes a brutal war.

It wouldn't be the first time I'd made a mistake when it came to my father.

It's my fault he was arrested at the funeral in the first place.

I should've realized my FBI informant was hiding information from me. I should've known they had enough evidence to make an arrest.

"Is that what you're trying to do?" Luca's brows pinch with stern inquisition. "You're looking for a way out? You know you don't have to do this. Not now. We can go home, wait it out, and come back when you're ready"

"Shut your fucking mouth."

He's judging me. Finding me lacking. Just like she does.

I'm not incapable of taking care of business. And that's all this is. Business. A righting of wrongs.

My father was once an asset, and now he's a liability. I can't look at this any other way.

"Get out of my face." I take another step, our chests almost brushing as I scowl. "And stay out of my fucking head or you'll find yourself in a worse position than Sayker."

14

ANISSA

I LINGER A FEW FEET FROM THE SHEER CURTAIN, MY PULSE heavy in my throat as I wait for war to break out beside the pool.

I should be searching for a weapon. A phone. An escape plan.

Instead, I'm transfixed by the ferocity on display.

I've never seen Cole this way. He's out of control. Spiraling, just like Luca said.

But it's more than that.

The volatility presents like vulnerability. It's raw. Brutal and honest. And God, I wish I wasn't bearing witness, because now I'm finally beginning to believe this situation isn't based on a string of intricately woven lies.

Cole plans to kill his father. And I'm here to watch the bloodbath.

He takes another step, the two men toe to toe. "Get out of my face. And stay out of my fucking head."

Luca stares down his boss. "I'm trying to help."

My ribs grow tight, my unease narrowing on the possibility of Cole desperately wanting a way out. Is he trapped in this situation? Has he made me a victim because he's one as well?

I glare, despising the tiny flicker of empathy working its way into my bloodstream. These men aren't entitled to anything other than my dedication to bring them to justice. They deserve four cement walls and a lengthy sentence, not my contemplation of their hardships.

"Help by doing your fucking job. Be prepared for when my father arrives. That's all you're here for."

Cole maneuvers around Luca, clipping his shoulder as he stalks toward the house. Toward *me*.

Shit.

I turn and run, fleeing the living area on the tips of my toes to race down the hall and into my room. I inch the door closed with exquisite patience, the handle making the tiniest click as it latches.

I shudder out a relieved breath, only to question my response seconds later.

Why am I hiding? I'm not scared of Cole. And now is the perfect time to poke him for more information. To push him toward the edge of honesty.

But I guess honesty isn't a necessity. Not when getting out of here is far more important.

I sigh and lean back against the door as the loud *boom, boom, boom* of his footfalls approach. He doesn't stop. Doesn't even pause. Those pounding steps continue down the hall until a door slams, the loud crack of noise plunging the house into silence.

I should be happy he's unravelling. If he's losing control it means he's more likely to make a mistake. And mistakes will allow me to gain the upper-hand.

The tailspin is great news. If only his volatility didn't unnerve me.

There was desperation in his eyes. A sense of him being cornered prey. Did he know I was watching? Is this yet another layer to his sophisticated plot?

My stomach twists, and this time it has nothing to do with rabid hunger. I can't figure out his motives. And without understanding, I'm lost.

The only option I can think of is to convince him I'm on his side. I don't know how else to approach this. Not when he sees me as an antagonist instead of a victim.

Taking on his warped sense of reality may be the key. I'm never going to change his corrupt foundations. But I can learn to understand them in an attempt to use it against him.

The door slams again and I hold my breath, waiting as those thunderous footsteps storm back down the hall in the opposite direction before I slide to the floor in a heap.

The silence returns.

I don't hear another sound apart from the heavy beat of my heart for what feels like an hour. There's no clock in here. I don't have any association with time apart from knowing mine is running out.

I need to work on a plan—to manipulate Cole, to get away from Luca, to escape this fucking island. But none of my thoughts have substance. Everything returns to Cole's anger. Its severity. His uncharacteristic show of emotion.

If the display was real, I want to know whether it's an everyday occurrence for those close to him, or something entirely out of the ordinary. Is this situation tearing him apart? Was the dominant display an outlet for the pain he's hiding?

"You're a fucking idiot." I bang my head gently against the door, hoping the soft brain massage will kick me out of my stupidity.

It doesn't.

I can't stop seeing him when I close my eyes. I even shove to my feet, stalk to the bed, and slump onto the mattress in the hopes a new position will bring a new outlook, but that doesn't work either.

I curl into the fetal position as I scrutinize Cole's face in my mind, when a gentle knock at the door sends me snapping upright.

I'm not ready to speak to him.

I don't know how to play his game yet, let alone win. And I sure as hell don't know how to stop clinging to the hope that he's just as vulnerable as I am.

"Anissa?" The knock raps again.

It isn't Cole, and I'm even less interested in talking to the man who stood by while a maniacal old Greek mocked me.

"Yes?" I slide my legs off the bed and sit up straight.

The handle clicks, the door opening slightly.

Luca's stern face comes into view. "You need to eat. I've made sandwiches."

I hold back a response, not succumbing to the ravenous way my insides tingle at the offer.

He left me on the pier yesterday. Alone. With a man filled with giddy excitement at the thought of blowing my brains out.

For reasons that don't hold a wealth of rationality, I find Luca's actions more despicable than Cole's. I'm well aware my prejudice doesn't make sense. And regardless of my own insight, I can't change my perception.

Cole has antagonized me for weeks. He's torn my life apart and sabotaged my career. But I'm not scared of him.

In contrast, Luca frightens me. He's an unknown entity. A threat.

"I'm not going to hold your hand." His expression hardens. "If you want them, they're in the kitchen. If not, it makes no difference to me."

He snaps the door shut, the noise reverberating around the room. I stare, dumbfounded, as I wonder if the sandwiches are meant as a peace offering.

Am I supposed to be grateful? Does he expect me to fall to my knees in thanks?

I scoff, mind-blown at his audacity, while I contemplate whether or not to play nice. Not only do I desperately crave food, I need answers, too, and Luca may be able to give me both. He's as deep in this mess as Cole. I won't leave either of them off a criminal report. So if he's just as likely to fry for his actions, but less invested in the family betrayal, maybe he's a better target for my questions.

I walk across the room and pull open the door to an empty hall. "Luca?"

"Kitchen."

I make my way into the open living area and find him leaning over the island counter eating one of those highly anticipated peace-offering sandwiches.

God, they look good.

All I can see is white bread, but damn, they're like clouds of heaven as he wraps his lips around them and takes a bite.

I inch toward him, moving to the opposite side of the island counter.

"Help yourself." He slides a clean plate toward me and I willingly take it, offering a look of civility in thanks. "I'll make more if necessary."

Next, he pushes over the tray of stacked sandwiches with a mass of the same type of filling—lettuce, tomato, carrot.

"Ham salad," he offers. "That's as good as it gets when I'm left in charge of meal prep."

I nod, letting his kindness sink in. "I'm not fussy. But I am starving." My mouth salivates as I grab one of the sandwich halves.

Then I'm forced to pause.

The inundating moisture evaporates, leaving my tongue dry and parched. I eye the offering dubiously and wonder if my impatience to fill my stomach is leading me into another trap.

"They're safe." He grabs the other half of the sandwich and takes a large bite, holding my gaze as he chews.

It's another offer of goodwill. A display of obvious assurance.

Maybe too obvious.

My insides gurgle, begging, pleading for something to fill the empty space, drugs be damned.

"Just being cautious." I throw that caution to the wind and bite into the puffy, soft clouds of bread-induced heaven. Flavors burst across my tongue like they're the most expensive delicacy.

He doesn't quit watching while I eat, downing the half in a few quick bites. The scrutiny is different to what I've come to expect from his boss. More cynical. Less provoking.

"Better?" he asks.

My nod is subtle. Even though the hunger pangs have slightly dissipated, I'm not going to gush with gratitude.

"Cole said you ran into some trouble with the boat driver yesterday."

I stiffen.

"That's my fault," he continues. "Leaving you alone with him wasn't a smart move."

"What was the alternative?"

He shrugs. "I should've waited with you until he left."

Staying on the pier may have stopped a gun being pointed at my head, but the conclusion would've remained the same. I'm still stuck here. Held captive.

"Cole wants you to feel safe. The sooner you realize you're not a prisoner, the easier this will be."

I grab another sandwich, not buying his line. "I'm not a prisoner, yet I can't leave. That doesn't make a lick of sense."

"Sometimes people need to be encouraged to make the right decisions. Would you have come here if you were asked? Would you have believed Cole if he trusted you with the truth?"

I don't have the truth. I don't have anything but confusion.

"The answer is no." He stares me down as he takes another bite, his jaw working overtime. "Don't even pretend otherwise. You might not agree with his tactics, but sometimes catching bees with honey takes a lot longer than—"

"Drugs and abduction?"

His jaw tics with the accusation, his stare remaining fierce as I blink innocently at him. I'm no stranger to antagonism. I know the ropes. Hell, I've been provoking tight-lipped narcs for years, but not once did I feel compelled to obtain what I needed illegally. I may have threatened something underhanded a time or two, doesn't mean I ever followed through.

"Where is he anyway?" I divert the conversation toward something that doesn't include judging me.

"Cole?"

No, Spiderman, asshole. "Yes, Cole."

"Why do you want to know?"

"I heard you two arguing by the pool." I take another bite and another, letting the silence build. "It seemed intense."

"And?"

"I was hoping for an explanation. I've never seen him out of control. It's not like him to be aggressive. It's uncharacteristic, isn't it?"

"Uncharacteristic?" Luca raises a brow and dusts his hands over his crumb-riddled plate. "You barely know him."

I want to refute his opinion. After what feels like a lifetime learning the ins and outs of the Torian family, the denial sits on the tip of my tongue, held back only to maintain our thinly veiled civility.

"Maybe not." I shrug. "But you know him, and you said it yourself: he wasn't acting like his normal self. He was spiraling. What does that mean?"

"What do you think it means?" His eyes narrow, scathing in their appraisal. "He told you what he's here to do. Did you expect him to carry out the job with a smile on his face and a fucking bounce in his step?"

"For starters, I expected this all to be a lie—another game—but I guess when I did contemplate the possibility, I imagined Cole committing the crime with his usual calm calculation."

Why wouldn't I?

He's always been a righteous villain.

"He isn't playing around. Torian is determined, and nothing will sway him once his mind is made up." He pushes from the counter and opens a cupboard behind him, grabbing two glasses. "Juice? Water? Soda?"

"Water. Thanks." The appreciation is grated. My pride takes a hit at having to thank an accomplice to my abduction. "If Cole is so sure of himself, why is he spiraling?"

He fills the glasses from the jug in the fridge, then turns back to slide one across the counter toward me. "I don't know about you, but where I'm from, killing your father isn't something most folks do for fun."

"I understand—"

He holds up a hand. "No, you don't. And if you have more questions, ask him. Not me."

"I would, but he's not the easiest person to speak to."

His features tighten, his lips pinching. "Neither am I."

Maybe this wasn't a peace offering after all.

"Can you at least tell me why I'm here?" I swallow over the last vestiges of ham salad in my mouth and the vile taste of the plea. "What he told me doesn't make sense. If I witness a crime, I'm obligated to report it. I can't let it slide, no matter which way Cole tries to twist the situation. It's cold-blooded, premeditated murder."

"Ask him." His tone hardens.

"Please." I've lowered myself to begging, and it fucking hurts. "You told him he needs to give me more information. What else is there to know?"

He grabs another sandwich half and glares at me as he takes a bite.

"Why do I need to be a witness? Why can't he use some other form of evidence? A photo? A recording? An account from someone else?"

He continues to work his jaw, his mouth pressed into a tight line. He can't possibly have to chew for as long as he does. I suspect he's buying time. Weighing his options.

"Luca?"

"Maybe you don't need to be a witness." He grins, his entire demeanor changing. "Maybe that's not why you're here at all."

My heart kicks up a notch. "It's not? Then why?"

"I don't know. It could be the same reason you kept going after him back in Portland even though you'd been instructed to stay out of the investigation. Neither one of you seem able to leave each other alone."

The accusation stabs right through me. It's severe. Harsh. And entirely off base. "The FBI has worked for years trying to get Luther behind bars. Of course I was going to find it hard to walk away from the investigation when Cole used me as an alibi."

"Turning up at the restaurant had nothing to do with investigating." He takes a drink, eyeing me over the rim of his glass before resting it back on the counter. "Just admit your interest in him goes beyond his criminal reputation."

I ignore the rise of my pulse. It's beneath me to rebuff the claim.

"Your cheeks are turning pink." He smirks. "Don't bite your tongue on my account. I'd love to hear your denial."

"Your understanding of the situation is embarrassing. I was only doing my job."

"Since when does your job include jetsetting with the infamous Cole Torian? Without backup?" His brows rise. "Should

I be taking a refresher on the FBI handbook so I can stop confusing an unhealthy obsession with official Bureau protocol?"

Obsessed?

No way. I'm focused. Determined.

"Where is he?" I slide from the stool, squaring my shoulders, then wince at the bite of pain that comes with the movement. My fall last night left me with tense, swollen muscles and a bruise dark enough to rival the night sky. But the last thing I should do is announce the weakness. "I need to see him."

He grins. "He's letting off steam in the weights room."

"Can you point me in the right direction?"

He jerks his head backward. "Down the far end of the hall. Last room. But I wouldn't suggest going after him until he's cooled down."

"I appreciate the concern," I drawl, "but you can shove your suggestions up your ass."

I walk toward the hall opening and take a right this time, heading into unchartered territory. There're more paintings down this way. More rooms, too.

I hear a clang as I approach the glass door at the very end. Then another. Weights colliding with metal. The impact sounds heavy, harsh, as if he's doing the complete opposite of cooling down.

I stop at the frosted glass and listen. The slightest sense of unease skims across my chest, the sensation igniting a mass of goosebumps.

I'm not sure if I'm about to prove Luca right.

Going in search of Cole could be misconstrued as obsession instead of investigation. And I have to admit, the man acts like a thorn under my skin. From the moment we spoke at his uncle's funeral, I've had an increasing thirst to learn more about him. To get under his skin. To understand the world through his eyes.

That doesn't mean I'm obsessed.

I press my hands against the frosted glass and push inside.

Cole is on the bench press, dressed in a white tank and black sport shorts as he locks the impressive weight back into the cradle before shoving to his feet.

He doesn't look at me, doesn't even acknowledge my existence as he stalks to the pull-up bar to start hauling himself up and down, a masculine display on repeat.

I drag my gaze from his sweat-slicked skin, showing a similar lack of interest as I scope out the room, his breathy sounds of exertion taunting me.

There's a mass of equipment in here. A treadmill. Rower. Medicine balls. Elliptical trainer. Spin bike. The list goes on and on. There even looks to be a wooden door leading to a sauna in the far corner.

I keep my focus on that door, watching Cole from the corner of my eye until he drops to the floor. I use the break in exercise to gain his attention, raising my brows at him in a silent question.

I don't know what I'm asking exactly. I don't know much of anything as he grips the hem of his tank, raising the material to wipe the sweat from his face. He exposes all those muscles normally hidden from view.

All the perfected strength.

All the beauty tainted by his personality.

"What do you want, Nissa?" Aggression coats his tone. There's no calm. No calculation. His voice is filled with barely contained rage.

"I want to talk."

He scoffs out a laugh. "We've needed to talk for twenty-four hours. What's the rush now?"

Yet again, I'm stuck on what to say—truth or lies, deception or brutal honesty. Which path will get me out of this maze?

"You're spiraling. I need to know what that means for me."

Those eyes narrow as he grips the pull-up bar, his fingers cinched tight. "You've been talking to Luca."

"I overheard you two arguing by the pool. You were upset."

"Upset?" He lifts his chin over the bar, then again and again, his arm muscles bending and flexing with the exertion. "I'm sorry my response to planning my father's death isn't to your approval."

He's wrong.

The response isn't unwanted. If anything, his reaction is what I've been searching for. Knowing he's not emotionless gives me hope for my future. "If you don't want to go through with this, why are you?"

He drops back to the ground, his chest rapidly rising and falling with aggressive breaths. "What's the point in explaining? You won't understand. Not when all you want to do is look down on me from your fucking high horse."

I jut my chin, unable to remain still at the insult. "Make me understand."

He laughs again, the sound bitter. "You have rose-tinted glasses, Niss. You think the justice system is this perfect utopia that punishes the bad and protects the good."

"No, I don't. I know there are faults."

"Then why do you fucking defend it? Why are you on the front lines, claiming victims?"

"Victims? You're—" I snap my mouth shut, biting back the remark. I silently count to ten, calming myself. "I put away criminals. I make the community safe."

"Like hell you do. You put away petty crims. Low-level scum. You imprison the fools who are too powerless to buy their freedom. Occasionally, you'll bag someone who can cause real damage, but it's rare, because anyone like me knows your system is flawed. Lawyers manipulate juries. Judges and authorities can be bought or threatened. Evidence is tampered with. There's nothing that can't be swept under the rug. I could sit here for hours and name people who have walked free from the harshest crimes because they have money and influence, yet you call it a justice system. And those who remain behind bars are nothing but a burden on society. Do you know how many people are currently incarcerated, Ms. Fox? Do you know the amount of tax-payer dollars spent every year to let rapists and murderers live? Because I sure as hell do."

He's smart. And informed.

His knowledge isn't a surprise. But the unwanted twinge of respect itching behind my sternum is.

The fact he pays attention means he's thought about the effect of his actions on the community. There's logic to his system. It may be severely unhinged logic, but it's there nonetheless.

"We need rules, Cole. Society would implode without them."

"Society is already imploding," he snaps. "And your system is to blame. At least where I'm concerned, I ensure those who break the rules are a burden to no one but themselves. My punishments are swift and impact nobody but the culprit."

"That's a lie." I step forward. "Your physical punishments impact hospitals. Nursing staff. Doctors. They change the lives of friends and relatives of those you find guilty. It incites more aggression and violence."

"It inspires loyalty and fear, which breeds compliance." He stalks to the padded bench press and positions himself beneath the weighted bar. "Imprisonment has a major psychological impact that goes hand in hand with the huge expense. How can you not see how it fails society?" He pushes out five repetitions, grunting with the lift and fall of the heavy weight.

"Okay, I'll admit our system is flawed. But you're looking at the situation entirely one-sided. Following the law is far better than an eye for an eye." I take another step, not sure if I'm inching closer toward conflict or common ground.

If I wanted, I could hurt him.

Kill him.

Right here. Right now.

All I'd need to do is grab that bar and press down with all my weight.

Simple.

Easy.

"Why is it better?" He struggles through more repetition, sweat beading his face, veins bulging in his neck. He clinks the heavy weight into the cradle, then lets his arms fall to his sides. "Give me one good reason."

"I could give you hundreds."

He glares. "I'm only looking for one."

I get it. He's lived with this mindset all his life. He doesn't understand my reasoning. He probably never will. He's been brainwashed by his upbringing.

"For starters, by my society's rules, nobody is ever placed in your position. Not one person has ever had to kill their own father in the name of justice."

"I can deal with my situation." He reclaims the bar and pumps the iron, harder, faster, punishing himself.

"Are you sure?" I continue forward, one step, two. I creep closer toward risky possibilities as the weight rises and falls, those arms trembling under the pressure. "Can you honestly say you feel comfortable killing your dad?"

He falls quiet, nothing but the aggressive pant of his breaths falling between us.

"There's more to this, Cole. And I need to know what it is. I have to know why I'm really here."

"I've already told you," he seethes.

"*No.*" I add steel to my tone. He's lying. *Always* lying. God, it drives me insane. "You haven't told me anything. Having me here as a witness isn't smart. And you're a smart man. There has to be another reason."

His jaw clenches, his movements becoming hostile, combative and unrhythmic.

"Tell me why the hell I'm here." I raise my voice. "*Tell me.*"

He doesn't respond. Doesn't even acknowledge my demand.

Fucking hell. I'm going to lose my shit.

My temples throb. My chest pounds. Adrenaline floods my system, and I move so far beyond frustration I have to clench my hands at my sides to fight a scream.

"It's time for you to get out of here," he mutters. "We can talk later."

"No." Goddammit. I can't be kept from the information a moment longer. I refuse to bend to his will.

He's fucked me over, time and time again.

He's taunted me. Threatened my career. Spat in the face of my privacy. Disregarded my safety.

Enough is enough.

I lunge forward, hiking my leg over the bench to straddle his waist and claim the weighted bar. I press down hard, his dark blue eyes meeting mine as I threaten to crush the life from him. "Tell me."

His gaze narrows to tiny slits. His lip curls in a vicious snarl.

I don't know what I'm doing other than living by impulse. I

climbed aboard him without a strategy or common sense. I'm not even sure of my aim.

I want answers. I want freedom. And apparently, autopilot is pushing me toward murder in an attempt to achieve both.

If I go ahead with this, it won't be a quick death. Or a quiet one. His face will turn red. He'll gasp and splutter.

Fuck. What the hell am I doing?

Even if I could stomach killing this man, I'd then have to deal with Luca. And find a way off this island.

What I've instigated is completely irrational.

Entire lunacy.

I'm about to raise a white flag and retreat when he quits fighting. His arms drop. He lets go of the bar, leaving me to struggle with the heavy load.

My injured shoulder screams in protest, the pain slicing down my muscles. "What are you doing?" My voice trembles as I lose strength, the bar lowering with my struggle, the agony increasing. I can't hold on.

"Don't stop now." He stares up at me, his face an emotionless mask. "You want me dead? Then kill me. This is the perfect opportunity. My arms are fatigued. I can't fight back."

I shuffle my feet, trying to stabilize myself as I straddle him. I throw all my strength into the lift and cry out when my shoulder screams with another painful revolt. "Cole, I can't carry this much longer. My arm..."

He doesn't offer assistance.

"*Cole*. Please." The agony shooting down my bicep is excruciating. Red-hot and blinding. "I didn't mean—"

I didn't mean what? To threaten him? To attempt murder?

He'll punish me. He'll use this as an excuse to retaliate.

Jesus Christ, what the fuck have I done?

The bar continues to lower as I succumb to the pain. My curled fingers brush his hard chest, the bar pressing into him. Soon, I'll lose all my strength. The bar will roll. The weight will suffocate him.

A million thoughts run through my head, each and every one

of them revolving around this man's death and how I'd give anything for it not to happen.

I fight harder and still I fail.

"*Luca*," I scream. "*Help*."

Cole's eyes harden.

In a flash, he raises his arms, shoving at the bar, the heavy weight lifting like a feather to clang into the cradle. I jerk back, yet again surprised by another form of his manipulation as he snaps upright. I slither down his body with a hollow sense of shame and come to sit in his lap, face-to-face, chest-to-chest.

"Pure stupidity," he seethes, his hatred engulfing me. "I've abducted you, drugged and tied you, yet you can't even come close to finishing me off. That's disappointing, little fox. Where's your self-preservation?"

My heart trembles behind tightening ribs.

I'm lost.

In those eyes.

In his vehemence.

In complete and utter confusion.

I still see his vulnerability. It's there. *Right* there. Beaming back at me with furrowed brows.

"Want to know why you couldn't follow through?" His voice loses the bitter edge and gains a taint of condescension. "It's because you know I won't hurt you. There's no fear because I'm no threat."

He's right.

I don't fear him. Not physically.

Not even when I'm held down on his lap, his ferocity staring back at me.

"You know I'm right," he growls. "You can claim to be a victim all you like, but you're here willingly."

I shake my head, sickened by his logic. "You *have* hurt me. Look at my wrists. And there's a track mark on my side, too. I don't even know if you used a sterile needle."

Something flashes behind those eyes. Regret? Disappointment?

I wait for an apology. I even hope for a viable explanation for his actions when the door swings open and Luca rushes in.

His eyes turn judgmental at the sight before him. "What's—"

"Get out," Cole yells. "*Now.*"

Luca complies in a heartbeat, leaving us alone, with me straddling the lap of a man who looks back at me as if I'm a disappointment.

I swallow, trying to fight the complete detox of moisture from my tongue, and lick my lower lip. The dryness only increases as Cole watches the action, his attention focused on my mouth.

The *thump, thump, thump* of my heart is a constant reminder I'm alive, but I'm entirely numb. Completely devoid of a suitable reaction to the rainbow of insanity tearing my insides apart.

There's anger and hostility. Frustration and exhaustion.

And something else, too. Something that builds the longer he looks at me this way.

Something I don't even want to define.

"You've never been scared of me." His hand raises from my waist, the touch trailing to my neck, his fingers wrapping around my throat. "Not even when I set out to claim your fear."

I tremble, the quake building in intensity.

There's no pain from his hold. It's light—so light it almost seems to be made with pleasurable intent.

My pulse pounds wildly beneath his palm, my rampant heartbeat increasing to the point it's deafening. I can't stop my quickening breaths, the short, shallow pants rasping from my lips.

I don't like this feeling. It's unnatural. It's in complete contrast to self-preservation.

Something is wrong with me.

He's threatening my life, his strength capable of crushing my windpipe, and I'm not trembling because of fear.

I'm... *God*, I don't know what I am, but it definitely isn't scared.

Maybe it's shame. Or a different taste of humiliation.

"You want to know why you're here?" he murmurs. "You want to know why you were my first and only choice to bear witness?"

I swallow again. I can't gain any moisture to speak. I can only nod in subtle acknowledgement.

His gaze holds mine, his stare sinking deep into my heart. Then the calm stops in an abrupt blink. His face hardens; his upper lip curls.

Finally, a tingle of caution niggles its way from the bottom of my spine, the awareness increasing the higher it climbs.

"I brought you here because I knew you'd argue your case, claiming you, with your infamous virtue, were right, and me, with my merciless reputation, are wrong. And I fucking knew all it would do is convince me I was making the right choice." His hand falls, his grip moving to my hips where he lifts and drags me off of him to stand beside the bench press. "I brought you here, Nissa, because I refuse to let myself fail with such a judgmental bitch keeping score."

15

TORIAN

I stalk away from the bench press, turning my back to her as I adjust my cock.

She's plotting to kill me, and here I am, rearranging the dick tenting my fucking shorts. If that's not psychotic I don't know what is.

But at least it's clear now. All the shit I've worried about has come to fruition.

My father's perverted afflictions must have been working their subliminal bullshit toward me for years. I've always been his perfect protégé—Luther's mini-me with bigger plans and even bigger ideas. And I naively thought his teachings had been limited to business.

Turns out he handed down the fetishes, too.

Sexualized brutality is new to me. Harming women has never brought a thrill.

Until now.

Maybe this is how the fucked-up shit starts. The twisted kinks are triggered by an event.

A woman.

This woman.

Bringing her here was fucking reckless. Indulgent. But the reasons I've told her aren't a lie.

I need someone reliable to relay the information of my father's death, because those who don't believe I'm capable will be hard to convince.

Luca's account won't hold merit. The word of anyone loyal to me, or easily bribed, is worthless.

But Anissa isn't either of those.

I didn't fabricate the truth about her being here to ensure my success either. Every time she looks at me with her narrow-eyed judgment, I grow more determined.

She's here to push me. Provoke me.

Her bitchy, self-righteous superiority will ensure I finish this thing with my father despite the guilt hovering close.

There's more though.

So much more it feels like she's the linchpin to this entire fucking operation for no justifiable reason. I'm propelled forward because of her. Not my sister's need for closure. And definitely not due to my father's nameless, faceless victims.

Anissa messes with my head to the point where I'm beating back a goddamn erection at the thought of her trying to choke me with a weights bar. I'm crazed with the need to get her back on top of me. Those wide eyes staring down at mine. That bated breath brushing my mouth.

And that fucking pussy. Nothing has ever felt better than her heat against my stomach.

"Cole?"

Gentle pressure leans into my shoulder blade. A hand. *Her* hand.

"What?" I jerk away.

"Did you hear what I said?"

I shake my arms, and it's not because of the building lactic acid. I need to get these toxic thoughts out of my system. I have to figure out where the fuck I went wrong and if there's any possibility of going back.

I'm not a weak son of a bitch who takes pleasure in hurting women. I'm not my father. I don't need to strong-arm the vulnerable to make myself feel powerful. Not for a fucking second.

"Sorry," I snarl. "I have other things on my mind. I guess when someone tries to kill you, it's hard to focus." I turn to face her and shouldn't be surprised when she straightens those shoulders and raises her chin.

"I didn't try to kill you. I just..."

"Just attempted to crush my throat, then pussied out at the last second."

She blinks at me, those eyes wider than usual, her lips slightly parted. She wants to reject my claim, but she can't.

This woman contemplated ending my life.

Maybe I would've let her, too.

Maybe I should've.

"Cole, please, I want to believe you, but your logic is hard to justify." She keeps staring. Pleading. "You know I'm loyal to my job. There's no way I could keep my mouth shut about this."

She's right.

There's no logic. No rationale. No sense. There's only impulse and instinct when it comes to her.

"If you report this, you won't live long enough to testify. Never forget that." I flash my teeth in a feral smile. "You should also realize I'm my father's son. So maybe think twice before you straddle my dick next time."

She recoils, her mouth agape.

Good.

The shock should keep her at bay.

"Come on." I stride across the room. "I'll show you where you need to be when he arrives."

I shove open the gym door, holding it wide until she enters the hall.

"You'll be in my room." I continue toward the other end of the house, her footsteps following behind me.

"Why your room?"

"You'll see in a minute." I don't stop until we reach my door, then push it open for her to proceed before me.

She stares, dubious, but walks ahead to pause near the bed. "Now what?"

"The walk-in robe." I jerk my head to the door at my left.

She sighs and does as instructed, sliding the opening wide.

"Pull the hanging shirts to the side."

"Which ones?" she drawls. "There's a whole heap."

I follow her into the cramped space, making sure to keep as much distance between us as possible. For my dick's sake. "Start in the middle."

She separates the hung clothing, the clink of hangers skittering along the rail as she exposes the door behind with a keypad lock on the wall beside it. She glances at me over her shoulder. "What's this?"

"A panic room."

A different kind of concern crosses her features, more speculation than worry.

"The code is eight-nine-seven-one. And only the two of us know those digits."

She keeps staring.

"Go on." I encourage her with a wave of my hand. "Eight-nine-seven-one. Pin it in."

She turns her focus back to the door and keys in the numbers, then the door panel slides across as she hits Enter.

"There's a light switch inside, on the right wall."

She reaches out, running her fingers along the inside of the frame to illuminate the panic room in artificial light. She inches forward, assessing the interior as she turns in a circle.

I remain in the middle of the wardrobe, not wanting to tempt myself with her close proximity. I already know what she'll find in there—a wall of six blank screens, each capable of exposing a real-life feed of any main room inside the sprawling mansion.

There's also a mini bathroom and a disabled communications station. At one time, anyone hiding in here could call for help. But I can't trust her with that option. Not yet.

"You'll stay in there." I lean back against the shelves. "You'll have access to the video and audio feed."

"How?" She pokes her head back out the door. "Can you show me?"

I contemplate denying her. I try to convince myself it's a fucking bad idea to insert myself into the small space beside her. But seconds later, I'm in there, almost shoulder to shoulder with this beguiling woman as I turn on the switch to illuminate the six monitors displaying the pool, yard, kitchen, living room, and my bedroom, along with two different angles of the hall.

"Are these the only rooms under surveillance?"

"No." I keep my focus on those screens, ignoring her as she turns to face me.

"Are there cameras in every room?"

"Apart from the bathrooms, yes. Every bedroom. Every square inch of livable space."

"How convenient." The words are grated, her anger crackling to life in the air between us. "I guess you've spent a lot of time in here."

A smirk slowly spreads my lips. Her anger is invigorating. Always has been. I bet it always will be. "Don't flatter yourself."

Her shoulders relax, her relief evident even from the corner of my eye.

"I don't need to be in the panic room. I get the video feed on my cell." I pull the device from my pocket, unlock the screen, and show her the view of her bedroom.

Her posture stiffens, snapping tight in a heartbeat.

She mutters something. A curse. A promise, maybe.

Again, I'm invigorated. Euphoric at the ease of angering her, and equally disgusted in myself at enjoying her reaction.

"The cell feed doesn't allow for audio. But you'll have access to it in here." I reach for the narrow counter and pull out a keyboard to tap in the necessary button combination. Brief flickers of noise filter through from the speakers in the corners of the room. The sound of Luca clearing his throat. The clink and clatter of plates as he piles them into the dishwasher. "You'll hear whatever my father has to say when the time comes. You'll bear witness to it all in the safety of this room."

I can already picture what she's going to see.

He'll greet me with a handshake, his designer suit flawless, his hair groomed and perfectly cut. He'll compliment me on something, then follow it up with a harsh insult. The kindness before the storm. It's how he's always been. With me. With my sisters. Reward then reprimand.

We'll talk about family. Money. Negotiations. And those women.

"Anything overheard is to be kept in the strictest confidence. I have friends in the FBI, so I'll know if you sing."

I think that's another part of this game. I like her being a threat. A constant devil on my shoulder. Once this thing with my father is over, the ball will be in her court. It will be up to Anissa if we play another round.

"You've made the threat clear, Cole. You don't need to keep repeating it."

"You sure? I have to admit, it's slightly enjoyable reminding you."

She sighs, remaining silent while her gaze is trained on the screens for long seconds. "How do you plan to...?" The end of her sentence hangs between us, her voice barely audible. Soft.

I know exactly what she's asking. It's the same question I've asked myself time and time again.

I have options when it comes to killing my father. Multiple alternatives. But the problem stems from the honor we've built our lives upon. Just because I don't abide by Anissa's justice system doesn't mean my world doesn't have a code of our own. One that demands respect.

Stabbing my father in the back is one thing. Killing him in cowardice is quite another.

I need to finish this face-to-face. Eye-to-eye. His power and authority command a full-frontal attack. An end-game of strategy, not a battle for strength.

"You don't need to know the finer details."

"All you want me to do is watch? I don't need to be involved?"

"Bearing witness is all that's necessary. For obvious reasons, it's best if he's kept in the dark where you're concerned."

She sucks in a deep breath and turns to face me, a mere foot of space between us. "Has he made contact?"

"No. But he won't be too far away. He could arrive at any minute. Either today or tomorrow. I doubt it will be much later."

"And what if he sees me? What if he arrives unnoticed and I'm found?"

"We'll hear the boat."

Worry breaks across her features. "What if we don't?"

"We'll hear it."

"But—"

"We'll hear him coming, Nissa. I promise you. That's why none of the televisions have been turned on. There's no music or noise to distract from what might be coming."

"What about when we're sleeping?"

She seems to inch closer with her apprehension. Or the space around us shrinks. Everything closes in. There's only her. Only me. And a fucking dick that won't stop with its incessant twitch.

"Trust me. I'll keep you safe. I know my father. The last thing people like us want to do is surprise assholes with trigger-happy fingers in the middle of the night. He'll make sure I'm aware he's on his way."

She nods, the movement almost imperceptible as she stares at me. Stares so deep I feel it in my bones.

Could she finally be letting down her guard? Is this fierce, spiteful woman succumbing to my charm?

I step back, giving myself a reprieve from the sweet scent of her shampoo. Or maybe it's her soap.

"Remind me why you're doing this. What's the aim?" she asks. "I understand why any normal person would want to stop your father but..."

"Just not someone like me?" I finish for her.

"You've built a crime-riddled empire. Why draw a line at sex offenses?"

"There's always a line. This just happens to be mine."

It's clear she doesn't understand why a heartless motherfucker like me would want to distance himself from a wealthy business opportunity.

This woman is a world away from having me pegged.

She has no fucking clue.

"I'm struggling to believe why your father's actions are such a hardship for you. Death and destruction shadow you, Cole. You seem to crave the horrors that stalk most people's nightmares."

I ignore the truth and focus on the words she makes seem

195

erotic—death, destruction, craving. Her fake purity sprinkles the evil with naive innocence. But she's not entirely free from sin herself. There're darker sides to this woman, and I'd love to expose them.

"I have many cravings," I admit. "Some I think you'd enjoy."

My mouth is running away with me. Saying things better left unsaid.

I can no longer deny my attraction. Both physically and mentally.

I want this woman. Her body. Her mind.

She needs to be beneath me. At my mercy.

"Is that a poor attempt at deflection?" She raises a brow. "I know there's more to this. Killing your father will have long-lasting repercussions. Your family allies will be torn. Nobody will trust you. You're risking everything. Why?"

"To most, my father won't be murdered; he'll simply disappear. It's not like he hasn't done it before."

"You still haven't answered why. You're deflecting again. You're trying to hide."

Her strike hits its mark.

A fucking bull's-eye.

"Cole?" She looks at me. Really fucking looks at me. Like she's a sympathetic shrink and I'm her unhinged patient. "I want to believe you're doing this for the right reasons."

"I'm killing a man, Niss. My own father. In cold blood. If I were you, I wouldn't spend sleepless nights searching for whimsical reasons. Just focus on the benefits his death will bring." I turn, needing to get away from her. "I'm hungry. We're done here."

She grabs my arm, her fingers sliding over the sweat still clinging to my skin.

I don't need to stop. Her hold is inconsequential. But my feet remain immobile. Unmoving.

"*Please.*"

She kills me with her plea.

This could be a ploy, a fucking FBI tactic. And it's working.

Her feigned need for understanding tears at me. Claws. I want to tell her everything. To shed the shame coating me like a second skin. To yell it right into her pretty face. To admit the remorse that has eaten away at me since I was a fucking kid.

I should do it. I should fucking succumb, exposing the depths of my own internal destruction for her to pick and prod.

"Quit the gentle act." I swing around and take a menacing step toward her. "We both know you don't have a tender bone in your body."

She inches back, bumping her ass into the counter as I continue to approach, looming over her, glaring. I attempt to siphon her misleading goodwill with a physical threat and I succeed.

Her expression changes, the gentleness seeping away until all I witness is interest.

Anticipation.

It might be my father's fucking perverted influence, but I see hunger staring back at me. Somehow this response is ten times worse.

I'm a breath away from taking her on this counter. From pulling apart those tight leggings and plunging deep inside her.

She swallows and licks her lower lip. "Tell me the real reasons." Her voice is filled with expectation. Delirium. She's dying for a taste of me.

I'm dying to give it to her.

It would be incredibly easy to lose a wealth of frustration in her body. The mindlessness would be cathartic. But incredibly fucking stupid.

"Why do you need me to convince you?" I grate. "Why even bother trying? We both know everyone lies. You, more than anyone, know those closest to us can lie the easiest."

Shock splits across her face, the sudden change in expression announcing she understands the subtle dig at her father.

"You will never know me, Nissa." I sink into those green eyes. I drown in them. "You will never understand me. All you can do is come to terms with what I've told you, and make peace with what's to come. It's either this way or nothing."

Her focus is intense. Confounding. Her breaths shudder

between perfect lips.

Her attention sweeps over me. Through me. She pokes at secrets I wasn't aware I had.

"And nothing isn't an option?" she asks.

I scowl at her. "You still think his freedom would be better?"

"I'm not asking for me. I want to make sure you know what you're doing. You can't come back from something like this."

I scoff out a snicker, denying her concern. "I know what I'm doing. Don't worry your pretty little head about me."

She wraps her arms around her stomach.

I want to unravel those arms and place her hands on her hips. To return her to a strong, commanding warrior woman because this fragile demeanor has a mirror effect. Her gentleness makes me powerless.

Defenseless.

She swallows, clears her throat, and raises her chin a smidge. "My concern is based on the aftermath. You'll change after this. Nobody can kill their own parent and not lose themself. I'm concerned this will inspire more violence. And in return, more crime."

I bite out a bitter laugh. I should've known. She has no concern for me. This was only part of her attempt to achieve the perfect crime-free Utopia. "You think you know me well enough to predict how I'll react?"

How can she when I have no clue myself?

I could be consumed with relief once my father is gone. Happy as fuck.

"No, I guess I don't know you well," she admits. "I doubt I know you at all. But I'd like to believe you're not capable of this."

The gentle disapproval strikes hard, punishing me with its subtlety. Her thorns are sinking farther, burying deeper.

"Then you're going to be bitterly disappointed, Nissa, because this is already a foregone conclusion. I'll pull the trigger without hesitation, and I won't look back."

16

ANISSA

I believe him now.

When he talks about his plan, I hear the truth in his words. I acknowledge the determination driving him to take drastic action. I see his conviction.

There's something deeper, too.

I feel his animosity for Luther, and it resembles the emotions I harbor toward my own father so closely I struggle to fight against the common ground.

What I lack is an understanding of how he can follow through with the crime.

I can't imagine contemplating the murder of my own flesh and blood. Not cold and premeditated. Not even if my father's actions meant the punishment was justified. I could never pull that trigger. And I'm not sure I should feel comfortable in the company of someone who can.

But I do.

There's no fear beating behind my ribs. No shock or devastation.

I want to detest Cole's plan, but I'm beginning to believe he's making the right decision.

If Luther has local police protecting him, I can't see a way to bring him down. Not efficiently. Or legally. And every minute ticking by is sixty seconds of torture for those women held captive.

This situation is a moral dilemma for me on innumerable levels. A crisis I'm sure Cole designed with pinpoint precision.

"Okay," I murmur. "I'll do it. I'll watch. I'll tell your connections whatever necessary as long as you can vow the information will never get back to the Bureau. I won't have this hanging over my head for the rest of my life."

The tightness coiled around him loosens. His shoulders relax. Those muscled arms lose their ferocity.

"That's not all." I hold his gaze and show my conviction with the hitch of my chin. "After I've held up my end of the bargain, we're done with this. There're no more games. No more tormenting or provoking. The stalking has to stop. The flowers and cards, too. We go our separate ways and never speak to each other again. I won't spend my days trying to take you down, and you won't spend yours trying to make my life a living hell."

I need to distance myself from him as much as possible. To flee the confusion his presence brings.

"You want to take back your promise?" His eyes taunt me. The curl of his lips, too. "You were the one who vowed we would spend more time together."

"Quit the games, Cole. I mean it." I clutch the counter at my sides and stare him down, feigning strength I don't have. "I can't do this if I think you're still toying with me."

For long moments he eyes me, stroking my unease with his devilish gaze.

"I agree to your terms." He steps close, leaning into me as he murmurs, "Being done with you will be a pleasure."

His response doesn't fill me with the relief I'd anticipated.

In fact, the tightening pressure nudging into my chest almost feels like rejection.

"Good." I swallow and freeze in place as his attention locks onto my throat.

The lingering effects of his touch still plague me. The tingle remains from where those fingers wrapped around my neck.

I suppress a shudder. I refuse to give in to the adrenaline sabotaging my system, making me react in uncharacteristic ways.

"I'm going back to my room." I walk out of the small space, determined not to slink away from his bulky frame when our shoulders brush. "Let me know when I need to be at your beck and call."

I take another step, only to be halted by his tight grip on my sore arm.

"You're not up to something, are you?" He narrows his gaze. "Is this sudden agreement a ploy?"

I contemplate provoking him again. The impulse is engrained.

Instead, I bite my tongue, staring deep into those dark ocean eyes. "It's no ploy, Cole." I yank my arm away and wince at the bite of pain lashing my shoulder. "I'm well aware my life is in your hands."

His jaw tics. Anger spikes in his expression.

I fall into confusion, wondering what I've done to antagonize him this time when his gaze lowers to my shoulder.

"Show me your injury."

The sudden change in topic has my mind spinning.

"Show me," he demands.

I shake my head and take a backward step.

He counters, lashing out, slinging an arm around my waist to drag me into him.

I'm close. So fucking close. I'm plastered against his muscles, his frustration bearing down on me.

Time. Fucking. Stops.

He doesn't move. Neither do I.

I'm caught up in those eyes. His scent. His hold.

I'm in the arms of my enemy, and I'm trembling for reasons that bear no resemblance to fear.

"I'm not going to show you, Cole."

"I thought you would've learned by now I'm not a man who appreciates being denied."

My knees threaten to buckle. My heart feels ready to explode.

Am I imagining the innuendo? Have I lost all grasp on reality?

"Here." I snatch at the short sleeve of my T-shirt and tug it down my arm, exposing my shoulder through the stretched neckhole. "It's a bruise. Now can I go?"

His gaze narrows on the exposed skin. His nostrils flare.

The tight hold around my waist doesn't loosen. I'm still stuck against his body. Pressed into a wall of hard muscle.

"Just a bruise," he repeats. "You don't need pain meds? Or a sling?"

"I don't need a damn thing from you."

Well, apart from maybe a phone, a boat ride off this hell hole, a plane ticket home, and a way to circumvent customs without my fucking passport.

The intensity fades from his features. A brutal smile curves his lips. "Not a damn thing?" he repeats with humor in his voice. "I'll remember that."

It's a threat—one that inspires a shiver I'm sure he can feel.

He releases me and I stumble forward into him, before I right myself and lunge back. My flailing triggers the soft rumble of his laughter.

I ignore the infuriating sound as I turn and stride from the walk-in robe.

I drag my feet into his bedroom, escape into the hall, and then into the sanctuary of my own room.

I reclaim my favored position, back against the wall, ass on the carpet, this time right next to the door I leave open.

He doesn't follow.

I'm left to suffer through a mental rerun of our encounter for long, painful minutes, my breathing rampant until he eventually strides past my room, freshly showered and wearing an impeccable suit.

Maybe I should do the same.

Washing away his touch might clear my head because as it stands, his gentle grip still haunts my skin. But I don't have the energy to move. I'm exhausted in mind and body. So I sit, listening to the world as time ticks by.

I hear everything—the lapping of the ocean. The whispers of the breeze through the living room curtains. The shuffle of feet and clink of crockery.

The thing I hear most is his voice.

He speaks to Luca, striking a conversation that ignores the tension they'd previously had between them. He doesn't mention me. There's no bite of hostility. Not an ounce of the discomfort consuming me.

He discusses inconsequential things. Business back home. The possibility of Hunter's wedding. A planned renovation to his restaurant.

I ignore the words as his rough, deep timbre hums in my ears.

I listen to him for hours wondering where the hell my despised hatred for this man has gone. He doesn't change the volume of his voice. Not when his phone rings and he speaks to his sister, lying to her about his location.

He doesn't change his tone as the day draws to a close and he continues his civil conversation with Luca. He doesn't even quieten his voice when he starts to discuss his father's upcoming arrival and how Luther won't be alone. There will be bodyguards.

More casualties.

I'm sure Cole knows I'm in listening distance. I'm positive he's checked the video feed on his phone to see I'm positioned close to the door, hanging off his every word.

And still he doesn't hide anything from me.

He doesn't whisper or step outside to hold the discussion away from prying ears.

"I'll greet them on the pier and make sure your father's men stay on the boat." Luca doesn't lower his voice either. "That way you can do your thing while I do mine."

I tilt my ear toward the open door, latching onto a more detailed part of their plan.

"And what about her?" Luca asks. "What will she do?"

My pulse increases.

"Don't worry. She will be safe."

There's a pause, a longer than necessary delay where I have the unfortunate opportunity to wonder if they're having some sort of silent communication.

Is it a scheme? Another trick?

Of course it is. Luca has no "worry" for me. He doesn't care about my safety.

"And once this is over?" he adds. "Will she be safe then, too?"

I hold my breath, the captured air burning in my lungs.

"That's up to her."

Me. I can be safe if I hold up my end of the bargain.

I need to watch a murder and follow his protocol afterward.

The former seems far easier than the latter.

I've seen a wealth of violence in my life and the act of murder isn't what daunts me. It's the morality. But the more I think about Cole's reasoning, the more I believe he has a point.

It's becoming a struggle to straddle the righteous high-wire. Maybe I shouldn't have stepped foot on it at all when innocents are still being tortured.

I'm sure other agents wouldn't hesitate to push for a speedy resolution. If the choice came down to Luther's freedom or his death, my fellow Feds might easily choose death without pausing for contemplation.

The murder of a criminal would've already happened. The cover-up would be taking place.

Unfortunately, I don't have that luxury.

When my father diverted off the path of justice, it ensured I'd have to watch every decision I made for the rest of my life. I don't have the freedom to make even slightly dishonorable choices. Every thought I have needs to be on the right side of the law.

I can't falter.

I shouldn't even waiver.

Which, I guess, means my conflict isn't entirely based on right and wrong. I'm looking at this problem and seeing how it will affect my reputation—my career—not the women held captive.

My stomach churns at the realization.

"Shit." I hang my head in my hands, my elbows rested against my knees.

I don't give a fuck about Luther. Nobody should.

And what is the alternative? A crapload of money spent on a manhunt for someone who would then cost the government more money when he was holed up in prison for the rest of his life.

I should be out there, helping to plot a foolproof plan instead of fighting this. My skills could be put to use to ensure nothing goes wrong.

But then I'd have the issue of aiding and abetting.

"Goddammit." I massage my forehead and battle my conscience. I drown in the tumultuous waves of my internal struggle while the sound of food preparation starts in the kitchen.

I hear the fridge open and close. Drawers, too. Then footsteps.

Cole enters my peripheral vision, his frame bearing down on me as he stops in the doorway, his suit-covered shoulder leaning against the frame.

"Would you like to help me prepare dinner?"

I raise a brow, unimpressed. But it's not only the invitation to be his kitchen bitch that pokes at me. It's everything else: the laziness in his stance. The relaxation. The calm. "You want me to be your slave?"

"I thought you'd appreciate being involved so you didn't have to worry about any secret ingredients."

My cheeks heat.

He's offering me a kindness, of sorts.

"There's no pressure, Nissa. I have no hidden motives."

There're always hidden motives.

Always.

"I'll leave the decision with you." He pushes from the frame, his presence escaping my periphery as he walks away.

It's not that I don't want to ensure he's not slipping something into my next meal. My hesitation revolves around my lack of hatred for this easily hate-able man.

I've lost my animosity. Fevered bitterness no longer boils my blood. All the venom is gone.

Nothing consumes me. Nothing but frustration.

I want to return to hating him. I want to be sucked dry of my knowledge so I can float back to ignorance.

But it's too late. We have something in common: our hatred for our fathers. And I can't stop my thoughts from wandering to admiration when I think of the struggle he's willing to endure to set things right.

We're striving toward a common goal and it feels wrong. Wrong, but so damn right. And entirely necessary.

I push from the floor and ignore the bipolar reactions of my inner voice while I walk down the hall and into the open living room.

Cole is in the kitchen.

Luca is stretched out on the couch, his head poking up to watch me. "You okay?"

His concern hits me like an assault.

"Super," I drawl, making my way into the kitchen. I position myself on the opposite side of the island counter to Cole as he pulls out a frying pan from the drawers beneath, the sound of it colliding with the stove clattering off the walls.

Luca pushes from the couch and walks for the glass doors leading into the fading sunlight. He's leaving me alone with Cole. Alone with confusion.

"Where's he going?" My voice is an agitated mess.

"Outside to make sure we don't miss anything while I'm cooking."

That doesn't ease my concerns as I watch Luca push aside the sheer curtain and disappear outside.

"Have you heard from Luther yet?"

"No." He peels an onion, then begins to dice, his large, tanned hands working in proficient strokes. Perfectly timed. Evenly spaced.

"You're eying the knife like a treasure." He drops the blade to the chopping board and discards his suit jacket, placing it on the kitchen counter behind him. "Have you had a change of heart about killing me?"

I raise my gaze to his, not showing an ounce of how far from the truth he is. "Why don't you hand it over and we can find out?"

He smiles, the expression transforming his face into that of a playful playboy. He's not threatened by me. Not even a little. "Maybe later. After the risotto."

He reclaims the weapon and continues making a dish I've never attempted before. Not that his superior culinary skills are surprising. There isn't much point being a master chef when I'm only serving a table for one.

I watch him in silence, taking in the mastery as he combines ingredients, melting butter, frying the diced onion and some garlic.

He does everything with perfect confidence and synchronicity. He heats rice, prepares shrimp from the fridge, stirs broth in the pan.

He's at home in the kitchen.

He seems almost normal.

Human.

Right now, Cole is an everyday guy, cooking an everyday meal, in an everyday environment.

There's no deception, no deceit, no horror.

All his atrocities are hidden. Shielded from view.

When it comes to adding the wine, he raises the bottle in my direction. "Would you like a glass?"

"Are you kidding?" I glare.

"Too soon?" His lips lift in that taunting kick he's perfected.

"Yeah. Too soon."

Asshole.

I roll my eyes and swivel my stool, diverting my attention to the glass doors, the daylight no longer in existence.

I want Luca to return. Having no buffer between me and Cole's attempts at humor is starting to get to me. I don't want to see him as a man. He needs to remain a criminal. A murderer. But with each passing second, I'm becoming more and more settled.

"After you kill your father, how long do I have to wait before I can go home?"

The rhythmic stirring of the pan doesn't stop; neither does the sound of him adding broth.

"As soon as I can accommodate it."

I turn back to him, raising a brow. "I want specifics, with your word being your bond and all that."

"I'm well aware of your urgency to get away from me." There's a gentleness to his voice. Understanding. I don't like it. "But the aftermath is unpredictable. There's the issue of cleaning up and disposing of evidence. Not to mention getting out of here with all our lives intact."

I ignore his attempt to scare me into submission. "Are we talking hours? Days? Weeks?"

He meets my gaze and holds it. "If I can't get you out of here within twenty-four hours, something has gone wrong, and the least of my concerns will be breaking any promises I've made to you."

Okay, so maybe I'm slightly daunted with the continued mention of danger. It's one thing to stare down the barrel of a life-threatening situation with a gun in-hand and a partner at my side. It's quite another to do it unarmed with the enemy as my only shield. "And how will you dispose of evidence?"

He sighs. "Is it too much to ask for us to enjoy dinner without talking shop?" He reaches behind him, pulling a spoon from the drawer on the far counter. "Here, try this." He scoops up a tiny serve of risotto and reaches over the counter toward me.

I stare at the offering, then him, not trusting either.

"Scared?" he asks.

He's baiting me. I know he is.

My assumption is confirmed when I snatch the spoon and take a taste, bringing his laughter to life.

I gave him exactly what he wanted—retaliation—but I don't care. Not when deliciousness consumes my mouth.

The risotto is good. Really good.

"Do you approve?" He watches me, waiting for praise I'm loath to give.

I take my time, finishing the food slowly before I swallow. "It's..."

"Delicious? Perfect? The best thing you've ever tasted?" He dusts his hands, then wipes them on a tea towel. "You know it's not a sin to pay me a compliment."

"How can you be sure?" I hand back the spoon. "What I was actually going to say is 'surprising.'"

"I own a chain of award-winning restaurants, and you're surprised I can cook?" The look he gives me is condescending.

"Okay, so I made an inaccurate assessment. Sue me."

"Don't worry. It's not your first."

I bite my tongue, unwilling to continue the verbal tennis match.

Maybe I have made false judgments. But so has he. I'm not the righteous bitch who's always peering down from her high horse.

"How long until you're done?" I push from my stool, needing

more space than the few feet of distance the island counter provides.

"Minutes, if not seconds." He pours the last of the broth into the pan and stirs. "Could you do me a favor and get the plates?"

I pretend reluctance isn't eating me from the inside out. I don't want to help him any more than I already am. But they're only plates. And I have to eat.

I make my way to the far wall of cupboards, opening one, then another, and another.

"Here." He closes in behind me, the gentle brush of his presence making me stiffen as he opens the cupboard beside my thigh.

He's there and gone in seconds. Close then far in a brutal case of nerve-tingling whiplash.

"Do you need anything else?" I grab the damn plates and dump them on the counter beside him.

"What kind of scope do I have with my answer? Because that's a loaded question coming from a Fed to someone about to commit murder."

I grind my teeth. I won't let him keep poking me.

I can't.

"Your scope is minimal. I'm talking about cutlery or salt and pepper."

"They're already on the table."

I glance at the eight-seater table near the window with its three place settings close together at one end. Nope. No way. I'm not going to spend unnecessary time with his sly grin haunting my periphery while he watches me salivate over the meal he's made.

"I'll eat in my room."

I'm not being antagonistic or petulant. I *need* space.

It's imperative.

I have to get away from all the confusion.

"Okay." He takes a risotto-filled plate to the oven, opens the door and uses tongs to place shrimp on top. "Here you go."

He holds out the plate and I grasp it, latching on like it's a prize when in reality, it's a temporary escape plan. But he doesn't let go. He holds tight, wordlessly demanding me to meet his gaze.

I don't want to comply. Not when I know cocky arrogance will greet me.

Only the standoff is worse.

He remains close. Silent. Entirely menacing with his calm patience until I raise my gaze and come face-to-face with concern.

"Are you okay?" His brow furrows. His lips thin. "You're tense."

Again, his confidence grates on me. His worry is even worse. He's not asking if I'm tense. He's already made the claim as if he can read me like a book.

"Sure am," I drawl. "Being here is better than Disneyland."

His lips twitch, and I tug on the plate before he hits me with a full-blown grin. Then it's straight to the cutlery drawer for a fork before I'm striding away, into my now dark room.

I leave the lights off, preferring the comfort of the moonlight through the window to soothe me as I eat on the bed.

Each swallow of risotto is an agonizing chore. I detest every time I have to refill my spoon, because the flavor is thoroughly delicious—the shrimp even better—and I don't want to acknowledge Cole is responsible for the brilliance.

I practically lick the plate clean, then glare at it with disgust as I place it on the nightstand.

Why does he have to be entirely normal in some moments and a monster in others? Why can't he pick a path and stick to it?

It hasn't skipped my attention he's never mentioned his concern for the women held captive. His motivation is based on reputation. To remove the perverted taint on his name from his father's actions.

I'm only here because his word can't be trusted, not even with his business associates, drug lords, or whoever else I'm meant to inform about Luther's death.

The world knows he's a liar.

A manipulator.

And I just downed a plateful of his cooking while daydreaming he was my personal chef.

I groan with the guilt and stretch out on the bed, my head on the pillow, with a perfect view of the stars.

I can't remember the last time I simply laid back and watched the night sky. It would've been a lifetime ago, when memories of my past didn't haunt me through the quiet.

Still moments overwhelm me, because the nothingness quickly fills with pain. After all these years, I can't forgive my father. His actions were the catalyst to the end of my happiness.

We'd been the perfect family—me, Mom, and Dad.

Then he changed.

It was as if a switch flipped and my level-headed, smart, caring father turned into a paranoid, possessive stranger who refused to discuss his personality change. The man I'd admired and shaped my future career around became a shell of who I thought he was.

So I found an apartment with some friends and moved out.

My mom soon followed, stating it was better to live with her sister in a rundown house with no money than to stay with a man she no longer recognized.

The separation only made my father worse.

He hounded me to move back home. Phone calls. Text messages. He even showed up at my apartment on a weekly basis.

I held out hope of things changing once I made it into the Bureau. I told myself I'd be able to understand him and the pressures of his position. But by the time I got my badge, he was gone.

Disappeared.

All he left behind were the whispers of him turning to a life of crime, and the one damning photo taken by an anonymous source of my father participating in a money exchange with a well-known Idaho criminal.

The reason for the transaction is still up for speculation.

Everyone has a theory. Some claim it was a drug deal. Others say it was payment for classified information. Nobody knew which way the cash went—from my father to the criminal or vice versa.

I was among many who tried to figure it out.

I spent months trying to clear his name. Each day it grew harder to maintain the workload when he didn't make contact. His trail died with a one-way ticket to Spain.

Not long after, my mother died, too.

Car accident. Heavy impact. Dead at the scene.

I'd been orphaned in the blink of an eye, although, technically my father is still alive.

He makes his presence known every now and then. Sometimes there are unsigned postcards or packages delivered from overseas. And I know he's responsible for the flowers on my mother's grave.

"Nissa?"

I jolt from the memories and rub my nose, wiping away the tingle.

"Are you still down here?" Cole's footsteps approach along the hall.

I close my eyes and remain still. I don't speak, don't even twitch, as he enters the room.

"Nissa?" he whispers.

The bed jolts. I don't know if he's seated on the far edge of the mattress or leaned against it. He's close enough for his aftershave to sink into my lungs.

"I know you're not asleep. I've watched you do the real thing for long enough to know the difference."

I don't bite. I keep my inhales measured. Deep.

The mattress jolts again. More footsteps follow, the pad of his feet coming around to my side of the bed. "You may not want to believe me, but we're on the same side. At least temporarily."

I suck in a longer breath and exhale with a whimper, bringing out my A-game acting skills.

He chuckles, friendly and masculine as hell. It's the most frightening sound I've ever heard because it seems genuine.

"Okay," he drawls. "Have it your way. I just want you to rest assured I'm going to get you home safely."

The plate scrapes across the nightstand, his footfalls recede, and I'm left alone to refute his claim.

There's no resting assured. There's no ability to rest at all.

I lie there through the sound of the kitchen clean-up and his soft conversation with Luca as the night carries on without me. I'm still lying there, plagued with thoughts of him, when they both retreat to their rooms. And I'm still thinking of him when sleep finally drags me under.

. . .

Nightmares wake me. I launch upright, gasping for breath.

The panic-infused dreams were of Cole.

He'd been shielding me from an unseen enemy, one arm wrapped around my shoulder as he fired his gun into the darkness. The betraying feel of his overwhelming protection continues to haunt me as I blink to consciousness and measure my inhales, trying to calm my pulse.

The sound of the gunshot still hums in my ears. The vibration continuous.

No, it's a rumble. A growl.

And it grows. Getting louder.

Shit.

It's not recollection. It's a fucking boat.

I scramble from the bed and rush into the hall. I reach Cole's door, the light from the other side glowing against the carpet.

"Knock. Make sure he's awake."

I gasp and turn to see Luca standing in the open doorway behind me, pulling a shirt over his head.

"It's time." He jerks his chin at me, telling me to hurry up. "Luther's here."

I'm not ready.

I need a weapon. My gun. I'm entirely vulnerable without it.

He disappears into his darkened room, leaving me to rely on autopilot. My hand rises to Cole's door, my knuckles rapping against the wood before I know what I'm doing. I knock. Hard. Over and over. My staccato pulse matches the rhythm of my banging.

There's no response, only the increased volume of the rumble from the approaching boat.

I grasp the handle and push inside, not sure what to expect, but it isn't an empty room. The bedside lamp is on, the room bathed in light, and he's nowhere in sight.

"Cole?" I take a step, swallowing my apprehension. "*Cole?*"

"I'm here." He stalks from the walk-in robe, suit pants the only thing covering his perfect body as he tugs on a collared shirt. "Don't worry, I got a call twenty minutes ago. I'm ready for him."

"You didn't think to wake me?" I'm shaking, fucking trembling from adrenaline.

"I didn't wake you because I didn't want this to happen." He flicks his hand in my direction. "You don't need to panic; we've got time."

"I'm not panicking." I'm not. This is...different.

He shoots me a look of disbelief and walks to the bed, grabbing the suit jacket spread out on the mattress.

"I'm unarmed," I offer in explanation. "I'm vulnerable. If something goes wrong—"

"Nothing will go wrong." He tugs his shirt collar into place, looking entirely suave while he does it. "By this time tomorrow, you'll be on your way home, relaxing in a private jet with a glass of unspiked Beluga while you reminisce on how I completed a task the Bureau failed for years."

My pulse spikes, my face heating from anger and frustration. "And what about you?" I step closer. "Will you be celebrating? Are you entirely immune to what's about to happen?"

His eyes harden. His jaw tics. "You know I'm not."

Do I?

I'd give anything to believe hell is raining down on his shoulders right now, but it's hard when he carries himself so well. He looks as if he's preparing for a day of business, just like any other.

"Scamper into the panic room, little fox, and don't open the door until I come get you."

I stare into those eyes, the ones now devoid of emotion.

He's deflecting. Again. Trying to hide behind animosity.

Has he done this the whole time? Does he poke at me when he's trying to deflect from something important—his fear or regret?

The realization is like a lightbulb bursting in the dull shadows of my mind.

"I won't ask again." He storms for the hall.

Shit.

I've fractured his calm.

He had his game face on, and was ready and waiting for

action, until I came in and fucked it up. I've added to his burden and gained a dose of guilt to go with it.

"Cole, wait."

He pauses, not looking over his shoulder.

I don't want to say anything else. I should leave this how it is in the hope I don't make a bigger mess. But my life is in his hands. And the lives of so many other women, too.

"What?" he growls.

"I'm sorry." The apology mumbles past my lips. It's pathetic, and probably entirely unbelievable, but at least it's out there, clearing my conscience. "I hope everything goes to plan."

17

TORIAN

Her apology makes me stiffen. The wish for good luck just pisses me off.

"Get in the panic room." I stalk for the hall, not looking back. Those pleading eyes and pained voice are putting me off my game.

I yank the bedroom door shut behind me and stand there, my hand clutching the handle as I rest my head against the thick wood.

Where the fuck is the conniving agent with the easily provoked spite? It's like she switched a dial and had the good fortune of finding the exact channel likely to bring me down.

Or was it tact instead of luck?

"You ready?" Luca's voice carries to me from the opening to the living room.

"Yeah." I stalk toward him. "I just need my gun."

He holds out the weapon as I approach, his face stark. I'm well aware he's on edge. He doesn't think I'm capable of killing my own father, and that's okay. He can doubt me all he fucking likes. As long as he's got my back.

I grasp the gun, check the clip, and shove it down the back of my waistband, covering it with my jacket while I continue into the bright light of the open living area.

"It sounds like they're almost here." He follows at my side, staying close.

"Go greet him and make sure everyone else remains on the boat." I keep my tone level, well aware I've got eyes and ears on me now. My audience screams loud through the silence, Anissa's scrutiny shadowing me through the pinhole camera on the far wall.

"I'll have outside under control." He starts for the glass doors. "I've got everything I need. I'll just wait for your signal."

"Good."

He leaves me alone, giving me the necessary space to regroup, yet all I think about is her. I'm caught trying to determine if her actions in my bedroom were a charade or if I've messed with her head enough to make her soft.

I approach the sofa, gliding my hands over the cushioned headrest as I stare at the tiny black dot of a camera disguised in the frame of a local artist's painting.

That woman isn't soft. But she's fucking smart. Brilliant.

I made the mistake of telling her I needed her antagonism—that fucking high horse—to get through this, so she gave me vulnerability and concern instead.

A grin pulls at my lips. The conniving bitch knew exactly what she was doing and the tactic worked. Good for her. Unless it leads me to show my hand with my father; then we're all as good as worm bait.

I focus on the camouflaged dot, sending a silent message to my adversary.

You're not in my head, little fox.

I'm focused.

Locked fucking tight.

This isn't my first rodeo. Switching off emotion comes easily. Why wouldn't it, when I spent my entire childhood being punished whenever my poker face failed?

The labored beat in my chest is adrenaline-based. There's no guilt or time to second guess. I'm done with that.

After tonight, my sisters can gain closure. My family will be safe. The tarnish of someone else's sins won't mark my name. Everything will ease.

Only the nightmares will linger.

I shove from the sofa and walk into the kitchen, turning on the coffee machine. I strengthen my conviction while I wait for the java to pour.

I recall the photos I'd been given by a private investigator. The haunted eyes of women used as objects by men without souls. I've seen one of those haunted faces up close. I've witnessed the sterility staring back at me from someone I love.

That's why my father's actions sicken me to my core.

This is personal. Not business.

This depravity goes against everything he taught me—strength can never be derived from the weak. You only gain power from destroying the strong.

My father should loathe his own actions. Instead, I'm led to believe he thrives on them.

It's a disease. One without a cure.

Death is the only option.

The coffee machine kicks in, the gentle gurgle filling the room as the glass door slides open behind me.

I concentrate on my breathing. My expression. My posture. Luther will scrutinize all of the above. I make sure my mask is perfectly in place, then I turn and hide my surprise at seeing Luca walk inside.

He's not meant to return. His place is on the pier. With my father's guards.

He had one job, and he's already fucked up.

I lock down my annoyance. "Forget something?"

His tight expression says it all.

There's been a change in plan. Something has happened.

I don't react. Don't falter.

I remain coiled. Prepared.

He moves to the side of the doorway, holding back the curtain, and from the darkness my father steps inside, the strong, sure stride of my family's patriarch heading toward me, his smile holding an air of superiority.

There's no fear in his features. Not a hint of concern to explain Luca's presence. Only the thinning hair of a man too old to be causing so many problems, and laugh lines that seem all the more sinister now I know his happiness has been siphoned from the suffering of women.

"It's good to see you, son."

I return his smile and walk toward him. "You, too."

"Although, it would've been better if you didn't look so weary. I gather I caused you a few headaches while I was in the States."

"Nothing I couldn't handle." I hide a frantic search for answers under a calm facade. I scrutinize him head to toe. I analyze his tone. His gait.

But it becomes clear he's not the cause of Luca's unease.

It's not Luther at all.

The gentle pad of feet in his wake are the issue.

The tiny, barely heard steps are torture to my ears.

I quieten my speculation. I refuse to react.

Then a small boy inches out from Luther's shadow and wide eyes blink up at me. The face of innocence threatens to destroy me and send this whole plan crashing to hell. I stare, angered beyond belief while I pretend the world hasn't opened up beneath me in an attempt to swallow me whole.

"I smell coffee." My father stops before me and thrusts out a hand to shake.

It takes all my effort to drag my attention from the child and clasp the offering.

"I'll make you a mug." Luca walks around us, his narrowed gaze pinning me, giving a warning, as he heads toward the coffee machine. "Do you both want one?"

My game face must be slipping.

"Yes. Coffee." I incline my head and release my father's hand.

Now, more than ever, I need to focus, but the child reclaims my attention, his tiny arms wrapping around Luther's thigh for protection. Those eyes. That bone structure. The dark hair.

It's like looking into a mirror from my past. My own reflection stares back at me.

"What have I told you about meeting people?" my father warns.

The boy hangs his head, wisps of mussed hair shrouding the purity of his face. "Never show fear."

Bile churns in my gut, growing toxic.

The gentle innocence in his voice assaults me. It fucking rips me open and tears me to shreds. But the heightened level of my father's betrayal is what slays me.

The boy isn't an infant. He has to be older than five.

Fucking *five*.

Five years of lies. Innumerable months of a secret life lived apart from me and my sisters.

"It looks like somebody has some explaining to do." I meet my father's gaze. "Care to tell me why you brought a kid out here in the middle of the night?"

He winces.

I know what comes next. I've wondered if this day would ever come. My father has been escaping to Greece for years. He's been living another life overseas. Evidently, with another family.

"Here." Luca returns, holding two steaming mugs of coffee. "I'm going to head back outside to keep Robert and Chris company."

He hands over my father's mug, then meets my gaze as he hands me mine. A silent question is asked. He's waiting for insight. Instruction. He doesn't know where to go from here, and I need him to know nothing has fucking changed.

"Good idea." I give Luca a taunting grin. "Get back to work."

There's a pause, the tiniest second where my words sink in, then he nods. "Shout out if you need me."

He returns outside, the whoosh of the clasping glass door confining me in a situation fast escalating out of my control.

I need to reclaim the wheel. I'm not going to nosedive.

This asshole won't get the better of me.

"I've wanted to tell you for a while," he speaks in his usual tone, as if our conversation doesn't require a change in pitch to mark the seriousness. "The time never seemed right."

He sidesteps and places a hand on the child's shoulder, encouraging the boy forward. "Cole, this is Tobias. Your half-brother."

The confirmation hits me hard, but I lock it down.

I anticipated the explanation the moment I stared into the

boy's tiny face. I knew this was coming. I won't let the words strike me with the force of a sucker punch.

"A brother?" I hold everything in check—my calm, my confidence, my fucking temper. My sisters will be beside themselves when they hear the news, but I can't think of them now.

"Hello, Tobias." I force myself to crouch, meeting purity at eye level.

He inches backward. Afraid. Of me.

His recoil is brutal.

"Tobias," my father warns. "What have I told you?"

The boy swallows, his shoulders drooping. "Never show fear."

"Exactly. Now what do you say?"

The kid hesitates, his mouth working like a fish before he finally finds his voice. "It's a pleasure to meet you."

My rage coagulates. My father is the most menacing prick to walk the earth, and yet he's the one who needs to convince my brother to fake a happy introduction.

"The pleasure is all mine." I grin, trying to ease the apprehension staring back at me. "But you must be tired. Does your dad usually wake you during the middle of the night to meet strangers?"

I glance up at Luther, no longer able to face one of his sins.

"Coming out at this hour was a safety precaution. We won't stay long. We can catch up more tomorrow."

I straighten, pushing to my feet, and ignore the spill of coffee escaping the lip of my mug.

"I understand." I swing out an arm, indicating the sofa. "Tell me everything. I want to hear all there is to know about this new brother of mine."

Luther leads the way into the living area, taking the farthest position on the three-seater while I take a seat on the opposite side.

"I learned a long time ago that I'd never be able to fully return to the US," he continues, ignoring Tobias as the boy shuffles onto the cushions, snuggling into his side.

I ignore the kid, too. I have to.

As far as I'm concerned, he doesn't exist.

If I want to succeed, I have to pretend my half-brother is nothing more than a physical deformity that needs to be disregarded for the sake of good manners.

"I had to start over in Greece, which wasn't easy. Being alone, without you and your sisters, was difficult."

"So you found yourself a new family?" I don't let anything other than curiosity mark my words. There's no wounded pride or bitter resentment. I push down all the animosity.

"Of sorts, yes. My business dealings kept me occupied enough, but I needed more."

What he needed was a victim. A mindless slave. Someone to look up to him and take in every lie as if the information were heaven-sent.

"You have your empire in Portland." He wraps his arm around Tobias. "And I needed someone to take over the family business I created in Greece."

That's comforting.

He had another child for the sole benefit of continuing the trade of sex slaves. This little boy was born to torture. How fucking delightful.

The bile pulsing up my throat no longer registers over the hatred coursing through me. I'm done with my father. I'm entirely finished with his manipulations. My continued civility is only for the benefit of gaining information.

"And his mother?" I take a sip of coffee. Slow. Measured.

"She was a complication neither one of us needed."

In other words, she's dead.

Just another victim.

I raise my brows. "You look after him on your own?"

"No." He chuckles. "My harem takes good care of the motherly duties. He's only with me for the business side of things."

I can't help joining in on the laughter. At the absurdity. At the fucking conceited way he boasts his depravity.

"But there's no need for you to feel threatened," he adds. "Not by Tobias, or the new family I'm creating. Nothing between you and I has changed."

I smile through the insults. "I assure you, I'm not threatened in the slightest. I'm just glad to hear you're safe. I wasn't sure what to think when you escaped without giving me any notice of your plan." I throw another one of his betrayals into the air, curious to see how he will hit it back at me.

"That was a tough decision." He cradles his coffee, raising it to his face and the aroma deep into his lungs. "I wanted to keep you as far away from the scrutiny as possible. I can handle my own mess."

I nod. "I know. But don't ever worry about what I can and can't handle. The authorities are the last of my concerns. They won't touch me."

"I used to think the same thing. Unfortunately, alliances change."

"Your business model changed," I correct. I won't let him sit here, blaming his arrest on the shift of treaties when he was the one who threw himself under the bus. He's responsible for his issues. Him and him alone. "There's a limit to police generosity, and you crossed it when you began abducting women from the country."

There's a beat of silence. A shift in his expression.

His lips tighten. His eyes narrow.

"Is that judgment I hear in your voice?" He cocks his head to the side. "I should've known. You made your lack of support clear when you declined my offer to join this part of the family business. What happened to the bloodthirsty entrepreneur I created?"

It's another insult. One that's hard to ignore.

I bite down my ever-growing rage and release the slightest scoff. "My concern is over your safety. It always has been. Drug distribution is different to trafficking women. You need to grease a lot more palms, otherwise you're going to wind up back behind bars."

"The only reason I was there in the first place was because of Richard. If he hadn't died, I never would've returned to Portland."

Never.

Would've.

Returned.

Not to see me. Or his daughters. Or his granddaughter.

223

He cut ties without us even knowing.

"But, son," He leans back, resting one arm along the head rest, exuding supremacy. "The benefits to my recent adventures go above and beyond anything the drug trade could provide. I'm living a new way of life. I'm a fucking king over here. Men want to be me. Women beg to sleep with me. Nothing could be better."

"Women beg to sleep with you?" I hide my skepticism behind another sip of coffee.

"They spread their legs eagerly." He smirks. "Because the alternative is far worse. My women can either take turns fucking me once or twice a day in an opulent setting, or I can send them back to work with the rest of the slaves where they will be brutalized once or twice an hour."

On instinct, I glance at the kid.

It pains me to find no surprise or confusion in his features. The topic of conversation isn't out of the ordinary. And I guess that shouldn't shock me. If his upbringing is at all like mine, he's probably heard his father talk uncensored about brutal crimes since the moment he was born.

"Don't worry about him." Luther ruffles my brother's hair. "He's not new to this. He's actually just like you when you were little—enthusiastic and excited to learn everything his papa has to teach."

Bless the naivety of Torian children.

"Speaking of teaching," I drawl. "How are you laying low here? Where do you keep these women without drawing attention?"

He shrugs. "They're moved often. If you change your mind and decide to come onboard, you won't need to worry about things like that. We're entirely covered."

It's my turn to kick back, leaning against the armrest while I eye him in contemplation. "What sort of money are we talking?"

"Are you thinking about changing your mind on my offer?" His brows raise, along with the curve of his lips. "You would love it, son. I know you've always had money, but the pussy and power are addictive."

He's ignorant if he doesn't think I've always had all three.

"I've been contemplating the pros and cons." I suck in a deep breath and let it out on a tired sigh. "I'm not entirely convinced the risk is worth the complication."

His smile grows. I can almost see a fucking twinkle in his eye. "I knew you'd come to your senses sooner or later. You've always been a chip off the old block."

"That's never been in doubt."

"I wasn't so sure," he muses. "For a while, I thought you may have become a disappointment. And I'll be honest, it concerned me. We've always been a family business. We work together, and you not having my back was an insult."

"It was an insult to have this business running under my nose for years without telling me," I counter.

"That was your conflict?" His face brightens. He's just found the pot at the end of the rainbow. "I thought you had moral issues. I actually feared you'd turned soft."

"I'm neither soft nor moral," I drawl.

"Well, regardless, the secrecy was your uncle's decision. You two rarely saw eye to eye, and because it was his brainchild, he insisted we keep it to ourselves."

The mention of Richard always makes my hackles rise, but to learn he's the reason I was kept in the dark is a fucking sucker punch. Even after death, that piece of shit has proven he can fuck with my life.

"That's all in the past now." I let the coffee soothe me, the hot liquid beating back the rage.

"Along with my disappointment." We drink in unison. Slow sip after slow sip. "When I got word of your arrival, I couldn't deny my pride for you returned."

"I've always been one flight away; all you needed to do was reach out." Maybe if he'd tried, this shit never would've happened. I could've got in his head before Richard. I would've diverted the taint to our family name, not letting it start in the first place.

"I'm not referring to your visit. I'm talking about the prize you brought along with you."

I stiffen.

The skin at the back of my neck prickles.

I hold myself in check, barely able to control the threadbare wisps of my anger at his knowledge of Anissa.

It's not that I didn't anticipate the capabilities of his spies. I knew my arrival was under surveillance. I just didn't anticipate how strongly I would want to protect her.

"A woman bound and sedated." He smirks. "You have no idea how pleased that makes me."

I snicker, because how else should I respond to a pride-filled moment surrounding the abduction of an unwilling victim?

"Where is she?"

I hold my smile in place. I nail that motherfucker down, not letting it budge an inch. "In my bed. Passed out."

I face him the way he's always taught me to face a challenge—without emotion or investment.

Anissa is nothing.

Not a woman. Or an asset. Or a fucking addiction.

My concern for her doesn't exist.

"Passed out?" He clucks his tongue, his eyes dancing with excitement. "Keeping them conscious and fighting is the best part."

I laugh and contemplate pulling the gun from my waistband.

The thirst for bloodshed beats through my veins. The desire to claim retribution for all his transgressions is a pulse throbbing through every organ, pummeling every limb.

But that kid.

That fucking kid is still here, staring up at me, taking in the horrors like a vacuum.

"Her enthusiasm to escape has grown tiring." I finish the last of my coffee and place the mug on the table. "Sometimes I need a break."

"Now your weariness makes more sense."

"I assure you, it's all been in good fun."

He chuckles again, and the pride I see in his face sickens me. He's never looked at me this way. Judgment has always accompanied his praise. Bitterness has come hand in hand with each of his compliments.

Until now.

He's finally seeing me as a worthy son to his inheritance when all I want to do is spit in the face of what he has to offer.

"I assume you've made preparations for when you grow tired of her."

I incline my head. "Yes. She's going to take a long walk off a short pier."

"Good idea." He nudges Tobias in the ribs. "People disappear easily out here, don't they, son?"

The kid nods, the movement wrought with hesitation.

It's fucking draining to watch the boy. He's this innocent sponge being filled with brutality. At what point will the damage become permanent?

I can't take my eyes off him as my father fills the passing minutes with whimsical stories about the women he's conquered. The beauties from Spain who were barely in their teens. And those from the US who are always harder to break because they're used to a life of freedom and unending human rights.

I sprinkle the conversation with my approval, convincing him I'm impressed while the need for revenge builds behind my ribs.

"And how are your sisters?" he asks. "I've told Tobias about them. Stella, too. I'm hoping you'll convince them all to come visit us soon."

"Of course." I don't comment on the ease with which he switches from the topic of rape to settle on his daughters and granddaughter. I don't let him know every breath he takes makes me grind my teeth harder. "All you need to do is tell me a suitable date and I'll have them on the jet."

He nods, seeming appeased, while Tobias yawns.

"Your boy needs sleep." I jerk my head in the kid's direction. "Do you want to set him up in one of the spare rooms?"

"No. I never planned to stay long. I should get him back to bed." Luther pushes to his feet and Tobias follows, dragging his weary frame upward to stick to his father's side. "We can catch up properly tomorrow."

"Okay." I stand and follow them both into the open space away from the sofa.

It's time to act.

Now or never.

Everything slows to the precious seconds between each thunderous pound of my pulse. The sound echoes in my ears, becoming a driving force. All I need to do is move the kid out of the way.

"You can come for a tour of the house." My father turns to face me. "And I can take you to one of the functions I host on a regular basis. You can see my business in action." He pauses, a grin spreading from ear to ear. "Bring your toy. She might enjoy the learning experience."

"I think she'd disagree," I grate. "The little bitch is hard enough to handle already."

"Like I said, that's the best part." He steps forward, holding out his hand. "I'll teach you a trick or two."

"And I'll appreciate the insight." I reach for him, holding his gaze as our palms clasp.

We won't connect again.

This will be the last shake.

The final goodbye.

I sink into the moment, letting the taint of his atrocities build my conviction. I recount all the betrayal he tried to hide, all the lies he used to cover the bullshit he caused.

Then it's over, his grip falling from mine to make way for progress.

I turn my focus to Tobias and crouch. "Goodbye, little brother." I hold out my hand, needing him to make the connection so I can drag him out of the firing line.

Instead, he shrinks into himself. Those tiny arms cling tight to my father's leg. His wide, petrified eyes start their own attack, beating into me with force, slamming my conscience.

I'm sure he knows what I'm about to do. Call it a sixth sense or sibling intuition, but this terrified child is looking back at me with so much fucking fear I can barely think through the building guilt.

"Come on, little man." I use all my strength to add humor to my tone. "You don't want to shake your brother's hand?"

I detest the sound of my own voice. I fucking hate it. I'm trying to coax a kid into a nightmare. My own fucking brother.

"*Tobias*," Luther snaps.

The kid jumps.

"No." I hold up a hand. "Don't push him."

Don't. Fucking. Push.

Goddammit.

Those eyes tell me he's already been through enough. Not just today, but every day since his birth. I can't add to his trauma. I fucking can't.

Not tonight.

"Is everything okay, Cole?"

I clench my teeth at my father's question. Every inch of me revolts in repulsion, not at him, but at myself. I've become a plague on my family.

A pathetic curse.

A fucking failure.

"I'm sorry." I can't stop the words from grating as I hang my head. "I guess the shock of having a brother has finally hit me."

"Don't apologize." Luther steps forward, clasps my shoulder, and gives a squeeze. His comfort is the worst punishment I've ever endured. It's hell on earth. Fucking purgatory. "Family is everything, son."

18

ANISSA

I STARE AT THE SCREEN IN CONFUSION, MY CHEST restricting.

I've second guessed myself so many times since Luther arrived that the reaction is a living, breathing thing behind my ribs. It's all there is. All I know.

I'd expected a vicious bloodbath. The carnage over and done with before I could think to make a protest.

I didn't anticipate my conscience having time to run havoc.

But it has.

It still does.

I stood here, leaned toward the screen showing the perfect view of the child in the living room, my hands gripping the counter, my throat closing over. Some of their conversation didn't make it to my ears. Their voices were too low or my heartbeat pounded too loud.

But the tones were coated in civility.

Everything was calm.

A planned family reunion.

I can't tell truth from fiction. Fact from deviously deceptive lie.

Cole is such a skilled manipulator I'm unsure if he's playing his father, or still continuing to play me. He'd barely reacted to the news of his half-brother. He took in Tobias's introduction as if it were a weather report for a city he never planned to visit.

There was no emotion. Very little interest. At least from my view on the pixilated screen.

I can only tell myself he must have known about the boy's existence prior. Tobias has to be what Cole referred to when he said there was more to Luther than the information in the FBI database.

Then he shared coffee with the man and talked shop. He sat there, enjoying a fucking beverage when he was meant to be claiming a life.

I remained riveted and horrified while they held an uncensored conversation in front of an innocent child. And the poor boy listened. Unmoving. Barely blinking. His tiny body nestled close beside Satan himself.

Cole only added to my confusion when he crouched to shake the boy's hand, then hung his head, claiming to be overwhelmed. Through the entire encounter, I wasn't able to get a read on him. There was no rage or intent to punish for me to bank my hopes on.

He acted as if he was going to join his father's business, not take it down. But was it an act?

The only words ringing true are those I should fear. The ones outlining me as a plaything.

A toy.

She's going to take a long walk off a short pier.

Like hell I will.

I watch with building dread as Cole stands and Luther escorts the child toward the glass doors.

I wait for something to happen. And wait. And wait.

All Cole does is stiffen while the sheer curtains are pulled aside and his father and brother disappear outside.

It's over.

There's no bloodshed. No victory or horror.

Cole has no plan to kill his father. Maybe he never did. And with the child's arrival, I'm not sure if I should be relieved or traumatized.

I don't know what the hell any of this means, and the questions only multiply when Cole reaches behind his back and pulls the gun from his waistband.

I swear his hand trembles as he begins to pace, raising the gun to tap, tap, tap the side of the barrel against his temple in an agitated rhythm.

His movements become hostile. The mask of calm disappears, making way for an expression of pure fury. The lack of emotion I've witnessed for long minutes changes with the force of a tsunami.

He's purging. Succumbing. Letting down his guard.

Then he stalks for the doors, slamming the glass panel aside and escaping out of view.

"Goddammit." I reach for the keyboard and tap buttons to cycle through the camera angles. I need to get eyes on him, but there's nothing. No more images of anyone.

Time stands still as I wait for gunfire to erupt.

The small room becomes a cell, keeping me from reality.

Pressure bears down on me. Pure panic builds.

What's going to happen to that little boy?

I switch off the screens with a hard slam of my palm against the wall switch and enter the pin-code to open the panic room door. The barrier to the world glides open in the silence and I step forward, waiting in the entry, each second without sound acting as painful torture until a boat engine roars to life in the distance.

My mind runs wild with speculation.

Is Luther dead? Did I miss the sound of a kill shot?

The purr of the boat grows distant, the rumble lessening when the familiar thump of footsteps enters my ears. The slam of a cupboard follows. The smash of glass. Then more pounding footfalls.

I was told to remain in here until Cole came to get me, but that's an impossibility. I can't stand by a moment longer.

I tiptoe from the walk-in robe, through the bedroom, and slowly down the hall. Nobody is waiting for me as I peek my head around the wall to see into the living room. The glass doors remain open, the curtains billowing in the breeze.

My steps are cautious as I start toward the glass and slip outside onto the tiled pool area.

The boat is now a far-off grumble in the night. A rumbling purr. That's all there is.

I can't hear Cole or Luca.

Not the child or his monster of a father.

I increase my pace around the pool, but the snap of a twig makes me stop in my tracks. I swing around, fists clenched, poised, and ready to fight.

Luca steps out from the darkness beside the house, his face stony. "Get back inside."

"What happened?"

"Get your ass back inside."

I lower my hands and my voice. "Are they still here?"

"No. But you need to leave Cole alone." He starts toward me, his posture threatening.

"No. I want answers."

"And you'll get them. Later. For now, you have to give him space."

That's not good enough. I don't have the patience to wait any longer.

I've done everything they asked of me. I hid in that room. I witnessed what I was led to believe would be a victory for the greater good. And now I want to know if the bad guys won, whether that includes Cole or not.

"Where is he?"

"Leave him alone," he barks. "You're not going to get what you want from him."

I disagree.

I'm sick of being a puppet. A *toy*.

I glance toward the trail leading to the pier, then back at Luca.

His expression tightens, letting me know what I need is down that path. All that remains here is irritation and impatience.

I can't take it anymore—the games, the psychological warfare. I need to know what's going on, consequences be damned.

I start for the path, Luca's frustrated snarl haunting my escape. "Don't say I didn't warn you."

My determination increases with each step into shrouded darkness. The house lights don't touch this part of the island. I'm well aware I'm walking toward a gun-toting criminal. But I don't stop.

As the trees and shrubs clear, I see the pier with Cole sitting at the far end, the moonlight gleaming down on his dark suit.

I continue toward him, measuring my approach, slowing just a little. "Is this the short pier I'm going to take a long walk off?"

"Not now, Nissa." His tone is brutal. Raw. "Go back to the house."

He grabs a liquor bottle from between his thighs and takes a long pull. When he lowers the bottle, his shoulders slump along with it. He places the liquor back between his thighs and hangs his head, making short wisps of hair frame the side of his face.

This isn't the fearless man I watched on the television screens.

This guy is something else.

Someone else.

"Yes, I failed, if that's what you're waiting to hear." He takes another drink and follows it up with a rough swipe of his hand over his mouth.

His devastation seeps into me, touching every nerve.

"I couldn't do a damn thing," he snaps. "Not with that kid staring up at me. God knows he's going to need a lifetime worth of therapy without having to witness his father's murder."

Puzzle pieces fall in place, but not enough to create a clear picture. "You didn't expect the child?"

He bites out a bitter laugh. "I didn't expect his existence, let alone his arrival."

My stomach clenches. I'm pretty sure the reflex is instigated from pity.

It doesn't stop me from despising the instinctual reaction and becoming a slave to it in the same breath. I'm torn apart. My sympathy and self-preservation collide.

"You made the right choice." The comfort is whispered from my lips. "You'll get another chance to deal with your father."

He raises the bottle, the pull of liquid long and dangerous.

I inch forward, reach the end of the pier, and sit a foot away. A wall of darkness surrounds me, both visually and emotionally. There's no hope. No confidence. Only black. "But drowning your sorrows isn't going to help."

"Like hell it won't."

"I'm serious." I reach for the bottle, spreading my hand around the glass. "It's just a minor setback."

"Finding out I have a brother is a minor setback?" He glances at me, his eyes stark, the inky depths gripping in their intensity as he tries to reclaim the liquid solace.

"The shock will wear off." I tug the bottle, pulling it from his grip. "The least you can do is share."

I take a large gulp of my own and wince as the scotch burns my throat, searing everything in its path.

He doesn't watch my struggle. Instead, he returns his stare to the water, letting me leisurely drink my fill until liquor warms my belly.

"How could I not have known?" His question is murmured. Barely spoken. "I had no fucking idea. All this time."

"I think people rely too heavily on the bond of blood," I whisper.

His uncharacteristic show of vulnerability gets to me. This criminal Goliath is on his knees, and I struggle to react the way an FBI agent should. "Some expect it will excuse any behavior. That despite betrayal and deception, all will be forgiven because they're family."

That's the only reason I can give for my father's actions. He must have thought I would let his criminal activity slide because we share DNA.

He thought wrong.

"Maybe you're right," he murmurs. "For once."

I smile, seeing the thin layer of his humor through the pain.

"Just when I think he can't stoop any lower." He shakes his head. "*Christ.* He has a new fucking family and didn't even think to tell the one he already had." He shoots me a look. "That kid had to be at least five or six, right?"

"I'm not sure. Kids aren't my schtick. But he did seem awfully young."

"Young, but too fucking old to have been hidden this long."

I wince. "Betrayal is always worse when it comes from someone you trust."

He bites out a bitter laugh. "I wish I could say this is the worst thing he's ever done, but we both know that's a lie."

"This is different. The crimes he's previously committed are against other people. I understand how hard it must be to have something aimed at you this time."

"Like I said," he mutters, "this isn't the first."

The conversation dies on the breeze. He doesn't offer more insight, and I don't push for an explanation.

We remain there, silent, as we share the bottle of liquor until footsteps approach from behind.

"How are things going out here?" Luca walks down toward us, stopping behind me. "I gather you forgot my invitation to the party." The words are somber, half-hearted banter to skirt all the doom and gloom.

"There's no party here." Cole holds up the bottle. "Only fucking resentment and a wealth of complication."

"We'll figure it out." Luca sits on the side of the pier closest to me and dangles his legs over the edge. "Have you got any idea what you want to do from here?"

"No. But I'll be taking Luther up on his offer to meet tomorrow. Any insight is good insight."

"We," Luca clarifies, handing back the bottle. "You're not going anywhere on your own."

I don't move my attention from the water. I act unfazed by the change in schedule. "Where does that leave me?"

"On the jet, headed for home." Cole's response comes without pause.

"Excuse me?" I stiffen, caught in shock.

Hours ago, I would've been excited at the prospect of freedom. Now, I'm not so sure.

"I thought I had to be here." I turn to face him. "What happened to me being a witness?"

"Things changed."

"Like what?" Luca asks.

Cole throws back the scotch, his gulp audible, before he lowers it with a sigh. "He knows she's here."

That part isn't a surprise. I already heard Luther talk about me. What I didn't hear was a problem.

"We covered our asses on arrival," Luca adds. "I thought we bound and sedated her for this exact reason—to stifle Luther's suspicion."

"That was the reason?" I narrow my gaze on Cole. "My traumatic introduction to the Greek Islands was done out of strategy?"

Not a blatant show of Cole's power? Not for his sadistic pleasure?

"God forbid you ever think I do something for your safety," he mutters. "If you willingly walked off the jet and word got back to my father, he wouldn't have stopped until he found out every last thing about you. You needed to look like a random victim."

"So why didn't you tell me this to begin with?" I grab the scotch from him, the dark liquid reaching the middle of the bottle. "You made me believe you did it for fun."

"No, I didn't." He snatches the liquor before I can raise it to my mouth. "I made it clear I didn't mean to hurt you. You chose not to listen."

With a few brief sentences I'm cast back to my arrival, seeing everything through different eyes.

"You heard the way he spoke about you. He doesn't consider you a threat. He thinks of you as a toy, which isn't something I considered. It means if he ever gets his hands on you, he won't want to kill you; he'll want to play."

Luca huffs out a defeated breath. "If she goes home, who's going to tell your sisters about Luther?"

Yet again, I'm confused.

"Tell your sisters what about Luther?"

Cole mutters under his breath, the words indecipherable as he pushes to his feet. "I'm done with this shit. We can talk about it tomorrow." He stalks for the path leading to the house, taking the bottle with him.

"What is he talking about?" I rush to my feet, my head swirling with the sudden movement.

"Fucking hell." Luca pivots, grabbing my thighs in a vain attempt to stabilize me. "How much have you had to drink?"

"Less than Cole." I shove at his shoulders and struggle to get my bearings. "What do you mean about his sisters? What do they have to be told?"

His face hardens. "You heard him. We'll talk about it tomorrow."

"No. We'll talk about it now. I'm sick of fighting and clawing to get any sort of clarity. I want the truth."

Luca crosses his arms over his chest. His mouth clamps tight. He's preparing to play hard ball.

"Luca, please." My tone is far from pleading. I can't hide my frustration. "I thought I was here to be a witness for anyone who believes Cole isn't capable of succeeding with Luther."

"You are." He speaks through clenched teeth.

"Then what does this have to do with his sisters?"

He crosses his arms over his chest. Unmoving. Barely blinking.

"Fine. I'll ask Cole." I move to walk around him only to have him jump to his feet in front of me, blocking my path.

"No, you won't."

"Watch me." I elbow his ribs, making him sidestep, then prepare myself for retaliation.

Nothing happens. He just stands there, glaring at me.

I nudge him again, trying to create enough room to get by him, but this time he doesn't stumble.

"I could do this all night." He holds up his arms. "I don't even have to use my hands."

I laugh. "What about your balls? Do you need to use them?"

I grab his shoulders and raise my knee, pretending to mount a full-scale attack on his dick. When he twists away to counter the move, I slip by him and sprint down the pier.

"Fucking hell, Anissa."

I make it onto the pebbled path and glance over my shoulder, finding him still standing on the wooden planks, not bothering to give chase.

He's watching me, arms at his sides, his face shadowed but not enough to hide his frustration. "Don't be stupid. He's drunk as fuck. That never works in anyone's favor."

I don't care.

I turn away and stumble along the rest of the path.

Truth be told, the scotch may have affected me in a not-so-subtle way, too. The liquor has cleared the deafening static from my head. I can process now. At least a little easier than before.

I don't like what I'm thinking though.

I don't want these things in my head to be real.

Not if it means Cole isn't the nasty piece of work I've always known him to be.

I make my way to the house, step inside, and flick the billowing curtain out of the way. "Cole?"

He's nowhere in sight. Not in the living area or the kitchen.

I slide the glass door shut, then lock it, buying myself some time before Luca follows.

"Cole?"

Again, no answer.

I stalk down the hall, toward his closed bedroom door, and fling it open.

He's walking from the robe to the bed in nothing but black boxer briefs with that bottle still in his hand, only a few inches of liquid floating at the bottom.

The scotch doesn't seem to have worked its magic on his brilliance. He's still a vision of masculinity. All muscles and strength.

"Do you have a problem with knocking?" He clatters the bottle down on the bedside table, glaring his anger my way.

"Do you have a problem with wearing clothes?"

"I'm going to bed." He grabs the covers, pulling them back. "Unless you plan on joining me, get out."

"I'll leave as soon as you confirm I'm here for no other reason than to inform your sisters about Luther's death."

His jaw tics. His knuckles clench tight in the bedding.

"Holy shit." I stare at him, seeing the powerful man with fresh eyes.

I'm not here to recount a murder to business associates or criminal masterminds. I'm here to let his sisters down gently.

"Why didn't you just tell me instead of dragging me through hell?"

"One, because you wouldn't have believed me. Two, I needed to sedate you in case my father's spies were watching, and you never would've given consent." He grins, the expression entirely sinister. "And three, it was more fun this way."

"You made me believe I was here to tell your drug connections."

"Bullshit." He throws down the covers and stalks toward me. "Don't go blaming me for your misconceptions. You and your high horse made those assumptions all on your own."

He's a wall of superiority. Tense muscles. Tight expression. Hard eyes.

He's almost scary, yet so entirely strong and unyielding I can't help admiring his conviction.

"So I've been wrong about you all this time?" My question is the slightest taunt. "I misconceived you as a murderous, conniving criminal when really you're, what? A saint? I don't get it. I don't get *you*. One minute, you're taking pleasure in manipulating me; the next, you claim you won't hurt me. It's clear you're hiding. I just don't know what you're hiding from."

"I'm not hiding shit." He doesn't stop his approach, not until we're toe to toe, almost chest to chest. "Your problem is that you can't fit me into one of your perfect little boxes. You want to label me as right or wrong, good or bad, moral or fucking corrupt, when all those tags apply at any given time."

He glares at me, the level of judgment sinking deep. "I don't follow your legal system, but I'm true, without fault, to the values of my world. I'm not heartless or merciless. I may not give a flying fuck about strangers, but I would die for my family and anyone in my inner circle."

He's so close, a mere whisper of space between us. His breath brushes my lips, the hint of scotch sinking into my lungs.

"I didn't tell you about my sisters because shielding them from outsiders is what I do. It's all I've ever done. I keep them safe. I maintain their privacy."

"Do they know what's happening?" I swallow over my drying throat as his intensity wraps around me. Tight. I'm almost suffocated. "I heard you on the phone to Keira. You lied about being in Greece."

He takes another step and I'm forced to backtrack, bumping into the door, making it swing shut behind me.

"She knows what will eventually happen." He scoffs out a laugh. "In fact, she wants Luther dead more than I do. That's why she can't know when it's going to happen. I don't want her or Decker involved."

Decker.

The reminder of the man who lost a sister to Luther's perversions washes over me like a bucket of ice-cold reality.

"Did you ever find out more information on Penelope?"

"You've asked enough of me tonight." His lip curls, the progression slow and vindictive. "I'm done with the subtle interrogation. And don't think, for one second, I've forgotten you tried your best to get us all killed tonight."

"Excuse me?" I take another backward step, my ass bumping into the door. "What the hell did I do?"

"I noticed how you tried to sabotage my plan, little fox. Do you really think I believed all your soft, emotional bullshit when the boat arrived?"

My cheeks heat, the shame from my needy outburst taking over my face.

"I told you I brought you here to inspire determination." He raises his arms, placing his hands on either side of my head, caging me in. "You knew your spite was my motivator. So you flipped the script, thinking I'd falter with the batting of your lashes. But I'll tell you right now, I'm not that fucking weak."

I don't answer.

I'm embarrassed to admit my emotional display wasn't a scheme. There was no sabotage. None at all.

"You're not the agent I thought you were." He leans closer, the glaze of intoxication making those dark eyes seem questioning. "The spiteful Anissa Fox isn't as tactical as she thinks."

"That wasn't a tactic." I tilt my chin higher, my shame and frustration colliding. "I've almost always told you the truth."

He laughs. "Almost always?"

"It's better than what you've given me. You can blame me for misconceptions all you like, but we both know you've deliberately tried to steer my thoughts in one direction. You've wanted me to fear you all along."

"If I wanted your fear bad enough, I'd have it."

A shiver skitters through me. It's not born from apprehension or panic. It's something different. Something I desperately have to ignore.

"I knew how important tonight was. I wasn't stupid enough to play games." The admission doesn't lessen the tingle searing through my veins. "I told you I'd do whatever you needed me to do, and I'm still committed to that promise."

He raises a brow, looking down his nose at me like I've done to him a million times over.

"I'm not lying. I agreed this was the best option for Luther, and I don't want to leave until it's done."

"Too bad." His jaw hardens. "You'll be on the jet at sunup."

His refusal acts like a match to a mountain of kindling. The tingle I'd been consumed with turns to vibrations. Heart palpitations. I'm sick of him throwing his weight around. It's fucking exhausting.

"No, I won't." I straighten my shoulders, giving him an up-close-and-personal view of my defiance. There's so much tightly coiled fury in his features and all it does is fuel me, making me buzz. "I'm not going anywhere until this is over. Not unless you plan on drugging me again."

"You'll do exactly what I want, when I want. Now get your drunk ass to bed."

My blood boils. I try to bottle it, to keep it deep down inside, but the spite bursts from me. "Yours or mine?"

His brows shoot skyward. I'm sure mine do the same.

It's the alcohol talking. The liquor puts words in my mouth. Emotions in my veins. And despite the danger, the temporary shock written all over his face is worth it.

"Cute." He eyes me, reading me, the glaze of intoxication bearing down like a threat. "Real fucking cute."

His gaze drops to my mouth, making my lips burn under the

attention. "You're playing with fire. If I were you, I wouldn't push boundaries when you don't know what's on the other side."

"What are you going to do? Take a page out of your father's book?"

His nostrils flare and his hand shoots up, grasping my throat.

History repeats itself. The feral stare. The blinding fury. And yet again, that hold is gentle. Non-threatening.

"Who's to say I won't? Like father, like son, right?" His breaths come in heaves, his chest rising and falling with the aggression. "You don't understand me, little fox. We both know I could destroy you."

I've pushed too far. I've made a mistake. I know this. I know it just as well as I know day follows night. And still, I want more.

It's as if self-preservation no longer exists. Common sense has evaporated.

"You could, but you won't." I raise my chin in defiance. "I don't know if you wish you were more like your father, or if you're glad you're not. But it's clear you're hurt by what he's done. I didn't notice it while he was here because your poker face is crazy-brilliant. But I noticed after. I saw your pain. I still see it now."

His aggression falters. His eyes flare with sorrow before quickly falling back under the shroud of anger.

"Leave. Get out of my fucking room, and don't disturb me again." He doesn't move. Doesn't allow me the escape he demands.

He confuses me, telling my head one thing while my churning insides announce something else entirely.

Neither reaction makes sense.

"I don't want to leave," I admit. "I want to see this through."

I'm not sure if I'm still talking about his father. About those women. About victory for the greater good.

"It isn't safe." He doesn't break our gaze, not even when his expression falls, exposing a mass of regret. He releases his hold on my neck, his fingers grazing my shoulder, my hip, for an instant of pure friction.

It's the liquor.

The buzz.

I can't help it. My body reacts without my consent.

Before I can think about the consequences, my hand rises to his face, my touch brushing the light stubble along his jaw.

He flinches, but doesn't pull away. He remains close, one hand pressed against the door, one foot between mine.

"You're drunk." He snatches my wrist, holding it in place. "You'll regret this in the morning."

"I already regret it now. That doesn't mean I can stop." I raise my other hand, gliding my fingers gently along the softness of his cheekbone, all the way down to the side of his mouth.

I don't know what's wrong with me. But it's clear something is loco-fucking-bat-shit in this head of mine because this devil of a man seems entirely redeemable.

I see the turmoil in his eyes, the battle waging war beneath his impenetrable exterior. I feel his conflict. His agony. I understand all the good he's tried to do through an entirely bad situation.

"Who are you?" I whisper.

"You know who I am." His grip tightens. "Don't let the alcohol cloud your judgment."

He's right. I do know. And the alcohol is.

I know both facts as if they're tattooed across my chest, and yet my heart overrules them, twisting and turning in the need for more.

More insight.

More connection.

More sizzle.

"How do you live like this? How do you do what you do?" I sound like Dr. Seuss, the words rolling off my tongue with the tiniest of slurs. "Explain it to me."

"Tomorrow."

"No." I drag my thumb along the exquisite softness of his lower lip. "Now."

"*Niss.*" My nickname is a warning. "I've had more to drink than you. I'm not playing games when I say my hesitation won't last forever."

Heat takes over my stomach and descends, pooling in a place that should be entirely off-limits to this man's effect.

I struggle against my body's reaction. I mentally fight for

stability. But the battle is too hard. *Everything* is too hard when I've never seen anything more beautiful. More stark and brutal and gorgeous.

My heart pounds behind my sternum, the beat carrying heavily to my ears. It's intuition and madness. Passion and impulse. Insanity and picture-perfect clarity.

I glide my hand over his chin, down to his neck to grasp his throat. My hold is like his has always been. Gentle. Soft. The only difference is mine doesn't elicit a reaction.

I grip tighter, harder, my fingers becoming a vise with each passing second, until I finally get what I want—a deep swallow beneath my palm.

He's not unaffected by me.

Whatever I'm feeling, he feels it, too.

"You don't want to do this." His words haunt me, the warning a kindness.

"Johnnie Walker tells me I do." My mind is consumed with those lips. My heart pounds with the thrill of just one taste.

He grins, the expression subtle, yet mocking. "Since when does Johnnie Walker cost eight hundred dollars a bottle?"

"You've got expensive taste." I can barely hear my own voice. It's breathy. A whisper.

"Exquisite." He releases my wrist. His hand moves to the sensitive skin below my ear, his thumb trailing back and forth along my carotid. "I have exquisite taste, Nissa."

My nerves catch on fire, sizzling, blazing.

"Are you trying to make yourself believe I'm a good guy?" He leans into me, hip to hip, his thigh between my thighs. "Do you want me to pretend, too?"

Everything is hard. His arms. His chest. His cock.

The thick length of his erection presses into my abdomen, making it difficult to breathe. My nipples bead. Every inch of my skin tingles. A flicker of fireworks skims along my senses.

"I don't know." I can already predict the aftermath. The mistake I'm about to make will haunt me forever, yet in this moment I'm willing to pay the price.

I can't deny myself.

I lean in, my mouth a breath away from his. A mere gasp. Then I steal the gentlest touch of connection.

It's the most delicate dance of pleasure. His lips are kind, placating, all the gentleness at odds with his ferocity.

I taste the scotch on his tongue. I drown in the flavor.

A hazardous thrill shoots through me. The temptation sinks into my marrow.

I kiss him harder, dropping both hands to his hips to grip the waistband of his underwear, and drag him tighter against me.

I grow dizzy with adrenaline. Enslaved by bliss.

I tingle everywhere—arms, legs, pussy. There isn't an inch of my skin unaffected by this man. At least until he pulls back, his eyes narrowed to spiteful slits.

"You've had your fun," he growls. "Now it's time to stop pretending you're not making a dangerous fucking mistake."

19

TORIAN

I inch back, getting a front-row seat to the indignant flare of her eyes.

She has no idea of the trouble she's getting into.

How deep the water is.

How easy it would be to drown.

She cocks her head, her expression bathed in liquor-induced ignorance. "*Dangerous* mistake?"

I would've bet good money on her scampering away. Even when I held back on the reins, not kissing her the way an indignant woman deserves to be kissed. But I could've sworn the hard press of my dick would've woken her up to where this is going to go if she doesn't run.

"You heard right," I growl. "This isn't high school. I don't fool around then walk away."

"And I do?" She pushes at me, punctuating her statement.

I clench my teeth, trying hard not to show how much I fucking love her bite.

Her animosity fuels me. Invigorates. Every inch of my skin is alive, waiting for her touch. Every nerve is raw and exposed.

"Stop provoking me." She shoves again and I backtrack with the spike of my pulse. "Stop messing with my head."

I want to beg her to do the same. To stop pushing buttons. Poking demons.

"You're fucking insane," I grate. "You've got no idea what you're doing."

She shoots me a grin. A fucking taunt a smile likely to trigger the strongest of men. "Don't I?" She shoves again. And again. And again.

I take retreating steps with her aggression, for *her* safety. For *her* protection. "Nissa," I growl.

She slams those palms into my chest, her sultry lips curving. My own burn in response, demanding another taste of her sweetness.

I plant my feet. "Do you really want to play, little fox?"

She shoves again.

This time, I don't budge.

I straighten my shoulders, square my jaw. I look straight down my nose at her, glaring.

She inches closer, sliding up to me. Hip to hip. Chest to chest.

I clench my fists, gnash my molars. I breathe slowly, try to force a sense of calm, but that shit is nowhere to be found.

"I think," she murmurs, "maybe you're the one who's scared about the danger of fucking with me."

Her spite. Her confidence. Her fucking instability. All of it works against me, building the force I've barely contained behind my threadbare restraint.

"Last warning," I snarl.

She chuckles, the alluring scotch scent of her breath brushing my skin. "How many warnings do you need to give before you understand I'm not going anywhere?"

I snap.

It's mental and physical.

Feral and uncivilized.

I grab her around the waist and storm forward, shoving against the closed door. Her back hits with a thwack, her entire body jolting. I hold her off the ground with the hard press of my hips and reclaim that delicate fucking neck of hers in my grip.

She shudders, her glossy lips parting, preparing to speak.

"Shut the fuck up." I smash my mouth against hers, drawing a gasp from her throat, a whimper from her chest.

I kiss her hard, fast, punishing us both with the ferocity. I release all my frustration into her body, nudging my cock against her, digging my fingers into her skin.

It's fucking brutal, made all the worse when she matches my severity, her hands grasping my shoulders, her nails digging deep. She wraps her legs around me, clinging tight, grinding the heat of her pussy directly over my dick.

She's a temptress.

A taste of heaven.

Or maybe an injection of hell.

Who the fuck knows?

All I'm aware of is the craving for more.

I hold her tighter, grind harder, breathing in her needy whimpers and moans.

"You're going to regret pushing me." I drag my teeth over her lower lip and pull back to stare at her. "I'll make sure of it."

"Maybe you're the one who's going to regret abducting me."

"Too late," I growl. "I already do."

She raises a brow. It's all the fucking defiance I need.

I haul her over my shoulder to carry her to the bed, then flop her unceremoniously on the mattress.

She looks up at me. Without regret. Without fucking fear.

"Clothes off," I demand.

Her sultry mouth opens and those eyes tell me she's poised to deliver disobedience I have no desire to hear.

I reach out, grab her ankles, and pull her closer, giving myself access to those tight pants. I yank them down, pulling them off.

Her chest rises and falls in quick succession. Her tongue darts out to moisten her lower lip.

I reach for her again, this time dragging her loose top over her stomach, her chest, her head.

It's not until I'm throwing the material to the floor that I realize she's cradling her fucking shoulder, holding her arm tight against her body as if I've caused her pain.

Fuck.

An apology clogs my throat. Choking. Suffocating.

I fucking ignore it.

I ignore everything apart from the body I'm about to dominate.

She's all smooth curves and flawless skin, her tits firmly cupped in a black-with-gold-trim bra. I've seen it before—the gorgeousness, the slim figure—and having an up-close view only makes me more determined to have her.

With rough hands, I grab the waistband of her matching lace underwear, yank the flimsy material down her thighs, and throw them aimlessly behind me. Then I stare, riddled with lust, at the trim patch of hair between her thighs leading to a perfectly smooth pussy.

She glistens.

Her core is fucking ripe and ready for me.

"Tell me to stop." I shove her knees apart, exposing more of her pretty pink brilliance. "Tell me you've made a mistake."

She stares me down, her teeth digging into her lower lip, her cheeks flushed.

"Tell me." I drop to my knees, wrap my arms around her legs, and make her squeal as I haul her to the edge of the mattress.

She's wet for me, dripping, her body reacting on instinct instead of her conceited fucking morality.

"No." She shakes her head. "I won't."

I lean down, pressing my mouth to the inside of her knee. "Why? You know it's true."

She shudders, her skin breaking out in goose bumps. "I think I want to see if your arrogance is justified."

"I'll take pleasure in proving it to you."

I palm her foot, adding pressure to her sole to gently lift her leg and guide it over my shoulder. I do the same with the other, making her my puppet.

My dirty little doll.

I never would've thought she was capable of compliance. I always imagined she'd be a handful in bed. An untamed tiger who fought and scratched her way to release. But this submissive side is intriguing.

I inch my head forward, my path marked by teeth scrapes and teasing kisses along the inside of her thighs.

She jolts. Shivers. Whimpers.

She's putty in my hands, entirely malleable to my touch.

This is usually where my interest wanes. Where I realize the hard-to-get challenge is no longer producing adrenaline.

Orgasms aren't my goal. The game is. The back and forth. The seduction. It's rare for a woman to hold my interest once she submits to the inevitable.

But this time it's different.

She's different.

I'm still wired. I'm fucking buzzing, my dick hard, my balls tight. Right here, staring down the barrel of her smooth thighs, I'm more challenged than I've ever been. More driven to prove my arrogance is fucking justified.

I slide my hands along the outside of her legs, slow, like I've got the patience of a monk on valium. I inch closer and closer to her pussy, the heat of her a dizzying temptation, but I won't fall victim to a quick conclusion.

I want to draw this out. Make her suffer in the sweetest possible way.

I reach the highest point on the inside of her thighs and nuzzle my nose against the burning skin. I lick, and suck, and devour, earning the quickening of her breathing without paying her pussy any fucking attention.

I ignore the temptation I want most. I pretend the glistening slit doesn't exist as I nip and graze my teeth along her bare flesh.

Her legs squeeze tight. Her hips buck and twist, demanding more. But I slow in response. I make my kisses long, drawn-out gifts, switching back and forth from one side of her cunt to the other.

"Oh, God," she moans.

I smirk, deliberately grazing her with my rough stubble. "You're calling out to the wrong team, little fox. It's the devil who brings pleasure."

She whimpers and claws her fingers into the bed coverings. "Stop teasing me."

"Not so fast. I need you to beg for what you want."

"Excuse me?" She stiffens, every muscle pulling taut. "What did you say?"

"Beg," I repeat.

She lifts onto one elbow, blinking away the lust-filled gaze to stare and stare and fucking stare some more. She's weighing her pride against the pleasure she knows I can give. Measuring the worth of a mind-blowing orgasm against her ego.

"Beg. Me." I enunciate the demand slowly, letting it sink right down into that antagonistic mind of hers.

She glares, her jaw ticking, her cheeks darkening.

My pulse increases while she makes me wait and wonder if she'll deny us both. Is her pride so deeply ingrained she's willing to stop this chemistry of madness? Fuck, I hope not.

Her lips part, her tongue snaking out to moisten the darkened flesh. "Please, Cole," she grates. "Stop being a pussy tease and make me come."

I snicker even though my dick is harder than stone and pulsing to the point of pain. "Not good enough. I want you to lose the death stare and beg me according to my worth. I won't give you another chance."

The ultimatum was an afterthought. An insane, fucking idiotic addition.

If she denies me, I can't walk away. I've just given her the perfect opportunity to turn the tables. I've set myself up to lose. To *her*.

The slightest hint of panic raises the hair on the back of my neck. I'm teetering on failure. With the right response she'll know exactly how much hold she has on me. But I won't give up yet.

I swipe my tongue down her core, just once, just enough to get a delicious taste and make a growl rumble in my throat.

She jolts, her lashes flaring with the spike in pleasure.

I won't be defeated.

I can't be.

She shudders out a shaky breath. "Please, Cole. You're killing me." Her throat works over an awkward swallow. "I want you to make me come... I *need* you to."

I gift her another teasing swipe. "More."

Her back arches, her head falling to the mattress. "I've never felt this way... and I... I'll never feel this way again. I know I won't."

"More," I demand.

"Please, it won't take much. I'm already close... And God, you feel so good... I hate it, and I don't know how you're doing it, but you make me feel so... Fucking... Good." Her nails find my shoulders, piercing skin. "I've never wanted anything like this before."

Victory suffuses me, pulsing through every vein, searing every nerve. She's never wanted anyone like she wants me. Has never experienced pleasure the way I can give it to her.

Little fox, you ain't seen nothin' yet.

I cover her clit with my mouth and suck. I lap and flick and tease the bundle of nerves while she moans and grinds into me. And still, it's not enough.

Her mindlessness needs to be bone-deep. Soul-shattering. I want to break her in the best possible way.

I devour her as I glide a hand between the bed and her ass, shimmying it in unison with her gyrations until my thumb finds her pussy. I slide back and forth along the bottom of her entrance, soaking the tip of my digit, making her squirm while my fingers nuzzle into her crack, applying pressure to her puckered hole.

I sink into her, her walls pulsing around my thumb.

She pants, her breaths heavy heaves of greed.

"Cole." She fucks my hand, eagerly seeking release.

She's ready. So fucking close.

I want to deny her. To drag this moment out forever, but *fuck*, my cock is killing me, the pre-cum sliding down my length in a silent cry for relief.

I pulse harder with my thumb, breech her ass with a lone finger, and clamp my lips around her clit.

She gasps. Jerks. Pulls taut.

Then that perfect pussy flutters, her orgasm spasming as her thighs nail me in place. She moans over and over, the sound a symphony to my ego. A fucking victory.

I don't stop until she begins to loosen and those convulsions of her core slow to a long grind.

Then nothing.

She doesn't move. Doesn't speak.

It's as if her bad decisions have finally caught up with her and she thinks going mute will save the day.

No way in hell will I let that happen.

She's going to own this mistake. Remember it. Dwell on the brilliance of succumbing to me.

I stand, wiping the heel of my palm over my mouth. "Now we can both agree my arrogance is justified."

She collapses onto the bed, her eyes closed, her lips quirked in a delirious, infectious smile. She fucking beams with afterglow. But still, she doesn't respond.

"Have I finally worked out the way to silence that snappy mouth of yours?"

She chuckles.

It's beautiful.

The sound.

The sight.

Anissa, on any given day, is gorgeous. But happy Anissa— playful, orgasm-high, Anissa—is fucking mesmerizing.

She leans up on her good elbow, her stomach and tits still bouncing with mirth. "Nothing silences this mouth."

I raise a brow. "Nothing?"

"Nothing."

I shuck my boxer briefs, letting my cock spring free.

Her laughter ceases as she eyes me. I don't anticipate my reaction.

Her hunger unravels me even though I know it's not really her behind those curious eyes. The interest is driven by liquor, yet it's equally hard to deny.

I climb onto the bed, over her, caging her body beneath mine. The stutter returns to her breathing. Her teeth reclaim her lower lip.

"Take off the bra."

She complies, arching an arm behind her back and wincing as she pivots the other side of her body harder into the mattress.

"Your shoulder..." I grind my teeth, not wanting to care and not being able to stop at the same time. "It fucking hurts, doesn't it?"

"Sometimes." Her bra loosens and those supple tits fall free. "But you're a good distraction."

I want to drag my lips over the lightly bruised skin. Nuzzle the swelling. Soothe the ache.

Instead, I grab her hips and rise onto my knees, aligning her pussy with my cock. "I would've thought by now that I'd become more than that."

"You're many things, Cole. A distraction is just one of them."

She piques my interest, all the while making my dick twitch.

"Tell me what else I am to you, little fox." I tug her farther along my thighs, then hold her in place with one hand while I guide my cock to her entrance. "Tell me everything."

She contemplates me, her breathing becoming ragged. "You're the son of Satan."

"Is that so?"

"And you're cunning." She holds my gaze, hypnotizing me with all the pretty green. "I also think you're incredibly smart. I just wish I understood your thirst for power."

There is no thirst, and I want to tell her why. I'm fucking drawn to explain my position was a birthright, not something I wished for. Nobody gets to step down from this throne. Not unless it's in a body bag.

In my world, I can only move forward.

"It's a hunger like no other." I end the conversation with a hard thrust into her heat. There's no protection. No fucking insurance policy to guard either of us against an STD or parenthood. And I don't give a damn. She's smart enough to be clean and covered. At least I hope so.

I revel in the way her back arches, her breasts reaching toward me. She's tight, her walls choking my dick in the best possible way as she releases a feminine whimper.

I can't stop myself from leaning forward, resting on one hand to hover over her. I need to get closer. Being inside her isn't enough. I want her touch. Her mouth. Her thoughts. Her future.

Fuck.

I look away, unable to remain staring into those mind-reading eyes as I continue gliding into her. Back and forth. Over and over.

"What is it?" She cups my cheek with a delicate palm.

The connection is so fucking soft. So fucking brutal.

I hate her gentleness.

I fucking loathe the way she weakens me.

"Nothing." I swoop down, stealing her mouth and a gasp along with it.

I pound my frustration into her. I buck hard. I fucking slam deep. And the brilliant woman matches me, wrapping her legs around my hips, scratching the shit out of my back.

I've never been this intoxicated, and it's not the liquor taking over my senses. It's her. A fucking Fed.

The reminder should make my balls shrivel. Instead, it brings a thrill. The world disappears through my compulsion to claim her.

I want to own her. Control her. And I itch to make her feel the same way. To bring her down with this mindless addiction.

"Waging war against you was the best decision I ever made." I drag my lips over her sweat-slicked skin.

"You fight dirty." She grinds into my thrusts, our rhythm perfectly synched. "How the hell are you doing this to me?"

I kiss her neck. I bite. I earn myself another gasp.

"I'm close again." She clings tighter, her pussy clamping like a vise. "So close already."

"That's because you were born to submit to me."

She shudders. "Don't be an asshole. I'm not submitting to anything."

"Then maybe you love slumming it on the wrong side of the tracks." I nuzzle her ear. "Do you enjoy the thrill of being fucked by a murderer?"

Her nails dig deeper into my back. "Stop it."

Her protest is in contrast to the truth of her body. There's no pause in her movements. The tightness of her legs doesn't ease.

"Admit it." I pull back, grasp her chin, and force her gaze to mine. Exotic green blinks back at me, dazed and delirious.

She's incredibly beautiful. There's never been a more alluring woman. Not in my bed or my consciousness. There's only her.

At this point, it feels like there will only ever be her.

"Tell me the truth, little fox." I kiss those lips, brushing my tongue over hers. "Tell me you're dying to have a criminal come inside you."

She shivers with a breathy exhale. Then those pretty eyes roll and her neck arches. She unravels, milking my dick with another orgasm.

For a brief second, I contemplate dragging this out, hoping to get her tally to three before I follow along with her, but her whimpers undo me. Her allure has me thrusting harder, pumping faster.

Pressure builds in my balls, the release hitting hard.

I force my mouth on hers, tasting her cries, each one of her breaths becoming mine as I lose myself. Over and over I come, and even then my mind doesn't stray from her.

There's only the need to mark her. To claim her as my own.

That's when the uppercut of unease hits me.

The clarity.

All this time I demanded she admit the mistake of fucking me. But as she lies beneath me, her eyes closing, her lips pulled in a smile, I realize I'm the one who messed up.

There was no error on her behalf.

Anissa Fox would never sleep with me out of weakness or drunken stupidity.

Hell no.

Not in a million years.

The Fed I know would've done it out of strategy. Pure manipulation. She aimed to achieve something by fucking me, and my obsession was the end result.

Shit.

I rest my forehead against her shoulder, letting her deception sink deeper than her nails, while my dick continues to jerk inside her.

Did she just win?

Did I just become mind-fucked by someone who will stop at nothing to place me behind bars?

20

TORIAN

I STEW ON MY PRECARIOUS POSITION ALL NIGHT.

It's clear she made a bad judgment call by sleeping with me.

She made it twice more during the early hours of the morning, when I succumbed to the need to have her again.

But I, by far, made the biggest mistake in letting her win this latest game of ours.

She played me with her body. Seduced me with her beauty. Brought me to my knees with her lack of inhibitions. Over and over.

I kept telling myself I'd grow bored if I tasted her again... Kissed her in one more place... Fucked her repeatedly. But here I stand beside the bed, showered, dressed, and still sporting a dick that can't be tamed. At least not by me.

Currently, my favorite bodily asset is leashed by the sleeping beauty who lies before me, the thin sheet molding to the curves of her breasts and the gentle groove of her hip.

She has a hold on me. A tight grasp she's woven intricately since the first day we met.

On cue, she whimpers and tilts her head into the pillow, her dark hair fanning over one eye as the sleepy sound continues to burrow up from her throat.

She'll be awake soon, and I'm too busy battling a raging hangover to deal with whatever attitude the new day brings.

From our brief early morning fuckfest conversation, I know

she remains adamant on staying, and even though I gave her a lust-filled promise of agreement, I still haven't made up my mind.

Breaking a promise to an outsider has never been difficult. I can turn on a dime for those who haven't proven their loyalty. But the truth is, I want her to stay.

Not for her benefit. Or the women she wants to help.

I need her here. For me.

To feed my growing addiction.

Despite the safety risks associated with my father's knowledge of her existence, and the myriad of complications fucking her has brought to the table, I'm not willing to let her go.

She wiggles, about to wake, which encourages me to move. I start for the door, not having the patience or restraint to listen to her fake excuses for fucking me when we both know it all came down to strategy.

I ignore the swish of sheets and another waking moan. I don't stop until I grasp the handle to the hall.

"Why didn't you wake me?" Her voice is husky. Sleep-riddled. "What time is it?"

I should keep my attention straight ahead, directly on the painted wood, on the only barrier keeping me from distancing myself. But I succumb, like I always do with her, and glance over my shoulder.

She's perched on one elbow, her dreamy gaze hitting me, her long lashes batting softly as her hand clutches the sheet to her chest.

She's a sight to behold. A vision.

One I need to wipe from my mind.

I plunge the lever, and open the door a crack. "I thought I'd do you a favor and leave you to make your walk of shame without an audience."

She groans and flops back on the bed, covering her face with a flailed arm. "The sex was inevitable, Cole. It's the scotch I regret."

I bristle. Tense. "Inevitable? That's interesting. I wouldn't have predicted an admission of guilt."

"Guilt?" Her arm falls, those eyes narrowing on mine. "What are you accusing me of now?"

I bare my teeth in a sinister smile. "The sordid scheme to try and take me down with the use of your body." I release the door handle and pivot to face her head-on. "How you planned on getting in my head by getting in my bed."

Her lips part on silent words, her look of pained defiance almost believable.

"Too bad I saw right through you. But I thoroughly enjoyed your attempt." My smile increases. "More than once."

She scoffs and diverts her attention, lowering her gaze to the bed. For a moment she seems lost in angered shock before she mutters, "Fucking idiot," under her breath.

"Don't be too hard on yourself. Ambitious is a more fitting term. Not many people would try to manipulate me with sex. Especially when it's one of my favorite tactics." I wink, just to piss her off. "If you're going to play a player, you probably shouldn't pit your novice skills against a master."

"No, Cole, *you're* the fucking idiot." She pushes up on both elbows, awkwardly keeping the sheet to her chest with one hand even though her modesty left the building hours ago. "This," she indicates the bed with a wave of her free hand, "wasn't a tactic. I can admit I'm manipulative, but I'm not a fucking whore."

For a second, I believe her.

I see the anguish in her eyes and take it at face value, but it doesn't stop me from looking at her with smug superiority to put her off her game like she's put me off mine.

She rolls her eyes and sighs. "What time is it?"

"Almost one."

"And you're leaving?" She drags her attention over me, taking in the business suit and polished shoes. "You're going to see your father?"

"Soon."

She slides from the bed, yanking the sheet from the mattress as she goes, the lengthy material trailing behind her like a sordid wedding dress. "And what about me?"

"You're packing your things."

"You're sending me home?"

Yes. No.

Fuck. I want both.

"That depends." I draw out the words as she continues closer, her sleep-roughened hair tempting me to guide the strands back into place.

"On what?"

"On your admission of guilt. Tell me the truth about why you spent the night in my bed. Explain the reasons for sleeping with the enemy."

"Why bother? You've already made up your mind."

Because I need to hear her lies.

I itch to believe them.

"There's no harm in trying." I succumb to the need to touch her hair, delicately gliding it behind her ear. "Spin me a web of fiction, little fox. Make me believe you're not a whore."

A delicate shade of pink enters her cheeks. "You're an asshole."

I incline my head. "That's always been crystal clear."

"Yeah, I guess you're right. I don't know what possessed me to forget." Her eyes soften with uncharacteristic sadness. "But I still don't want to leave. I need to see this through. Don't you think I'm owed that much after everything you've put me through?"

I owe her nothing.

Not a damn thing.

"If you want something from me, Nissa, I'm afraid I'm going to have to ask for something in return."

She balks, clutching the sheet tighter. "What now?"

I hold her gaze and force a smirk. She's different this morning. Not brimming with confidence like I'd expected. I thought she'd boast her victory, when in reality she's exuding failure.

"Drop the sheet," I demand.

She blinks at me, unmoving. "That's what you want in return?"

I'm as shocked as she is. I hadn't planned on making demands. It's her fault for throwing me off balance.

"I'm a simple man. With simple requests." All I want is a subtle humiliation, which is nowhere near the level she inflicted upon me last night.

261

"And if I drop the sheet, I get to stay?"

I incline my head, my pulse ramping with impatience for her to submit. "Temporarily, yes."

The muscles in her jaw flicker. The narrowing of her eyes is barely seen. Regardless of both, I can feel her animosity. It pulses from her in waves as she straightens her shoulders and drops the long length of material to the floor.

I brace myself for the burst of enjoyment at her humiliation.

I wait, and wait, and fucking wait, my gaze holding hers, but the taste of victory doesn't come. Instead, I'm the one who battles shame.

My actions resemble something my father would dictate.

A pathetic perversion.

Pure weakness.

The only thing stopping self-loathing from coating me like a second skin is how I refrain from lowering my attention. I don't add a visual violation to my pitiful demand. Instead, I stand there for long moments, silently cursing a conscience that is at its loudest around her, as I stare into those spite-filled eyes.

She's tainting me. Turning me into a fool.

"Get dressed," I growl. "You can stay until Luca and I return to the island."

She crosses her arms over her chest, the plump of her breasts taunting my peripheral vision. "You wanted me at my most vulnerable so you could reject me? Is that it?" She scoffs and shakes her head. "You're such a prick."

Yes, I'm a fucking prick.

I'm far worse, too. Especially when she continuously pokes my volatility.

"A fucking sociopath," she spits.

I clench my fists. "And what does that make you? You're the one who fucked me to claim victory."

"I didn't *fuck you* for anything other than pleasure. You're the one who keeps continuing these mind games when I stopped long ago. I've had enough, Cole." Her voice waivers. "I can't take this anymore."

I can't accept her accusation, not when she's the most recent contributor. I'm not the one who's lying here. If I'm a sociopath, I've certainly got likeminded company.

I step into her, my shoes bare inches from trampling her delicate toes.

"You're wrong," I snarl. "I'm the one who stopped the mind games."

She throws up her hands. "You just—"

"*I just tried to fucking test myself,*" I roar, the sound ricocheting through the room. "I wanted you naked because I was trying to prove I could fucking resist you. But if I lower my gaze, it will only confirm I can't."

She rears back as if I struck her.

I guess I did.

I hit her with a dose of painfully regretful truth.

"Get dressed," I repeat. "And make sure you're ready to leave once we return."

She doesn't respond, not other than the swipe of her tongue against her lower lip, which is made with blatant apprehension, not seduction.

Good.

She should be apprehensive because I've never been this unstable.

I storm for the door, forcing my attention back to where it needs to be—on my father. On the necessity to make him pay.

"Cole?"

Fuck. I pause, and this time I don't make the mistake of looking back. "What?"

"I can't resist you either." Her voice is a whisper. "You could've asked me to do a lot more than drop the sheet and I would've complied."

The admission stiffens my dick. "I know. Last night you made it clear you'll go to great lengths to stay."

I stalk into the hall and pound out the distance to the living room, ignoring how badly I want to believe her.

She almost has me convinced last night wasn't a ploy. My entire consciousness is contemplating the possibility of her malleable body being beneath mine purely for pleasure, not manipulative profit.

And that, in itself, makes her fucking dangerous.

The amount of power I've given her is insane.

"Trouble in paradise?" Luca sits forward on the recliner, elbows on his thighs, head in his hands. He stares at me as I walk farther into the room, his scathing expression telling me exactly where his thoughts are.

"Don't say another word," I warn.

"I shouldn't have to," he mutters, "but I will. You're not doing something fucking stupid like falling for her, are you?"

I answer him with a glare.

"Good." He rests back in his chair. "I thought you might have forgotten she works informants for a living. It's her job to screw people over to make an arrest."

"Your lack of faith is insulting." I continue toward the kitchen in search of something to numb the hangover. "You're also getting really close to overstepping your place in life."

"I'm watching your back. That's what I'm here for. The way you two were eying each other on the pier last night set off a whole heap of warning bells. The subsequent fucking only cemented my concern."

I grip the counter and hang my head. "I hope, for your sake, you stayed off the video feed."

"Rest assured, your lily-white ass isn't something I want to see. The acoustics were more than enough, fuck you very much." He shoves to his feet. "It's a big house and all, but I don't think you realize how easily sound travels through the rooms."

"You were the last thing on my mind." I yank open a drawer, then another, and another until I find a plastic bottle of pain relief. "And don't you dare judge me for fucking her when the alternative was to drink myself into a coma."

"It's after lunch, so it seems like you did both."

I open the pill bottle, throw three capsules in my mouth, then use my hand to cup water from the tap to swallow them back. When I straighten he's still appraising me, his gaze digging deep.

"But neither choice is any of my business. All I'm saying is that you're giving her more ammo to put you behind bars."

I stiffen, hearing an accusation of rape in his tone. "It was fucking consensual."

"I know. Believe me, I heard her consent. Continuously. For too damn long. But it's not going to stop her from fucking us over once she gets back to Portland."

"No, I won't." She inches from the hall, wearing nothing but my suit jacket cinched around her middle by her arms. My guess is that she grabbed the closest item of clothing before leaving the room in a rush to snoop. "I believe in what you're trying to do. And if you're successful, all the good you've done will outweigh the bad."

"You truly believe that?" Luca shoots her a look of scorn. "Your abduction, being sedated and hog-tied, having a gun pointed at your head? All that shit will be wiped off the slate?"

"I built my life around a career that brings monsters to justice. Who am I if I'm willing for Luther to remain free just because he can't be punished by the authorities? It's better for him to be dead since you've made it clear there's no other alternative."

I don't pay her any attention. I watch Luca instead. I notice how he straightens, his brow furrowed in dawning belief.

He believes her.

It's not only me she has wrapped around her little finger.

"There's something else I need to say," she continues. "Cole, you wanted me to admit last night was a mistake, and you're right. It was."

Fuck.

My hangover increases tenfold. My brain pounds. My gut churns. I keep my focus on Luca and jerk my chin at him. "Have you eaten?"

He nods.

"Then give us a minute." I won't let her air our dirty laundry in front of an audience. Not if it's another attempt to create humiliation. "I'm going to make some coffee, then I'll be ready to leave. Call a boat to come pick us up."

"Amar is already on standby. He won't take long to get here."

He sends a skeptical glance at Anissa, then focuses back on me. "I'll wait for you on the pier."

I dismiss the instinct to demand a different driver. I don't want the old fucking Greek anywhere near here, but I also don't have the luxury of showing any more weakness toward the feminine snake in the room. I have to keep my mouth shut as Luca makes his way outside, sliding the glass door closed behind him.

"Continue," I drawl, meeting Anissa's gaze.

She cringes, a whole heap of discomfort marring her features. "Yesterday, I was convinced your plan was the right thing to do. Any alternative the authorities could provide would be too risky and time consuming. Let alone the money associated with that type of operation when the Greek police would block US officials at every turn."

"Get to the point." I drop the pills back to the drawer and slam it shut.

"The point is that nothing has changed. I'm still convinced. And I still think this is the only way to take him down."

"And your mistake last night? What does that have to do with all this?"

She remains silent for a moment, her forehead creased with concern. "The mistake is that I became a distraction. I've complicated things."

I trek my attention over her body, down along the expanse of thigh exposed beneath the jacket. "If that's your concern, maybe you should think about putting more clothes on."

"Stop it. I'm not messing around." Her eyes plead with me. "I was worried for you before your father turned up last night, and that was when I thought you were prepared and ready for what had to be done. Now, your head isn't in the game. You're too angry with me to possibly think straight, and that's scaring the hell out of me."

She doesn't look scared. After all this time I've spent craving her fear, she doesn't look anything other than a little anxious.

"Is this another tactic?" I lean against the kitchen counter, relaxed, hiding all the anger she's created. "Is there a strategy to this pity party?"

"No. This is me trying to tell you I care." Her voice grows in strength. "I'm fucking worried about you."

She attempts to stare me down, to illicit a reaction I won't give.

Eventually, she gives up, wiping her hands down her face, letting the jacket sweep open and expose a wealth of creamy skin.

My dick instantly grows hard.

A smart man would think the erotic show was right on cue for another perfect distraction. And I'm definitely a smart man. Most days.

"You don't need to worry, little fox. I'm not going to make a move. It's too dangerous to take action on his turf. I'm meeting up with Luther for nothing more than information."

I turn away and grab a mug from the cupboard to place it under the automatic coffee machine.

"Cole?"

I hear her approach. The soft pad of footfalls heightens my senses.

I don't look at her. I can't anymore.

She's too stunning to deny.

"I need you to believe last night wasn't a strategy."

I shake my head. I refuse to have this conversation. Not again. With every word she undoes me, turning me into a pathetic slave. But the question leaves me anyway. "Then what was it?"

"I don't know," she murmurs. "I guess it was a result of the intense situation. Or the alcohol. Or chemistry. Maybe it was a combination of all three. But it wasn't a trick or a betrayal. I'd sooner slit my wrists than fake an orgasm for you, or any man."

"I never said you faked it. I fucking felt your pussy melt for me." I tilt my head, glancing at her from the corner of my eye.

"Well, I don't whore myself out either. I slept with you because, at the time, I wanted to."

At the time.

I scoff, hating her need to insert the unnecessary proviso. "Thanks for clarifying."

I want to demand she revoke the defensive part of her admission. I itch to make her admit she fucked me because she needed to—*had* to—because she couldn't get through the fucking night without my dick.

But continuing this conversation will only send me into a tailspin. I'm already fucking nosediving.

Instead, I start the coffee machine and detour to the pantry, pulling the door wide to retrieve a box from the highest shelf. I remove one of the burner phones stashed there and shove the box back in place before shutting the door. "Here."

I walk toward her and lob the cell in her direction.

She catches it in both hands, then stares at the device in confusion. "What's this?"

"A phone. People use it to communicate."

She scowls. "I meant, why are you giving it to me?"

I shrug, downplaying how monumental this mistake could be. "You'll need it in case of an emergency."

If Luca and I run into trouble and don't make it back, she'll be stuck here. At least temporarily, until my father remembers the toy he can play with. Leaving her open to that situation isn't an option, even with the risk of her stabbing me in the back.

"But what if I call home?"

"Then I guess we all pay the price. You included."

Her brows pull tight as she runs her fingers over the cell. "Is *this* another game? Are you testing me?"

"*No,*" I growl. "No more fucking games, Nissa. Okay? I'm done. And you are, too."

She straightens, seeming to gain some sort of strength from my animosity. "Then I don't want it." She storms forward and shoves the cell against my chest. "You need to take it back because I'll be tempted to use it."

"Then that's a battle you're going to have to fight." I push her wrist down, moving her arm away. "If you're as invested in this as you say you are, you shouldn't have a problem keeping your mouth shut. I'm only giving it to you in case I don't come back."

Her eyes widen. "Is that a possibility?"

I breathe in her concern. It sinks under my fucking skin.

No woman has ever looked at me like that. Like every blink is etched in the phantom pain of never seeing me again.

"It's unlikely. The cell is only a precaution. The last thing I want to do is die today and have your abduction stain my reputation for eternity."

She shakes her head. "I'd never admit that's what happened."

Fuck. She's killing me.

Fucking. Killing. Me.

"But I appreciate the safety net." She lowers her head and shoves the device into the jacket pocket. "Thank you."

Fuck the coffee.

Fuck waiting here within reach of her.

"I need to go." I sidestep, slapping a hand against the coffee machine to turn it off. "I'll see you later."

Her head snaps up. "You're leaving? The boat's not even here."

"Yeah, but you were right." I soften my voice, trying to bite back all the frustration. "You've become a distraction."

She cringes, her face filling with apology. "I'm—"

"Don't." I wrap my arm around her neck, pulling her into me. "Be ready to leave when I get back." I place a kiss at her temple, holding the connection longer than necessary. "Stay safe."

21

TORIAN

I SPEND EACH MINUTE OF THE RIDE TO THE NAXOS PORT trying not to glare at the back of Amar's head. I can still smell Anissa, can still feel my mouth against her temple, and this fucker dared to greet me with a smile after the disrespect he paid her.

The only thing stopping me from ripping out his throat is Luca's judgmental stare.

The scrutinizing SEAL can see right through me, and his focus isn't on the distraction of a man who threatened something belonging to me. Luca knows I'm mind-fucked by the Fed.

He goddamn knows.

It takes all my hangover-depleted energy to focus on ignoring thoughts of her. Even then my subconscious refuses to stray from Anissa more than momentarily.

I want to get back to the island. She's too exposed out there on her own.

"What's the plan today?" Luca keeps his voice low, no doubt making sure we're not overheard.

"Information. That's all. We're not making a move. It's too risky."

Amar guides the boat alongside the jetty and cuts the engine.

I don't hang around to give the asshole a tip. I'm shoving to my feet and jumping onto the walkway before the gangway is put in place.

"Because the Fed will be a loose end on the island?" Luca jogs to catch up with me. "I don't know why you didn't send her packing like you promised."

"She has nothing to do with this. The risk of attacking from here is based on my father's protection. He's going to be covered from all angles." My statement is confirmed when I see Luther waiting on the rocky shore, two men flanking him. "His home has always been his fortress. And those two guards are merely the tip of the iceberg."

"They're the guys from last night—Chris and Robert." Luca remains at my side, matching me step for step. "They were also at your uncle's funeral."

"Yeah. I remember. What sort of vibe did you get from them?"

"A whole heap of arrogance with an added dose of fuck-off."

"Meaning?"

"They didn't see me as an equal. I was nothing. And I have a feeling they'll regard you with the same contempt."

"I'd like to see them try." I straighten my lapels and stride ahead to greet my father with a handshake. "Morning."

"Afternoon," he corrects, his smile forced. "I thought you would've made contact earlier."

"Blame the liquor." I laugh off his annoyance and clap him on the shoulder. "We had a big night celebrating my brother's existence. I didn't crawl from bed until lunch."

"Well, I'm glad to hear you enjoyed yourself, even if it was at the detriment of those who waited around for you to call."

Comfort and criticism. He's nothing if not predictable.

"Now that you're finally here, I'd like you to meet Robert and Chris." He waves a hand, indicating his goons. "I owe everything to them."

"Everything?" I offer my hand to the guy on the left—the steroid-infused mammoth. He doesn't have a flaccid vein in his body. Everything bulges with an overabundance of testosterone. "Chris, is it? You look familiar."

"Robert," he grates, his ice-blue eyes emotionless as he grips my hand harder than necessary. "You would've seen me in Portland at the graveside service."

271

"And you didn't think to introduce yourself when my father was arrested?" I step away, turning my attention to Chris. "I assume you two are the ones responsible for the escape."

"That was us." The leaner of the two grins at me, like he's earned himself an Olympic medal. "We needed to lay low. We didn't know who we could trust."

We shake, the act dismissive on his side. He's not threatened by my presence.

Bad move.

"In future," I sneer, "You can rest assured Luther's son is trustworthy."

"Sons," Robert clarifies. "Don't forget you're not the only one."

Bitter irritation throbs through my chest, making it almost impossible not to glare as I drop Chris's hand. "Don't correct me. Not unless you want a lesson in manners."

"They're protective. That's all." My father defuses the growing tension with a soothing tone. "And they did a great job in Portland. You should be grateful I have such an exceptional team."

"So the dead prison guard was part of the plan?" Luca's tone drips with sarcasm. "That's hardcore."

I fight a grin and ignore the chastising glare my father shoots me. If he expects me to make a reprimand he's going to be waiting a hell of a while. "How many of you ran the job? Witness accounts are conflicting. Some said two. Others mentioned four."

"It was only the two of us." Robert matches my smirk with his own. "That's all your father has ever needed while we've been on the job."

"You're confident. I like it. Although, you wouldn't hear my team running their mouth if they allowed me to get arrested in the first place."

"And maybe we wouldn't have needed to bring your father home at all if you'd protected Richard properly."

My hackles rise, my hands clenching into fists. "What did you say?"

"That's enough," my father warns. "Let's get back to the house.

Robert, you can get started on the project I mentioned earlier. We can meet up later."

I dig my fingers into my palms, itching to take this further into hostile territory.

"Come on." Luther strides for the row of cars parked a few yards from the end of the jetty. "We've got a lot to discuss."

I shoot a scowl at Luca, letting him know I'm far from appreciative of the warm welcome and follow after my father. "Robert isn't joining us?"

"I'd prefer not to cram five of us in the car. He can catch up later."

"What a shame," Luca drawls. "He seems like a stand-up guy."

"He's a worthy asset." Luther pulls a car fob from his suit jacket and unlocks a polished sedan, then throws the fob to Chris. "Speaking of worthy assets, I thought you were going to bring your toy along?"

The hairs rise on the back of my neck. Every nerve stands at attention. "She's not worth the frustration. I'm growing tired of her struggle."

"That's a shame. It's been a while since I enjoyed the thrill of breaking in a newbie." He opens the rear driver's side door. "Luca, you can sit in the front with Chris while I talk with my son in the back."

I follow my father's lead as we climb into the luxury car and make our way onto the narrow streets.

Luther fills the drive with idle chitchat. We discuss my sisters and niece. For a few brief moments, we skim over Richard's funeral and the upkeep of the burial plot. Then the conversation switches to my half-brother and the twinkle in Luther's eye irks me in a way I can't describe.

It isn't jealousy. My father could have a million sons and I wouldn't give a shit.

It's the way Tobias was created as an asset which has me questioning God's existence.

The boy was conceived in brutality and baptized in sin. No child should have to carry those mental scars.

"You should spend some time with him while you're here."

Luther meets my gaze. "The two of you are likely to work together in the future."

"Not too soon I hope. Give the kid a chance to grow up."

He laughs. "The boy is smart, and despite being shy, he's strong. It won't be long and he'll be making me retire."

"Then I look forward to getting to know him." I bite back a curse.

That child keeps creating problems, and the complications will only grow once he's an orphan.

It's not like I'm parental material.

I won't be looking after him. But he's also family, which means one of my sisters will have to mother him—her rapist father's illegitimate, parent-less kid.

Jesus Christ.

I push back the building mental struggle and force myself to focus on the here and now. On the immaculate view. Everything here is pristine and picture-perfect. It's the company that taints it all.

I don't want to speak to my father anymore. I'm not sure I can keep opening my mouth without spewing hatred.

The pressure only builds when I consider how easy it would be to end his life right now. All it would take is a quick slide of hand into my jacket to retrieve my gun. A turn of my wrist. Then two quick squeezes of the trigger.

Luther, then Chris.

Dead.

I could do it, too. I *would* do it if I knew where Robert had gone.

If I had to place a bet, I'd say he's tailing us around every corner, providing a hidden safety net. The backup wouldn't help my slain father, but I'm sure the steroid junkie would cause enough trouble to stop me from reaching Anissa.

I wouldn't be able to get us all to the jet before reinforcements caught up to us. And even if I did, the aftermath would be riddled with complications.

The whole idea of making a move in Greece is so my father

274

can go missing. The isolated island provides a buffer to dispose of evidence, and it also means there'll be no witnesses.

Luther would've sunk to the bottom of the ocean by now if I'd followed through last night. The three of them would've become fish food. One minute, they're building a thriving empire. The next, I'm taking over and shutting it down.

"Cole?"

"Hmm?" The car slows as I turn back to my father. "What is it?"

"Chris asked for your gun."

The driver holds his hand over his shoulder, waiting. "All weapons need to be surrendered before you enter the property. We don't allow visitors to be armed."

"Visitors? Since when is your son a visitor?"

"It's necessary." My father winces out an unspoken apology. "We had problems a year ago with one of my girls. She stole a gun from a guest and created unnecessary bloodshed. We've taken strict precautions ever since."

I don't like it. I fucking hate the idea. And the stiff posture of Luca in the front seat announces he feels the same way.

"Maybe we should go somewhere else then." I swirl my finger in the air, motioning for Chris to turn the vehicle around. "Find a cafe or a restaurant."

"Don't be ridiculous. We're almost home. And no son of mine is going to come all this way and not see where I live. I'm sure you can survive without your weapons for a few hours."

Can I? I'm not so sure.

"Cole?" Luther frowns at me. "What's gotten into you? Since when don't you trust your own flesh and blood?"

I scoff out a laugh. "Since you demanded to take my gun."

He continues to frown, his scrutiny increasing. It's only a matter of time before he realizes my uncertainty is a reflection of myself, not him.

"Okay, okay." I reach into my jacket and pull my weapon from the holster. "Look after her."

I slap the warm metal in Chris's hand and watch as Luca does the same. Both weapons are placed in the glove compartment.

When the car moves again, it's only a few yards along the road until we pull up before wrought-iron gates, the overbearing barrier guarded by a lone man with a rifle.

"Welcome to my home away from home." Luther nods his appreciation at the guard as we're allowed entry, passing security cameras and a head-high brick wall. "This is my personal paradise."

The gardens are lush. The lawns manicured. The trees blooming with flowers. All of it is a perfect frame for the massive white building coming into view as we round the curving pebbled drive.

Tobias stands at the top of the few stairs leading to the large double doors of the mansion, his innocent face pale. The poor kid seems awkward in his dress pants and collared shirt, the formal attire daunting his tiny frame.

"There's my boy." My father releases his belt, and the car pulls to a stop. "Come on. I'll show you around."

We climb out, all four of us walking toward the house, my father and Chris in front, Luca eyeing me with trepidation as we walk behind to meet the kid at the top step.

"Hey, little man." I crouch on one knee, not bothering to offer my hand when I can already see the anxiety in his features. "It's nice to see you again."

He nods, the movement jerky until he settles in against my father's side. He gains strength from Luther. Protection.

I used to feel the same.

"The two of you are strikingly similar," my father drawls. "Both worrying unnecessarily. It's a useless waste of time. I have men walking the perimeter twenty-four/seven. You've got nothing to worry about while you're here."

"I trust you." I shove to my feet. "But I'm beginning to question whether these women are worth the hassle."

"Believe me, they are." He shoos Tobias with a wave of his hand. "Go get them. Tell them we have guests."

"Yes, *Baba*." Tobias backtracks with a nod and slips between the front doors, his running footsteps echoing from inside.

We follow, my father leading us down a wide hall, through an opulent living room, past a sparkling kitchen, then outside to a stunning pool area with an unfettered view of the ocean.

"Chris, get one of the women to arrange something to eat." My father looks at his right-hand man. "I think we could all do with a drink, too."

The guy jerks his head and makes his way back inside, leaving me and Luca to pretend to take in the atmosphere while we scope the security.

"Well?" My father descends onto a cushioned outdoor chair and retrieves a remote from the coffee table in front of him. With the press of a button an overhead fan starts to spin, releasing a cooling white mist. "What do you think?"

"You've done well for yourself." It's the best compliment I can offer. I'm tired of the lies and fake placations. Every breath Luther takes is a taunt to my failure, not only last night, but years ago. "How long have you lived here?"

"A while. At least since Tobias was born. Chris and Robert used to run the household and look after the women when I was still travelling back and forth from the States."

"Look after them?" I take a seat opposite him.

"Yes. A certain level of routine needs to be maintained, otherwise the slaves slip into bad habits."

Luca takes the seat beside me. "Meaning they're serviced on a regular basis to stop them fighting back after a long stretch of relative freedom?"

"Correct. Although, I do enjoy a good fight." Luther grins. "But Robert and Chris also made sure the women saw to Tobias's education and welfare. He's home schooled, and it's a fine line between them treating him like their own son, and having him realize they're assets, not maternal figures."

"Well, from what I've seen, you've raised a good kid." Luca kicks back in his chair, a picture of relaxed calm.

"He's exceptional. With Cole, I had his mother to contend with in the early years. She made me soften the truth of the family business until she thought he was old enough to handle reality. With Tobias, I haven't had those restrictions. And it's made a world of difference."

"I wouldn't disregard the importance of balance." I spread my arms wide, indicating his riches. "No matter how much money you have, it won't be enough to pay for the therapy the kid will need if you expose him to too much too soon."

"Children are resilient. And most important, they're easily molded. You'd be surprised what he can withstand."

No, I wouldn't.

My imagination has already run wild with what the poor kid has had to endure.

"But what about you, son?" Luther asks. "Have you put any thought into expanding the family name?"

"Children?" I laugh. And keep laughing. "I wouldn't hold your breath for more grandbabies. Not from me, anyway."

"What about Layla or Keira?"

I shake my head, not willing to get his hopes up for more minions to work under his control. "Not in the foreseeable future."

"I disagree." Luca clears his throat. "Keira and Seb go at it like rabbits."

I look at him. Smile. Blink.

None of it is kind.

Not when he's discussing my sister's sex life.

"Who's Seb?" My father sits straighter. "Do I know him?"

"No. His name is Sebastian." I continue to stare my annoyance at Luca, as if the aggression has the power to force his mouth closed. "He's a tech guy who's been working on the fringes for a while. He's valuable. Knows his shit. And has saved my ass on more occasions than I'd like to admit."

"But?"

That's a good question.

I've held tight to my animosity for so long the reasons don't hold much weight anymore. He *is* a valued part of my team. His skills with a computer are beyond my comprehension. And he can handle a gun better than most.

Then there's his devotion to family. I learned the hard way he'd go to war for the sake of those he loves.

"I'm protective," I admit. "And she's been through a lot. I couldn't stand to see her suffer again."

I sprinkle history into the conversation as a test.

My father may not be aware of what Keira has been through recently, but that's not what I'm referring to. I want to trigger the past. Her childhood. Once and for all, I need to know if he's aware of what his failure as a parent did to her.

"Their relationship is serious?" His brows rise. "That's surprising. I've never seen her with a man before apart from the guy at Richard's funeral."

I want to tell him he's responsible for her abstinence. That her mistreatment as a child is to blame. It won't help, though. His predictable dismissal would only increase my thirst for blood.

"They're joined at the hip," Luca adds. "There's no separating them."

Numerous sets of footsteps approach, breaking our conversation. Tobias leads three women toward us, all of them trailing behind him in a line.

They're victims—my father's slaves—who walk forward, their faces deadpan as if they've done this strut of shame a hundred times before.

"Here they are." Luther encourages them forward with a jerk of his head. "My gorgeous beauties, I'd like you to meet my special guests."

The line stops. The women turn to face us, almost military like, while Tobias remains in the lead, his focus on my father, waiting, wanting recognition.

"Who do we have here?" Luca inches forward with a sly grin, his act unsettling.

There's no reaction from the victims. They remain in formation, staring straight ahead over our heads at the white brick wall behind.

They're attractive. Seemingly healthy. Impeccably dressed. Their hair is styled, their clothing immaculate. Even their makeup is on point.

There's no sign of the brutality they endure. Not one hint of the horrors they've faced.

"This is Nina." Luther points at the blonde on the left with her pursed lips and narrowed gaze. She's wearing a casual sundress, her hair loose around her shoulders, her skin sun-kissed with a healthy tan.

"Then Abigail and Chloe." The two brunettes are similar in appearance. Both slim. Attractive. Fashionable.

They're trophies. Not just slaves, but pretty decorations to promote my father's deviance.

"You've got a nice collection." Luca eyes the women with appreciation.

"This isn't the entirety of my stable. Lilly is resting. And I assume the apple of my eye is arranging drinks."

Tobias nods. "She's getting food, too."

"Five women?" I raise my brows. "I'm impressed by your stamina."

"I'm like a fine wine, boy." He spreads his arms along the backrest of his seat. "I only get better with age. Isn't that right, ladies?"

They voice a chorus of murmured agreement, the "yes", "of course", and "definitely" a drone of sound.

"That's not very convincing, my loves." He pushes from the chair, his approach causing them to stand taller. Straighter.

"You're remarkable, Luther," the blonde says in a rush.

"And very generous," the one next to her adds with conviction.

"We're lucky to have you." Chloe practically pleads with her eyes.

"That's more like it." He walks around them, the lazy stroll predatory. "I'm going to check on our drinks and take a quick bathroom break." He leans in to grasp the blonde on the ass. "Get moving, ladies. It's time to stop distracting the men."

He ushers them into the house, sliding the door shut behind him.

"Your dad is a piece of work," Luca mutters under his breath.

"Keep your opinions to yourself." I shoot him a warning glare. We have no idea who's listening. This place could be bugged down to the foundations for all we know. "If you can't stomach your job, go wait in the car."

He snaps his gaze away, his teeth clenched, his nostrils flaring.

"This is business." I keep my voice low, still playing the game in case I'm overheard. "Consider it a learning opportunity."

In other words, dig deep and gain information. Make this bullshit worthwhile.

He juts his chin in acknowledgement, his jaw ticking with each passing second.

"Why don't you go for—"

The whoosh of the sliding door cuts off my words. The tap of heels puts me back on edge.

I force myself to lazily sink back into the chair as a new woman walks forward with a wooden tray. She's like the others, slim, beautiful, with a braid of long dark hair resting over her left shoulder.

She meets my gaze briefly, her dark brown eyes striking me with a sense of déjà vu.

I give up on the lazy posture and sit straight, trying to get a better view of her downcast face.

I've seen her before. I'm sure I have.

She places the tray on the coffee table before us, the loose dress gaping at her chest as she bends to pick up two of the three glasses, each filled with a finger of scotch. She hands the first to Luca, her attention remaining on the floor.

When it's my turn, I reach out, about to retrieve the drink but stop before making contact, letting my fingers hover close. "Aren't you going to introduce yourself?"

She stills, her long lashes fluttering as she blinks.

There's no other outward reaction. No sign of distress, apart from the way her throat works over a tormented swallow.

"I'm Cole," I offer. "Luther's son."

She stiffens, her chocolate eyes hollow as they meet mine.

I'm not offered a greeting. Not in words. But the underlying "fuck you" in her tight expression speaks loud.

"Have we met?" I drag my attention over every inch of her, trying to find a birthmark or tattoo that might spark more familiarity. "I'm sure I've seen you before."

"You're mistaken." She shoves the glass into my hand and backtracks with the sound of the nearby opening door.

"Ahh, there she is." My old man sidles up to her, wrapping an arm around her waist to pull her close.

She doesn't stiffen or bristle. She follows the movement, flowing with the motion like water in a stream.

"I see you've already met my pretty penny." Luther's fingers tangle in her dress, deep and possessive. "I shouldn't have favorites, but it's no secret this woman has claimed all my attention."

"I can see why." I keep racking my brain, trying to pinpoint the familiarity. "Is there a reason why I feel like we've already met?"

My father seems to consider my question, glancing between us, back and forth. "I don't know. Maybe you've seen her on the television. Penny's not from Oregon. But the news of her disappearance may have crossed state lines."

"Penny?" Luca repeats. "That's her name?"

Hell opens up before me, threatening to swallow me whole.

If this woman is who I think she is, she's meant to be dead, her body dumped in a mass grave, her teeth and hair found among the remains of other sex slaves.

"Is something wrong?" My father grabs the last remaining glass of scotch from the tray and reclaims his seat. "Have you two met before?"

"No." I take a sip of liquor, gripping the glass like a motherfucking lifeline and still, the rage intensifies. "She must have a familiar face. That's all."

"I'm not sure about her face, but she has a truly unforgettable mouth." He laughs, the sound crawling over my skin like lice. "Don't you, baby girl?"

She smiles, the expression forced as she retreats.

"Where are you going?" He pats his lap. "Come here."

Penny eyes me, Luca, then my father before daring to approach with cautious steps. She considers every one of us a threat. My guess is that she's been exposed to group violations in the past.

"Come on." Luther reaches out, grabs her wrist, and yanks her onto his lap. "There's no need to be shy." He places his hand on her thigh, dragging it higher, beneath the hem of her yellow dress.

Every inch of skin he touches acts like a red-hot poker to my rage.

I want to hurt him. Torture him. I could rip his heart out with my bare hands.

Because if I don't, Decker, who I suspect is her brother, definitely will.

"I don't mean to cock block, but is that food still on the way?" Luca's words brush along the edge of my consciousness, barely breaching my growing instability.

"I'm starving," he adds, his gaze finding mine. "And you haven't even eaten today."

He's trying to pull me back. To drag me away from the tight grip of insanity.

But my father's hand keeps creeping higher and higher, on a path to violation right in front of my fucking eyes.

"Yes. Food." Luther slaps the inside of Penny's thigh then shoves her off his lap. "We need to feed our guests."

Penny stumbles to right herself, then hustles to escape inside.

"I didn't mean to spoil your fun." Luca gulps down the rest of his alcohol. "But, God, I'm hungry. I've been awake since dawn, while hangover Harry slept like a log." He jerks his chin at me. "Then he crawls out of bed and demands to leave before I can eat lunch."

He's picking up the slack. Succeeding where I'm failing.

I'm losing the battle to remain composed.

"I'm not hungover. But I am intrigued." I let the sentence fall, and take a generous gulp of liquor to help me finish. "These women of yours, are they for sale? Or hire?"

There's a tweak to his lips. A sly, overly arrogant tilt. "Yes. The women I'll show you tonight are all available for whatever you want."

"No. I'm talking about the women here. The ones I've already seen."

"My personal harem?" He frowns. "You're interested in sleeping with *my* women?"

"Maybe." I hedge my bets, but I'm not sure what for. There doesn't seem to be a level of deviance he finds unsettling.

"There's no maybes from me." Luca places his glass back on

the tray. "I'm definitely interested. I'd part ways with a lot of money for just a taste."

My father snickers. "Sorry, lads. I don't give up my toys until I'm good and ready."

"You're telling me no amount of money would tempt you to hand one of them over?" Luca rubs his hands together. "I thought you were in this business for the riches."

We're getting nowhere. Fast.

"I don't think his reluctance has anything to do with money. I'd take a guess the old man is worried he'll be quickly forgotten if a newer model takes one of his toys for a spin." I smirk. "Ain't that right, old goat?"

He narrows his eyes on me, taking the provocation and raising it with a conniving curve of lips. "For interest's sake, who do you have your eye on?"

I take another sip of liquid, letting the burn take over my tongue. "The jewel in your crown, of course. What's the point of the game if I can't have your best and brightest?"

"Is that what this is? A game?" He crosses his arms over his chest, the liquid jostling in his glass. "If so, maybe your amateur skills would be best suited for someone with a little less bite. Penny's a fighter. You wouldn't be able to handle her."

"He might not," Luca adds, "but I could. I've got more patience than your son."

"Really?" He drinks down his scotch and wipes a hand over his mouth. "Then how about you go speak to her so Cole and I can finally talk business?"

My pulse kicks at the small victory.

"It's more of a tease, if anything," he continues. "But if you're eager to get close to her, by all means, try your hand. Just don't blame me when she bites."

"And when I seduce her out of those panties? What then?"

"Then you back away slowly," I drawl. "Before my father gets a hold of you."

"Yes, sir." Luca pushes to his feet, grinning from ear to ear. "Consider me forewarned."

I watch him leave, taking the jovial vibe with him.

Tension settles between me and the man I once idolized. It coils tight, wrapping around my chest until I can't stomach looking at the son of a bitch who has become unrecognizable.

"What's this Penny thing all about?" Luther lowers his voice. "It's not like you to push for something that's not yours."

"We're having a bit of fun. That's all." I glance away, out past the pool toward the ocean-filled horizon. Anissa is out there somewhere. Alone. Hopefully packing her bags so I can get her as far away from this monstrous fuck as soon as possible.

"I know you, Cole. I'm well aware there's something more at play."

I turn back to face him, not bowing down to the judgment in his eyes. "I'll admit this isn't what I expected."

"You've changed your mind about the business opportunity?"

"No. That's not what this is about." I lay the bait, dragging it out slowly. "It's been a long time since Mom died. Seeing you enjoy yourself with a stream of women isn't fucking easy."

"I'm..." His expression loses the annoyed edge. "I didn't think this would affect you after all these years."

"It shouldn't. I'm not a kid anymore."

"But you're still my son."

I hold his gaze through the fake family moment. I don't let that motherfucker go while he's trapped in my sights. Every second immersed in this bullshit is more time for Luca to talk to the girl. "Don't spare it another thought. Just be aware Keira and Layla will take it harder than me. They were closer to Mom."

"I agree. And I apologize for blindsiding you for a second time." He pushes to his feet and straightens his jacket. "On that note, I think it's best if we get out of here."

"No. That isn't necessary."

"It's for the best. I can take you to the location for tonight's event." He waves at me to get off the sofa. "If we leave now, we'll have at least half an hour of privacy until the assets arrive to prepare."

Fuck his assets.

Fuck his location.

Fuck his ability to take another unhindered breath.

Luca needs time with Penny. Time that is quickly running out.

"Don't be ridiculous." I spread an arm along the backrest of the chair. "It's better to get over the shock now. There's no point running from it."

"I insist." He starts for the house. "We will have less interruptions this way. I don't want any more distractions while we discuss business. And let's not forget that woman of yours. We need to discuss her, too."

The mention of Anissa has me blinking back rage. "She's not worth mentioning."

"Really?" He continues to the house, forcing me to push to my feet and stalk after him. He doesn't pause until he reaches the door to wait for me. "I think your toy may have a vital role in establishing a new partnership between father and son."

"What kind of vital role?"

He glances over his shoulder, and paranoia leads me to believe he's testing me. His lazy scrutiny digs deep, searching for secrets to expose.

"*Stop.*" The feminine scream carries from inside. From Penny. "*Stop.*"

I don't have time to think before my father shoves the door aside and stalks forward. I follow close behind, reaching for a gun that isn't there.

"What's going on?" he bellows.

Penny stands in the corner of the kitchen, the counter clutched behind her as Luca holds up his hands in surrender from the other side of the room.

He looks guilty as fuck, the red stain of a slap mark on his cheek turning the taste in my mouth sour.

"Someone better start talking," I seethe. "My patience is growing fucking thin."

"He didn't do anything." The innocent voice of my brother comes from the doorway on the far side of the kitchen, his head poking around the frame from the hall.

"You saw what happened?" my father asks.

"I was snooping." Tobias takes a tentative step into the room. "I know I shouldn't, but Penny sounded upset and I was worried."

"And?" I grind my teeth to lessen the aggression in my tone. "What happened?"

"Nothing." He shakes his head. "The man was being nice and Penny was..." He glances at her with guilt, then quickly looks away, hanging his head.

"What, son?" Luther approaches him, placing strong hands on tiny shoulders. "What was she doing?"

The boy keeps his head lowered. "She was being mean."

Luther stiffens and stands to his full height. "You dare to make a guest of mine unwelcome?" He swings around, approaching her, making her cower.

She turns her face away, her arms wrapping around her stomach. "I'm sorry. I don't know what came over me."

"Fucking stupidity, that's what." He looms over her, his fists clenched at his sides. "Do you need to go back to basic training? Maybe I should send you to the farm so you can be reminded how well you're treated here."

"Please." She drops to her knees and grips his trousers. "I didn't mean it. I apologize."

I can't step in. Whatever the fuck she's done, I can't save her. I can't show my cards until I'm ready to shoot my way out of here. And I can't fucking do that without a goddamn gun.

"It's my fault." Luca's voice is calm. There's no hint of panic. "I got carried away. I tried to make small talk, and when I mentioned her past, I think she took it as a taunt."

Luther grips her chin, forcing her tear-soaked eyes to meet his as he raises a hand. "You need to be punished for your disobedience."

"Dad," I warn. "I'm growing tired of the adolescent distractions from these women. Can't we get the fuck out of here already?"

I pray he hears the insult. The subtle stab at his pride is the only thing capable of lowering his hand. Yet the threatening position of his arm doesn't lower.

"Fine. We'll leave." I start toward Tobias, offering my palm for a high-five he barely taps. "Until next time, little man."

287

I walk by him and into the hall, Luca following behind.

I only make it a few yards before he grabs my arm.

"I can't leave." His voice is low, his eyes wild, his nostrils flared. "He's going to hurt her."

"This isn't the most opportune time to fall victim to your conscience," I snarl under my breath.

His admission is dangerous. Fucking reckless. If we're overheard—if my loyalties are questioned—I'll make it out of here because I'm blood. He won't.

"Just keep walking. My father will follow."

"And if he doesn't?"

I shrug off his hold. "We just keep walking. We have no other choice."

22

ANISSA

I sit on the living room floor, my back against the sofa, my legs outstretched before me as I cradle the cell in my hand.

I never should've agreed to take the device. Not when I knew the temptation would eat me from the inside out.

I've battled indecision since the moment Cole walked from the house, and it isn't because I want to be rescued. I'm past that. What I require is grounding.

I slept with Cole Torian. A criminal. And not just any criminal, a high-functioning, incredibly successful, lawless entrepreneur.

There's no sense. No regret. No guilt.

I'm trying to encourage thoughts of disgust and shame when the only thing consuming me are memories of shock and goddamn bliss.

It's insanity.

Nobody in their right mind would look back on what happened last night and crave more.

But those lips.

The reverence.

He was another man. One who brushed his mouth over my injured shoulder with such exquisite adoration it still brings an enjoyable shiver to my skin.

I can't quit sinking my nose into the collar of his suit jacket to breathe his scent deep into my lungs. Each inhalation is a hit that fills me with warmth. With sizzling flashbacks.

I'd snatched his jacket from the dresser because it was the first thing within reach when I rushed from the bed to snoop on the conversation in the living room.

Now I can't bring myself to take it off.

Not when the Cole from last night wasn't the heartless mastermind I'd grown to despise. They're two contrary people—entirely different souls trapped in the same body.

And the split personalities aren't the only reason I should dial home.

Common sense demands I contact the Bureau. It's necessary on multiple levels. I can't be entirely sure of my timeline since boarding the jet, but I'm confident I'm meant to be back at the office by now.

Easton will wonder where I am. Taggert will take my no-show as a silent resignation. And both are likely to mount a full-scale search for answers.

I don't want to lead them here. Not when I'm certain Cole will finish Luther more efficiently than any organization ever could. He already has the means and the determination. If it weren't for that poor little boy, I'm sure this nightmare would already be over.

So now, I don't know what to do.

The more I contemplate reaching for the outside world, the more affirmative reasons compound. But thinking about betraying Cole makes my stomach hollow.

I can't even bring myself to stop seeing him whenever I close my eyes. He's always there, staring right back at me with his smug gorgeousness.

Taggart was right not to trust me. He knew one day I'd act exactly like my traitorous father. Maybe everyone in my department could see my weakness better than I could.

I unlock the phone, the *click* sound filling me with guilt.

I focus on the square call icon until my vision blurs. I keep staring until it's Cole that stares back at me.

"Goddammit." I relock the screen and shove the cell along the carpet, sliding it out of reach.

Betraying him doesn't feel right.

Being loyal to him brings the same discomfort.

"What the hell have you done to me?" I thump my back against the sofa, hoping the jolt will lead me in the right direction. I keep rocking into the cushions, the *thud, thud, thud* oddly soothing until the sound is accompanied by a far-off rumble.

I pause.

Listen.

It's a boat.

"Shit." The only thing that noise has ever brought is trouble.

I shove to my feet and glance toward the hall. I should get dressed, but I'd prefer to assess the risks before spending precious moments worrying about clothes.

I rush for the glass door.

Cole hasn't been gone for more than an hour. I'm not sure if that means the meeting didn't go as planned. Or something fell into place.

My pulse increases at the possibility of his success. A subtle kiss of excitement settles into my stomach before I think better of celebrating murder.

I pull the door wide, listening to the growl of the boat approaching, getting closer and closer with every passing second.

He told me to be ready in case something happened, but I'm not. My belongings aren't packed. I haven't showered. I'm still naked beneath the suit jacket.

I thought I'd have more time.

I walk outside, the beat of my pulse building. I break into a jog around the pool and continue down the gravel path, my pace increasing the more I convince myself Cole has come back to get me.

I'm halfway down the path when I see the boat. The same speedboat from the first day I arrived.

Any hint of optimism flees at the memory of the gun pointed in my face.

My steps falter.

My heart stops.

I can't see who's onboard, and I didn't have the foresight to

291

check what boat escorted the men from the island earlier. Maybe the threatening old man is their chauffeur. Or maybe he knows I'm alone and has returned to have his fun with me.

I slow, creeping forward, shielding myself behind bushes and trees.

I keep approaching the pier, not stopping until I've reached the last waist-high shrub, then I wait as my shadowed guests pull up a few yards away.

The engine is cut and the boat bobs into place while I scrutinize the shaded area underneath the upper-deck canopy, trying to make out the two silhouettes.

I'm not sure if it's Luca. The height of one person is similar to his. Big. Bulky.

I contemplate calling out. But what should I say?

If it's Cole, I want to run to him. To find out what happened to have him returning so soon. And if it's not, it's imperative I prepare for the worst. I need to know if I should be scrambling for the protection of the house before any danger approaches.

I stand, wrapping the jacket tight around me with one arm while I raise a hand to my brow, shielding the sun from my eyes to gain a better look.

An unfamiliar man steps out from beneath the shelter, his gaze fixed on me. He climbs onto the pier, tall, broad, and sporting an entirely blank expression. I've never seen such an emotionless face promote such pure hostility before. The man hurls bad juju without so much as a sneer.

I swallow, lick the dryness from my lips, and tell myself my fear is unsubstantiated. He could be here to help. This man, with his ice-cold stare, could have been sent by Cole.

"Hello?" I squint into the sun. "Who are you?"

"The name's Robert," he grunts. "You need to come with me."

"What? Why?" I backtrack, breathing through the panic.

"Ih-mur-juhn-see." The old Greek slides into view on the back of the boat, his smile wide. "Ih-mur-juhn-see. Ih-mur-juhn-see."

Fuck.

I quit fighting fear.

I turn.

Run.

Sprint.

My hair flicks in my eyes. My lungs burn from exertion. But I don't stop, don't even pause as pebbles bite into my feet and heat lashes my throat.

I head for the house, hoping it will be my savior.

I can grab the cell, call Cole, and shield myself in the panic room until he arrives.

Oh, God, how long will it take for him to get to me?

The thunder of faster footfalls follows me, the frightening sound increasing as I reach the pool.

I sense his darkness. His cruel intent. I don't want to know what this man hides beneath the blank expression.

I push myself harder, throwing myself at the glass door to yank it open. I'm inside, about to slam the barrier between us and lock him out when his arm launches through the closing space and snatches my wrist.

My heart lurches. My breathing stops.

I stare deep into those soulless eyes as I twist and tug, finally scrambling from his grip. But there's no time to close the door. It's too late. He's shoving my only protection wide to stalk inside, his shoulders broad and menacing.

I swing away and dash ahead, determined to make it to the panic room.

I don't even reach the hall.

He yanks me backward by my hair. Pain slices through my skull as he spins me around, slamming my face into the back of the sofa. My cheek breaches the cushioning and collides with the hard wood beneath, the impact buckling my knees to send me toppling to the floor.

Everything vanishes. Thought. Feelings. Consciousness.

Then it all comes rushing back in a tangled mess of panic and agony as my tormentor continues to drag me by my hair.

I kick, punch, and launch my elbows in every direction. I fight, fight, fight, never pausing. Not for a second. Not even when his hand latches onto my neck and squeezes.

The hold is nothing like Cole's.

This man's touch isn't a pleasurable grip. His fingertips dig deep, his strength tightening to restrict my breath.

I claw at his hands, scratching and flailing while fire burns a trail down my throat.

I let my legs fall out from beneath me, becoming a dead weight in the hopes he will drop me.

He doesn't.

He holds me like a rag doll, choking, suffocating while I scramble to regain my footing and ease the pressure.

"I could do this all day, bitch. But we've got somewhere to be."

I try to scream and only produce a squeak.

I need air.

I need help.

I need Cole.

"Do you want to come willingly or are you going to let me have more fun?" His gaze treks my body, over the exposed skin beneath the gaping jacket.

I struggle for air, gulping with no relief.

Darkness edges into the corners of my vision as my toes grasp for grounding. Everything moves incredibly fast and eerily slow at the same time.

I'm disoriented. Dazed.

I don't realize I'm dropping to the floor until my ass hits the hard tile and my palms slap against the soothing cold. I fall into a mass of tangled limbs, gasping, heaving, gulping. My chest rises and falls as I clamber to reclaim oxygen.

"Get up," he demands.

I don't know how.

"I said, get the fuck up." He kicks me, his booted foot launching into my ribs. The pain spreads through my lungs, bringing a dose of adrenaline-filled clarity.

He doesn't have a foreign accent. He's American.

"Who are you?" My voice is a weak rasp. "Do you work for Cole?"

"Cole?" He scoffs. "That man has no power over me. My orders come from someone with far more influence. Someone who is going to make Cole look like a puppy in comparison."

Luther?

Oh, God.

"What do you want with me?"

He grabs a fistful of my hair, dragging me to my feet. "I want you to get your ass on the fucking boat and quit wasting my time." He shoves me toward the glass doors, following a foot behind. "Keep moving."

I won't go. I can't bring myself to willingly follow.

If I get on that boat, I'm dead. Never to be found.

I make another attempt at escape, not thinking, just running. I spin, lunge, and sprint faster than I've ever sprinted before.

"Fucking bitch." He chases me, his booming footfalls tattooing my mind.

I aim for the hall, the archway within reach when he barrels into me from behind, launching me forward.

I can't divert my trajectory.

I can't stop the impact.

My head hits the wall. Hard.

Then blackness takes me away.

23

TORIAN

I lean against the hood of my father's car, Luca next to me, both of us waiting.

It's been five minutes since we walked outside, the time passing like an eternity as I glare at the front doors of the mansion.

"I'm going back in." Luca pushes from the car.

"No." I keep my focus on those doors, despising every second Luther remains inside. "It's fucking stupid to attempt saving her when we still don't know who she is, and it's obvious Luther isn't going to kill his prized possession."

"Sometimes death isn't the worst punishment," he snarls.

I know.

I fucking know.

But going in there to retaliate when our guns remain locked in the car will endanger the other women, too. Along with Tobias.

"She's survived this long." I shove from the hood and move to stand in front of him. "She's strong. A little while longer won't change her position."

He glares at me—glares right through me—until the sound of the front door opening has us both pivoting to watch my father and Chris walk outside.

"Sorry for the delay. I got stuck on a call." My father doesn't show an ounce of concern as he stalks for the car, and we all claim our previous positions in the vehicle.

We don't talk about what happened. The only reminder is Luca's hatred, which thickens in the air around us.

We're at the end of the street when Luther breaks the silence and starts telling me about the profound success of his business. He throws figures at me. Large numbers. Impressive stats.

I play along, acting interested in his scheme, pretending I'm considering taking a piece of the pie, while the hunger for retribution builds in my blood.

"My success has been built on trust. I'm known for my discretion. That's why the majority of my income is repeat business." He pivots his body to face me. "When I host parties, I don't just mingle among my clients. I participate. Not only for my own gratification, but to reassure my paying customers their actions aren't going to come with consequences."

I frown, feigning confusion when his perversions are crystal clear. "You openly indulge in the activities so everyone in attendance knows you're confident nobody will get caught?"

The strategy is business savvy. If only he didn't enjoy every vile fucking minute of it.

"It's more than that. They see me enjoying myself and understand they're among like-minded people. They're free from judgment." He waves a hand toward his window, indicating the pristine waters. "Solicitation is legal here. Pussy is easy to buy. But that's not what men are looking for. They want power and the ability to express their God-given instincts. These women provide that opportunity. Without restriction."

"None at all?" I raise a brow. "I'm assuming some of them have extravagant taste."

"Almost all of them do. There's a preference for young girls among the newer clients. And those who've been around longer tend to be sadists. Some even pay for the luxury of necrophilia."

"And you provide whatever they want?"

"There hasn't been a request I've denied."

I focus on the road, the quiet seeping under my skin. My father holds no shame for his actions. He doesn't care how Luca is now privy to his perversions. But I do. I despise the thought of anyone knowing what this man has done. What my own flesh and blood delights in. "I bet you've earned quite a reputation."

"True." His face breaks out in smug satisfaction. "I like to experience my clients desires firsthand. So whenever there's a new request, I always try it for myself."

I keep my focus out the window. I do everything in my power not to let my expression waiver. I play pretend like a fucking pro, holding my need for revenge so fucking tight all my muscles ache in protest.

I try not to picture his crimes, and fail.

I'm consumed with revulsion.

His sins are a disgusting taint on my mother's memory. So much so that the grief feels like I'm losing her all over again.

"Which brings me back to the conversation I brought up at the house." Luther relaxes into his seat. "Before we dive any deeper into discussions of a partnership, I want to see you with this shiny new toy of yours. I need to make sure you're fit for this lifestyle."

"See me with her?" I can't hold back the disgust from my voice.

"My clients need to trust you. They'll want confirmation you're one of them."

I clench my teeth, my fists, my muscles.

"It's not an issue, is it?" He eyes me with impatience. "We can sort this out today."

"That's not going to happen." My refusal holds too much anger. I can't rein it in.

"What's the harm?"

"The harm?" I grasp for a fucking tactic, scrambling to deflect this bullshit whatever way possible. "As far as I'm concerned, this is a business opportunity. One that shouldn't depend on the way I treat my toys."

"Normally, I would agree." His ageing face tightens with a myriad of wrinkles. "But my recent arrest is a blatant example of why I need likeminded people on my team. I can't risk trusting those who don't believe in my vision."

His vision? Of what? Female slavery?

He's lost his fucking mind.

"You don't trust me?" I seethe. "I didn't need to be a fucking addict to help you run the multi-million-dollar drug empire. Why the hell would you put restrictions on me now? Is this a test? Or maybe an attempt to push me away so you don't feel guilty distancing yourself even more from a family you no longer care about?" I throw the verbal punch as hard as I can, hoping to deflect attention away from Anissa. "Admit you're cutting us off. Have the balls to fucking say your adult children are out of the—"

"Stop being dramatic." He scowls, his lips pinching.

I can't stop. There's no peace to be found in this war zone. All I can do is glare at my father, wondering who the hell he's become.

"My answer is no." I hold his gaze, staring him down. "I don't have to earn your trust or prove myself. If a lifetime of servitude isn't enough, you can drive us straight to the fucking jetty and we'll be on our merry way."

He doesn't respond. Not in words.

Instead, he turns his judgmental focus out the window as Chris continues along narrow streets lined with more expensive houses.

I seethe in silence, my frustration and concern growing the longer I remain in the shrinking space.

My father won't give up. Not easily. He never does.

He'll want another round of negotiations. He won't stop until he gets his prize, which means I have to get Anissa back to the States before he grows tired of asking and transitions into taking.

I should call her and make arrangements for her immediate return home. The pilots are on standby. I can get a boat to pick her up. Hunt could meet her when she lands. He would escort her to my house, where she would stay until I have the opportunity to mold her story into what I need it to be to appease her fellow agents.

The lack of control is the only thing stopping me.

I want to see her board the jet. I don't like the thought of her travelling on her own.

"We're almost there." My father taps on his window, pointing farther along the street to another gated property. "We can discuss this inside."

"No, we're done with this discussion." I mark my line in the sand. "I'm too hungover for this shit. Either tell me to leave or quit with the domineering bullshit."

He smiles at me, the expression far from comforting. "You're right. We'll find another way to prove your loyalty to my clients."

He pulls a cell from his jacket pocket and makes a quick call, telling the person on the other end of the line we've arrived.

The car inches closer, the gates opening on our approach.

The property is a minor-scale version of the place we just left —manicured gardens, oozing extravagance. The only thing lacking is the heightened security. I don't see any cameras and there are no rifle-toting assholes walking the perimeter.

"The women live here?" Luca's scopes our surroundings, checking every angle. "Spreading their legs has to be a small price to pay for all this luxury, right?"

"No. It's cheaper to house the women offsite." My father releases his seat belt. "This place is rented by the night. We're always switching up locations, both with where the assets are held and where we hold our parties."

Chris pulls in behind another expensive SUV and cuts the engine.

"Do we get our guns back now?" I ask. "You said there aren't any women here yet."

"No, but there will be." My father opens his door. "It's best to leave the weapons where they are."

I breathe through my anger. I fucking seethe through each breath as he climbs from the vehicle, Chris following straight after. They head for the house, waiting for us at the front door.

"I don't like this." Luca glances over his shoulder at me. "Something's not right. We should call for a car and get out of here."

I agree. If only the threat of Luther's motives weren't raising the hairs on the back of my neck. I have a feeling running with our tail between our legs might be more dangerous. "Give me half an hour. I need to work out what he's up to."

We get out of the car, the doors being locked seconds after, and make our way to my father's side.

"Everything okay?" His question is probably meant to be filled with concern, but all I hear is suspicion. He's closing in on me. Taking stock of my reactions.

"Other than having the hangover from hell, I'm fine." I approach the front door and pull it wide. "I still haven't eaten. I think I'm going to have to call an early end to this clusterfuck of a meeting and come back tomorrow."

"Don't be ridiculous. The caterers should have already stocked the fridge for tonight. There's plenty to eat in here." My father steps into the house and continues down the hall.

Great.

Fucking great.

Chris passes me as I continue to hold the door.

Then Luca approaches, his silent "what the fuck" loud and clear. He's lost his patience. He lost everything back at the house with the pretty Penny.

I pull the door shut behind us and follow along the hall, heading toward Chris's laughter. A ruckus of conversation builds with each step, but it's not my father and Chris. The other end of the discussion comes from someone else. Another man.

"Is that Robert?" Luca shoots me a glance.

I cock my head to confirm his suspicions.

I guess the asshole wasn't tailing us after all.

"We need to leave," Luca mutters under his breath. "This feels like a trap."

I know it does. Unease crawls over my skin, heightening my awareness.

The laughter continues, the mumbled conversation indecipherable.

"Head back outside," I tell him. "I'll meet you there."

Luca doesn't move. He keeps watching down the hall, waiting, until the sound of a feminine whimper breeches the boisterous amusement.

"Did you hear that?" He stiffens.

"Yeah, I fucking heard it." I jerk my head in the opposite direction. "Go. I'll meet you outside."

The whimper turns to a cry.

"I don't have the restraint for this shit." He clenches his fists. "I'm ready to—"

"Stop," the woman begs. "*Don't.*"

That voice. That tone.

Anissa.

I run, leaving Luca in my wake as I make it to the end of the hall to find her standing in the middle of the open living room, Robert's hand clenched around her suit-covered arm.

"What's going on?" I roar.

All eyes turn to me—my father, his men. Worst of all, Nissa.

At one time, I craved her mental torment. I wanted nothing more than to see her undiluted fear. And here it is, the horror intricately laced into her beautiful features, and the sight sickens me.

Her terror threatens to bring me to my knees.

"I said, what the fuck is going on?" I wrench my gaze from her and glare at my father as Luca closes in by my side. "What the fuck do you think you're doing?"

"Calm down." Luther gives me a dismissive glance.

"*Calm down?* You fucking stole from me." I storm forward. "That asshole has two seconds to get his hands off my property before I—"

"Before you what?" Chris blocks my path. "What are you going to do?"

I cock my fist and launch.

I don't think. I don't contemplate.

I send my knuckles into that motherfucker's nose, dropping him to the ground as I heave through panted breaths.

"That's what I'm going to do, asshole." I straighten my suit, trying to rein in the crazy. "If you dare to question me one more time my reaction won't be as kind."

"Cole," my father warns. "Control your temper."

How can I when Robert's continued laughter threatens to send me postal? The son of a bitch still doesn't see me as a threat as he slowly releases his hold on Anissa, his chest vibrating with barely contained laughter.

"You *stole* from me," I repeat.

Luther sighs. "We didn't steal anything. I told you I hoped this woman would help to cement our business agreement. That's the only reason I asked Robert to retrieve her. I didn't anticipate you making a childish refusal to prove yourself."

"That's because he's not like us." Chris spits blood onto the tile and glares as he climbs back to his feet. "It's an act."

"Jesus fucking Christ," Luca mutters over my shoulder. "What's he gotta do? Rape her in front of you?"

Chris pinches his bloodied nose. "Why the hell not? What's stopping him?"

Anissa gasps, the sound of fear almost strong enough to steal my attention. But I won't look at her again. I can't. I'll show my fucking hand if I stare into those eyes. They'll see she's my weakness, if they're not already aware.

"I'm not a fucking dog eager to perform." I work my fingers at my sides, preparing to make another strike. "That sounds more like your style."

"It definitely is." Robert waggles his brows and reaches out, running his hand through her hair. "So let me fuck her instead. You can watch."

My breaths come short and shallow. Every second his fingers touch her opens the floodgates to my rage.

"I'm done with this. We're leaving." I wave a hand at Luca, instructing him to escort Anissa. I still can't look at her. The image in my head is punishing enough. "We're going to take the car. You can pick it up at the port." I turn for the hall, ready to flee like the dog I claimed not to be.

"See? I told you he was a traitor," Chris drawls. "He set you up in Portland. He knew the Feds were making a move. Who's to say he didn't have Richard killed, too?"

Fuck.

I freeze in place.

Today wasn't about a business proposal.

My father is questioning my loyalty. He's testing me—and not my perversions. His sights are set on my obedience.

"You think I betrayed you?" I turn around. "How dare—"

"*Enough.*" Luther straightens to his full height, becoming the threatening tyrant from my childhood. "All I asked for was a

303

show of allegiance. A fucking sign of your commitment to the family business, and you gave me nothing. All I get from you, Cole, are the whispers from people who say you've turned on me."

"Whispers?" I raise my voice. "There are always fucking whispers. You know that as well as I do."

I'm being buried, the heavy weight of dirt compacting on top of me.

I don't know how to find safety. Not for me. Not for Luca. And fuck, definitely not for Anissa.

I have to give my father what he wants—a sign.

A fucking show.

"True." He inclines his head. "But whispers backed up by your refusal only make me question who you've become in my absence."

"You want proof?" I throw my arms wide. "I'll give you fucking proof."

Luca curses under his breath as I storm for Anissa, hating myself with each inch I approach.

I no longer fight my punishment. I can't. I deserve to look into those petrified eyes, the ones that also contain defiance, and a fuckload of hatred.

She clenches her fists at her sides. Her chin hitches in a worthless show of strength.

She's still so fucking strong, staring me down, questioning my motives. There's no hint of her thinking I'll be her savior. There's only loathing and desolation beaming back at me.

I've reclaimed the villain status in her story, and that's okay. I'll pay whatever price necessary to keep air in her lungs.

"I'll show you the hits she's taken at the price of my enjoyment." I stop in front of her and steel myself, straightening my shoulders, tightening my jaw.

I pretend she's nothing.

Not my woman.

Not the air I breathe.

"Here's your fucking proof." I shove the jacket from her shoulders, pushing it from her body to fall to the floor.

But the evidence staring back at me isn't something I inflicted.

The myriad of blacks and blues marring her once milky skin aren't my doing.

I didn't create the mottled bruise covering her ribs. Or the scratches along her legs. And not once was my hold against her throat worthy of creating the red marks that perfectly form the imprint of a hand.

The fading proof of rope burns on her wrists are nothing in comparison to the brutality before me.

"Well?" Chris asks. "What are you waiting for? Move out of the fucking way so we can see."

I sneer, sheer menace pulling at my lips as I meet her gaze and wordlessly promise retribution. But the woman staring back at me doesn't resemble the same person from seconds ago.

Those eyes are now glazed, her tears barely bottled.

Her lips tremble. She pleads for help without a word, and all I want to do is slay the fucking world to make this right.

"It looks like I've been outdone." I suck in a breath and force myself to turn away from her. "Here I was thinking I could show you my handiwork, but it's obvious your dog has ruined my masterpiece."

I grab Anissa's wrist and yank her forward, exposing her.

"Holy fuck." Luca's curse doesn't sink in. Nothing breeches my internal battle.

I want their blood.

I want their pain.

I want anything and everything that will strip me of the fucking guilt tearing me from the inside out.

"He laid hands on her." I glare at my father. "What would you do if someone tainted your pretty Penny like this?"

He presses his lips tight, not buying into my anger.

"Answer me," I demand. "Tell me how this is acceptable."

"My concern is *your* actions. Not his."

I'm still losing, the dirt compacting harder to bury me alive.

Anissa's breaths become audible, the tiny pants of panic undoing me.

I'd die to tell her how strong she is. To remind her of the shit she's already lived through. To show her what she looks like through my eyes.

Instead, I step away from her—away from the numbing hitch accompanying her inhales—and approach Luther. A throb builds behind my sternum. It's common sense trying to alert me to an impending mistake, but I have no other choice.

"Do you want to know why I refused to jump through your hoops today?" I get right in his face. "Do you want me to explain why I'm above all this unnecessary bullshit?"

"A legitimate reason is all I'm waiting for, son."

I scoff out a laugh and shake my head. "It's because I've already done a lifetime worth of parlor tricks. And I know how to fucking pre-empt them. I came here looking to join your partnership after already providing my evidence. Dragging this bitch here, abducting her, drugging her, and using her fucking body is my testament."

"We do that shit on the daily," Chris mutters. "It's nothing special."

I hold my father's gaze and swallow over the tightening vise around my chest. "She doesn't look familiar to you?"

Anissa gasps.

She knows where I'm going with this. She understands the risks.

"Should she?" Luther glances behind me, his brow furrowed as he takes her in. "I don't recognize her at all."

"That's a pity. Maybe none of this shit would've happened if you did."

He returns his attention to me, his eyes narrowing. "Who is she?"

"Special Agent Anissa Fox, William Fox's daughter, and one of the arresting agents from Richard's funeral."

"You brought a fucking Fed into the heart of our operation?" Robert asks. "Are you fucking insane?"

"We brought her to an undisclosed island, you fucking piece of shit." Luca stalks toward him. "You assholes are the ones who brought her here."

I ignore the build of their animosity as I continue to stare at my father. I can't read him. I don't know which way he'll swing.

I can only hope—and fucking pray—I've anticipated the correct reaction.

"You're not going to respond?" I growl. "You don't think I knew I'd need to prove my worth to you when I've spent every day of my life doing the same damn thing?"

I backtrack, returning to Anissa's side as my father watches in avid fascination.

"I knew you'd want some type of proof." I grab her wrist and force her to do a spin, flaunting my control. "So I went above and beyond. I put all your men to shame by abducting an FBI agent—a woman who helped to put you behind bars, for fuck's sake."

Nissa yanks her arm from my grip, and I pretend her rejection doesn't stab me through the fucking chest. Out of all the people I'm trying to convince of my sincerity, she isn't one of them.

"You put a lot of thought into this." Luther continues to eye her as he steps forward, reaching out to touch.

"Don't even think about placing hands on her." I block his path. "You don't deserve to play in my league."

He doesn't react. The seconds tick by in painful increments. Then finally, with excruciating lethargy, his lips lift into a grin. "Touché."

"If that's an apology, it's a fucking pathetic one." I glance down at the jacket on the floor, then jut my chin at her. "Put it back on."

"I won't apologize." My father's voice remains strong.

He doesn't need to tell me. I already know from a lifetime of experience.

"But I will admit I'm impressed. I never would've crossed the line to work off William's debt through his daughter."

"I didn't cross anything. The line no longer existed once she helped put you in jail."

He nods. "Again, I'm impressed."

"It's a little late for that." I wait for Anissa to shrug into my overbearing jacket, then grab her wrist. She fights again, trying to yank herself from my grip, slowly killing me in the process. "You can keep your business to yourself. I no longer want a part of it."

"Don't take my actions personally." My father placates me

with one of those chastising parental looks. "You know as well as I do it's not smart to ignore rumors."

"Maybe that's true if you're not questioning your own flesh and blood. But you've gone too far this time, old man. You betrayed me. You stole from me. And you let that piece of shit brutalize my property. As far as I'm concerned nothing but a seriously impressive act of apology will undo the damage you've done." I hold out a hand, palm up. "Now, give me the fucking keys to your car. We'll drive ourselves out of here."

24

ANISSA

I'm a heartbeat away from hysteria. The delirium looms close, ramping up my pulse as I wait for either side to crumple.

Cole and his father stare each other down. And Luther's men are just as hostile with their unshakable glares.

Tension crackles in every direction and all I can do is wait for a spark to ignite the situation into a raging inferno.

"The keys," Cole demands.

Luther raises his chin, his nostrils flaring with a deep inhale until finally, he inclines his head. "Chris, hand them over."

Hope builds wings inside my chest, lessening the craziness and smothering my internal screams for revenge.

I want them to pay for what they've done. Someone needs to answer for my injuries. For my humiliation and potent fear.

"*Chris*," Luther warns. "The keys."

The henchman bares his teeth. "If I hand them over, they'll have access to their guns."

What? A sob thickens in my throat. Cole is unarmed? He announced my FBI status without a safety net?

"It's not hard to see where the rumors are coming from." Luca shakes his head. "These assholes would make anyone paranoid."

"These assholes are the ones betraying my father," Cole adds. "Not me."

"This has gotten out of hand." Luther attempts to placate the room by raising his hands in surrender. "Walking away on bad terms won't do either of us any good."

"Then it's up to you to make this right. Fix it."

"How?" Luther grates. "What do you expect me to do?"

Cole laughs, the low grumble vibrating through my chest. His gorgeousness is lost under brutality. The harshness of his features resembles those of the devil. He's a menacing, furious predator.

"I expect you to do what's necessary. What *he* deserves. What you would insist if the situation was reversed."

Nobody breeches the void of silence. Not for long seconds as concerned glances are shared between Chris and Robert.

"Your men don't know their place," Cole continues. "Either show them the error of their ways or consider this the dissolution of our relationship."

Again, Luther remains quiet. He doesn't even change his expression.

It's Luca who breaks the gridlock by stalking to Chris. "Keys. *Now*."

The unfamiliar man complies, slapping the car fob into Luca's palm. "Safe travels, motherfucker."

"Until we meet again, asshole." Luca turns and stalks for Cole. "Are you ready?"

"Yeah. Let's get the fuck out of here." My protector focuses on his father, his mouth breaking into a sardonic smile. "Make your decision, old man. But realize if Robert is left standing, you're as good as dead to me."

He walks for the hall, dragging me along with him, my feet fumbling as if they're painted on.

"Son—"

"Don't fucking 'son' me." Cole doesn't stop our progression across the room. "Make your choice. I won't wait forever."

Each step we take adds a layer of vulnerability to my precarious position. I don't appreciate having my back to the enemy—not when there's no protection other than the threats of the vigilant defender at my side.

We're all out of our depth. None more so than me.

"Keep moving," he mutters. "Hurry up."

We reach the shadowed hall and I glance over my shoulder to see Luca following right behind.

His focus is intense. Pained.

He pities me. The emotion is potent enough to make my skin crawl.

Fuck those monsters. Fuck them and the ease with which they broke me.

I didn't stand a chance.

Not when I was stranded on an island without a weapon or a chance of escape. I was an easy target, and it's all Cole's fault.

I yank my hand from his grip, earning another dose of pity, this time from the man himself. Those dark eyes hit me even harder than Luca's did, smothering me with their guilt.

"Robert..." Luther's ominous tone carries toward us. "You were out of line."

"Quick." Cole places a hand on my lower back, providing gentle pressure. "We need to get out of here."

The panic returns. The fear and lack of control collide with enough force to have me running for the door.

"You can't be serious." Robert's words are filled with incredulity. "The bitch put up a fight."

The bitch.

Me.

He continues to argue how I deserved what I got, his voice growing animated, his fury escalating.

My own volatile emotions build. Rage curdles among the self-pity and panic. I want to hurt him like he hurt me. To see the horror in his eyes and the shake in his limbs.

"Luther, what the hell are you doing?" Robert raises his voice. "What the fu—"

A bang bursts around me, the noise attacking my ears and reverberating off the walls.

I scream.

And scream.

And scream.

The mania I've been fighting finally takes over.

I lose all grasp on reality. I can't see. Can't hear. Can't think.

A hand clasps over my mouth. An arm is wrapped around my waist.

I'm lifted off the ground and dragged outside into the sunlight while Luca storms ahead, leading the way to a black SUV parked on the pebbled drive.

Cole murmurs in my ear. He says words I don't understand. Soothes me with things that don't make sense until Luca pulls open the back door of the vehicle and I'm guided inside.

The moment Cole releases me, I crumple. I miss his protection as soon as it's gone. I'm exposed and weak without him.

The seconds he takes to climb into the front passenger seat seem like a lifetime spent on the frontlines of a world war.

"What's the plan?" Luca sinks behind the wheel. "What are we doing?"

"You're going to start the fucking car and get us out of here." Cole opens the glove compartment and retrieves two guns, handing one to Luca before placing his own beneath his jacket.

"There's only two of them now. We could take them. We could end—"

"No." Cole slams the glove compartment shut. "Not with her here. I won't risk it."

I want to sob at his conviction. But I won't. I refuse to remain in this weakened state. I'm not a spineless damsel.

What I need to do is tell them I'm okay. I have to side with Luca and make it clear this has to end now. But the words won't form.

"Drive," Cole demands. "*Now.*"

My heart lurches as the engine ticks over. Relief tingles its way through my belly with the slow inch of the car creeping forward. The acceleration increases. Going, going.

Then stops.

Luca taps the brakes, his muttered expletive filling the car interior.

I'm hit with another dose of sickening adrenaline, my gaze darting everywhere to seek answers until my focus finds the mini bus pulling into the drive, each window filled with a new nightmare.

Pained eyes stare down at us, the pale faces of female passengers filling me with an emotion far beyond description. There have to be more than twenty women on that bus. Twenty sex slaves, their haunted features tattooing my mind.

They pass slowly as I stare into the dull blue eyes of a woman who can't be older than eighteen. There's concern in her features —concern for me—when I'm the one leaving hell as she's about to enter.

"Move," Cole growls. "Get us to the port."

I shake my head, needing to deny the instruction, but my voice is lost in a deep and consuming void. There's nothing inside me. No conviction. No determination.

I close my eyes as the car rolls forward and all I see is that woman. That *girl*.

She's going to go through far more than the trauma I endured. The things they will do to her... The horrors...

"Stop," my voice is croaky, barely recognizable. Not that my attempt to speak matters. I'm ignored. Nothing changes in the tense interior of the car. Pebbles continue to grate under the slowly turning tires. The engine purrs without pause.

"Cole," I rasp, inching forward in my seat. "We need to go back."

"We can't." His tone is frosty, so damn cold as Luca accelerates onto the road.

Guilt makes me tremble—my arms, my hands, my feet.

How can I escape to find sanctuary when other women are about to endure far worse?

It's not right.

It's beyond redemption.

"We can't leave them behind." I grab Cole's shoulder, demanding attention. "*Please.*"

"It's okay." Luca meets my gaze in the rearview. "We'll help them once you're safe. But we need to get you away from here first."

"No." I shake my head. "I can't. Please, Cole."

He doesn't respond. The car doesn't slow.

"Fine." I slide to the door, grab the handle, and shove, flinging the heavy weight wide.

"Jesus. *Fuck.*" Luca slams on the brakes, the wheels screeching with the sudden impact.

I don't wait for them to deny me again. Once the car stops, I scramble outside and start running in the direction we came, ignoring the ache from every inch of my brutalized body.

I'll make it back to that house. I don't know what I'll do once I get there, but I'll do something. Anything.

I'll find a phone. I'll contact the embassy.

Rushed footsteps approach behind me. Strong arms engulf my waist. I'm lifted, hauled off the ground and into a hard body.

The restriction is suffocating.

"Don't." I thrash. I beat at the familiar arms enslaving me.

"We can't go back, Niss." Cole's voice brushes my ear, the apologetic tone tearing me to pieces. "You need to listen to me."

"We can't leave them." I kick. I fight.

"You don't think this is fucking killing me, too?" His hold tightens, squeezing me to his chest. "But we can't help them right now. If we go in there guns blazing, we're only going to get them killed."

"*No.*"

No. No. *No.*

I deny him even though logic stabs through me, the truth in his words too brutal to handle.

My eyes burn. Tears consume my vision. I'd rather die than be responsible for their continued torture.

"I'll make this right." He lowers me to the ground and grabs my arms, turning me to face him. "Believe me, Nissa." He continues to hold me, not letting go. "I'll make them fucking pay."

I clench my fists and thump his chest. I fight against myself. I battle the injustice one punch at a time.

"It's okay." He pulls me close, cradling the back of my neck. "We're going to help them. You just need to trust me. But right now, we have to go. I don't want anyone seeing you."

"I don't know how to leave them behind."

"You can." His hands slide away, leaving me empty as he steps back. "And you will. Trust me enough to believe I'll get them out of there."

"Today?"

He winces. "No, but eventually. I need to get you Stateside first. We'll go back to the island, grab our things, then head home where I can work out a better plan with Hunt and Decker."

"That will take days. If not weeks."

"There's no other choice." He grabs my hand and leads me to the car. "Not unless you want to risk some of them dying in a shootout, and that's not something Luca needs on his conscience."

"What about yours?"

A lone brow rises. "You think I've got a conscience?"

"I know you do."

"Then I guess mine has taken enough of a beating today to last a lifetime." He directs me into the back of the car, this time following in beside me. He holds me close against his side as he slams the door shut, then barks an order to get us to the boat.

I can't switch my brain off as we speed through the narrow, winding streets. My stomach roils with shame at every corner. Guilt accompanies every breath. And the worst part is the relief. Every mile we move away from Luther makes me stronger.

It helps when Cole huddles me close, his arm never losing its protective hold as he bundles me against his side.

Yes, in the heat of the moment I blamed him for today, but I'm the one who fought to stay. I begged not to be sent home. I wanted to be here. And I can't pretend I didn't know the risks.

I relax into him, running my hand over his shirt-covered stomach, my fingers brushing his holstered gun.

He stiffens and remains taut.

He doesn't trust me. I guess he has no reason to.

But I trust him.

He could've left me with Luther instead of risking every future opportunity to take his father down. He didn't have to fight for me. He did some crazy shit in an effort to help me escape.

"Your dad could've demanded my death when you announced I was with the FBI."

He strokes my hair, his fingers tangling in the knotted strands. "I know."

The confirmation makes my stomach turn. "You weren't worried?"

"I was fucking petrified."

I close my eyes and wince through the pain in my ribs as I sink farther into his warmth. "He's not going to let you keep a walking, talking liability. At some point, he will want to make sure I'm silenced."

Cole doesn't answer. He doesn't do anything apart from drag his fingers through my hair.

"Cole?" I push back from his chest to look at him, but he doesn't meet my gaze. "He's going to come after me, isn't he?"

"He can try. I won't let him anywhere near you."

The adrenaline rollercoaster reaches another peak. My pulse intensifies. My throat tightens.

"Don't worry." He shoots me a half-hearted grin, his gorgeousness not doing anything to appease my churning insides. "He's going to take stock of what happened today and realize he fucked up. If he has anything planned for you, he won't set the balls rolling until we're long gone."

"Are you sure?"

He drags me back into his side and plants a kiss on my forehead. "You're safe, little fox. I promise I'll get you home in one piece."

25

TORIAN

She lets me guide her from the car and onto the jetty, the jacket huddled close around her chest.

I keep a hand on the low of her back, the touch soft but just as easily construed as threatening if any of my father's vultures are watching. We need to maintain the pretense of her being my captive, which shouldn't be hard when she's as edgy as a beaten snake.

"Are we riding with Amar?" Luca shadows Anissa from the other side. "His boat is still docked."

I nod. "I want the quickest option."

If he didn't have a duffel full of suspect items like bleach, explosives, and wireless detonators back at the house, maybe we could cut and run without this additional trip. Unfortunately, I know how thorough my father will be once I'm gone.

His men will snoop and I don't want to give them more ammo to build their suspicions. Returning to finish this will be hard enough already.

"Shit." Nissa stubs her toe on an unlevelled board and stumbles forward, her jacket billowing open.

"I've got you." I grab her with both arms and haul her upright, positioning myself in front of her to cover her exposed body. "We're almost there." I hike a thumb over my shoulder toward the boat a few yards ahead. "It won't be long, and we'll be out of here."

She cinches the clothing back around her waist and glances in the direction I pointed, her eyes widening.

"That's the boat?" Her gaze cuts to mine, her pupils dilated.

"What's wrong?"

"I can't go on that thing." She jostles her arms from my grip and steps back. "Not again."

Again?

A rumble of a storm builds inside me, dark and thunderous.

"That's how you got here?" I keep my voice low. "You came on Amar's boat?"

She returns her focus over my shoulder, her skin losing the slight tinge of color she only just started to regain as she stares for long moments.

"Anissa?" Luca steps in beside me, facing her head on. "You need to tell us if it was him."

"I don't know who Amar is. But if he's an old Greek piece of shit who delights in the suffering of women, then yes, that's him." She sucks in a deep shuddering breath. "He drove Robert out to get me."

I'll slaughter him.

I'll slit the motherfucker's throat and watch the shark frenzy when I throw him overboard.

"I'll find us another boat." Luca turns in a slow circle, searching our surroundings. "We can—"

"No." I lean toward her until her gaze meets mine. "We're taking Amar's boat."

She blinks at me, confusion and fear accompanying every bat of her lashes.

"It's okay." I return my hand to her back, gently coaxing her forward. "We're going to use this as an opportunity."

"For what?" She frowns. "I don't want to go anywhere near him."

"We're going to get you some closure."

"Let's be honest," Luca drawls. "Revenge is a more accurate description."

Her eyes flare. Her lips part. She stands there for long moments, seeming lost in an internal struggle that keeps the blood drained from her face. All her features become brighter against her ivory skin. Those green irises are more luminous. Her lips are deep red and fucking inviting.

"No." She hugs her arms around her waist. "I can't."

"Can't?" A vicious bite laces my words. That asshole is just as responsible for her injuries as Robert. They both deserve death. "Why not?"

"We need to leave it to the authorities." She raises her chin, her determination returning. "I won't be a part of this."

I itch to shake some sense into her. To grasp her shoulders and rattle that deluded brain of hers.

But she's so fucking fragile.

The woman is glass. One sudden move and she'll shatter.

"What are the local cops going to do?" Luca grates. "And how the fuck do you think you're going to get anywhere near a station to make a statement? If Luther sees you—"

"This is the way we do things." I cut him off, not wanting her spooked by any more threats about my father. "This is our justice system."

She stares back at me with pleading eyes, her internal struggle loud and clear.

Our lack of similarities has never been more apparent. We're worlds apart. Polar opposites.

I've always refused to be shoved into one of her perfectly judged boxes, but when it comes down to it, she's the good and I'm the bad.

She's the light to my dark.

And no matter how much I wish I could give her common ground to cling to, I can't turn my back on giving Amar at least a taste of what he deserves.

She shakes her head. "This isn't me. I won't be responsible. I can't."

"You don't need to do anything." I lean closer so it's just the two of us. "This is my score to settle."

I know she's battling demons. Fighting her nightmares. All while she stands there blinking back at me.

"He's going to be punished regardless," Luca murmurs. "At least if you're here the retaliation will be restrained."

That's true.

If she wasn't with me I'd take my time torturing him. He'd lose fingers and toes. Maybe even his tongue. And he'd deserve it. But I can't do that now. Not with her judgment and disapproval smothering me.

I won't add to her torment.

"What will you do?" Her question is an accusation. "How far will you take this?"

After everything she's been through, she still sees me as the bad guy. It's who I am to her. It's who I'll always be.

A fucking villain.

"How 'bout I go easy on him? Just for you." I don't wait for an answer. My admission of leniency is bad enough without coddling her any more. I grab the crook of her arm and lead her forward, my gaze turning to Luca. "Go ahead and tell him we want to leave. Make sure he knows we're in a hurry."

"I'm on it." He jogs ahead.

"Cole..." Anissa grows taut beneath my touch, the tension growing tighter the closer we get. "I can't do this. I feel..." She splays a hand over her jacket-covered stomach. "It's wrong... I shouldn't... My job..."

"Sorry, little fox. I'm not giving you a choice. He needs to pay."

She stares at me. Stares and stares and fucking stares as she drags her feet as slowly as possible. "I..."

"What? Get it out of your system."

She sighs. "Do you enjoy it? Are you hungry for it?"

Again, she's making me into a monster when all I want to be is her savior. She refuses to understand how the justice system needs to be different in the underworld. We dance to a different rhythm. Sing to our own fucking tune.

"I know you like to believe I'm the devil, Niss, but taking action is a fucking necessity, not the highlight of my day." It's a lie. One I hope she doesn't see for the blatant mistruth it is.

Hurting Amar will be the pinnacle of my week after what he did. My fucking year.

"That's not what I was implying." She winces. "Revenge can cloud your judgment and—"

"I'm not clouded. Not in the slightest. Nobody steals from me, Nissa. Not if they want to live to tell the tale."

We approach the boat where Amar stands behind the wheel, revving the engine to life.

I feel the moment she sights him. Her body revolts. Her breathing quickens.

"You're safe." I glide my hand to her wrist. "He's not going to do anything to you."

"It's not me I'm worried about. I'm just..." She sighs. "I'm strung out on adrenaline and can't think straight."

"Keep quiet, and you'll be fine."

"I know. I won't say another word." She lowers her gaze as I drag her onto the boat. The closer we get to her tormentor, the more she huddles into herself, bowing her head. It's fucking torture to watch her suffer from his toxic presence.

I don't want her to wilt. Not for anyone.

"Mr. Torian," Amar greets me with a grin. "Did you enjoy your visit?"

"Unfortunately, there were complications." I glare, making it clear I'm in no mood to talk. "Just hurry up and get us back to the island."

"Of course." He nods and returns his attention to the wheel to start reversing the boat from the jetty.

I make a show of dragging Anissa to the bench seat and sit her down beside Luca. Once seated, she doesn't raise her focus above waist height. She places her hands in her lap and plays with the quicks on her nails, rubbing them back, over and over.

I stand before her, my feet between hers, our legs brushing. It's strange how much I need the contact. Even the slightest connection reminds me she's okay. And the farther we move into open water, the more I realize she isn't entirely vulnerable.

She sits a little straighter with each passing minute. Her expression grows fierce. She becomes emboldened before my eyes, her lips setting in a thin line, her forehead creasing. And those hands stop fidgeting and turn into clenched fists.

She's gains strength with the isolation, her focus raising to meet mine. "Have you changed your mind?"

"Soon." I curb the need to soothe the growing bruise on her cheek with a delicate brush of my hand. "It won't be long now."

I kid myself into thinking she's growing disappointed with my delay. That she's ditched the cloak of integrity and wants to dabble in the ways of my world.

But my mind isn't creative enough to imagine her as anything less than entirely ethical. She's too virtuous. I doubt she'll ever change, no matter how much I want her to.

"Stay with her." I glance at Luca. "Make sure she's all right."

He nods. "What's the plan?"

I shrug, despite already knowing my actions are going to be mild. I can't stand the thought of her having more confirmation of my satanic status. She despises who I am enough without more evidence to fuel her judgment. "Just watch her, okay?"

"I will."

I step away, her heat vanishing in an instant as I make my way to the helm and mimic Amar's stare across the open expanse of deep blue water. "Do me a favor and kill the engine."

There's a beat of silence. A tense pause.

"Excuse me, Mr. Tor—"

"Kill the fucking engine."

He stiffens, his knuckles turning white with his tightened grip against the wheel. "Sure. No problem." He eases back on the throttle, slowing our movement, then turns off the ignition. "Is something wrong?"

"That's exactly what I hope to find out." I turn to face him, leaning my hip against the cockpit as we bob in open waters. "Is it true you returned to my island this morning and assisted in robbing me?"

He has a "holy shit" moment. One of those brief eye-widening, lip-parting shows of shock which is quickly hidden behind fake confidence.

"No. I drive the boat. Nothing else. I don't steal from you."

"You escorted a thief to and from the island where he committed the crime, making you an accomplice."

"No. I did not know." He holds up his hands. "I thought you sent him. I thought he work for you, Mr. Torian."

I raise a brow. "Really?"

"Yes. *Yes.*" He nods rapidly. "That man, he works for your family. Your father. I thought you send him."

"You thought I sent one of my father's men to retrieve something I could've easily brought on my own? Is that the lie you're going with?"

His eyes bug. "It's no lie. I promise you. No lie at all."

"Do you know what I do to liars?"

"I'm no liar. I swear to you. I would never—"

"How was the woman taken from the island, Amar? Did she willingly walk onto the boat? Was she forced? Was she hurt?"

Panic starts to set in. His hands fidget. His gaze darts to Luca who stares with intent, appraising the situation from his position beside Nissa.

"Answer me," I growl. "Tell me what happened."

"She was sleeping. The man carried her."

"Sleeping?" I chuckle through the rage. "In broad daylight? You must have thought she was a heavy sleeper."

He doesn't respond, not apart from the agitated twitch of his fingers at his sides.

"And what about the other day? What excuse do you have for threatening my property by holding a gun to the woman's head?"

I realize the mistake of my question as soon as the words are out. I've encouraged his attention to stray to Nissa, his gaze narrowing on her.

"Eyes on me." I lash out, grabbing him by the throat, my fingers squeezing tight. "Don't even fucking breathe in her direction if you want to live to see another day."

Her gasp brushes my ears in yet another sign of our differences. Her disgust must be building, yet I revel in the retaliation. The frantic beat of his pulse beneath my fingers is cathartic. Fucking thrilling.

"I mean no disrespect." He clasps his hands in prayer. "Please. I made a mistake."

"You made many." I dig my fingers deeper. "You threatened something of mine. Held a gun to her head. Then you had the audacity to return and help someone steal her from me."

"I was only—"

"*Stealing from me,*" I snarl.

He shakes his head. "No. No, sir. I would never—"

"But you did. You drove a thief to my island and stood by, watching him commit the crime. Then you gave him safe passage to Naxos." I inch closer and breathe in the fear ebbing off him. "Do you know what he did to her? Did you know he hit her? Hurt her? Choked her? Now she's damaged goods, Amar."

"I did not know." He bobs those praying hands between us. "I swear I did not know."

I release his throat and watch him stumble backward. "You're not a stupid man. You knew exactly what you were participating in."

He returns his attention to Anissa, his deeply tanned skin growing pale.

"I said, don't fucking look at her." I snatch my gun from the holster and shove it against his forehead.

I itch to pull the trigger. I fucking throb with the need to end his life.

The only thing stopping me is her.

Fucking Anissa and her goddamn morality that hovers over me like a toxic cloud.

"*Please.*" Amar lowers to his knees before me, his head bowed. "I have children. Grandchildren. They rely on me."

I keep the barrel aimed on his skull and my mind set on revenge.

I can't let him walk away. He doesn't get to hurt her and then escape unscathed.

"I understand." I suck in a calming breath. "I have people who rely on me, too. Their income is dependent on my success, and that success is dependent on my power. My entire empire would crumple, affecting all those in my employ, if people thought they could get away with disrespecting me."

"I beg of you, have mercy." His eyes glaze, the hint of tears almost sickening me. "I have a daughter. She has three sons. Growing boys. I help them every day. I give them—"

"*Enough.*" I can't deal with his sob story. The pathetic

weakness only increases my loathing. "You can relax, old man. I'm not going to kill you. You're only going for a swim."

"A swim?"

"That's right." I holster my gun and wave a hand for him to stand. "You steal from me. I steal from you. And this boat seems like the perfect payment."

"Oh, no." He begins to sob. "Please, no."

"Hurry up, Amar." Luca walks toward us. "We don't have time for your crocodile tears."

"No, I won't go. I'll drown. This is murder."

I reclaim my gun, my patience entirely lost, and place the barrel on his temple. "No, this will be murder."

"*Get up.*" Anissa's scream splits the ocean silence as she pushes to her feet. "Swim, you heartless piece of shit."

"Anissa." Luca is the one to warn her of the precarious position she's putting herself in.

I don't say a word.

I keep my mouth shut because the storm of strength she exudes isn't something I'm willing to stifle.

"Get on your feet and fucking swim," she snaps.

Amar looks at me, then Anissa, and back again. But this time, it isn't in fear. His eyes are scrutinizing. Calculating.

"You heard the lady." I jerk my gun skyward. "On your feet. Now."

Finally, he complies, moving like a ninety-year-old as he climbs to his feet instead of the active man he's always been. "You would sentence a grandfather to death for doing his job?"

"I would slit your throat in a heartbeat for far less." I grab his arm and drag him starboard. "You should be grateful I'm being lenient."

"Let me take it from here." Luca joins me, grabbing Amar by the back of the shirt to encourage him to straddle the side of the boat.

"But my shoes. My clothes. Please, let me take them off." The old man attempts to kick off one of his loafers.

"No. Leave them on." I exude sympathy with a feigned smile. "I'm a fair man, Amar. I only want the boat. I wouldn't dare to take anything else from you. Not your clothes or your wallet. Not even your cell. You need to make sure you take it all with you."

He shakes his head, over and over.

I incline mine. "Enjoy the swim."

Luca gives him another shove, sending the man tumbling into the water with a rewarding splash. He bobs in the deep blue and struggles to remain afloat as he kicks off his shoes and maneuvers out of the clothes weighing him down.

Anissa watches every second, her arms crossed over her chest, her face a mix of anger and guilt.

"Want me to get us out of here?" Luca asks.

"Yeah. We don't have time to watch the show."

"I agree. She made her position all the more precarious by throwing her weight around. If Amar makes it ashore and word gets back to Luther that—"

"That I value a toy over the asshole who stole from me?" I shove my gun back inside my jacket. "I'm not afraid to admit her worth is more than Amar's."

"Right," he mutters.

He makes for the cockpit and turns on the ignition while I remain in place, my attention glued to Anissa as she stares at the slow-moving swimmer.

"You spoke up for his benefit, didn't you?" I move toward her, drawn closer by her internal struggle. "Your demands were an attempt to save his life."

"I don't know."

"You're too soft, Anissa."

It's that remarkable softness that has me settling in behind her to wrap my arms around her waist. I let her compassion ease my rage, my thirst for blood dissipating with her warmth.

She gives a slight shake of her head. "That wasn't softness."

"I wasn't going to execute him. I told you I'd be lenient and I was. The old man escaped without a single scratch."

She doesn't respond. She barely breathes as the boat accelerates, gliding over the water's surface to gently rock us back and forward.

"For a second, I thought you were enjoying the power trip."

"Maybe I did." She turns into me, her arms still clinging tight around her waist while she rests her head on my shoulder. "I don't know what I'm feeling anymore. Everything is so heavy."

"You should sit down. The adrenaline is wearing off."

She nods but doesn't move.

"Come on." I slide my hand over her arm and lead her back to her seat. "Sit."

She slumps onto the padded bench and stares up at me. "Will he make it back to shore?"

"Do you want him to?"

She hangs her head.

The show of guilt pummels me. There's no place for it. Not here. Not after what he did. But I need to remember she's not like me. She set up camp on the opposite side of the law and has no plan to cross enemy lines.

"He was born and raised in the Greek islands, Nis." I run a hand through her hair, gently soothing her. "He lives and breathes this ocean. I'm sure he'll be fine." I glide my touch over her jaw to her chin, raising her face to meet my gaze. "Is that what you wanted me to say?"

"I don't know." Her eyes implore me. "Nothing makes sense anymore."

"Your guilt is unjustified."

She shakes her head. "You don't understand."

"I may not be prone to the emotion. But I'm not immune, either. I've made mistakes that haunt me."

"Over what?"

"It doesn't matter." I stroke her jaw, succumbing to her tenderness.

"I don't need details, Cole, I just want a distraction. Tell me a story. Tell me about *you*."

"I don't think you need more ammunition to hate me, do you?"

She winces, her beautiful face changing into a mask of pain. "I don't hate you. I don't think I even understand you. I still don't know why you're doing any of this—fighting your father, taking down a money-making operation—it doesn't make—"

327

"Because when I was a kid I caught a man raping someone I cared about."

Her expression slackens. "I'm sorry. I didn't mean to pry."

"But you want to understand, right? So let me tell you."

I shouldn't elaborate. It's nothing but pathetic weakness encouraging me to spill my secrets. A blatant desire for her understanding.

"I walked in on the situation too late and had to drag the man off her. But that's where my help stopped. Instead of taking matters into my own hands, I told my father and hoped he would deal with the perpetrator."

"He didn't?"

"At the time, I thought he had. The sick bastard who hurt her disappeared from my life for a while. I knew he was still around, but he wasn't part of the organization like he once was."

"He worked for your family?"

"He *was* family. They all are. Everyone who makes their way into our circle is one of us. Luca. Hunter. Sarah. Even Decker. They may not have the same blood in their veins, but their loyalty makes their bond even stronger."

"What happened to the girl?" She blinks up at me, her eyes holding sympathy I don't deserve.

"I kept watch over her for a long time. I made sure she was doing okay. But it wasn't enough. I told myself she was moving on with her life when in reality she was bottling her anger, letting it fester for years until it became too much and she took revenge into her own hands."

She pulls back, her concern making way for shock.

"I should've dealt with him as soon as it happened. If I'd had the balls to take care of the situation back then, my father wouldn't have found a like-minded deviant. Then maybe they never would've built this empire together."

"Wait?" She frowns "They built it together? But I thought your father and uncle..."

I let the information sink in. The depravity, too.

"Jesus, Cole. It was Richard who raped her?"

"My lineage doesn't leave much hope for me, does it?"

A heave of breath leaves her lips as she sinks her head against my stomach and curls her arms around me. She hugs me tight, as if she's trying to keep the vulnerability wrapped around me, not letting an ounce of the weakness escape.

I return my touch to her hair, stroking the delicate strands. "I'm the cause of all this. One moment of weakness inspired more women to be violated."

"You said you were a kid."

"In body, not in mind. Just like Tobias, the reality of this life has been my constant since I was born. I was raised as an adult. I should've acted like one."

She clings tighter, as if her hold can save my soul. "You're being too hard on your—"

"Don't," I warn. "Don't say another word."

The punishment I live with is nothing in comparison to what I deserve. I let revenge slip through my fingers, and not a day goes by when I don't wish I'd acted differently. Just like I'll probably grow to despise letting Amar free. Because of her. All due to the instability she encourages.

"I'm sorry." Her voice is barely heard over the splash of waves against the hull.

I wish I didn't hear her at all.

"You feel sorry for *me* now?" I chuckle. "Minutes ago you were disgusted by what I wanted to do to Amar."

"I wasn't disgusted." She raises her head, resting her chin on my chest to stare up at me. "And no, I don't feel sorry for you. I'm sorry for the boy who grew up without a mother to soften him and only had a father whose influence never should've been inflicted upon a child."

"Save your pity, little fox. I'm not a kid anymore. I may have spared Amar's life but that was temporary, and only for your sake. Once Luca and I return to Greece without you, the old man will be dead."

Her eyes flare. Her lips part.

I wait for her to yell at me. To demand Amar's life be spared.

But she doesn't say the words. She knows there's no hope of us seeing eye to eye. Not on this.

We will never share common ground. Will never hold similar values.

Will always be at odds with each other.

The slowing of the boat is a welcome reprieve, the island up ahead announcing an end to our conversation.

"Don't worry. This will all be behind you soon." I keep stroking her hair. I commit the texture to memory because I'm well aware these niceties won't return to Portland with us. "You can pretend it never existed."

The engine dies, the forward momentum decreasing as the vessel bobs in the water.

Luca ropes the boat to a pillar, then jumps out onto the pier. "I'm going to start packing. Do you need me to do anything else?"

"No." This time when I meet his gaze, there's no judgment. No disapproval. Only focused determination. "We'll be inside in a minute."

He nods and stalks away, his walk turning into a jog as he reaches the gravel path.

"We should get organized. I need to get in contact with the pilot so we can be placed on the flight schedule asap."

She glances away, her tongue gently sneaking out and moistening her lower lip. But she doesn't move. She remains nestled in front of me, her breathing gentle, her skin soft below my fingers.

"Come on. We've got time for you to have a shower or soak in the bath. It might do you the world of good."

The longer we remain on our own, the more the urge to kiss her drags me under.

The need for possession, the desire to claim, it all builds in my veins.

I tug her to her feet and grow tempted to haul her into my arms. I could carry her inside. She deserves to be held.

"Wait." She drags her hand away. "What happens once we get back to Portland?"

"I don't know yet." I start for the side of the boat, but she doesn't follow.

"I need to know, Cole. Will we be enemies once we get back? Will all this change?"

All this—the lust, the mindlessness. Without the adrenaline to spur the madness, maybe things will be different for her. But I won't leave unscathed.

No matter where I go or who I'm with, Anissa will remain with me. She's fucked with my head. Burrowed deep. She's a chronic illness I'll never overcome.

"Tell me what you're thinking." She inches up to me, placing her hands on my chest. "Because all I can think about right now is being with you."

"That's survival mode kickin' in, sweetheart. You'll get over it."

"Will I?" She leans close, her palms sliding up to my neck. "What if I don't?"

"Then that will make two of us." I press my lips to hers, unable to deny myself.

If she needs a temporary distraction I'll give it to her.

If she needs an outlet, I'm here for that, too.

I grip her hips and grind into her, parting her lips with my tongue. I'm already hard as stone, my lust on a hair-trigger.

I fucking want her.

Now. Tomorrow. Next week.

I want inside her body. In her mind. I itch to claim everything. All the thoughts. All the nightmares.

This woman was made to be mine, my needy little fox.

If only our values weren't worlds apart.

"I need you," she whispers into my mouth, her hands gliding back down to the buttons of my shirt.

"I need you, too." I grip her wrists and pull back. "But we're not doing this here. Not today."

"Why?"

"The first time we fucked, you were drunk. The next time won't be because you're scared and free falling with an adrenaline detox. Tomorrow will be even more of a bitch slap of reality if you do."

"That's not true."

"It's not?" I step back. "You're telling me on any given day back in Portland, you would've fucked me? Why? Because I'm such a nice guy?" I raise a brow, waiting for a denial she can't give. "Admit it, Niss. This is fucked up."

"I don't care."

"Maybe not now, but you will. When you're walking back into the Bureau, wearing one of those ugly-ass pantsuits like it's your shield of morality, you're going to think of this moment and hate yourself."

Her throat works over a heavy swallow, her strength dissipating with the movement. "I still don't care."

"Well, I do. You can hate me for a lot of things, but fucking won't be one of them."

She glances away. Sighs.

Believe me, I hate my restraint more than she does.

But it's her fault. She's rubbing off on me after all, her virtues tainting what could've been the perfect conclusion to a disastrous day.

"Come on." I grab her fingers. "Let's go."

"Wait."

I pause, recognizing a shift in her mood. "What is it this time, sweetheart?"

"I need something from you... Two things, actually."

I turn, finding the lust gone from her features and a glimpse of the determined agent taking its place. "I'm listening."

"For starters, don't ever call me sweetheart again. I'd finally gotten used to the Niss, Nissa, and Nissie that I originally despised, but calling me sweetheart only points out how fragile you think I've become."

"I don't think—"

She holds up a hand and the return of her stubbornness is a relief. No doubt it will soon become a pain in my ass, but for now, it brings me pride.

"Whatever you say, little fox."

She nods in appreciation, her hand falling back to her side. "Now I need you to tell me what you know about my father."

26

TORIAN

I knew this moment would arrive since William Fox was brought up in conversation.

What I didn't anticipate is my compulsion to lie to her.

"Luther said something about you working off my father's debt through me. What does that mean?" She blinks up at me through thick lashes. "And why didn't you say something earlier? All this time my family has owed you money, and you never said a word."

"You owe me nothing. Women and children are never dragged into the mistakes of men."

"What mistakes? What did he do?"

I contemplate hiding the truth. I could even drip feed the information over the passing days. Or weeks. Maybe even months. The ability to hold the insight hostage, ensuring she always has a reason to remain close, isn't beneath me.

"We can discuss your father once we're in the air. We'll have hours without interruption."

"No. I can't wait. After everything that's happened today, I just need...something. I don't care if it's bad news, or information I don't want to hear. I just have to know." She pleads with her eyes, unravelling me one bad habit at a time. "Cole, please."

I waiver between a cruel plan and blatant truth.

I question my motives and the possible benefits.

"I already know he was dirty." She waves off the comment as if its meaningless. "Days after he disappeared, a photo was handed in to the Bureau. It showed him involved in a money exchange with a known criminal. So you're not telling me anything new. I just want to understand the specifics."

There's strength in her tone. Backbone. But she can't hide the pain in her eyes.

I see the emotion clearly. My pretty little fox still wants to believe in a father she doesn't think exists.

"This photo convinced you he was dirty?"

"The photo convinced the entire Bureau. Colleagues he'd worked with for years gave up on him in a heartbeat."

"You didn't answer my question."

She holds my gaze while indecision flickers in her expression. She's considering lying to me. Falsifying the truth to save face.

"You don't want to admit it, do you?" I answer for her. "Despite what everyone says, you're still trying to cling to the man you looked up to as a child."

I understand the compulsion. I've been there myself.

"Just tell me." She refuses to open up to me, keeping herself locked tight. "Confirm it once and for all."

"That he was dirty?" I shake my head. "I can't. Because he wasn't. Not in my opinion."

Her teeth dig into her lower lip, the depth deep enough to cause pain. "Tell me what you know. And don't placate me. I can handle the truth."

"Do you really think I'm the placating type?" I raise a brow, almost insulted by the accusation.

"No. I guess not." She places her hands on my hips, her warmth sinking into me. "Your skills are more focused on manipulation."

The sucker punch hits me without warning. It's another reminder of the vast differences that will always separate us.

"Your dad was in trouble." I hold her focus. "He pissed off some bloodthirsty people and his life was on the line."

I wait for a reaction. Agreement or surprise.

I get neither.

She's locked tight, keeping me from the battle waging war behind those eyes.

"He came to my father asking for help. He had no other option."

"How is that possible? If it was a safety issue, why didn't he go to the Bureau? He would've been offered protective custody."

"He did. And he was."

"Then why the hell would he approach your father?" She hurls the question at me like an accusation. Like a fucking insult. She's climbing aboard her high horse again, sitting tall to look down on me and mine.

"Maybe because your holier-than-thou Bureau only offered *him* protection. As the story goes, they wouldn't budget the expense of protecting you and your mother. Not when you weren't living together. They either didn't believe the severity of the threat, or they didn't fucking care."

She shakes her head, the grooves in her forehead digging deep. "That wouldn't happen."

"You prefer to think your father switched sides than to question your beloved FBI?" I scoff. "Come on, little fox. Don't be naive. They don't give a shit about you. They never have. You're just another badge—easily replaceable and not worthy of financial support."

"Naive or not, your story doesn't add up. You haven't explained why he would go to your father for help. Or why he was seen giving money to someone your family isn't even tied to."

"I have all the answers you need, but I don't think you're ready to hear them." I grab her hands and lower them to her sides. "We'll finish this later. Go have a long shower. You'll think clearly afterward."

I make for the side of the boat and climb onto the pier.

"No. *Please.*" She scrambles after me, pulling on my jacket. "Just tell me."

"I'm not going to waste my breath when you don't trust me." There's still a wealth of hostility coiled inside her. Her judgment and scrutiny are quick to pounce. "You're committed to seeing everything in black and white. Right and wrong. Good and bad. I can't help you when you're not prepared to listen."

Her fingers cling tighter to my jacket, tugging. "Because it doesn't make sense."

"It makes perfect sense."

"No." She shakes her head. "He could've told me. He could've gone to a security firm—"

"He didn't come to us looking for protection, Nissa."

She stiffens. "The guy my father paid was a hitman?"

"Yes." I palm her cheek and witness the devastation seeping into her soul. "My father respected yours. Apparently, the way your dad conducted himself during the investigation of my mother's death meant he was worthy of help. But that didn't mean Luther wanted to touch a job contracted by a straight-laced agent. Instead, he put in a good word with a reputable contractor. Which wouldn't have been a problem if your dad didn't take off before paying the remainder of his debt."

"He didn't pay?"

"He ghosted as soon as the contracts were fulfilled, which meant my father felt liable for the betrayal and paid the amount owing."

"Why would my father do that? He had to know it would put me and my mother in more danger." She turns rigid, her eyes widening, mouth gaping. "My mother..." She steps back, staring at me in horror. "She was killed in a car accident. The driver fled—"

"Don't go there," I warn. "Whatever happened to her had nothing to do with us. I didn't even know she was dead or that you were a Fed until after Richard's funeral. You weren't on our radar. When it comes to retaliation, women and children are off-limits. They always have been."

"You're kidding, right?" She takes another retreating step, approaching the side of the pier. "Your family has amassed a colony of innocent victims—women and children alike—and you expect me to believe me and my mother were let off scot-free?"

I clench my teeth as she accuses my family of more crimes.

"Are you done?" I glare. "Or is there more blame you'd like to lay at my feet?"

She crosses her arms over her chest, shutting me out.

"Fine." I start walking. "I guess we're done here."

I make it to the end of the wooden planks, the lap of the ocean against rocks the only sound.

"*Wait.*" She rushes toward me. "I know you're not to blame."

"No, you don't. You hold me accountable for my father's actions. Which is fucking ironic when you refuse to be Amar's judge, jury, and executioner even though he dragged you to hell and back." I continue forward, stalking my way along the path. "Yet when it comes to me, there's no hesitation to bang the fucking gavel."

"And I should know better." She moves in front of me, walking backward to keep up. "I've lived with the same scrutiny since my father disappeared."

"Then why do you do it?" I snarl. "Why the fuck do you keep blaming me for what Luther's done?"

She stops, forcing me to do the same. The answer lingers in her eyes. She knows exactly why; she just doesn't want to tell me.

"Fucking say it, Nissa. Why hold back now?"

"Because I want you to be guilty," she admits. "I want a reason to hate you, because then I wouldn't feel the way I do."

"What way?" I snap. "How the fuck do you feel?"

She lowers her gaze.

"How do you feel?" I grab her chin, demanding her attention. "Tell me."

"Confused," she rasps. "I feel completely and utterly confused."

"About me being guilty?" I glare. "Nissa, I'm no knight in shining armor. That's a foregone fucking conclusion. You know that. But I stand apart from my father. I'm not him."

"I'm not talking about Luther." She winces and yanks away from my hold. "I'm confused about how I feel for you. About how I feel when I'm around you."

Fuck.

That's not where I thought this conversation was headed.

Not even close.

She wipes her hands down her face with a sigh. "I shouldn't have said that. See, I'm not thinking straight."

"This type of situation doesn't breed clarity."

"Just tell me one more time. Help me understand what my father did."

I shouldn't. I already regret what I've told her, and tearing open old wounds is the last thing she needs. But again, I can't fucking deny her. "Your father hired a hitman to protect you and your mother. He never worked for my family, Niss. And I'm sure he wouldn't have taken the path he did if the Bureau would've given him the help he needed. But all he did was try to keep you safe. He just didn't have the money to pay for what was done, because that shit don't come cheap."

A weary sigh escapes her. "Okay." She nods, coming to terms with the information while she sweeps the bombshell of her feelings about me under a metaphorical rug. "Thank you."

I keep my distance, not wanting to trigger any more mind-numbing conversation.

I'm done. Fucking drained.

"You need to get ready." I tilt my chin toward the house. "Take a shower. Pack your things. And grab some pain relief for the plane."

Tylenol won't help the heartache, but she's going to need something once the adrenaline clears her system and all that remains is the agony of her injuries.

"Are you coming?"

"Soon." I pull my cell from my jacket pocket. "I need to call the pilot to set the ball rolling."

She nods, seeming entirely defeated. If her expression was a torture technique, I'd spill all my secrets to make her misery stop.

"Go." I jerk my head again. "I'll come and get you when it's time to leave."

"Okay." She continues toward the house, her bare feet crunching on the path.

Relief doesn't come once she's out of sight.

The toxicity in my veins only increases.

For once, I feel like the monster she accuses me of being. The weight behind my convictions grows weak. She's fucking poisoning me.

"Jesus Christ." I swipe a hand through my hair.

I can't have her.

This woman isn't capable of being the docile puppet I need at my side. I don't have time for complications. Or issues of integrity. All I want from a partner is a place to shove my dick, and Anissa is above and beyond that.

Above and fucking beyond.

I keep a hand fisted in my hair as I dial the pilot's number. I clench my teeth as the call is left to ring on a continuous loop until the message service cuts in.

I disconnect and try again, and again, my lack of patience growing with each beat of my pulse.

"Mr. Torian, I'm sorry I missed your—"

"Meet me at the airport as soon as possible. We're leaving. I only need to pack my things and we'll be on our way."

"Sir..."

I close my eyes at the hesitation in his voice. "Thirty minutes, Jefferson. I swear to God, if there's a holdup, heads will roll."

There's a pause.

A blatant issue.

"What is it?" I growl. "How long is it going to take to get us in the air?"

"I'm sorry, sir. It's going to be a while. I'm about to land in Portland. I need to touchdown and refuel. I'm at least fourteen hours away, and that's if I fly straight back."

"You're in Portland?" I clench the cell in my grip. "Why, for the love of fucking God, would you go back there?"

"Your sister, sir. I was told to pick her up. She said you approved the plans."

27

ANISSA

I slowly peel Cole's jacket from my body as if it's a layer of skin. Every muscle aches, each movement making me want to whimper in protest.

The vulnerability accompanying my nudity doesn't help either.

The reminder of being stripped bare to stand before an audience of rapists makes my limbs break out in a toxic shiver. Then there's the evidence of the trauma staring back at me from the mirror, proving how defenseless I'd been.

Reds, purples, and pinks line my neck. My shoulder is puffy and swollen. I'm pale, my cheek bruised, my eyes lifeless.

I'd given Cole the impression I hadn't wanted him to hurt Amar, but that's only because the truth had scared me.

I'd wanted that man punished.

Tortured.

Killed.

I'd craved the sight of his blood. The sound of his screams. The taste of his panic. I didn't experience an ounce of reluctance due to morality.

My pleas were due to fear. Anger etched itself through every one of my nerves, the compulsion for revenge potent enough to frighten the hell out of me.

I still fear it now.

I'm scared of becoming Cole. Of succumbing to this need for

revenge that feels more natural than a set of handcuffs, a lengthy court process, and wasted time behind bars.

I'd wanted Amar's humiliation.

My scream for him to swim only came out because I couldn't let the darkness win.

I would've watched his execution without an ounce of disgust, and I would've lost my soul in the process. Instead, I got a taste of what I wanted and disguised it as a reprieve.

Cole still thinks I'm this perfectly intact agent, when death without conviction is all I want for any bastard who makes women feel the way I do—hopeless, helpless, and entirely at the mercy of mad men.

I step into the open shower, turn on the water, and wait for ribbons of steam to inch their delicate fingers toward me.

I breathe in the warmth, dragging the moisture deep into my lungs. The heat needs to fill the hollow space carved into my soul. It has to make me whole again. But it doesn't.

After long minutes I'm still empty. Still broken.

I step under the spray and hope the peppering water will wash away the dirt and grime. Only there's so much filth left behind.

I'm not sure I'll ever be clean.

All the toxins are still there. Coating me. Smothering the light to fill me with darkness.

I can't imagine losing this sickening demand for retaliation. It's as if my body thinks the damage will be healed if I return the evil gift I was given.

I want justice, and for once, I understand that will never come from somewhere that provides shelter, amenities, and three solid meals a day. My perpetrators can't be sentenced and have an end date to their suffering when I don't know if mine will ever stop.

"Oh, God." I close my eyes and raise my face to the heavens.

I'm not this person. I don't want to succumb to the poison.

I *can't*.

I slump against the tiled wall and slide to the floor, every muscle aching in protest.

Water dances over my feet as I bend my knees, hugging my

legs to my chest, and bow my head. The falling shower rains over my hair, creating a curtain to shield my face from the world—a world where I turned my back on my own father.

If I'd been the virtuous woman I claimed to be, I would've fought harder to seek the truth about him. I wouldn't have stopped when humiliation seemed like the only option waiting for me on the other side of my investigation.

I should've fought.

I should've clawed.

I should've screamed in the face of all those who took me in with judgmental eyes because they thought the blood flowing through my veins was tainted with criminal genes.

It was the system who failed me. Not the man I should've believed in.

The Bureau betrayed me. Not my father.

My stomach churns, the guilt having a building effect. Heat licks at my eyes, the sting of building tears increasing my anger.

This isn't me either. I'm not a crier.

I'm not weak.

To prove it to myself, I let the onslaught of childhood memories I'd previously disowned come rushing back. I relive the precious moments, allowing the grief to burn inside me.

I remember all those birthdays when he was the first person waiting for me when I left my bedroom. I hear him singing as he cooked dinner, his voice a deep, calming timbre. And I recall the moment that started it all—the day he attended the scene of Cole's mother's murder.

I can imagine my father paying Luther respect for his loss despite them being on opposite sides of the law. He always had a heavy sense of integrity. He wanted to help, not hurt.

He was a good man.

I guess he still is.

I'm the one who's defecting. Failing. And sweating like a pig with all this hot water.

I sit up, the skin on my toes now wrinkled after I disappeared into a black hole of thoughts for too damn long.

Stark eyes meet mine from across the bathroom. My avenging

angel sits perched on the elegant white tub, his shoulders drooped in defeat, his lips set in a thin line.

He fills me with conflict. He always has. But I can't deny the connection. The pull.

I'm drawn to him. It's like the cliched moth to a flame. It's so much more than that, too.

He suffuses me with strengthening breaths. With new curious life.

He also punishes and destroys.

He makes me feel whole and empty. Right and wrong. Invigorated and eviscerated all at the same time, with every varying sensation in between.

He showed me the sliding scale of gray when I'd been used to seeing black and white for so long. He's encouraged me to think outside the constraints of what I've been taught. To question everything. To challenge anything.

Now the Anissa I once was is becoming a stranger.

"Do you feel any better?" His eyes turn sympathetic, his comfort attempting to fill the hollow ache inside.

I nod, unwilling to speak and expose any more weakness.

"Good. Are you hungry?"

There's something different about him. Something wary.

His knuckles are white as he clutches the tub on either side of his thighs. His defeat is etched into the very fiber of his being.

"What's wrong?" My voice croaks. "Has something happened?"

"There's been a change of plan. We're not going to leave just yet."

Adrenaline injects itself back among my mix of melancholy and self-loathing. I brace myself to stand, only to have him halt me with the raise of his hands.

"Sit. There's nothing to worry about. Everything is fine. There's been a holdup with the jet. Keira called it back to Portland, but it's returning now."

My breathing increases, the tendrils of steam filling my lungs to the point of suffocation.

"It's okay." He pushes to his feet, discards his suit jacket, and toes off his shoes and socks to walk into the shower. "You're safe." His frame towers above me as water soaks the cuffs of his pants. "It's a slight delay; that's all. We'll leave in the morning."

"Can't we take another jet? Or fly commercial? We can't stay here."

"We'll be fine." He gives a sad smile. A placating, condescending curve of lips. "There's nothing to worry about."

"That's not the impression you gave on the boat. You wanted us out of here as soon as possible."

"Then things changed."

He continues to appease me with a calm facade. I don't buy it. I know our safety is at risk if we remain in Greece.

"Tell me."

He lets out a breath of a laugh. "It's a delay. That's all."

"So why can't we find an alternative?"

Silence.

He doesn't appease me anymore. He just ignores me as those dark blue irises drag me in.

"Cole?"

His jaw tenses. "Because you don't have a passport."

Oh.

I let the information sink deep, the ropes of claustrophobia pulling tight.

I'm the one keeping us captive. Luca and Cole could leave, but I'd have to stay.

"It's okay." He steps closer, his protection bearing down on me as he glides a hand through the soaked mess of my hair. "Like I said before, Luther will take his time stewing over what happened. We'll still be long gone before he decides to make any sort of move to reconcile his actions."

"What if he doesn't want to reconcile? What if he looks into the day we left the States and finds out I came willingly?"

"Then he'll have evidence I used the same tactics he does when abducting women." His touch lowers to my cheek, his thumb wiping away the water droplets. "It's always been his strategy to entice women abroad with offers they can't refuse. I did the exact same."

344

Yes, he did. He lured me with the promise of justice, and now the concept seems laughable. But none of that dissolves the threat.

"I need a weapon." My voice breaks, my words raspy and weak. "I want a gun."

His thumb continues to stroke my cheek, his comfort sinking marrow-deep. "A gun won't help—"

"Cole, please." I place my hand over his and rise to my feet, standing naked before him. "If I'd had a way to defend myself earlier, I never would've been attacked."

"No, you never would've been attacked if I'd put you on the jet like I promised." He steps closer, the shower spray beating down on his shirt and clinging to his skin. "I don't know how you did it, but you found a way to make me buckle to your demands. That hasn't happened to me before. And it can never happen again. From now on, I'll do what's necessary to protect you, despite your protests."

"I don't want to be protected. I need to be able to look after myself."

"I know. I've figured you out enough to see you don't like relying on anyone. Not a partner, or friends, or relatives." His hands find my hips, his palms sliding over my waist to my back and pulling me close. "My little fox is a solitary predator."

All my pain and fear dismantles under his touch. The heat from the shower becomes nothing against the burn of his contact.

"I'll get you a gun." He glides his hands lower, cups my ass, and drags me forward, stomach to stomach. "I'll unlock the knives and chemicals, and anything else I tried to keep away from you, too. I'll make sure you feel safe."

There's no room for relief. The hard length of his cock against my abdomen becomes my only focus.

He wants me. Despite his earlier refusal, he needs the connection as much as I do.

"I thought we weren't doing this," I whisper.

"Doing what?"

I close my eyes and shake away the doubt.

I'm not the only one consumed by attraction. I can't be. "You want me, Cole, even though you denied me earlier."

"I denied us both. And that was when I only had to pack our things and get you on the jet. Now we're stuck here, I'm not going to pretend I don't want you when it's all I can think about."

"But what about your speech on this being panic-driven, and a repeat of our first drunken disaster?"

He leans closer, his lips a breath away. "I never said it was a drunken disaster." He lifts me, carrying me backward until the kiss of cool tile brings relief to my smoldering skin. "And you should know my morality is flimsy at best. Those excuses were for you, not me."

He grazes his stubble against my cheek as he speaks into my ear. "They're still valid, though. You fucked me once because you were drunk. And this time, the lust is due to survival instinct. It's up to you whether you succumb."

I already have.

I need him.

Not out of spite or retribution. Not even due to pure lust.

I want him because I've never experienced hunger for common ground with such ravenous ferocity as I do right now. I've never felt this mindless connection for someone and wanted it deepened. I haven't craved understanding—for a man to know all the intricate details of the good, the bad, and the ugly—as much as I do with Cole.

I want more.

I want *everything*.

The yearning is emotional as well as physical.

"I'm not succumbing." I cling to his shoulders and wrap my legs around his waist. "I'm taking what I need."

He pulls back, grinning. "There's my wicked little fox." He grinds into me, the hard steel of his cock igniting tingles through my core. "How the fuck did we end up on opposite teams?"

"Because you picked the wrong side." I glide my hands to the buttons of his shirt, undoing them with restrained patience.

One... Two... Three.

I run my fingers over the mass of exposed muscles.

Four... Five... Six.

I slide the material from his shoulders to fall into a sodden heap on the tile. He lets me look my fill, my fingers learning the grooves of his muscles, my nails scraping the softness of his skin.

He's so gorgeous.

Utterly perfect.

Attraction intoxicates me. I'm consumed with a thickening pulse of anticipation, the beats growing longer, the vibration humming through my limbs.

"Why are we doing this?" I meet his gaze and search for answers I may never find.

"I explained before. For you, this is survival instinct."

He's wrong.

Survival instinct wouldn't have me scrambling to glimpse the future in the hopes we might be together. Survival instinct would be focused on the here and now. Not on my fears of this possibly being our last time together.

"And you?" I whisper over the ache in my throat. "Why are you doing this?"

He holds me steady with his hips and weaves those large hands down my sides, his thumbs brushing the curve of my breasts, then lower, all the way to the inside of my thighs.

"Because I can." He inches those thumbs closer to my sex, inspiring tingles. "And because I have no choice." He parts my folds, the slide exquisite in its softness. "You've become the only drug I crave."

I feel the same way.

It's all I feel.

"Then let's make the most of the chaos." I reach for his belt and fumble with the clasp.

"Here." He grabs my wrists and places them on his shoulders. "Let me do it."

He glides his hands to my hips and steps back, helping me to stand before he makes quick work of his belt and zipper. I can't drag my gaze away as he shoves his pants and underwear to the floor, allowing his cock to escape the confinement.

Every inch of him is hard, none more so than the brag-worthy length pointing between us. He's thick, the veins bulging along his shaft making me salivate.

I want him inside me. I want to have him filling me.

But first I need to taste him.

I fall to my knees, the shower's spray caressing my back as I run my hands around his hips to clasp his ass.

"Niss."

I ignore his attempt at a protest and give his length a tentative swipe with my tongue.

"Shit."

I press my lips to his shaft and smile, loving the sound of his struggle.

His thighs clench with every lick I tease along his cock. A sharp breath escapes him with every swipe across his sensitive head.

I never considered how euphoric it would be to turn such a powerful man into a panting mess. But I'm drunk on his pleasure, my bruises no longer existing, my emotional scars fading to a distant memory.

I clasp my mouth around him, working the intrusion to the back of my throat. I glide back and forth, over and over, one hand still clasping his ass, while I bring the other to grip the base of his cock.

"Fuck." His fingers find my hair and the harsh grip, along with the deep growl from his chest, makes my pussy tingle. "If you keep doing that I'll never let you go."

I close my eyes, wishing it was a possibility even though the thought is entirely foolish.

I suck harder, beating back reality. I twirl intricate patterns with my tongue. I rub my palm along his shaft and sink my nails into his ass.

"Niss." Those fingers dig into my scalp, the pain such a thrilling sensation that my arms break out in goose bumps.

"You need to stop, little fox."

I don't want to.

This needs to last forever. His protection has to remain coiled around me for longer. His strength is a guiding force through this crazy mess of my unrecognizable life.

I don't want to be alone. I can't return to a hollow existence.

"Hey." He steps back, clasping the base of his cock in a tight hold. "What's going on?" He grips my chin, dragging my face upward until I'm enslaved at the sight of those worried eyes. "Tell me what you're thinking."

I'm lost.

I'm scared.

And he's the only one who makes me feel powerful.

"I want you." I close my eyes, fighting the building burn in my vision. "That's all."

He hauls me to my feet, dragging me into his arms to place me back against the wall. "You've got me."

I hold him tight around the neck, circling his hips with my trembling legs. I cling to him, burying my face in his shoulder, my lips against his skin.

"You're better than this, Niss." He pulls back until we're face to face. "You're not weak."

"I know."

"Then snap out of it." He wraps an arm around my shoulder to grip my hair, yanking my head back, exposing my throat. "You're a fucking warrior. And if I hadn't left you vulnerable today, you would've brought Robert and Amar to their knees."

"I know."

"Good," he growls. "Then show me that bitch who likes to wear my balls as a fucking necklace."

A laugh forms in my stomach, not quite big enough to make a sound. "When have I ever worn your balls as a neckless?"

"Since the moment we met." He steals my mouth, attempting to punish me with passion.

Our lips dance. Our tongues tangle.

My nipples ache with the need for more. My pussy pulses, demanding to be filled.

"Don't make me wait," I beg. "Give me what I need."

"Always." He grips his dick from between my thighs and drags the head of his shaft through my slickness.

It's the faintest touch. A mere slide of friction.

I want to combust.

"Cole." I grow impatient, scratching my nails into his shoulder.

"Now, now, Niss. You're a fox, not a fucking cat." He thrusts into me, his cock sinking deep.

I gasp with the harsh jolt, my injuries protesting the ferocity. My ribs burn, the agony sinking into my lungs.

"I hurt you." He stops. He doesn't budge an inch.

"I don't care." I dig my nails into his shoulders. "If you don't keep moving, I'll return the favor."

"There she is." He smirks. "There's my snarky little witch."

I leverage myself against the wall, seeking selfish relief. I grind into him, over and over, while he remains still, peering down at me with devilish eyes. "Give me what I want."

"Or what? You're just going to use me like a piece of meat?" He quirks a brow. "Is that how it's going to be?"

"Maybe."

"I'm not complaining. Just asking." The tilt of his lips increases, the curve incredibly wicked. "I could watch you fucking me like this every damn day for the rest of my life."

I stifle my shock, masking it with a whimper.

He didn't mean what he said. It was a heat-of-the-moment compliment. Of sorts. But the possibility of unending days with this man leaves me breathless.

"What's wrong?" He begins to move, his hips rocking back and forth in teasing thrusts. "Are you tempted by the dark side?"

"No," I lie. "But you could always come to the light."

"You make it sound like a death sentence." He cups the back of my head, keeping his movements smooth as they grow in force. "I could change a lot of things to keep you at my side, but who I am isn't one of them."

"You don't even know who you are. You're not as bad as you claim to be."

"Don't kid yourself. I know exactly who I am." He brushes his lips over my cheek, the caress moving close to my ear. "I know what I want. What I'm capable of. What I'll do if anyone dares to touch me and mine."

He bites my shoulder, then sucks to soothe the sting, over and over, branding my skin with his marks.

"I'd kill for you, little fox." He reclaims my mouth, holding my jaw tight to trap me in place. "I'd die for you."

I shudder.

They're mindless promises in the heat of passion. Exquisite lies. And I believe them regardless.

His devotion becomes a fraudulent truth. His intensity tethers me to my waning strength.

"You could be my queen." He drags his teeth along my neck to my earlobe. "I'd be your fucking slave."

"No." I shake my head, denying his deception. That messed up reality could never exist. There's no future where we're on the same team. Where we wake every morning under the same roof.

There's no possibility of dreamy domestic bliss.

"You're tempted." He nuzzles my cheek. "I know you don't want this to end."

I deny the fantasy any more room in my thoughts. "What I want is for you to make me come."

"I can give you that, too."

He grinds harder, his hand leaving my face to slip between my thighs. He sweeps the pad of his thumb over my clit, and I buck with the resulting frenzy of sensation.

He applies more pressure, eliciting more pleasure, all the while thrusting his cock into me so slowly my walls clamp down around him.

"I want to fuck you so damn hard," he admits.

"Do it."

He presses his forehead to mine. "No. Not today."

There might not be another opportunity. This is all we have. It might be all that's left.

"Do it." I buck into him, making him sink to the hilt.

"*Not. Today*," he growls. "Fucking you hard is a promise I'll leave for another occasion."

My whimper is the only protest I can give.

I'm close, bliss tingling the tips of my nerves. I jerk my hips harder, making him groan and increasing my own madness. He pumps faster, his thumb pressing harder.

I shake my head, not ready for this to end, but entirely at the mercy of a body that is coasting forward without my approval.

"Clamp your pussy tight, little fox," he murmurs in my ear. "Milk my cock."

I come undone, my back arching, my core fluttering.

I cling to him, our rhythm perfectly synchronized, our panted breaths a mimicked symphony as he moans into my cheek.

The rough grate of his voice grows louder, deeper as we orgasm, the slap of flesh on flesh filling the space around us until eventually, it slows.

We both recede from the bliss together, our bodies slicked with sweat.

"I love how you obey me." His tone holds a hint of humor. "We should do this more often."

I scoff out a derisive laugh. "Let me down."

"Not yet. I'm not finished with you."

I crumple, my head sinking back against the tile, my hands falling to my sides as exhaustion takes over.

He carries me from the shower, our bodies still joined when he places me on the basin counter.

"Be my queen." He issues the command on a whispered breath. I don't doubt his sincerity. "Take over the world with me."

"No." I would give anything to accept his offer. Anything but my soul. And that's the price I'd have to pay.

He chuckles, the sound sinister. *Dark*. Entirely Cole. "It was worth a try." He steals my mouth with a contrasting kiss so heavenly and soft my heart bleeds for more. "Are you sore?"

"You're not that big." I push him away, needing to separate myself from the gentleness threatening to make me weak again.

"That's not what I've been told." He smirks.

"And I bet those compliments came from mafia bunnies striving to be Mrs. Cole Torian."

"Point taken." He opens a cabinet under the counter and retrieves a washcloth to give to me. "Unfortunately, I don't like bunnies. Turns out I prefer ball busters."

"For such a monster, you really are a shameless flirt."

"Guilty as charged." He steps close again, grasping my neck to give me a quick kiss before he walks his naked ass to the door and pulls it wide. "Do you want me to get you some clothes?"

"Yes. Thanks. That would be—"

"Torian." Luca's shout carries into the room.

Cole stiffens, his hand shooting up to warn me to remain in place. "What is it?" he calls back.

"You need to come see this."

28

TORIAN

"Stay in the bathroom." I tug on pants and yank up the zip. "If something happens, get in the panic room."

She nods and scoots from the counter to wrap a towel around her phenomenal body.

I stalk down the hall, not sure what I should expect when I enter the living room, but it sure as hell isn't Luca in the kitchen making sandwiches.

"I need to see this?" I stop at the counter and glare at the food. "You called me out here for ham fucking salad?"

"No." He meets my gaze with mirrored annoyance while he places two sandwich halves on a tray. "Does she look familiar to you?" He dusts his hands on his jeans and slides his cell across the counter to me.

A picture of a brunette stares back from the screen, her dimples deep, pure innocence beaming from her bright smile.

It's the woman from today. My father's slave.

"It's her." Luca grabs the chopping board and throws it at the sink, food scraps and crumbs flying everywhere. "Penelope fucking Decker."

"What about Penny?" Anissa's voice travels from behind me. "What's going on?"

Her padded footsteps approach until she stands at my side, wearing nothing but a fucking towel as she glances down at the cell screen. "That's Sebastian's sister. What are you doing with her picture?"

Luca snatches leftover vegetables from the counter, making his anger evident as he yanks open the fridge door and shoves them inside.

"Cole?" Anissa murmurs. "Has new evidence been found?"

Big green eyes implore me from my periphery as I keep staring at Penny. I can't drag my gaze away from what she used to be—before my father. Before horror tainted her features.

"Has her body been located?"

Luca scoffs out a laugh. "Yeah, you could say that."

"Where?" She glances between us, her scrutiny frantic. "Who found her?"

"We did. She was at my father's house this morning." I shove from the counter, needing space to think.

This situation is impossible. I have to get Nissa out of here when there's no jet. And I can't leave Decker's sister at my father's mercy. I can't betray Keira like that.

I've kept her boyfriend in my inner circle for a reason. He's valuable. He's got enviable loyalty toward family. He's a fucking asset no matter how much I want to deny it. And the worst part is the unwavering devotion he's given my sister.

The two of them will marry. It's a foregone conclusion.

Fuck.

I grind my teeth, unsure how I'm going to stop Luther from tainting Keira's future any more than he already has.

"Cole?" Anissa approaches slowly, her hair dripping water onto her shoulders. "Are you saying she's still alive?"

"Yes. She's still alive. Still being tortured. Still living hell on earth because of my fucking father."

"But she's alive." Her eyes brighten. "That means there's hope."

"Hope for what? A future for her with every mental issue under the sun? And that's if we can get her out."

My father won't give her up willingly. The only way to free her is to instigate war.

"Luther was meant to disappear." I stalk to the window to

355

focus on the long expanse of nothingness. "That way, our allies don't have to pick sides. There's no retaliation. No fucking death and destruction. It was meant to be a simple disappearance."

"It doesn't have to be you," she murmurs. "I could make a call. You can let the authorities—"

"Don't even start that shit with me." I swing back around, glaring at her. "I'll let her die before I involve the fucking Feds."

She straightens, taking the insult with a deep breath. "Then what do we do?"

"*We* do nothing. You're going to get on the jet as soon as it arrives, and in between now and then, I'm going to figure out a way to fix this fucking mess."

Luca carries his tray of sandwiches to the table, dropping the plate to clatter against the wood. "I need a drink."

"No alcohol," I demand. "We have to stay alert."

Anissa starts for the kitchen. "I'll make coffee."

"No." I follow after her. "I'll do it. You need to get some clothes on."

She sucks in another one of those I-want-to-stab-you breaths and pads her bare feet from the room, leaving me to bite back anger, frustration, and fucking guilt.

"Since when did she start feeling comfortable enough to make suggestions?" Luca walks into the kitchen, pulling three mugs from the corner cupboard.

"She wants to help." I start the coffee machine, snatching one of the mugs to place it under the nozzle. "We both know the Feds will never be involved."

"Do we?"

I pause and grip the counter. I don't need to be questioned. Not now. "If you've got something to say, spit it the fuck out. I don't have time for you to pussyfoot around shit."

"I'm just wondering if you're going to switch sides."

My pulse quickens, my annoyance becoming a bubbling threat in my chest. "For your sake, I'm going to pretend I didn't hear that." I turn to him, cocking my hip against the cupboard. "And if we're going to start questioning motives, why don't you start by explaining what the hell you did to cause Decker's sister to risk her

356

life by slapping you? Did the thought of an easy lay become too tempting?"

"Fuck you."

I raise a brow. "It's fun being insulted by idiotic questions, isn't it? If you don't know me by now, you should fucking leave." I jerk my chin toward the door. "God knows I've been doing this shit a hell of a lot longer than you."

The muscles along his jaw flex. "I tried to let her know I was there to help. But that isn't fucking easy when I couldn't say anything incriminating. I didn't know who was listening, and as it was, your little snitch of a brother overheard every word."

"What did you say to make her lash out?" I open drawers, pulling out medicine bottles, popping two Advil while I search for something to help Anissa's recovery.

"I don't know. I was speaking in fucking riddles. The only information I could think to use were references to her life back home with Decker. Clearly, she didn't like the reminder."

"That's all it took?"

"That's all it fucking took. I mentioned her brother, and she went from meek kitten to crouching tiger in seconds."

"So even if we do make a move to break her out, she's not going to trust either of us?"

He shrugs, his jaw still tight. "I don't know."

Christ.

The coffee gurgles into the first mug while I prepare a caffeine-free alternative for Anissa. It's going to be hard enough for her to sleep tonight with the nightmares waiting to take over.

Once all three mugs are filled, I slide Luca's along the counter toward him. "Here. Go have something to eat. We need to be on top of our game."

"I thought there was nothing to worry about?" Anissa returns to the living room, her hair towel-ruffled, her loose tank and sports shorts crinkled. "You said Luther wouldn't make a move so soon."

I lied.

I fucking bluffed my ass off hoping she would breathe a little easier.

"You think he's going to come out here, don't you?" She

357

continues to the table and takes a sandwich from the tray. "What will he do?"

"The likelihood of him coming here before morning is slim." Luca takes the hit, stealing her attention. "That doesn't mean we won't prepare for every possible situation."

I grab the remaining mugs and take them to the table, sliding hers in front of her and holding tight until she meets my gaze. "You need to eat, then get some rest. Don't worry about anything other than letting your injuries heal."

"And what about Penny? I can't forget she's here." She takes small bites of sandwich, chewing slowly. "I've known about her disappearance for a long time. I was one of the first to hear about the DNA the Greek police found at a mass grave. I saw her teeth. There were clumps of her hair. I was invested in her case, Cole."

"I'm invested, too," I growl. "I'm well aware she's likely to become Keira's sister-in-law. As far as I'm concerned, she's family. But that doesn't mean I'm going to ignore the risks. I'll get her out when the time is right."

"Then you need to call Sebastian." She takes a sip from her mug. "He needs to know."

I huff out a tiny fraction of my overbearing frustration and take a seat beside her. "*Eat.*"

"Why do you even care about Decker?" Luca scowls at her. "He hates you."

"He has reason to hate me. But it doesn't mean I want his sister to remain a prisoner. Everything he's ever done has been for her."

"He'll find out soon enough," I grate. "Until then, I don't need any more distractions."

She sucks in a deep breath and takes another sip, her nose scrunching with the gulp. "What type of coffee is this?"

Great. Just what I fucking need—a woman who can sniff out an imposter.

"Yours is decaf," I admit.

She gives me a look of incredulity. "Why?"

"You don't need to be wired. You need rest."

"I think I can make up my own mind." She shoves to her feet. "Thank you very much."

An ache forms under my sternum. I'm close to snapping. So fucking close.

I place a hand over her mug before she can think to throw the contents down the sink. "Sit."

Tension crackles to life between us, our adamant pride colliding.

"I'm not a dog to be ordered around, Cole."

I incline my head. "But you also haven't shown the necessary loyalty to hold a seat at this table, yet here you are, gaining insight into topics you shouldn't be privy to."

"So you're telling me I need to drink decaf if I want to remain at this table?" She scoffs. "That's ridiculous."

"No. I'm reminding you I'll do whatever it takes to protect you, and if that includes making you rest when you're determined not to let your wounds heal, then so be it." I slide my hand back to my mug. "Now sit. And drink the fucking coffee."

She remains in place.

My stubborn little fox is loath to succumb and too determined to walk away from the information loop.

"We're going to continue with the schedule as normal." I meet Luca's gaze and pretend she's not seething beside me. "Once the jet arrives, we'll go back to Portland to regroup."

"We're going to leave Penny here?" He shakes his head. "Are you kidding? What would you do if that was Keira, and Decker made the call to leave her behind?"

I'd kill him.

I'd fucking gut the bastard and leave his corpse to rot in the sun.

But we're not talking about Keira.

If there's any hint I've killed my father, the ensuing unrest would cause havoc. I wouldn't be trusted. Rumors are fine. There's always gossip and speculation, but proof is an entirely different matter.

I can't be seen attacking Luther.

I can only play into his disappearance and dismantle his operation afterward.

"All it would take is a phone call to the Bureau and we'd have help within hours." Anissa slumps into her seat and takes a juvenile slurp of her coffee, the sound a conniving taunt. "If you weren't so stubborn you'd realize it's a viable option."

I'm not going to argue with her again. I'm done.

We're all tired. None more so than her.

I keep my mouth shut as we all fall into uncomfortable silence.

Luca slinks low in his chair and stares into space. Anissa does the same as she alternates between taking bites of a sandwich and less-provoking gulps of coffee.

No matter how hard I try, I can't see a way out. Not without risking everything.

"You can't call Luther and work out some sort of deal?" Luca keeps his focus across the room. "Is there anything he would trade for the girl?"

"No. You heard him; Penny is his prized possession. He's not going to give her up."

"What about me?" Anissa places her empty mug on the table. "Would he trade her for an FBI agent?"

Both of them look to me for a confirmation I'd never fucking give. "No."

"You didn't even consider the possibility." She pleads for understanding with the long bat of her lashes. "I'm sure there'd have to be some interest if you continued to work the angle of using me to pay off my father's debt."

"Are you insane?"

I know she's tired. Her exhaustion is clear in the dark bags forming under her eyes and the loose slump of her shoulders. But even if she was on her death bed, she would have to realize I'd never use her. Not like that.

"But what if we didn't actually do the exchange?" Luca sits forward. "It's a way to bring him out here, on our turf, so we can end this the way we planned."

I bare my teeth. "Don't make me repeat myself."

Anissa sighs and Luca collapses back into his seat, the silence returning as the sun slowly sets to bathe the room in darkness.

We sit in the shadows for too damn long, the quiet stretching until Anissa pushes from her chair to turn on the light. She drags her feet, her face ashen.

I puff out a breath of frustration. "You need to get some rest."

"Yeah." Luca frowns at her. "You look like shit."

"Thanks." She returns to her seat, leaning on an elbow to cradle her face. "That's what every woman wants to hear."

"He's right." I stack our plates and grab her mug to take them to the sink. "Your body needs to heal."

"I'm fine. Just tired, that's all."

"It wasn't a suggestion." I walk back to the table and pull out her chair. "Come on. I'll walk you to bed."

"I can sleep once we've decided on a plan."

"You're not deciding anything." I tilt her chair forward, forcing her to stand. "I'm the one who will figure out what's going to happen." I hold out a hand which she refuses to take.

"I don't need a chaperone." She walks for the hall, her posture slouched.

"Fucking hell." I scrub both hands down my face, then meet Luca's unimpressed stare. "I'll be back in a minute."

He nods. "I'm going to make more coffee."

I stalk after her, catching up as she reaches her door. "Sleep in my bed."

"No, thank you." She grabs the handle and plunges the lever.

"My bed, Nissa." I close in behind her, wrapping an arm around her waist before she can escape inside.

She stiffens, growing inches with her annoyance.

"I won't apologize for protecting you," I murmur in her ear. "You need time to recover." I press into her, breathing in her anger. "And you'll do it in my bed. Either now, or when I carry you there later."

She shudders, her entire body responding to me. "Don't be an asshole."

"I'll be whatever I have to be. Just for you, sweetie."

She turns into my chest, her eyes narrowed to spiteful slits. "You know I hate when you call me that."

"Then let me take you to my room, and I won't have to resort to any more dirty tactics."

"I'm too tired for this, Cole." She wiggles from my embrace, wincing with the movement. "I just want to crash."

"That's okay." I scoop her into my arms and expect a protest that doesn't come.

Instead, she sighs and nestles into me, her head falling onto my shoulder. She's not merely exhausted. She's barely able to function.

"I should've taken you to a doctor." I walk us to my room, kicking the door wide with my foot.

"I feel okay. I just can't keep my eyes open."

I settle her on the bed and turn on the lamp to pull the covers out from beneath her. "Things will be better in the morning."

It's a lie. We both know it. And I'm thankful she's too tired to call me on it.

She nestles onto her side, her blinks becoming longer and longer.

"Before you pass out, I've got something for you." I retreat to the walk-in robe and open the safe hidden behind the same wall of clothes concealing the entry to the panic room. After a four-digit pin-code entry, I retrieve a pistol from the stash of weapons and make my way back to her.

"Here." I hand over the gun.

She sits up, blinking away some of the lethargy. "You're letting me have this?"

"You said you wanted one."

"Yeah. I just didn't think you'd allow it." She nibbles her lower lip, trekking her attention over the weapon as she tilts it back and forth. "Which is kind of a shame, because I was hating you just fine until now."

"You didn't give me much choice. It turns out I don't like you hating me all that much."

"Then maybe you should stop being a dick."

I grin. "I wouldn't hold your breath." I reach for the weapon and release the clip to show her the bullets. "It's fully loaded. So be fucking careful, okay? No pulling it out when something hard rubs up against you later."

She rolls her eyes and slinks under the sheet, sliding the pistol under her pillow. "You better believe I will."

"You wouldn't do that to me. You love my cock too much."

"With my current level of annoyance, I'd shoot you in a heartbeat."

I chuckle and lean forward to steal a kiss.

She grumbles for a brief second but those sultry lips still part beneath mine. "Get out of here."

"I'm going." I backtrack. "But I'll be back later."

I walk for the door, the rustle of sheets following me.

"Cole?"

I stop in the hall and glance over my shoulder. The sight of her in my bed is too fucking natural. Like she's meant to be there. "Hmm?"

"No matter how much I think about it, I still can't picture you killing your own father. I don't want to believe you can do it."

There's that inescapable divide again. The one thing standing between us.

"Who knows? Maybe I can't."

Her brows pull tight. "Are you questioning yourself? Are you thinking you can't go through with it?"

"I'm thinking only time will tell. Now get some rest." I trudge into the living room, trying to ignore how things will change between us once I take Luther down.

She'll see me differently. Worse than ever before. And there's nothing I can do about it.

"How'd you do?" Luca asks from the table.

"She passed out before her head hit the pillow." I reclaim my seat and latch onto the freshly topped mug of coffee.

"Did she figure out you sedated her?"

"Not yet." I grab a sandwich and sink my teeth into the stale bread. "But I'm sure she will."

He copies what I do. Bite for bite. Drink for drink. "You like her, don't you?"

"Jesus Christ." I contemplate lying. Or denying an answer. Both would work as well as pleading the fifth. "She's an indulgence."

"Is that all?"

I ignore him and take a larger bite, filling my mouth to capacity.

"You let Amar jump from the boat without so much as a fucking bruise when I've heard you make an execution order for far less."

I take another bite. "Would you have preferred if I made you an accomplice to murder right in front of a Fed?"

"You were going to do it with Luther. Why was Amar different, apart from Anissa making it clear she didn't want you to kill him?" He leans back in his chair, relaxed. "You drugged her. Abducted her. Made unending demands of her. Yet you're worried murder is crossing the line? That excuse is bullshit, and a clear attempt to hide the fact she has your balls tightly grasped in her fist."

"I'd be careful where you take this conversation. My patience is threadbare."

"I never said it was a bad thing," he mutters. "Only something I hope you're conscious of."

I'm fucking conscious. Her hold over me hasn't left the forefront of my mind since she came into my life.

"Do you think it was a smart move to sedate her considering the looming threat?"

I sedated her *because* of the threat. "I gather I'm not the only one who thinks Luther isn't done with us."

"You made demands of him today. Whether he's your father or not, I think he's going to want to do something to save face."

"Well, whether he does or doesn't, it's best for her if she sleeps through it. If he comes here, I'll put her in the panic room."

"And if we're gunned down and unable to save her?"

"Then I'm going to hope like hell nobody finds where she is until Hunt and Decker arrive."

Luca straightens and leans forward, his elbows pressed to the table. "They're on their way?"

"I assume so. The pilot said my sister made travel arrangements for herself and three others. It doesn't take a genius to figure out Hunt and Decker are behind the jet's disappearance."

"It couldn't be Layla and Benji?"

"They wouldn't risk bringing Stella here, and Keira is the only person they trust to look after their kid. It has to be Deck, Hunt, and Sarah."

"Which will bring even more issues."

"Yep." If Decker shows up here, I'll have to tell him about Penny. Then all hell will break loose, and we'll have a madman on our hands—someone unlikely to think rationally about danger when his sights will be set on rescuing his sister.

"But," Luca continues, "with seven of us able to work together, maybe we could finish this."

"If we don't get ambushed between now and then."

"Yeah." He sighs. "That's a big if."

He's more adamant of the danger than I am, which doesn't sit well with me.

I'd like to think I know my father better than anyone. Only problem is, my head is now clouded with worry for my FBI agent.

"Why don't you go get some sleep?" He yawns and stretches his neck from side to side. "Rest while you can."

"There's no way I can switch off right now. You go." I jerk my chin at him. "I'll take first watch."

"You sure?"

"Yeah." I deserve to spend more time thinking about what I dragged Anissa into. I need to let that shit percolate as long as possible to get a full dose of punishment.

"Call out when you want to switch." He pushes from the table and walks across the room, leaving me alone with my regret.

"Luca." I focus on him as he reaches the hall. "Before you go, tell me why you think Luther is likely to come out here. Do you anticipate he'll want to make amends or will he want to drag me over the coals for calling him out on his bullshit?"

"I think it's neither." His expression becomes bleak. "If he comes out here, my bet is that it's for Anissa."

Dread slithers its insidious fingers down my spine. "Why?"

"Because she intrigued him enough to get one of his men to take her away from you. Then you went and told him she was a Fed, and the daughter of someone who owed him a stack of money.

And whether it was from liking her as a person or a possession, you made it fucking clear you would guard her with your life."

Then I made demands for him to punish the prick who dared to touch her.

I encouraged Luther's interest with every single one of my reactions.

Fuck.

"Honestly, Cole, if Luther comes out here, I'm not worried about us. My concern will only be for her."

29

TORIAN

I DIDN'T SLEEP.

Caffeine, the threat of my father, and the fact I stayed in bed until lunch had me powering through until the early morning hours.

I spend my time trying to ignore what has to be done—I have to say goodbye to Nissa.

She needs to return to Portland while I stay to finish what I started, and secure Penny's freedom along the way.

Problem is, I don't want to say goodbye.

For starters, Anissa needs to be watched. For her protection as well as mine.

Secondly, I'm not ready to let her go.

I need more time to... I don't know. I just need more time.

But I don't have any. The sun is about to rise, meaning the jet should be here soon.

"Why the hell didn't you wake me?" Luca slinks into the living room in jeans and a T-shirt, squinting as he scratches the top of his head with the butt of his gun.

"I had no chance of sleeping. I thought you might as well get the rest."

"What about Anissa? Is she still knocked out?"

"Yeah. I've checked on her a few times, but the sedatives are working wonders." I push from the dining table and head for the kitchen. "Coffee?"

"Fuck, yes. Make it strong." He slides onto a stool at the island counter, placing his gun in front of him. "Any word from Luther?"

"Nope. I'm starting to think I'm going to have to figure out a plan to get him back here."

His brows tighten. "So, we're staying?"

"Yeah."

"And Anissa?"

I grab two mugs from the dishwasher and start the coffee machine. "I'm sending her home."

He doesn't respond.

I don't look to him for answers. I don't need his opinion. I don't want the questioning stare he gives me when I slide his steaming mug of java across the counter.

"I've already packed her things. They're in a duffel at the door. All I have to do is get her to the airport."

"When are we doing that?"

"Soon." I check my watch. "I called the pilot for an update a few hours ago. They shouldn't be too far away. But once I finish my coffee I'll call again to confirm."

"What's the plan after that?" He palms his mug and takes a sip. "Did you decide what to do about Penny?"

I pretend not to notice his invested interest.

One conversation and a slap across the face, and the guy is fully absorbed in her rescue.

"Once Hunt and Deck arrive, we'll chat it out together. Like you said, if it were my sister, I'd kill anyone who didn't put their life on the line to save her. So, for the sake of Keira and her bad taste in men, I'm going to have an open discussion about the options."

"That's more than fair."

"And if Decker can't keep a cool head, I'll contain him however necessary. But at least I'll have given him the choice."

He nods. "I wouldn't expect anything less."

Good, because that's the extent of my generosity.

Decker will be a fucking nightmare once he finds out his sister is alive, but I can admit he deserves to know.

"On second thought, I'm going to make the call now and speak to Hunt." I push from the cupboards. "It will be better if one of them isn't blindsided."

I snatch my cell from the counter and walk outside into the barely dawning light, not wanting to wake Anissa.

Like yesterday, my call isn't answered. I'm left to listen to the ongoing dial tone.

I try again and this time something else accompanies the ringing.

There's a faint hint of added noise. A hum.

I disconnect the call and hold still, listening to the whir of sound in the distance.

It's almost negligible. But it's there. Approaching.

I stalk back to the door and shove my head inside. "Luc, come out here for a sec."

He slides from his stool and strides toward me. "What is it?"

"Listen. Do you hear something?"

"Barely." He cocks his head. "Do you think it's a boat?"

"I'm sure it is."

"Keira?"

"I doubt it." Something uncomfortable builds in my chest. A bad feeling. Maybe I'm being paranoid. Or trying to delay sending Anissa home. But I don't think so. I shouldn't have tried to convince myself the passing hours were my first stroke of good luck. Luther always knows when to turn up at the worst possible moment.

"It could be a fishing boat, but I'll check it out." Luca jogs for the path, fast disappearing behind the vegetation.

I remain in place, contemplating whether to go after him.

I should wake Anissa. And I also shouldn't leave Luc on the jetty without protection. It didn't skip my attention he ran off without his fucking gun.

"Shit." I slide my hand inside my jacket and touch my pistol for confirmation before I stalk for the path, striding out the distance as the noise approaches.

It isn't hard to find the boat with its bright light illuminating the inky black water. I don't divert my attention as I walk onto the pier, trying to determine who's onboard.

"For confirmation, if this is Luther we're ending this, right?" Luca turns to me. "And if it's Keira, we're taking Anissa straight to the airport?"

"Exactly."

He nods. "Can you see who's behind the wheel?"

"I can't see a damn thing." The slight glow from the approaching sunrise isn't enough to dilute the headlight. The back of the boat remains hidden in differing shades of darkness.

"*Look.*" He shoots me a grin. "There's a woman. Port-side."

I squint, seeing the silhouette of a slim figure. Seconds later, I make out the long hair billowing in the breeze.

My bad vibe intensifies. The reality of saying goodbye to my little fox hits me with full force. This fun-filled adventure with her is over. Once she gets to Portland, I'll be nothing but a bad memory.

"Go wake her." I jerk my head toward the house. "Tell Anissa she's got two minutes to get down here because she's getting on this boat as soon as it stops."

"You got it."

"And next time, don't go anywhere without your fucking gun."

His brows snap tight. "Shit. I—"

"Never again," I warn.

He nods and jogs for the house as I turn toward the approaching boat.

This is it. The end. The moment where I stop tormenting someone who turned out to be more than I expected.

More bright.

More determined and admirable.

More fucking woman.

I never should've brought her here. My excuses for the abduction were messed up to begin with, when in reality, I think I only dragged her here because of my addiction.

I spent so long following her it became impossible to stop.

But I risked her safety. I stole her freedom. And I deserve to fry for her injuries.

Maybe she'll ensure I do.

I move to the end of the pier, preparing to help moor the boat in place opposite Amar's when the outline of the woman's silhouette becomes crisp.

Her frame is thinner than I thought. The free-flowing hair is longer.

I don't drag my attention away. I don't even blink as her features come into view—the shadowed face of misery, the eyes narrowed with spite.

It's not Keira.

Shit.

It's Penny, with Tobias nestled against her hip.

"*Luca,*" I shout toward the house. "*Luc, it's not her.*"

I can't hear a response over the approaching roar of the boat.

I'm stuck.

Fuck.

I won't run and show my surprise. I refuse to let my father think he has the upper hand. All I can do is straighten my shoulders and face him head-on as Chris cuts the engine and the vessel bobs into place.

"What are you doing here?" I cross my arms over my chest, strategically nestling my fingers close to my holstered gun.

"Morning, son." My father holds out his palm to help Penny from the boat, her loose black blouse waving in the slight breeze. "We need to talk."

"And if I'm not interested?" Obviously, I am. Despite my concern over Luca dragging Anissa back into the thick of this, I'm done waiting.

This shit ends now.

"I've already lost a brother." Luther continues his gentlemanly act, helping the kid disembark. "I can't live through losing a son."

I give a bitter laugh.

That's not why he's here.

Luca was right.

I showed my hand yesterday. I let this asshole know how important Nissa is to me, and after I made light of taking Penny from him, it's clear he wants to prove how easy it is to take what's mine.

He needs to reassert his power.

"We're unarmed." He steps onto the jetty and flicks open his jacket, exposing shadows beneath. "Feel free to pat us down if you like."

Now he's adding a game of chicken, daring me to refuse the offer.

"Thanks." I bet he thinks my pride will get in the way of checking him for weapons. At one time, it would've. But I can't be self-serving anymore. I refuse to let Anissa get hurt again.

I walk toward him, a smile stretching my lips as I skim my touch over his arms, waist, back, and legs. I check everywhere and come up empty.

He's clean.

Confusingly vulnerable.

"I've never known you to go anywhere unarmed, old man."

He inclines his head. "And Chris is as well. It's a show of good faith. I'm here to apologize."

"I'll believe that once I check him, too." I motion for Chris to get off the boat and then follow the same routine, checking his arms, waist, back, and legs.

He snickers as I pat his ankles. "While you're on your knees..."

I rage against my pride. I fucking battle self-control when all I want to do is slit this asshole's throat.

"Don't start," my father growls. "Cole, an apology isn't the only reason I'm here. We need to have an important conversation that should've happened a long time ago."

I stand and take a backward step, placing necessary space between us. "If you came to talk, why did you bring a woman and child as a shield?"

"A shield?" He balks. "Do I need one against my own son? Because I brought her here as a peace offering. The woman is yours."

He pushes Penny toward me, her spine snapping ramrod as she stumbles forward.

No. This isn't right.

There's an ulterior motive to his submission.

He must have found out why I want her, and now he's dangling success in front of me.

"You're handing her over?" I scrutinize the woman's face, seeing the undiluted panic in her eyes. She's filled with fear. More so than yesterday. I don't know if that means she's truly panicked over being handed over, or if there's a bigger picture sparking her horror.

Either way, I guess it doesn't matter.

They're unarmed and I'm sick of second-guessing his intent. I reach into my jacket, no longer willing to play a role.

"Cole, I need you to listen. There's something I have to tell you. It involves you and your sisters."

I pause, my fingers brushing the grip of my pistol.

He's triggered the only thing capable of making me hesitate. The only fucking thing.

"What about my sisters?" I return my hand to my side, granting him a temporary reprieve.

"Can we at least sit inside? The boy is tired."

I scoff. "Probably because you brought him out here when he should be in bed."

"Well, I couldn't sleep after yesterday, and there's something on my mind that can't wait."

"Fine." He might think he's manipulating me, but being inside works in my favor. I'll have an extra gun on my side. Two if I count Nissa's. "Go ahead." I indicate for them to start walking.

"Penny." Luther does the same, instructing her to lead the way. "You first, my sweet."

She complies, holding out a hand for Tobias to join her.

Chris continues a step behind, then my father starts his progression, stopping a few feet later to glance at me over his shoulder. "Are you coming?"

"Of course. I wouldn't miss this for the world." I lag back, not getting within arm's reach for the duration of our friendly stroll.

Chris remains quiet. Penny maintains her stiff posture, while the kid is skittish, anxiously clinging to her hand. None of them act any different than I would expect. Tobias is always a few breaths short of a panic attack, and the woman has every reason to be rigid.

There's nothing out of the ordinary. No hint of betrayal as Penny reaches the glass sliding door and stops to await instruction.

"Go." Luther shoos her forward. "Get inside."

"Wait." I claim control, deliberately throwing my weight around. "You, the woman, and the kid can go inside, but your dog isn't welcome."

My father bristles, a few heartbeats passing before he nods. "Whatever you say."

I don't understand the compliance. I refuse to believe yesterday triggered the respect I've always struggled to earn. He shouldn't feel comfortable being separated from his thug-for-hire. Not unless he truly is here to talk.

"I guess I'll stay here then." Chris steps out of my way. "Just so you can feel like more of a man for keeping me outside."

I clap him on the shoulder as I pass. "If I were you, I wouldn't forget your best buddy ate lead yesterday because of me."

"Don't worry. I'll never forget."

"Good." I follow everyone inside, locking the door behind me and sliding the sheer curtain across to block his view.

Luther has already claimed the recliner, while Penny stands tall at his side. It's Tobias who shocks me with his perched position in the middle of the sofa.

He eyes me, as if waiting for company.

"The boy's no longer glued to your side?" I ask.

Luther shrugs. "We heard you're leaving. I guess he wants to make the most of the moments you have together."

I'm about to call bullshit when Luca walks into the room, his face a mask of indifference.

"What's going on?" He eyes me casually, not showing a hint of panic.

"I'm not sure yet. But apparently, my father comes in peace."

He doesn't react, neither in belief or concern. I'm not given a hint to his mindset or what was happening inside the house before our visitors arrived.

"Is my little fox still sleeping?" I need to know what he's done with her. Is she safe?

He holds my focus for long moments. "She's back to the same tricks as she was on her first night here."

Her first night? When she hid outside?

Shit. Did I lock her out with Chris?

"Is there anything I need to be concerned about?"

He pauses. Shrugs. "No."

The response took too long.

He's worried.

"Go check on her," my father encourages. "By Amar's account, she took quite a beating yesterday. She probably shouldn't be left alone."

"You spoke to him?" My face heats, the anger quick to infuse my veins. I approach the sofa, taking a seat beside Tobias to look my father in the eye. "How is my old friend doing?"

"I received a call from him last night. He mentioned you might be enjoying his boat."

"I'm surprised that fucker survived the swim." I stretch my arms along the back of the headrest, flaunting my lack of concern.

"A boat of tourists picked him up. But I appreciate your leniency. I would've understood if you took harsher measures."

No, he wouldn't. For reasons unknown, he's telling me everything I want to hear.

Luther has no protection. No weapons. Nothing.

I'm in control, yet he's entirely calm.

"Tell me why you're here," I grate.

"First, why don't you let Luca make use of my peace offering so we can talk in private?"

The woman sucks in a breath.

"What's he talking about?" Luca approaches, stopping beside my armrest. "What peace offering?"

"I'm handing Penny over as a symbol of my apology. Why don't you take her to one of the bedrooms and get her accustomed to a new way of life under my son's reign?"

Luca glances at me with a raised brow.

"Go." I wave him away. "Enjoy yourself."

Penny doesn't move. Neither does Luca.

"*Go,*" I bark. "Teach her what she needs to know."

Her lips tighten, pure spite entering her features.

"Remember what will happen if you don't behave." Luther slaps her on the ass. "Now make me proud."

She grows an inch, her shoulders rigid. "Of course." She maneuvers around the coffee table and waits for Luca to join her before they continue to the hall.

"Right." I rub my hands together. "It's just us now. You can quit the act."

His mouth lifts at one side. "You've always lacked trust."

"I learned from the best." I lean back, stretching my arm along the headrest. "Now tell me why you're really here."

"I heard you're leaving and I wanted to confirm, in person, that there's no future of us working together. I wanted you to tell me face to face you're turning your back on the opportunity."

"That's not true." I match his smile. "I'm turning my back on you, Dad, not the opportunity."

"And your brother, too. You've just met him, yet you're pushing him away."

"I'm not pushing anything." We maintain our friendly facade despite the bitter meaning behind our calmly spoken words. "You're the one who kept his existence a secret."

"For his protection. You have no idea the safety risks you kids faced when you were young. You'll never understand the lengths I went to for all of my children."

My restraint vanishes as I sit forward, glaring my resentment. "What lengths did you go to when I told you your own brother molested your daughter? What fucking lengths were there then?"

"Is that what your badly bottled animosity has been about? You're holding a grudge over something you don't understand?"

"Something I don't understand? I was *there*. I dragged that son of a bitch off of her. And all you did to protect her was encourage Richard's fucking perversions."

He scoffs. "Did you ever think I was sating an addiction in a controlled environment so he wouldn't look elsewhere?"

"*You—*" I snap my mouth shut, my hands fisted.

"I handled your uncle," he reiterates. "I contained him."

"No, you only encouraged him to fuck other little girls."

He holds my gaze, the cogs turning in that messed up brain of his before he finally cuts his attention to Tobias.

Shit.

The fucking kid.

His tiny frame sits beside me, his shoulders curled inward, his head slumped. He clings to the cuffs of his long-sleeve shirt, trembling with quick breaths.

He's a mess.

"Tobias, have you got something to share with your brother?"

I scowl at my father. "Leave him alone. There's nothing he could say, about you or Richard that could cause me the slightest sense of vindication. I'm done."

I reach inside my jacket.

"*Tobias*," Luther warns.

I wish things were different and I didn't have to do this in front of the kid, but his life will be all the better without Luther in it. I curl my fingers around my gun when something stabs my thigh, a warm sensation spreading beneath my skin.

"*Fuck.*" I shove to my feet, my weapon drawn. "What the hell do you think you're doing?"

The kid stares up at me with wide eyes, his pupils tiny pinpricks. He clutches a plastic tube in his hand, his fingers white from the tight grip.

"Lower the weapon, son."

"No." My brain swells. It fucking tilts.

Everything slows—thoughts, breaths, heartbeats.

"What the fuck is this?" I snatch the plastic tube, the device similar to an EpiPen. "What the hell are you...?" My train of thought sways.

"It's a sedative. Don't worry. The effects will eventually wear off, but they're going to get worse before that happens."

A sedative.

A fucking sedative.

I bark out a laugh at the poetic justice.

"Burn in hell." I raise my gun and aim at my father's chest as my muscles stiffen. My body becomes heavy, each limb weighing a ton, my arm shaking.

"I didn't plunge it all." Tobias curls into himself. "I didn't do it right."

"What?" My father stands, his blurry frame barreling toward me.

He grabs my wrist, shoving it downward and twisting to lever my arm behind my back. He manipulates me like a puppet.

I have no control to stop him. No power to protest. All my strength goes into clinging to my weapon. It's all I focus on.

I won't let go.

I won't fucking fail.

"You're a piece of shit." My words are mumbled. "You steal from your own son. Then what? Attempt to kill him?"

"If I wanted you dead, I wouldn't waste time with theatrics." He speaks against my ear. "I told you I'd do anything to protect my children. This included. You're being softened by the people you surround yourself with. You've grown weak. It's time you went back to basics and learned what it's truly like to be a Torian."

"I know exactly what it's like. You're the one desecrating our name." I launch my elbow into his ribs and dive forward, hoping he'll release his hold. Instead, I lose my fucking balance. I stumble into the coffee table, the corner of my vision darkening.

Fuck.

I'm weighed down by air, the pressure intense.

But I don't lose my grip on the gun. I keep holding tight, fighting to tug it from Luther's grip. I close my eyes and force myself to focus. I concentrate everything on stopping the sway of consciousness.

The kid said it himself; he didn't succeed in injecting me with a full dose. I can pull myself out of this nosedive. I just might not be able to do it on my own.

"*Luca.*" I'm a pathetic piece of shit for having to call for backup. "*Luc.*"

"He can't help you."

I climb to my feet, the gun held between me and my father. "You sedated him?"

"Out of courtesy, yes, but he's one of the pathetic men you've entrusted with my legacy, and you're going to need to cut him loose."

He doesn't struggle with his grip on my gun. He's confident. Strong, while I'm flailing to hold tight.

"Your guy was being *nice* to Penny yesterday." He scoffs. "Fucking nice. Is that the sort of pathetic weakness you want your men to portray? Have I taught you nothing?"

"*Luca*," I roar.

Luther sighs. "Tobias, go get Penny."

The boy scampers from the sofa and runs for the hall.

I sway on my feet as I wait for hope. But there's no pounding steps coming in the opposite direction. I don't hear Luca or the sound of help on the way.

"It's time to go, son." My father grips my upper arm. "Let's make this as easy as possible."

"Fuck you." I launch a fist at his face and barely feel the connection. There's no pain in my knuckles. Only tightness.

He stumbles regardless, staggering backward, his grip leaving the gun.

Pull the fucking trigger.

My brain doesn't send the message fast enough. I'm stuck in a holding pattern as he rights himself and lunges at me, twisting the gun from my grip.

"*Luther*," Luca yells from behind me. "Drop it."

His voice is heaven to my ears. Fucking bliss... Until the shots ring out. My father fires.

Once.

Twice.

I turn to see Luca shove Penny down the hall before running in my direction, his large frame diving behind the sofa as more pops blast the room.

One minute he's there; the next he's gone. The only thing left behind is the blood splatter plastered against the wall.

He was hit.

Fucking shot.

Adrenaline consumes me. Anger and fear collide, clearing some of the fog from my head.

"Luther," Chris calls from outside. "You okay?"

My father grins. "Perfect. Couldn't be better."

I charge him, stumbling over my feet to drop my shoulder and send him flying. I reel with the onslaught of vertigo and struggle to

379

remain upright as he collapses to the floor, the gun remaining tight in his hand.

"It's too late. I got him." He laughs as he pushes onto his elbows. "Penny, check to make sure he's dead."

"Don't go near him." I swing around to face her, my vision taking seconds to catch up. "Get the fuck away."

"Luther, I'm sorry." She creeps from the hall, the kid nowhere in sight. "I'm so sorry. I tried to stab him with the sedative but he stopped me. He was too quick." She rambles, one word tumbling over the other. "I didn't know what to do. I thought maybe I could—"

"Just check him."

Luther crawls to his feet as I latch onto the recliner for stability. If I could get my head to stop spinning, I'd be able to take control.

If the world didn't keep tilting on its axis, I'd kill him with my bare hands.

"There's blood." Her voice trembles. "It's coming from his head."

I can already hear the answer etched into her tone.

Whatever she's looking at is fucked up.

Then she crouches, descending out of my view.

"Penny," Luther warns. "What are you doing?"

"His pulse... I-I'm checking his pulse" She remains in hiding, the sentence held hostage for pained heartbeats. "I can't find it... He's... I think he's dead."

"Fuck." I raise my hands to my head, trying to keep all the crazy inside. "*Fuck.*"

I messed up.

I killed him, and Anissa will be next.

"Get his weapon." My father reclaims a harsh grip on my wrist. "Then unlock the door and hand it to Chris."

"Don't do it." I yank my arm back and stumble. "Don't fucking do it, Penny."

"She does what she's told," Luther seethes in my ear. "Otherwise she knows the consequences."

"What's to stop her shooting you?"

"She could try." He digs his fingers into the material of my suit. "But she'd be dead before she had time to aim. And then I'd kill all her friends just to spite her."

"I've got the gun." She stands, the weapon clutched in both hands, blood staining her fingertips.

"Keep it. Protect yourself. Don't give it to Chris." I should make a run for her. Tackle the pistol from her grip. Take charge of the situation.

"Don't even think about it." Luther jabs me in the shoulder with his gun. "You're predictable. Always have been."

"Too bad you've already admitted you won't kill me, old man."

"No, but I have no problem hurting you. It'll toughen you up."

I stagger to face him, my vision pixelated. "What do you hope to achieve? What the fuck are you going to do?"

I need to delay him.

If I slow things down, maybe I can draw this out until Hunt and Deck arrive. It's a fucking pussy's plan, but I can't get my brain to work out another option. I can't think.

"Tell Penny not to give him the gun and we can talk this out. That's what you want, right? To show me the error of my ways?"

Penny reaches the sheer curtain and pulls it wide.

"Tell her to stop," I repeat. "Do it."

Luther smiles at me. Chris does the same from the other side of the glass.

I can't let them get their hands on another gun.

"Penny. Don't." I keep my tone low. "Don't be stupid."

"Shut your mouth." Luther slams the butt of the gun against my cheek, connecting with bone.

Like a bitch, I fall to my knees, my ears ringing as Penny pulls the door wide.

"No."

Fuck. No.

I battle to get back up. I plant my hands and sway as she raises the gun, barrel first, her aim in the right direction, but her orders are clear.

I'm done for.

Anissa clouds my mind. All I can see is her and the torture she will endure. I can't let that happen.

I stumble to my feet as Chris reaches for the barrel.

"Don't fucking do it, Penny." I wobble with each step toward her.

"*Cole*," my father cautions.

I don't listen.

I don't stop. Not until the *pop*, *pop* shocks me still, her arm jolting with each pull of the trigger.

Chris turns white, all color seeping through the bullet wounds in his chest as he falls backward.

Penny sobs, the weapon slipping from her fingers to clatter to the floor.

"I'll fucking kill you," my father snarls.

I swing back to him, dazed, confused, but certain he will retaliate. "Get down," I yell at Penny and run to block Luther's aim. I sidestep when he does and struggle not to stumble. I tilt when necessary and fight to keep consciousness. I don't let him get a clear shot despite the shit affecting my brain. "*Hide*."

"I've got her." Luca lumbers to his feet from behind the sofa, his face strewn with blood.

"Luca?" He's alive.

He looks like he should be dead. But he's fucking alive.

Luther changes the focus of his aim, resetting his sights on Luca who shoves the sofa toward us, then rushes for Penny.

Pop. Pop.

The burst of noise from my father's gun assails me.

I hurry to get in front of the weapon, my steps faltering as Luca collides into Penny, taking her to the ground.

"*Move*," my father roars at me. "I'll fucking shoot you."

Luca scrambles behind the kitchen island, dragging Decker's sister with him.

"Do it. This will be your last chance." I raise my arms wide and smile when I realize I have the strength to hold them there. The shit poisoning my veins is wearing off. "It's over, Dad. Your new protégé failed to inject me properly. Your dog is dead. And you fucked up when you thought you took Luca out."

"You forget I'm the only one with a weapon, son."

There's a scrape of sound behind me. A shuffle of noise. Then I hear her. The most welcome reprieve and the greatest punishment all at once as Anissa says, "I'm sorry, motherfucker, but you're mistaken."

30

ANISSA

I CLUTCH THE GUN IN MY HANDS, THE METAL WARM AGAINST my palm as I aim at Luther over Cole's right shoulder.

My pulse pounds in my ears. My chest beats an agitated rhythm. It doesn't help when all eyes turn to me. Even Luca and Penny's, from where they're crouched behind the island counter.

But there's relief. The sight of Cole fills me with hope after torturous minutes spent thinking the worst.

I'd been trapped outside, weaponless, hopeless, and forced to hide behind the house yard shrubs while an unseen battle took place inside.

I hadn't known who instigated the gunfire. I wasn't sure if Cole was safe or if Luther had been taken down.

Then Penny pulled the curtain aside, opened the door, and dropped Chris like a domino, his head hitting the outdoor tile with a stomach-turning thwack.

"Lower your weapon, Luther." I fall back on my training and force the panic out of my system. "Hand it over and this may not have to end badly."

"Don't shoot, Niss," Cole demands. "He won't kill me."

I take stock of the room, knowing full well he's not my only concern.

There's blood on the far wall. Spots on the floor. A mass all over one side of Luca's face along with smears on Penny's cream pants.

Luther clucks his tongue. "I knew she wasn't a toy. You'll never understand the disgrace you've brought me, son. It's a fucking shame."

I continue my visual search of the room, but I don't see the boy. "Where's Tobias?"

I keep my aim on Luther's shoulder and remain thankful Cole isn't covering his father completely. I can take a clear shot from here. The only thing stopping me is the uncertainty of stealing Cole's closure from him.

"Don't concern yourself with my son." Luther takes a backward step, moving toward the kitchen. "If you were smart, you'd worry about your own life."

"He's safe, Anissa," Luca offers. "Give Cole your gun and let him finish this."

For a second, I contemplate compliance.

I could simply hand it over and remove myself from a position of power. But what if Cole can't follow through?

"He's right." Luther grins. "Give Cole the gun. Entrust my son to do what's right."

"Lower your weapon," I snap. "Put it down or I'll shoot."

"Your hesitation already speaks volumes, bitch."

He's wrong. I haven't pulled the trigger because this isn't my situation to finish. I'm risking my own life, and so many others because of my weakness for a man I never should've fallen for. I need to stop. "Cole, where's your gun?"

Luther chuckles and raises the weapon in his hand. "You're looking at it, Agent Fox. He got bested by his papa. And if you don't lower yours, I'll take pleasure in making you regret it."

"He's not going to kill me." Cole stumbles the tiniest step and exposes more of his father. "He won't fucking do it, Niss."

"You're hurt." It's not a question. Clearly, he's swaying on his feet.

"He's about to have a nap." Delight spreads across Luther's face. "And as soon as he falls, you're going to have nothing to shield you." He takes another retreating step and Cole follows, always keeping himself in front of the barrel. "But I think I might start the fun with the scared little piece of shit who would prefer to hide instead of helping his boss."

"I'm not hiding, asshole," Luca grates. "I'm giving Cole space to finish this his way. And if he can't, I'm on standby with a knife in my hand, ready and willing to slit your throat."

I glance at him to confirm.

He's not lying. A hunting knife is on the tile beside his thigh, lying in wait.

"A knife isn't going to help you. Not when I have a gun."

"Says the man who shot at me multiple times and still couldn't take me down." Luca scoffs out a laugh. "All Cole has to do is say the word and I'll happily fuck you up."

"It's over, Dad." Cole reaches out, his hand gliding toward the gun. "We're done here."

"Do you seriously think you've got the balls to kill me?" Luther brings voice to my fears. "You couldn't even kill your uncle when he messed around with your sister."

All the air leaves my lungs on a heave.

I'd questioned myself on who Cole's loved one could've been. I'd wondered and contemplated. Not once did I think his regret surrounded someone so close.

I hurt for him.

I'm pained by the betrayal.

"Don't worry. I'm still the monster you created. I always will be." Cole slaps his hand down to his side. "But your hold on me is over. I no longer believe family is everything. Not when it comes to you."

Luca waves at me from his hiding spot. "Give him your gun. Let him finish this." His tone is urgent. Demanding.

I ignore the instruction.

I still don't believe Cole is capable of killing his father. Not after he spoke of his hesitation last night. He may be brutal and malicious, but he also has a heart. One far bigger than I think anyone can imagine. And I won't risk all our lives on an uncertainty.

Luther retreats again, getting closer to the kitchen, encroaching on Luca and Penny's hiding spot.

"Cole, I'm going to shoot." I grip the gun tighter. "I can't let him take another step."

Cole stumbles again, his head swaying as he exposes Luther's chest. God, he's struggling to remain upright. He's giving me no choice.

"Cole?"

Luther takes another step, taunting me with a smile.

"Stop." I pin my aim to his body mass. *"Luther. Stop."*

Cole rushes him, hauling him around the waist to slam him down to the floor.

They fight for the gun, chest to chest on the tile.

I have a clear shot. It's right there. Open. "Release the gun or I'll shoot."

They grapple. They grunt and heave and yell.

The direction of the barrel slowly pivots, pointing toward Cole. He's weakening. Luther's aim is so close.

"Cole?" I can't wait. I can't risk—

A burst of gunfire slams through the room, the shock making me stumble.

My ears ring. My pulse pounds.

Luther bucks, his mouth open, his eyes wide and rapidly blinking.

I got him. I shot him right through the side, the bullet hopefully piercing a mass of vital organs.

Cole scrambles backward, staring as his father gurgles and splutters while Luca and Penny rush to their feet.

They all stare at Luther as blood seeps from his mouth.

And still, he doesn't release the gun. He clings tight, inching his sights toward his son.

Pop.

Pop.

Pop.

I don't stop shooting until the clip is empty. Even then I keep pulling the trigger, over and over as he falls limp, never to move again.

But relief doesn't come.

The satisfaction I hoped would overwhelm me isn't there.

There's nothing. Only panic over Cole who rises to his feet to stare down at his father's lifeless body, unblinking, barely breathing.

I wait for him to break the silence. To react. To grieve. All he does is keep his focus on the pool of blood seeping its way across the tile.

"Cole?" I creep forward, my hand shaking with the need to reach for him.

He drags out the torture, the silence getting thicker.

"Baba?" Tobias's sweet voice wails from the hall entry. "*Baba?*"

"Tobias, no." Penny dashes across the room, maneuvering around Luca and Cole to scoop the boy into her arms and rush him back into the hall.

The boy's screams follow, the unending torture of a child losing a parent sinking into my ears and down to my heart.

And still, Cole doesn't move.

"Torian. You need to focus." Luca approaches him, the blood from his face soaking his shirt. "We've got stuff to do."

The closer he gets, the clearer the damage becomes. He was shot in the head, the bullet grazing his skull.

"Are you okay?" I start for him.

"It's a scratch." He waves me away. "Do us all a favor and grab the duffel from my room."

I nod, inching forward, bumping into the sofa before turning and fleeing down the hall toward the sound of a sobbing woman and child. I retrieve the duffel from Luca's room and drag it along the hall, the contents too heavy to carry with my protesting ribs and shoulder. "Here."

Luca rushes forward, falling to his knees to yank open the zipper and pull out tarps and numerous bottles of bleach.

"You need stitches." My voice is barely audible as I peer down at the side of his head. The gash has to be two inches long. The barest nudge to the right and he would've taken a bullet to the brain.

"Stitches are the last fucking thing on my mind." He bundles the items into his arms and stands. "Because unless this shit is cleaned up, you're going down for murder."

"It was self-defense."

"And how are you going to tell that story?" He scowls. "Are you going to throw Cole under the bus by saying you were a prisoner?"

"No. Of course not."

"So you're going to announce to the world you were working together? A Fed and a drug lord?" He scoffs. "Wake up, Anissa. These bodies need to fucking disappear. So if you're not going to help, get out of the fucking way."

I watch in a daze as he staggers to Luther's side and lays out the tarp along the tile.

Still, all Cole does is stare. No movement. No hint of what he's thinking.

"Cole." I start toward him, needing to be close. I don't care if he doesn't speak. His touch will be enough to tell me everything is all right.

I reach for him, about to run my fingers along his arm when he snaps from his daze and jerks away, his eyes filling with spite. "Back off."

All warmth seeps from my body. With two words and a scathing glare, he reduces me to nothing. "I—"

"Get away from me."

A panicked breath escapes my lips.

I don't understand. I saved his life. I saved *all* our lives, and now I've been reduced to a leper. If the feeling wasn't entirely familiar from my time in the Bureau, I'm not sure I could stop myself from breaking into a fit of sobs. "He was going to—"

"Get. The fuck. Away." His lip curls. "*Now*, Anissa."

My heart breaks.

Everything does—my strength, my pride, my confidence.

I shuffle back, placing more and more distance between us until I bump into a wall.

Maybe I should've waited... Listened... Ignored the building panic.

But I don't believe, not for one second, that Luther wouldn't have shot his own son. That monster was capable of killing anyone who stepped foot in his path. And if it wasn't Cole, it could've been anyone else.

I slither down the wall, sinking into a heap as Luca and Cole work together, lifting both bodies onto separate tarps, then wrapping them over and over. Then they carry one away, disappearing momentarily around the pool area before coming back for the next.

I should start cleaning up evidence, but I can't bring myself to do it. I can't move with the emotional pain leashing me in place.

Even when a boat revs to life, I remain shackled by invisible bonds.

I'm left alone for what feels like hours, staring at a pool of blood while unending suffering echoes from down the hall. I relive everything, over and over, the continuous loop punishing.

One minute I'd been asleep, the next, Luca woke me and demanded I get to the boat.

I hadn't had time to get the gun from under my pillow. *No.* I hadn't been fully awake to think about it until the open air hit my cheeks.

I'd sent Luca back to get it, leaving me to start the trek to the pier on my own.

That was when I'd heard them. The sound of voices in no way similar to the people I expected.

I hid, crouching behind the shrubs on the opposite side of the house yard, peeking through branches and leaves while I was locked outside with Chris.

I hadn't known what to do. But I was certain I didn't want to drag Cole's attention away from his task.

Then Penny had pulled the curtain aside, opened the door, and fired.

My world had shrunk to pure instinct.

That was when I ran for the open door, sidestepping the bloodbath at my feet to swipe the gun Penny dropped.

I hadn't spared a second thought about staying in my safe place. I'd risked my life to help Cole. I hadn't been able to spend another moment wondering if he was dead or alive. I'd needed to contradict my pessimism and see for myself that he was okay.

I scoff out a laugh.

I entered a war zone for him and now he hates me.

I pull my knees to my chest and bow my head.

I don't know how long I wait there, worrying about them never returning and even more concerned about what will happen if they do, until the familiar sound of shoes on gravel crunches outside.

I glance up to see Luca walk through the glass doorway, the blood now dried on his face, while Cole follows behind.

"What did you do with the bodies?"

"That's not your concern." Cole stalks to the kitchen, his face set in a tight scowl.

"Wait." I scramble to my feet. "Please talk to me."

He winces, a pained expression crossing his features for the briefest second before it turns to rage. "I don't think you want to know how I feel right now."

"Yes, I do. Tell me. Yell at me. But don't ignore me. Not now." Not when I'm drowning in guilt. "He was going to kill someone. You know that."

His jaw tics.

"Did I do the wrong thing?" My voice is a pathetic rasped plea. "Should I have let Luther keep aiming his gun at you?"

He ignores me and walks for the hall, not sparing me a backward glance.

"Why don't you wait outside?" Luca scoops a bottle of bleach from the floor and cracks the lid. "We need to focus on the cleanup."

"No. I'm not leaving him."

"I think you're doing more harm than good by staying." He pours the liquid onto the pool of blood where Luther fell, then places the bottle on the kitchen counter. "Come on. This shit is intense. You've gotta let the dust settle."

He indicates for me to follow him to the doors with a wave of his hand.

I still don't want to go.

I need to speak to Cole. He has to understand. "You can't tell me all our lives weren't in danger."

"We can talk outside." He stops at the glass doors.

Goddammit.

I feel sick. Worthless.

I follow after him on numb legs and walk outside, bypassing Chris's blood on the tiles. "What am I supposed to do?"

"Give him space." Luca moves into the doorway, blocking any possibility of my return inside. "You should be celebrating. This is over. You get to cut and run."

I don't want to cut and run.

I need closure.

I need Cole.

"Anissa..." Luca gives me a placating smile. A pathetic, deprecating curve of lips. "Being held here has fucked with your head. You've gotta realize the way you're feeling probably has a lot to do with Stockholm syndrome."

My world narrows to two words. One psychological condition.

No. The way I feel isn't dictated by mental instability.

"I think it's best if you wait at the pier," he continues. "We'll get word of Keira's arrival any minute now."

"I'm not going anywhere until I speak to Cole."

"I'm not giving you a choice." He jerks his chin toward the path. "I'm not Cole. You don't have me by the balls. This right here," he waves a hand between us, "is a kindness despite the mess you've made."

"The mess—"

"You took down a kingpin," he grates. "You just earned yourself a world of enemies. And who do you think is going to do everything in his power to protect your stupid ass when you fucking betrayed him?"

I suck in a breath. "I didn't—"

"Keep your mouth shut. Pretend Cole finished this. And go wait at the fucking pier."

My chest pounds with punishing beats. The way he looks at me—the disgust and annoyance—it's so fucking familiar.

I'm a pariah again.

"I don't need his protection," I whisper. "I can look after myself."

Luca scoffs. "We'll see."

A scream builds behind my sternum. I itch to lash out. To vent my frustration in a shriek. Instead, I turn and walk around the pool, hearing the slide of the glass door and the definitive *click* of the lock.

I don't stop along the path. I keep going, keep moving until I reach the end of the pier and sit to dangle my legs over the edge.

I did the right thing. I refuse to believe otherwise.

There was no other choice.

I continue to build on my argument as the sun creeps higher in the clear blue sky, beaming down on me from overhead.

The perfect weather mocks me. Everything does. And there's nothing I can do about it.

I remain in solitude, the numbness taking over through the passing morning until the low rumble of a boat approaches.

There's no motivation to panic anymore. I'm hollow. Empty.

I killed a man, thinking I was saving someone I care about, and instead, I've been accused of sabotage.

I don't even move when the boat approaches, the engine cut before it rocks into place beside the pier.

Decker climbs out first, his heavy boots thudding onto the wooden planks. "Sitting with all your friends, Agent Fox?"

He helps Keira from the vessel, Sarah and Hunter following close behind, all of them scowling their hatred at me.

I don't blame them. We have a convoluted history, especially Decker and I. Just like with Cole, they took opposing sides of the battlefield.

At least temporarily.

I no longer have any idea what team I'm on. There's no side for me.

I'm lost.

I push to my feet, wincing from the ache in my ribs as I face their judgment.

"You're beat up." Keira's scrutiny increases, her gaze trekking me up and down. "Cole didn't do this."

It sounds like a question. A pained plea for more information.

"No, he didn't touch me." Well, that's not technically true. We did a lot of touching, but not the kind she's referring to. And not the type I want to think about when he's made me an outcast.

"Are you all right?" she asks. "Who did this to you?"

"It doesn't matter."

She quirks a brow in offence. "Right... Okay, then. I'll leave you in peace."

I scoff as they start toward the house. There's no peace here. There never was. Not even in those precious moments spent alone with Cole.

But I was brought here for a reason. Cole dragged me into hell to tell Keira her father was dead, and now I understand why.

Luther's kids hated him. They despised everything he did. And they loved him in equal measure.

They didn't want his murder. They just had no other choice.

"Wait," I beg. "There's something Keira needs to know."

They pause collectively, then Hunt steps forward, his stance dominant. "If this is going to be some thinly veiled threat—"

"Quiet." Sarah claps him on the chest. "Let her speak."

They all stare, watching, waiting.

"He's dead, Keira." The admission lifts from the hollowness carving out my middle. "Luther is gone."

She stares at me without reaction. Without acknowledgement. As if I didn't speak.

"When?" Decker breaks the awkward silence.

"Earlier. Less than an hour ago. They're still cleaning up."

Keira turns, her stride determined as she continues for the house.

Her crew follow.

"Decker, wait."

He stiffens, his brutal glare hitting me from over his shoulder. "What?"

"Can I have a minute?"

He bares his teeth, not hiding an ounce of his hatred, then glances back at Keira. "Go ahead without me. I'll catch up." He crosses his muscled arms over his chest and stalks toward me. "What do you want?"

"There's something waiting for you inside."

He pulls a face—a mix of incredulity and annoyance. "Thanks for the ominous insight. Care to clarify?"

I open my mouth, but pause, unsure how to continue.

Maybe I'm not the person he should be hearing this from. The euphoric news shouldn't be tainted because it came from the lips of an enemy.

He deserves to believe the information as soon as he hears it. After everything he's been through, I want him to fully accept the relief without hesitation.

"It's something good."

His frown deepens. "Like a fucking present?"

I chuckle despite the seriousness. "Yeah, I guess."

"And you're not going to explain?"

He's such a strong man. A hero in his own right.

He went through hell with Penny's disappearance, then the misinformation of her murder. Thinking of his upcoming relief makes my eyes burn.

"I'll leave that up to Cole." I want to tell him everything. To salvage some of the memories from my time here with the purest glimpse of happiness. But it's not my place. "I just want you to know I'm happy for you."

31

TORIAN

I'm on my hands and knees, scrubbing the last vestiges of my father's blood from the tile when the glass door slides open and my sister pulls aside the sheer curtain.

"Do my eyes deceive me?" she drawls. "Could my brother actually be cleaning?"

I sit back on my haunches and wipe the sweat from my brow with the back of my hand. "Macabre jokes aren't your style. I guess that's Decker's influence rubbing off on you."

"He's not rubbing anything off on me." She glances away, hiding the faint hint of tears in her eyes.

"I beg to differ." Hunter walks in behind her. "There was definitely a lot of rubbing on the flight here."

"It would've been a blessing if rubbing was all we had to witness." Sarah follows after him, shooting me a wink. "Congrats, Cole. It seems like you got the job done."

"I always get the job done." I shove to my feet, my head throbbing from the after-effects of whatever shit Tobias stabbed into my leg. "Luther's dead. His henchmen, too. Now all that's left is to dismantle the fucking huge operation he has going."

Keira nods, her attention turned toward the sterile kitchen. "Thank you."

I don't want her appreciation. Not when I should've done this a long time ago. And besides, she's giving me a front, and I don't appreciate the show.

She just lost her father after recently burying her uncle. Both of them betrayed her throughout her life. There's no way she's okay with any of this.

"Come here." I step forward and drag her into my chest, wrapping my arms around her. "I could've fucking killed you when the pilot told me what you'd done."

She leans into me, resting her head against my shoulder. "I know. The poor guy even tried to tell us we weren't allowed to board, but he didn't stand a chance."

"Not when I shoved a gun in his face." Hunter smiles, all teeth and no charm. "In his defense though, he did try to maintain a fake bravado for at least five seconds. He crumpled to shit after that."

"You'll haunt the guy's nightmares for years to come. All for nothing." Sarah glances around the crime scene, unperturbed by what's happened. "It looks like we didn't need to be here to help after all."

"If I needed anything, I would've asked." I place a kiss in Keira's hair and step back. "Where's Deck—"

"Right here." He slips between the curtains and makes his way to the front of the crowd. "I'm told I have some secret present waiting for me, but I swear to God, if that bitch was referring to the bloodbath that needs to be cleaned up, I'm not going to be happy."

"A present?" Keira frowns, glancing from me to Decker, then back again.

They all look at me. Silent. Even Luca stops cleaning his own blood off the wall to watch the show.

I shouldn't be the one to tell Decker the life-changing news. I'm not subtle. I don't have the patience or kindness to relay the information. It's not my thing.

"Hey, Luc." I jerk my chin at him. "Maybe you should explain the situation."

"Oh, no. *Fuck* no. You're on your own." He returns to cleaning, turning his back on me.

Asshole.

"What's the surprise?" Sarah cocks her hip against the sofa. "And do we all get one?"

"It isn't a fucking surprise or a present," I grate. "You all need to stop acting like this is all fun and games, because it's not the time for it."

"So the bitch *was* referring to the cleanup." Decker scoffs. "I fucking hate her."

"No, she wasn't."

Jesus Christ.

Any minute now Penny could walk down that hall. In fact, maybe I should just wait for that to happen and let nature take its course.

"Are we meant to guess?" Hunt asks.

"Just shut up, okay?" I huff out a breath and search for understanding that doesn't seem to exist.

"Oh, goodie." Decker rubs his hands together. "What delights do you have in store for me?"

"You might want to tone down the sarcasm," I grate. "This is serious."

"No shit. It's not like you get me presents on the daily. I'm kinda expecting to get shanked."

And I'd seriously prefer that alternative. "Fine," I huff. "I'm just going to spit it out."

"Don't worry. I tell Keira to do that all the time." He shrugs. "Honestly, if you spit or swallow it doesn't bother me either way."

"Oh, shit." Hunter snickers. "Blow job jokes with the boss man about his own sister. That's likely to get you killed."

Yeah. It fucking will.

I cock my fist and convince myself one swift uppercut will snap the sarcasm right out of him.

"Cole, just tell us." Keira begs with her eyes. "What's this all about?"

I throw my bloodstained cloth to the floor and look the sarcastic prick right in the eye. "Luther took me to his house yesterday."

Decker stiffens, the humor leaving his features. *About fucking time, asshole.*

"And?" Keira steps closer.

"And Penny was there."

The room erupts in chatter, multiple questions hurtled in every direction while Decker remains stone still.

"Are we talking about her remains?" Hunt asks. "What do you mean she was there?"

"I mean she was fucking there. Alive. Not necessarily well, because I've got no idea about her mental state, but she looked healthy enough."

Decker turns white, looking like a ghost of the man he was moments earlier. He rubs a hand over his mouth and sucks in a breath. "Where is she now?"

I loosen the top buttons on my shirt, needing more room to breathe. "Before we talk about that, you need to know—"

"Where. The fuck. Is she?" He storms forward, getting in my face, his chest rising and falling with heavy breaths.

There's nothing stopping me from putting a gun to his temple and telling him to back the fuck off. Not one damn thing after the shit I've gone through in the last twenty-four hours, but I'm smart enough to realize the next twenty-four he'll go through will be just as tough.

"Cole, please." Keira pushes between us, keeping her seething boyfriend at her back. "Where can we find her?"

"In one of the rooms down the hall. I don't know which one."

"She's here?" Decker storms past me.

I don't bother holding him back. He can work out his own way to deal with the reunion, but I latch onto Keira's arm as she tries to follow. "Wait."

She stops, tilts her head, and meets my gaze. "I need to go with him."

"I know. But first you need to know she's not alone."

"What does that mean?"

"There's a kid."

"That son of a bitch," Sarah hisses. "He knocked her up?"

"No. She hasn't been gone long enough. But I know he's ours."

"Ours?" A shaky breath escapes Keira's lips. "Meaning?"

"We have a half-brother. And to make matters worse, we just killed his father."

She clamps a trembling hand over her mouth. From fearless to faint-hearted in the space of minutes.

Yep. That's my sister.

She shakes her head, her eyes bleak with shock and confusion. "What do we do? Where's his mother? Is he okay?

"First, I don't know. Second, from what our father told me, the mother is dead. And third, he was anxious as all hell when Luther made him stab me in the leg with a fucking sedative. But now I'm not so sure."

Her shock increases, the tremble in her hand turning to a full-blown shake.

"Just go to him." Luca walks toward us. "Try to show him as much support as possible. I'll come with you." He leads her to the hall and both of them continue out of sight.

I should probably follow, but I can't bring myself to face Tobias yet. Not until the evidence of our father's murder has been cleaned up. Maybe then we can both pretend he never existed.

"It sounds like Luca did good." Hunt focuses on the few remaining spots of blood on the floor. "Lucky for him."

I shrug. "He did okay. Who knows if you would've done better."

"*I* know," he mutters. "We both fucking know."

I'd probably laugh at his wounded pride if I didn't feel like my time in Greece has been one big kick to the balls. My father may be dead, but his clusterfuck of a legacy is still left behind, his orphaned kid included.

"If only you hadn't stabbed me in the back, you could've been here."

"Don't fucking start." Hunt stalks for the kitchen. "Do you have more bleach around here somewhere?"

"In the duffel. Near the table."

He doesn't need any more instruction. He makes for the chemicals and starts cleaning, doing the job he's perfected for years, while he leaves me alone with his fiancée, one hand on her hip, her lips pursed.

I should throw my dirty cloth at her and demand she get to work. "Are you just going to stand there?"

"Probably." She cocks her head. "I'm trying to figure out what's going on in that messed up mind of yours. By any chance, does the big, bad Cole Torian need a cuddle?" She smirks, beating the emotional bullshit out of the room like she's wielding a stick.

"It's always great to see you, Sarah." I'm tempted to take her up on the offer only because I'm well aware she's not the comforting type. Even more so when it comes to me. "You can save the cuddle torture for Hunt. But I changed my mind about what I said earlier. I think I do need your help."

"I'm listening."

I contemplate my next move, hating the indecision I feel now more than I ever did when it came to the plans for my father's punishment.

"I want you to take Anissa to the jet and accompany her back to Portland."

She shrugs. "No problem. I can do that."

"Good, because I need you to do it now." Before I have to see her again. Before I have a chance to tell her all the messed-up shit going on in my head.

"Okay..." Sarah's eyes narrow. "And what do I do with her once we're Stateside?"

I stand a little taller, breathe a little deeper. "You let her go."

32

ANISSA

WEEKS LATER

I RUN ALONG THE TRYON CREEK TRAIL, THE DENSE NATURE comfortably surrounding me as I push myself harder to pass two shirtless men jogging upfront.

I've taken this path for a while now, no longer appreciating the familiarity of the city streets. I need desolation. I can't even follow my early morning café routine because holding a brief conversation with the barista puts me on edge.

I want to be left alone. To quietly bathe in my mistakes. To hate the world from my darkened isolated corner.

Work hasn't been easy.

Taggert wasn't suspicious of the extra days I spent away from the office. Instead, he thought I was throwing a childish tantrum and used my disappearance to build bigger walls between me and my colleagues.

The entire department has made it clear they've grown tired of my drama.

All except Easton.

Anthony had my back the whole time—sending e-mails, leaving messages on my voicemail, hassling my apartment building manager for possible details of my whereabouts.

Even now, weeks later, he's the only person who checks on me.

402

There hasn't been one word from Cole.

I shake my head free from thoughts of him and punish myself harder, demanding more from my legs as I round the bare-chested male joggers and speed ahead.

It's a constant struggle not to suffocate in the past while also needing to analyze every second I spent on that island in an attempt to figure out where I went wrong.

I lost the game—that much is certain.

But it isn't all bad.

Numerous missing women have returned home. The stories they recounted to authorities and news outlets were clearly fictional—their disappearances explained by anything from running away, to going on drug benders, and even an elopement with a man who left a twenty-one-year-old high and dry in a foreign country—but regardless of whatever story Cole concocted to divert attention from his family, they're home.

And I'm thankful.

A snap of breaking undergrowth erupts from the bushes beside me, the hidden forest creature sending my hackles rising. I've been on edge since returning to Portland. Every shadow is Cole. Every bump in the night. Every private number that hangs up before I can connect the call.

Even now, surrounded by nature and calming solitude, my sixth sense is on alert.

I slow and glance over my shoulder, finding nothing. There're no shirtless men. No animals. Not even a bird flittering from tree to tree.

It's peaceful.

Too quiet.

I slide a hand over the canister of pepper spray held in the slim pocket of my skin-tight running pants and jog for the bend in the trail.

There's nothing to worry about out here.

Nothing but the waking nightmares I can't seem to shake.

I speed up, rounding the curve in the path only to skitter to a stop at the threat waiting in the small clearing.

My breathing catches. My pulse quickens.

Heat suffuses every single inch of me, the warm tingle a welcome sensation after weeks spent numb.

"Hello, little fox."

It feels like years have passed since his gorgeous face was more than a fading memory. A lifetime of misery since this foreboding man in his stunning suit, with his midnight eyes, stared at me.

I place my hands on my hips and straighten my back and shoulders, opening my lungs in an attempt to lessen the heaving gulps of air.

I don't speak. I can't. If I could, I wouldn't even know what to say. There's too much heartache.

And animosity.

Not to mention blinding rage.

He drags his gaze over me, slowly, the appraisal a tease even though his expression remains an emotionless mask. But he's not the only person with eyes on me. I can sense someone else, the tingle along my neck becoming a full-blown throb that descends down my spine.

I chance a glance over my shoulder, scrutinizing the mass of trees.

"It's Hunter," Cole murmurs. "He'll keep his distance and make sure we're not disturbed."

I continue to pant out my need for oxygen. "Is that meant to be comforting?"

A slow smile spreads across his gorgeous lips. The sight is punishing, the attack cutting deep. I'd almost forgotten how easily he lures his prey with that devilish appeal.

"I've missed your spite."

His admission rocks me, foundations and all.

The bliss lasts a split-second before I remember he was the one who discarded me like filthy garbage.

"What do you want, Cole?"

"You." He puts his hands in his pants pockets and lazily strolls toward me. "I think that's always been obvious, don't you?"

His lie doesn't warrant a response.

I refuse to participate in another game.

The way he played me still keeps me up at night.

I fell for him like a stone into murky waters, never to be seen again.

At one point, I couldn't picture returning to Portland without his protection wrapped around me. But that was before I came to terms with my Stockholm syndrome. Now, I know the sensation clawing beneath my sternum is nothing more than mental fuckery.

"What do you really want?" I cross my arms over my chest, building emotional barriers. "Because if you haven't noticed, I'm in the middle of something here."

"We were in the middle of something, too. Remember?" He raises a brow, continuing forward. He circles, walking behind me, setting me on edge. "We made a good team." His words brush my ear. "We were perfect together."

"You mean before you banished me?"

"I may have been quick to send you home, but don't forget that's exactly what you asked for." He continues around my other side, looking at me from the corner of his eye. "You wanted to get out of there as soon as possible. You made me promise to cut ties—no more games, no more flowers. Nothing. That was your stipulation, Nissa. Not mine."

He's manipulating the past, trying to rewrite history.

Yes, I made that deal with the devil, but that was before... Before he became the only air I wanted to breathe.

"You don't remember?" He stops in front of me, hands still in his pockets, his demeanor suave as hell. "It was after you tried to kill me with a loaded weights bar. We were in the panic room, and you were breathless and flushed. I'd wanted to fuck you up against—"

"Stop it," I snap. "You knew I didn't want to leave. Not after what I did. I was a mess."

A brief glimpse of regret pulls at his brows before quickly fading. "I needed time."

"And what about what I needed?" I slap a hand against my chest. "I was trying to save your life. Luca's and Penny's, and that little boy's, too. But you treated me as if I'd stabbed you in the back. The way you looked at me—" I shake my head, refusing to continue.

My recount doesn't matter.

Nothing does.

What I went through wasn't even reality. It was just another game.

"I needed time" he repeats, his voice softening. "When you shot him, I—"

"Regretted setting me up to take the fall?"

He turns quiet, cementing the suspicions that have torn me apart for weeks.

"Did you think I wouldn't work it out?" I glare. "You *wanted* me to kill him. You *planned* for it."

The silence stretches between us, building the anger I've kept tightly bottled.

"I admit it took me a while to put the clues together. I spent days locked in my apartment, staring at the ceiling, going over and over what I thought was a mistake on my behalf. But it was never a mistake, was it, Cole? It was your plan all along."

His mouth curves in a sad smile. "I should've known you'd figure it out."

The confirmation squeezes my heart before ripping it in two.

I'd known. God, how I'd known. But I didn't want to believe.

I'd hoped and prayed and begged to be wrong.

"Fuck you." I storm forward, grazing his shoulder, only to be stopped by the tight grip of his hand around my arm.

"You're not going to ask me why?"

I raise my chin. "I already know—it was a game."

"No, little fox. That part was never a game."

"Bullshit. You accused me of sleeping with you because of some fucked-up trickery. But it was really you who flipped the board that night."

"No."

"Yes. You worked me like a pro. That bullshit when you told me you weren't sure you could pull the trigger was pure gold." I tilt my head to face him. "But it was the day of reckoning where you really played your A-game. You kept repeating your father wouldn't shoot you—*you, Cole*—but you weren't the only victim in the room, and you would've known I was scared to death of Luther hurting any of us. And still, you kept saying it over and over. He won't shoot *me*, his own son. You predicted the subtlety would work its way into my psyche."

He doesn't answer.

I don't need him to.

Not anymore.

"And there was your strategic stance, too." I square my shoulders, thrilled to have the opportunity to get this shit off my chest. "You could've easily saved your father by blocking him with your body. You knew my aim. You were well aware I had an open shot. Yet you kept stumbling out of the way."

"You're a smart woman, Niss."

A sob inches its way up my throat, just waiting to be released.

I hate him. God, how I hate him. But I'd loved him, too.

It was a dizzying, heart-palpitating, Stockholm love. But love regardless.

"Not smart enough to understand why you continued the act after I pulled the trigger." I sniff and hate myself for the pathetic sound. "That part still has me stumped. Along with why you didn't just ask me to do it in the first place. But..." I shrug. "The past is in the past. And I no longer want to spare you a single thought, apart from wishing you all the best on your trip to hell."

I yank my arm from his grip and walk away, only to be hauled around the waist and pulled into his chest. Face to face. Hip to hip.

In an instant, I'm dragged back into fond memories, when I mistakenly thought the look in his eyes held hunger.

"Being away from you was hell on earth." He growls. "I have no plan to go through that again."

I fight his hold, shoving and scrambling.

He smothers me tighter, wrapping his arms around mine to hold them down at my sides.

"I'll scream."

He grins. "And you think I couldn't shut you up?"

I should be scared. Instead, the familiar burn of desire slides through me, scorching everything in its path.

I want him. After everything—all the pain, all the betrayal.

I.

Still.

Want.

Him.

"Scream, little fox," he whispers. "Give me the opportunity to silence that pretty mouth of yours."

My heart pounds beneath tightening ribs. My lips dry. My breathing becomes shallow.

I don't want to be like this, with every nerve in my body hyper aware of his touch.

I hate it. I loathe it. Yet, I no longer know how to feel alive when we're apart.

"You're going to listen to me." He leans in, his mouth a breath away from mine. "You're going to hear every word I have to say. Then, and only then, will you get to walk away from me."

I scoff and stare over his shoulder, refusing to submit. We both know he won't hurt me. The only thing he can break is my self-control.

I'm struggling to fight the need to have his mouth on mine. His hands on my body. His words in my ear.

I need it all, and the longer I remain captured against him, the more likely I am to succumb.

"I didn't break my promise to you," he murmurs. "I said no more games, and I meant it."

"Then why?" I focus on the trees, the leaves, the winding, weaving vines. "Why manipulate me?"

"Because you made it clear you hate who I am."

I turn rigid.

"After everything that happened, you still didn't understand my life, Nissa. You remained on that high horse, looking down on me."

I meet his gaze. "What does that have to do with me killing your father?"

"Everything." He stares at me, his eyes stony, his mouth tight. "I was determined to take Luther down. I would've killed anyone who dared take the closure away from me. But that day in Naxos changed everything. I wanted to torture Amar for what he did to you. I would've stripped the skin from his body, layer by layer, because of the part he played. But the horrified way you looked at me when I suggested punishment made it clear you were still stuck in your fairyland where justice is only served by someone holding a badge."

"That's not true."

"It's not?" He raises a brow. "Up until the very last night, you kept asking me how I could kill my own father. How I could possibly pull the fucking trigger on my own flesh and blood—"

"Because he was your father. At one time, he was everything to you."

"He was a fucking rapist," he snarls. "A sex trafficker. He ruined the lives of hundreds, and sending him six feet under would've brought me relief, *not* anguish." His anger is clear. His intent, too.

"Then why did you get me to do it?"

"Because of this." He jerks his head at me, narrowing his gaze. "Because of the way those judgmental eyes strip me to my core."

I shake my head. *No.*

"It's true, little fox. You messed with my mind. You, with your snappy mouth and perfect body, did things to me I couldn't undo. I knew I didn't want to let you go once my work in Greece was over. I couldn't stomach the thought of letting you out of my fucking sight, but I was also fully aware you and your high horse wouldn't be able to stand the sight of me once I murdered my own father."

I keep shaking my head. *No. That's not why.*

That couldn't be why.

"I manipulated you, Niss, because I couldn't let you go."

"Liar." I shove his chest. "You *did* let me go. You banished me in the blink of an eye. *You* looked at *me* with the same disgust you accused me of."

"Any disgust I had was for myself. Not you. I couldn't stand you looking at me when I'd been lowered to the point of letting a woman do my dirty work. And not just any woman. The *only* fucking woman I've ever given a shit about."

"Well, it's a bit damn late to tell me that now when I've lived with the guilt for weeks. I thought you hated me for what I'd done."

"I hated *me*," he snarls. "I hated being unable to get you out of my head. I hated my addiction to you and the inability to let go. I hated how your judgment tore me to fucking shreds. But most of all, I hated the fucking danger I put you in."

My pulse pounds in my throat, the thunderous beats wracking my body. I step back, not willing to believe him.

"I needed you." The admission is whispered from my lips. "I needed you to tell me you were okay. That I hadn't ruined your attempt to gain closure. And that the news reports of another mass grave of women found in Greece was untrue. But you wouldn't even speak to me. I called. So many times."

"I wasn't going to have this conversation with you over the phone."

I take another retreating step. "I went to your restaurant."

"I know." He nods. "They told me. But I was still in Greece tying up loose ends. I only returned Stateside an hour ago."

He's been gone this whole time?

I have so many questions. It kills me to keep my mouth closed and not bring voice to the curiosity surrounding those women. Surrounding *him*. It's pride that keeps my lips sewn shut.

"You're the first person I've seen since we landed, Nissa. I've thought of nothing else this entire time."

"Well, that's too bad, because I stopped thinking about you a while ago."

His lips kick up, silently calling me on my bullshit.

Asshole.

I look away, unable to face the truth. "How's Tobias?"

"I'm not entirely sure. He returned to the States a while ago. Keira and Layla have been helping to look after him. But they think he's feeding off Penny's trauma."

"And what do you think?" I whisper.

"I think I want to quit talking about shit that doesn't involve you. Instead, we should talk about your agent friend. I'm told Easton has been spending a lot of time at your apartment."

I bark out a laugh. "I'm not going to dignify you with a response."

"It's okay. You don't need to. I'm sure you're well aware he'll go missing if I find out he's laid hands on what's mine." He leans close, his mouth hovering near my ear. "And you're mine, Nissa, just in case you're confused about our situation."

I shudder, my entire body igniting with painful familiarity.

I want to be his. I ache for it every day. But the price is still too high.

I won't sell my soul for him.

"Like hell I am." I slide my arm away.

"You're mine," he repeats, his voice rough and ragged, the brutality filling my chest with a mass of tingles. "And I'm yours. It's always been that way. You know it as well as I do."

I shake my head, denying what I've tried to ignore for four weeks. Even longer. Since the day at the coffee shop. From the first day our eyes locked.

"I didn't report what happened in Greece," I admit. "I didn't tell anyone. Can't you be grateful and move on?"

"Can you move on?" It's not a question. It's a taunt. "Easton keeps hanging around at your apartment, but he never stays the night. He's made it clear he wants you. But you've never let him get grabby. Why's that?"

"Just how closely are you watching me?" I wish I was disgusted at the thought of him invading my privacy.

I wish.

I wish.

I wish.

Instead, my belly fills with butterflies. My lingering Stockholm issues have me concluding his stalking is a romantic gesture.

His lips lift in a lazy smirk. "He's not going to come around anymore."

"Because you say so?"

"Exactly." He inches away, leaving me cold. "I'll give you a week to let my return sink in. In that time, you need to tell him to walk away. Then you're going to meet me next Sunday morning at our coffee shop at eight."

"I'm not going to do any of that, Cole."

The smirk increases, the expression entirely devilish. "And why is that?"

"For starters, there are enough questions about my loyalties within the Bureau without being seen with you in public."

"Then quit and come work for me."

Everything inside me reacts. Stomach. Heart. Lungs.

Each organ squeezes. Twists.

I've thought long and hard about our differing morals. I've stewed on the way the FBI stabbed my father in the back. And yes, I've questioned whether I have what it takes to switch sides, ditching one corrupt organization for another. But the indecision over Cole has been everlasting. The frustration and confusion are always there. "Very funny."

"Funny?" He quirks a brow. "Do you know me to be the humorous type?"

No, I don't. He doesn't do jokes. He does taunts.

"Think about it." He takes a backward step. "Think about me. Think about how I haven't left your mind for a second all month. Then meet me next weekend. Eight o'clock. Sharp."

"I won't be there." My heart says otherwise, but I'm determine to succeed this time.

No more games. No more provoking.

I need to cut ties and move on.

"We'll see," he purrs.

I scoff and stalk along the path, my steps getting longer. "Goodbye, Cole."

This doesn't feel like goodbye. The tingling taking over my stomach resembles the excitement of a new beginning. A fresh start, despite the craziness.

"For now, Nissa. Goodbye for now."

EPILOGUE

TORIAN

ONE WEEK LATER

SHE'S NOT COMING.

I knew she wouldn't.

That's why I'm sitting in my car out the front of her apartment building one minute before we're meant to meet.

I need to give her the opportunity to humiliate me. I get it. It's payback.

I did the same to her when I demanded she drop the sheet after we slept together. Then again after she killed my father.

I hurt her. And I sure as shit can man up enough to let her even the score—at least temporarily—because it's not like this thing between us is over.

While I'd been stuck in Greece, I hadn't been able to predict how she would react to my return. I'd wondered if she'd be angry. Would those handcuffs of hers be ready and waiting for a long-overdue arrest?

I'd thought about her every damn minute of every damn day. She'd clouded my vision while I'd spent weeks dismantling the intricate details of my father's operation. I'd even contemplated her placing me in the rearview and moving on with her life.

Then news got back to me about the visits from her agent friend, and the spiral of jealous rage I'd descended into made me work around the clock to get back to Portland earlier than predicted.

I'd needed to see her for myself. I couldn't keep questioning what she was thinking.

But that first glance on the trail in the woods had answered all the unknowns.

She'd caught sight of me and reacted with relief.

I'd seen her hope. Witnessed the brief glimpse of excitement.

Despite our differences, and the hell I'd dragged her through, it was clear she still wanted me.

She'd tried to hide the spark with tough words and tougher mental shields, but I'd seen the truth. I'd also felt her tremble under my touch, the same way she did on the island.

Nothing between us had changed.

"You said eight, right?" The young florist delivery woman leans against the window ledge of my Porsche and smiles down at me. "Are you ready for me to deliver the arrangement yet?"

"Give her one more minute."

As much as I previously enjoyed the predatory parts of my time with Niss, I'd prefer to set that aside and delve into new territory.

"Oh, gosh." The woman steps back and pats her pockets. "I forgot to write on the card. You said there was a message, right? What do you want me to put on it?"

She pulls an envelope from her jeans pocket, then continues to rummage until she finds a pen.

"Just wait a little while longer," I mutter.

If Anissa decides to meet me, the flowers will become redundant, which means the card isn't necessary. I just need to wait.

I know she'll show.

"No problem." The woman nods. "What made you decide to send an arrangement of poppies? Is the woman a veteran?"

I grin. "No. It's more of an inside story. One of those things that only has meaning to the people involved."

Her eyes light up. "I love those stories. It makes the gift so romantic. I live for that stuff. Would it be incredibly rude if I asked

414

for details? How did poppies become the flower to symbolize your relationship?"

I bite back a laugh. The woman is in her early twenties and clearly spellbound by whimsical thoughts of romance. I'm sure she's expecting a tale filled with candlelit dinners and nights spent gazing at the stars.

I shrug. "It's simple, really. She's an FBI agent. I'm a notorious drug lord. The poppies are more of a taunt than anything. Alluring but deadly. Simplistic, yet the source of a multi-billion-dollar industry. The deep red color is also important because the temperamental times we've navigated together have been bathed in bloodshed."

She blinks at me, her face growing slack.

"We're a match made in heaven, don't you think?"

"Yes." The envelope and pen tremble in her grip. "Of course."

"Don't look so scared, sunshine. I'm only messing with you."

"Oh." She straightens and gives me a bashful smile. "For a minute, I thought you were serious. How crazy is that?"

"It's definitely crazy." I turn my attention back to the doors of the apartment building. "I just want to wait a few more seconds."

Thirty, to be exact.

I start the mental countdown, the tick of the metaphorical clock increasing my pulse.

Twenty-eight... Twenty-seven... Twenty-six...

Any moment now, my little fox is going to walk out those doors.

She's had her fun. She's inflicted her retaliation.

Now it's time to move forward.

Nineteen... Eighteen... Seventeen...

I can't wait to see her.

The last week has been torture. Watching her through the added security measures Decker put in place wasn't enough. I need to touch her. To fuck her. To hear her needy gasps against my ear.

Nine... Eight... Seven...

The doors swing wide and familiarity walks out.

Unwanted fucking familiarity.

An asshole in stone-washed jeans and a knitted goddamn sweater strides outside, not a care in the world as he increases my pulse, infusing my veins with a volatile dose of jealousy.

I shove the car door open, making the delivery woman scamper out of the way, and stalk toward the conceited prick. "Agent Easton, what brings you to the neighborhood?"

He pauses, his judgmental gaze trekking from my head to my toes. "I could ask you the same question."

I smile, hiding the venom surging to break free. "It's a beautiful day. I wanted to soak up the sunshine."

"What a coincidence. I'm about to do the same thing. I just had to check on my girl first. You know, priorities and all that."

His girl?

His fucking girl?

"You've got yourself a woman?" I want to kill him. Right here. In front of innocent witnesses and Sunday morning traffic. "Congratulations. She wouldn't happen to be the illustrious Agent Fox, would she?"

"How'd you know?" He smirks.

Fucking smirks.

My face heats, the need to act building like a furnace.

"Between you and me," he mock whispers, "she's been going through a tough time lately, and I'm enjoying spending every spare minute comforting her."

He's baiting me. And I'm devouring every morsel, even though it acts as poison.

"What a gentleman." I incline my head in approval. "I hope this tough time of hers isn't too serious."

"You know, Mr. Torian, it's a funny thing. She fell off the grid weeks ago. Just completely disappeared. Days later, she returned, battered and bruised on her arms, legs, and neck." His calm facade remains in place. "She claims it was an accident she received while vacationing on the coast. But I know her. Really well, in fact. So it's clear she's lying."

It's also clear he is, too.

If he's only aware of the damage on her limbs, this smug fucker hasn't had the pleasure of sleeping with her. No way in hell would the injury to her ribs have skipped his attention.

He might want to believe she's his girl, but that woman is most definitely still mine.

"I'm going to find out what happened to her, Mr. Torian." He steps forward, his sense of superiority all up in my face. "I'm going to break down those walls of hers until she tells me her juicy secrets. Then I'm going to go after the person responsible and tear him to pieces."

I raise my brows, impressed by his enthusiasm. "It sounds like you've got a tough task ahead of you."

"Not at all. It's only a matter of time." He leans closer, as if preparing to tell a secret. "Do you want to know the best part?"

I clench my jaw, growing tired of this cock-measuring competition.

"Once I make the arrest, I'll be her savior—the one she runs to in relief. Have you ever been someone's white knight, Cole? Do you know how generous a woman can be when all her demons have been slayed?"

"I'm more of a dark prince kinda guy," I growl.

"That's too bad, because unbreakable bonds are formed in those types of situations." He shrugs. "That's what I'm counting on, anyway."

Fuck him.

Fuck this straight-laced, badge-wearing prick.

He's not going to form any bond with Anissa. Not today. Not tomorrow. Not in a million fucking years. At least not while I'm around.

"Good luck." I clap him on the shoulder, my fingers digging into his jacket.

"Don't worry. I won't need it." He shrugs away from my grip and bumps into my shoulder as he starts down the cement path. "I'll see you around, Cole."

The poor bastard is delusional. Pathetic and fucking deranged.

He's no threat to what I have with Anissa.

I earned her trust under the harshest of conditions in only a matter of days. And by the sound of it, this asshole hasn't been able to get close in weeks.

"Be careful, Easton," I call over my shoulder. "You don't want to end up going off the grid like she did. Who knows if you'll return?"

I keep my focus on the building and raise my attention to her window, finding her staring back at me.

She doesn't retreat. She doesn't grant me a welcoming expression, either. But those gorgeous eyes drink me in. There's the faintest hint of hunger in her features. The tiniest glimpse. And that's enough for now.

I grin at her. I fucking beam my intentions her way.

Without a word, I let her know this isn't over. Her little mutt doesn't scare me. Not when she's made it clear she still wants me.

"Until next time, Niss."

I blow her a kiss, bidding her a silent farewell, then make my way back to the florist now waiting beside her white van.

"Are you ready for me to make the delivery?"

"Yes. It's time."

"And the card?" She holds out the crisp white envelope. "What would you like me to write on it?"

I contemplate my options, wondering if I should change my plan now Easton's entered the battlefield.

Should I approach her with caution? Maybe try a softer angle to beat the prick at his own game?

No. To hell with that.

I'm no white fucking knight.

Never have been. Never will be.

I hold out a hand. "Here, let me write on it."

The woman retrieves the slip of cardboard from the envelope and passes it over, allowing me to pen my message against the hood of the van.

If you want me to stalk you, then that's what I'll do.
Be careful, little fox. The big, bad wolf is coming for you.

Also by Eden Summers

Hunting Her Series

Hunter

Decker

Torian

———

Reckless Beat Series

Blind Attraction (Reckless Beat #1)

Passionate Addiction (Reckless Beat #2)

Reckless Weekend (Reckless Beat #2.5)

Undesired Lust (Reckless Beat #3)

Sultry Groove (Reckless Beat #4)

Reckless Rendezvous (Reckless Beat #4.5)

Undeniable Temptation (Reckless Beat #5)

———

The Vault Series

A Shot of Sin (The Vault #1)

Union of Sin (The Vault #2)

Brutal Sin (The Vault #3)

———

Information on more of Eden's titles can be found at
www.edensummers.com or your online book retailer.

ABOUT THE AUTHOR

Eden Summers is a bestselling author of contemporary romance with a side of sizzle and sarcasm.

She lives in Australia with a young family who are well aware she's circling the drain of insanity.
Eden can't resist alpha dominance, dark features and sarcasm in her fictional heroes and loves a strong heroine who knows when to bite her tongue but also serves retribution with a feminine smile on her face.

If you'd like access to exclusive information and giveaways, join Eden Summers' newsletter via the link on her website - www.edensummers.com

For more information:
www.edensummers.com
eden@edensummers.com

Printed in Great Britain
by Amazon

82048719R00243